RACERS
of the NIGHT

RACERS of the NIGHT

Science Fiction Stories
by Brad R. Torgersen

WordFire Press
Colorado Springs, Colorado

ISBN: 978-1-61475-232-5

Cover painting by Nick Greenwood

Cover design by Nick Greenwood
www.nickgreenwood.com
and
Art Director Kevin J. Anderson

Book Design by RuneWright, LLC
www.RuneWright.com

Published by
WordFire Press, an imprint of
WordFire, Inc.
PO Box 1840
Monument CO 80132

Kevin J. Anderson & Rebecca Moesta, Publishers

WordFire Press Trade Paperback Edition 2014
Printed in the USA
wordfirepress.com

Contents

Introduction 1

by L.E. Modesitt, Jr.

When Brad asked me to write an introduction to *Racers of the Night*, I was certainly surprised, but more than happy to do so. Not only because I appreciate and admire his work, but also because we both share one prominent similarity—each of us came comparatively late to our writing careers. If my calculations are correct, Brad published his first story when he was 28. I was 30 when I published my first story, and 39 when my first novel came out—while Brad will be 40 when his first novel, *The Chaplain's War*, is published by Baen. Also, both of us continued working full-time (and more) for others, even after years of regular publication.

I wouldn't go quite so far as to say that Brad burst upon the science fiction scene, but over the past five years he's gone from virtual literary invisibility to being a winner of The Writers of the Future contest, a finalist for the 2012 John W. Campbell Award for Best New Writer, a Nebula award nomination, three Hugo nominations, and two AnLab readers' choice awards from *Analog Science Fiction and Fact* magazine. Not only that, but he got *all* of those awards and nominations for his short fiction. Which is hard to do, and is especially impressive given the short time span in which Brad did it. He's also known for an even-handed and considerably less-than-inflammatory web blog that discusses not only writing-related issues, but a range of other topics as well.

What makes Mr. Torgersen so well-rounded?

Like me, Brad's had several careers, and still maintains three—as a medical technologist, as a United States Army Reserve Chief Warrant Officer (including a not insignificant amount of time on active duty orders), and as a writer. Brad's stories are therefore edged in an often gritty, realistic manner; something that's more than occasionally missing in much contemporary science fiction. What Brad's learned from occupations (and life) suffuses his stories.

In "Peacekeepers," Brad shows you all sides of the life of a professional soldier, including the impact of politics. In "The Flamingo Girl," there's the combination of success that only comes from relentless law enforcement-learned routine, and an understanding of all sides of human nature—even when one of those involved isn't even considered truly human. Another and totally different riff on law enforcement comes via "Blood and Mirrors," with a twist on what aspects of artificial intelligence become most marketable (and why) and where this leads. As for thrills, how about "The Curse of Sally Tincakes"—racing on the Moon on a track considered fatal for any woman who tries, because of another woman who is long-dead. Or what about "Life Flight," an interstellar travelogue which explores the impact of unknown genetics on a young crew member bound for the stars?

Whatever story is your favorite—and you may find several—reading Brad R. Torgersen should not only entertain you, but make you think ... and think again.

— L.E. Modesitt, Jr., May 2014

Introduction 2

by Kevin J. Anderson

When I was just starting as a writer, I hung out with other newbie authors, exchanging ideas, learning the ropes, sometimes sharing breakthroughs, sometimes sharing ignorance. I also knew a few big name authors who took an interest in me and offered their advice.

One of my greatest early mentors was Dean Koontz, who was willing to offer suggestions, listen to problems and questions, and lend a helping a hand. I could contact Dean with a contract concern, ask his opinion on a pending deal. He was instrumental in getting me my agent, and he even gave me a cover blurb for a very important book.

Dean was a huge name in the field and he certainly didn't need to go out of his way to help one particular aspiring author; in fact, the more I thought about his generosity, the more astonished I was. When I finally asked Dean why he had noticed me in particular, he explained that he had given a lot of advice over the years, "and you were one of the only writers who actually listened."

I remembered that, and as I became more and more successful myself, I also spent time teaching writing students: passing along my knowledge and trying to help other newbies avoid making the same mistakes I had made (so that they could make brand new mistakes all on their own).

Brad R. Torgersen is one of the ones who listened.

I first met Brad in 2010, when he was part of a group of a dozen new winners at the Writers of the Future gala and workshop. I've been a judge and instructor at Writers of the Future since 1996, and I've noticed that it's typical for several writers in each year's group to establish successful writing careers of their own, while most others vanish into obscurity—you never know which will be which.

I therefore had no reason to notice Brad in particular. He was cheerful about his win and excited for the future. But then, they're *all* like that. So you—as the judge—give them your wisdom and you wish them well, and you go back to your professional life where deadlines and projects multiply like kudzu.

Except, Brad showed up at our Superstars Writing Seminar—an intensive career-building workshop taught by bestselling writers—in Salt Lake City, just a few months later. He had a story in print with *Analog* magazine by then; his second professional sale. What was more, *Analog* had taken two more stories on top of that. Later in the same year I met Brad for the third time, at the 2011 Writers of the Future event, where Brad had come back to act as a sort of ambassador to the new winners—showing them what was possible, if you put your mind to it.

Clearly, this was a new writer determined to be noticed.

Brad and I struck up a relationship after that. He continued selling stories to *Analog* magazine, and he went out of his way to ask me for advice online. He also built a group of followers through social networking, and he made additional sales to other short fiction venues, such as *Orson Scott Card's InterGalactic Medicine Show*. Brad was also collaborating with fellow Writers of the Future judge and friend of mine, Mike Resnick, and when in 2012 Brad returned to Superstars—this time in Las Vegas, helping me out as one of our Superstars volunteers—he was a triple nominee for three of science fiction's top awards: the Hugo, the Nebula, and the Campbell. On top of the nominations, he'd also won the *Analog* AnLab—a readers' choice award chosen by the magazine's subscribers.

This collective swell in notoriety ultimately got him the notice of Toni Weisskopf, chief editor and publisher of Baen Books; to whom Brad sold his first novel in 2013. A transaction I proudly oversaw, as one of Brad's counselors on the affair. My blurb is on the front of his book, as a matter of fact (hat tip to Dean Koontz.)

But Brad had a problem. The novel wouldn't be published until late 2014, and with all his convention appearances there were fans who kept asking Brad for a book *now*. He therefore got the notion that he wanted to publish a collection of his award-winning and award-nominated short work. A very good idea, I thought. There was clear demand for his stuff, and Brad aimed to satisfy that demand. Simple businessman economics.

But short fiction collections are a tough sell to traditional publishers. And even if Brad could successfully pitch his project to an editor, it would take years for the book to reach print. Brad wanted something he could put into fans' hands immediately. So he was openly talking of self-publishing the collection.

I wasn't quite sure that self-publishing was the right route for him, since Brad has a full-time job, is also a Chief Warrant Officer in the Army Reserve, had other books to write, and self-publishing the book—correctly, to professional standards—would consume time Brad honestly didn't have. He also wouldn't know how to navigate the various distribution channels, nor have access to proofing and formatting and the other necessities of a professional label.

I therefore offered to publish Brad's first story collection, *Lights in the Deep*, at WordFire Press. We had the resources to do it right, and I thought we could find the right readers for it too. Ergo, capitalize on fans Brad had already earned, and get him a flotilla of new readers to boot.

That turned out to be exactly the case. The book, when done, looked beautiful. Brad got a gorgeous cover painting from award-winning artist Bob Eggleton—the same painting editor Stan Schmidt had previously commissioned for one of Brad's stories in *Analog* magazine—and we released the book at the inaugural (and very successful) Salt Lake City Comic Con, in September 2013. Brad did a signing at the WordFire table behind a small mountain of his books— a stack that rapidly diminished over the course of the weekend.

Brad's fans rallied on-line too, and the book sold quite well, hitting several Amazon category bestseller lists. Enough so that within thirty days Brad had earned enough royalties from *Lights in the Deep* to pay his mortgage that month—a terrific performance for a first short story collection from a relatively new author published by an independent press.

So of course we were interested in doing his second collection, when he floated the idea at Superstars in 2014. A collection which you now hold in your hands.

Brad is a prolific short story writer with the chops of a pro. I published one of his novellas in my second *Five by Five* military science fiction anthology, and also invited him to contribute a story for my second *Fantastic Holiday Season* anthology. (Of course that may be just a devious ploy to get him to write more short stories, so WordFire can put together the contents for yet another volume.)

Racers of the Night is therefore a strong collection showcasing the work of a rising author on the move. Dip in, read one or two at a time, or devour the whole collection straight through.

Then? You'll surely be ready for more. Goodness knows readers are. As of the writing of this introduction, Brad has secured a second AnLab award, and two more Hugo nominations; for stories Brad published in *Analog* magazine, and which he re-printed in *Lights in the Deep*.

Racers of the Night contains more of the same. I think you will enjoy.

—Kevin J. Anderson, May 2014

Introduction 3

by **Dave Wolverton**

I f you're familiar with Brad R. Torgersen's stories, you'll probably just want to skip this introduction and get right to the good stuff. That's what I'd do.

If you're not familiar with him, then maybe I can convince you to quit reading this now.

Brad is an unusual author. Not only is he very popular with other authors, vying for respected awards like the Hugo and Nebula, he's also hugely popular with fans, consistently winning awards like the *Analog* AnLabs.

That isn't easy to do. There are people that we might call "writer's writers," people whose storytelling skills are so stellar that other writers gaze upward in awe, as if at a fireworks display.

Then there are authors who are more "of the people," writers whose homespun simplicity charms us and delights us and fills us with warmth.

Rarely do we see an author who can captivate both audiences.

So Brad writes the kind of tales that science fiction readers love, with earthy heroes who remind us again and again what it is to be human, all the while writing about tough people facing impossible situations, in worlds that rigorously conform to scientific principles.

In looking at his stories, he reminds me most strongly of Robert Heinlein, yet in making that comparison, I would be doing a disservice to Brad. Somehow, Brad's characters are more likeable and human than Heinlein's. So if you set two stories in front of me, I'd grab the Torgersen.

In that way, he reminds me of another of my favorite authors, Lois McMaster Bujold, who also writes about ordinary people facing monumental challenges.

As an editor, I've read tens of thousands of stories—or at least the first few pages of tens of thousands of them. Sometimes I feel as if I've read too many of them. There aren't many authors these days that I will pick up and read for my own personal enjoyment, and there are even fewer that I will go search out to read. My weary eyes feel over-worn.

But Brad has made my short-list. If I see a magazine with his name on it, I want it.

And an anthology full of stories with his name on them? Ah, now there is a treasure indeed.

Brad R. Torgersen is quite simply one of the finest science fiction writers alive.

If you haven't read Brad R. Torgerson before, I envy you. You're about to discover something wonderful!

— Dave Wolverton, June 2014

The Curse of Sally Tincakes

She was brunette, with dark eyes, 100 meters high, and stacked like a pin-up model. The red thermal paint of her bikini had begun to flake after decades spent broiling in the lunar sunlight, but her smile never wavered. Both arms stretched above her head into the black sky. The empty first-stage of an ancient Tokawa moon booster rocket sat balanced across her palms. The cylinder of the booster was parallel to the roughly-graded regolith at the statue's base, where the statue's silvered platform heels sent anchor spikes deep into the lunar basalt below the surface. Across the cylinder the words CAZETTI RACEWAY were emblazoned in massive, royal blue lettering.

Jane Jeffords grinned at the sight.

It had taken years of effort to make it to the top.

Though her eager mood was not shared by her driver.

"What's wrong?" Jane asked Bill. The old man was frowning as he slowly navigated their suborbital moon car over the lumpy, gray infield—patiently waiting for traffic control to clear them for landing. A cloud of other cars, all belonging to competitors, had begun to swarm in the airless space above the track.

"You racing here is a bad idea," Bill said. "Sally Tincakes is watching."

"*Who?*"

"The giant broad down there. Sally Tincakes. That's what we used to call her, two generations ago; when I was still a racer."

Bill's liver-spotted hands smoothly worked the car's controls as he talked. Age had taken his hair and his looks, but not his surety with machines. The car moved with precision.

Jane shook her head, bemused.

"How in the heck did you come up with that ridiculous name?"

"The *real* Sally—Mrs. Frank Cazetti—was the darling of the racing circuit when I was your age. Her billionaire husband made a show of her everywhere he went. Liked to rub it in other guys' faces—how hot she was."

"To the point of making a huge effigy?" Jane said, eyebrow raised.

"That was strictly for publicity," Bill said.

"Why not just put up an LCD billboard?"

"Any idiot can stare at a screen. Sally down there was an experiment in throwback marketing. Something special. From a time when there just weren't that many women on the moon."

Jane felt her stomach shift as the car suddenly dropped, the lunar gravity tugging them gently towards the ground. The race track itself was a wide, shallow, concave half-pipe. It formed an irregular pattern of long straightaways, occasionally punctuated by a series of wicked-looking twists—like an outsized Earth bobsled course. On steroids.

Jane imagined herself hurtling along the route. Goose bumps momentarily formed. This was it. This was the *big time*. Cazetti was the toughest track on the lunar racing circuit. If a lady wanted to make a name for herself, this was the place to do it. The most publicity—and the sweetest purse, too.

The mere thought of it was like rocket fuel in Jane's veins.

She'd come a long way from her delinquent years as a foster kid, bouncing from settlement to settlement in the asteroids. She could still hear her last foster mother screaming at her, as Jane's few belongings were thrown out the door of the crummy family module on Ceres: *no wonder your real parents never came back for you, you'll never amount to anything, do you hear me? Nothing!*

If old Bill noticed her momentary reverie, he didn't show it. His eyes were fixed on the instruments—fingers making subtle attitude adjustments, and their car falling towards its assigned parking spot.

Jane could make out the domed bleachers that ran along the inside of the track, and the various pit assemblies which lay just inside the bleachers.

One of these pit assemblies had an empty stall that beckoned with flashing yellow lights.

Bill guided them in by instinct more than sight—Jane barely felt it when the landing struts finally touched down.

Even though he was ancient, Jane had to admit, Bill still had the right touch. She just hoped that, as crew boss, he'd be the man to help her take the Armstrong Cup. She'd spent a lot of money bringing him out of retirement—at the grudging suggestion of her old crew boss Mike Lomba, who'd quit the circuit and gone back to Earth.

"Let's hurry," Jane said. "I'm ready to give the new Falcon a whirl."

Bill reluctantly took off his headset and pressed the button for the revolving dome lid, which began sliding up from one side of the parking stall.

"You think that'll make a difference?" he said.

"I spent almost as much money on that bike as I did on you. It better be money well-spent."

Bill stared at her, and a shuddering in the car's frame told them the stall was being pressurized.

"First rule I always tell my drivers, it 'aint the crate, it's the ass sitting *in* the crate that matters most."

"You come up with that one yourself?"

"Nope. Richthofen."

"Who?"

"Baron von," Bill said.

Jane just shrugged her shoulders.

"Lord, Jay-Jay, don't you read history?"

"Unless it helps me win, it's a waste of my time."

Bill sighed, never taking his eyes off her.

"Mike told me you were the most single-minded, ferociously competitive driver he ever worked with. That you don't back down and you don't take no for an answer."

"Mike was right," Jane said firmly.

"Would it matter to you if I told you the real reason Mike quit?"

"He said his mother was ill and he had to go home."

"Mike's mother's been dead for ten years."

Now it was Jane who stared.

"Mike didn't have the heart to see you come here and get killed."

"What the hell is *that* supposed to mean?" Jane said, voice raised.

Bill didn't answer right away. He simply sighed again.

"You really don't read your history, do you?"

"Like I said—"

"I heard what you said," Bill snapped, cutting her off. "Everything you've done up to this point—every track you've ever won on—was practice. Cazetti is the real deal. Time for you to finish your edumacation."

• • •

Jane was doing 200 kilometers per hour. A breezy trial pace. The Falcon hummed reassuringly through the fabric on the insides of her knees—her legs gripping the machine tightly. The repulsors on the machine's underside kept a comfortable distance between the machine's lower hull, and the hurtling surface of the track.

Speed was freedom. Jane had been going full-throttle her entire life. In more ways than one.

None of her foster homes had liked her for that reason, nor she them.

A bad fit. That's what the social workers had called her. Couldn't hold her mouth, nor her temper, and the harder some of those families had cracked down, the more energy Jane had put into defying their rules. Until, at last, she'd been put out on her rear. And thank goodness for that.

If she'd once harbored dreams of Mom and Dad—the real Mom and Dad—returning from deep space to rescue her, Jane had learned that there would be no rescuing in this universe, except the kind she made for herself.

The Falcon was proving to be a delight.

Sally Tincakes approached on Jane's left—a looming comedy from the days when men alone had ruled the moon.

"How's it feel for yah?" Bill's voice said in Jane's helmet.

"Liquid," Jane said, smiling.

"Happy so far?"

"So far," she said.

Sally came up fast, and then was gone to Jane's rear. She glanced once over her shoulder, watching the old racing icon begin to shrink in the distance. She snickered quietly.

"What's so funny?" asked Bill.

"You really think that stupid thing's killed five people?"

"All I know is when Frank's wife caught wind of the fact that Frank had been sleeping around with one of the few female drivers then on the circuit, there was hell to pay. Big press conference. Sally threw her ring in Frank's face and said the offending driver would never win a series on Frank's track as long as Sally had something to say about it. Then she divorced him and went to Mars."

"And that's it?" Jane said.

"No," said Bill's voice, crackling. The way he'd said it told Jane the other shoe was about to drop.

"Two weeks after the divorce, Frank's girlfriend had a bad spin-out on this track and augured in at 400 KPH. No chance of survival. Not at those speeds. Three years later, the woman's sister came up in the ranks and she raced here too. Explosive engine failure at 375. They were picking up the pieces for days."

"Bad luck," Jane said, hunching down on her machine as she took it through a series of challenging turns, the gee pulling ferociously at her while she dug her toes into the boot clips and hung on to the control bars with clawed hands. A driver didn't sit *in* the Falcon so much as *on top* of it.

"Bad luck my ass," Bill said. "Six years after that, another woman came up in the standings, and she died here too. Collision with two other bikes. Ten years after that, same thing. A dozen years later, and the very next woman—"

"I know about her," Jane said, pulling out onto a significant straightaway. The throttle on the Falcon glided, pushing Jane up for an extended speed run just prior to the next set of tight turns. "Ellen McTaggert was a legend on the junior tracks. Youngest woman to ever win the Imbrium and Crisium Cups in the same year. She'd have taken the big one if she hadn't been killed."

"Did you know that she died *here*?"

"No," Jane admitted.

"They don't like to advertise this stuff because it's bad for the track and it's bad for the senior circuit overall. But I'm telling you, Jay-Jay, this track is death on women drivers. And old Sally's got something to do with it."

"I thought you said the original Sally went to Mars?"

"Went, and never arrived. To this day nobody knows what happened to her, or the clipper ship she was on."

Jane felt a sudden chill run down her spine. Her parents had vanished in a similar fashion. It was supposed to have been a short trip. Asteroid to asteroid. Their ferry had simply disappeared. A rare but not unheard of event in deep space. Hazard of the business, she'd once heard a veteran astronaut quip.

Which didn't make Jane feel any better. Even now.

"So Sally disappears," Jane said into her suit's helmet-mic. "What's left in it for Frank?"

"He kept the statue up because it was too much of a crowd-pleaser. Frank and the other track co-owners didn't dare take it down. Then, after the third female death on this course, none of us on the circuit thought it was a coincidence or simple bad luck. Not anymore."

"Nonsense," Jane said. But she still felt a chill.

Time to burn it off.

She approached a new set of turns with eagerness, slewing the Falcon with a hip-shake, then tapping her reaction control thrusters to fix her angle. Instead of spinning like a paddle on an air hockey table, Jane's bike stayed nose-down as it went up the banked length of the turn. She was dead-on for the next turn, slewed again, then came out of it and hammered the accelerator with her thumb.

"You ever wonder why we've never had a woman win the Armstrong?" Bill asked as Jane rocketed past an empty set of bleachers.

"They weren't good enough," Jane said.

"Like hell. They were all smart enough to decline an invitation."

"If this is your idea of a pep talk, you're doing a horrible job. Why did you even agree to be my crew boss if you think this is such a lousy idea?"

"Because when Mike told me what your goal was, to win the Armstrong Cup at all costs, I knew I had to try and keep another talented young woman from making the same mistake as Ellen."

"What's it to you?" Jane said. "Fewer women on the top course in the circuit means less competition for the cash and prestige. And it's not like men don't die here as well."

"They do, but not at 100% failure rate. And Ellen wasn't just another racer. Ellen was special."

"A girlfriend?" Jane said, her voice raising just enough to serve as a verbal poke at the curmudgeonly crew boss.

"Worse," Bill said. "She was my daughter."

• • •

The raceway ready room was empty, save for the one racer and the one crew boss.

Jane's undersuit was darkly damp at the arm pits and around her neck. She stared into empty air as old Bill stood near her. Occasionally another racer wandered past, taking note of the fact that Jane was a woman, then averting his eyes when it became clear that the old man and the lady weren't exactly up for company.

"You should have told me," Jane said sternly.

"I just did," Bill replied.

"If you're going to be my crew boss, I need you with your head in the game, not whispering in my ear all the time about how I need to quit. I'm sorry about what happened to Ellen. I really am. But if I'd known it was your own flesh and blood that died here—"

"Almost nobody knows she was my child, because she chose to keep her mother's name. Adara and I weren't the most copacetic couple God ever saw fit to put together. Ellen was probably the best thing we ever did. She lived with her mother until she was 18, then when she left Earth, she came up here to spend time with me. One look at the racing scene, and she was hooked."

"And you didn't warn *her* about the curse?"

"She knew the truth. About all of it. But she was so good. A natural. It was impossible not to encourage her. Then, when she started sweeping the juniors, I got my hopes up. That maybe, just maybe, she'd be the one to do it. To pull it off."

The pain and sorrow in Bill's heart brimmed at the edges of his eyelids. Jane looked up at him, not blinking, trying to decide if she should take his advice, or send him packing.

"It wasn't your fault," Jane finally said.

"Like hell it wasn't," Bill replied. "Mike can tell you, I tried pulling crew boss stints with different drivers, but my heart was never in it. Not after what happened to my girl. It would have been better if she'd stayed on Earth and gone into chemistry like her mother wanted. But no, she had to come play Mario Moon-Rock Andretti with her daddy. Adara never forgave me."

Bill turned away, wetness on his cheeks.

Jane had to admit, if this was all Mike Lomba's way of trying to convince her to avoid tackling the Armstrong Cup, it was a heck of a good try. Her resolve to come to Cazetti—to take the big purse, and hold the big trophy over her head—was slowly softening. A few more days with Bill talking and acting like this, and he might actually start to sway her.

Then she remembered how hard she'd worked. To come from nothing, and get all this way.

17 years old, kicked out of the house; nowhere to go but up.

Other girls might have hung out the proverbial shingle. It would have been easy. Life in the colonies wasn't like life on Earth—choked by so many laws and rules, a person couldn't turn around without getting fined. No. Life in space was free—or about as free as could be managed, within the limits of necessity.

There were still far more men knocking around the solar system, than women, but a girl with a body and a business mind could make quite a bit of money if she liked. Jane hadn't ever been interested in putting on heels and going to work. At least, not *that* kind of work.

Having stowed away on a freighter bound for Earth's Moon, she got a job as a custodial chump at one of the junior-circuit tracks. Cleaning up tables and chairs in the track's miniscule food court. It hadn't paid much, but it had provided the first real independence Jane had ever had. And at night, stuffed into the boxy confines of her rent-by-the-day migrant housing dorm room, she'd dreamed up her plan.

When she wasn't working she hung around the racers' lounge. Nobody at that level was particularly famous, nor wealthy. They weren't much older than Jane. Which made it both easier—and harder—to fit in. All of them hoping desperately for a chance to level up: to graduate to the seniors.

Most never made it. Turnover was common. Guys either quit, or moved on.

Eventually Jane convinced one of them to show her the ropes, which led in turn to her being signed as a backup driver.

Her ability—once unleashed—spoke for itself.

Now, ten years later, Jane ran her own outfit. A one-woman show. Just as she'd always wanted, ever since the first time she'd stood in that crappy little food court on the junior circuit, a wet table rag forgotten in one hand—her eyes watching rapt through the single-pane, curved window as the racers flew around the track, the movement of men and speeding machinery blending to form a thing of unique and intoxicating beauty.

If Mom and Dad could see her now—wherever they were, if anywhere at all—she hoped they were pleased. Jane was on the brink.

Just a few more races to go ...

Jane stood up, flicking a towel around the back of her neck.

"Enough," she said. "Mike swears you're the best at what you do, and Mike is the kind of guy I trust to know what he's talking about. But I don't want to hear any more of this crap about curses and death and how I need to quit. Okay? If you can't do that, then I'd better hire myself a new man. Because I'm racing on this track, and I am winning that trophy. Got it?"

· · ·

When the first race of the series came around, Bill was in the pit with the tech team, suited up and thoughtfully jawing on a wad of gum. There were over five hundred teams putting drivers on the track for the first round, and at twenty drivers per heat, it would be days before the initial cull was complete and Jane could get on with the business of moving up the pyramid.

Not that she took the first heat for granted.

She'd seen other drivers get cocky like that, and wash out. Or worse. If illogical fear was an enemy at one end of the spectrum, foolhardiness was the enemy at the other.

Jane pulled her Falcon out of the pit and lightly maneuvered it into formation with the other drivers circling the track—grid position being determined by comparative standing in the last cup race any of the drivers had competed in. Her breath was even, controlled, and her limbs wiry and strong, but with flexibility to spare. Some drivers got tight on the bike and tried to force the machine to do their will. Jane was a pure flow theorist: best results achieved by blending body to the bike in as natural a symbiosis as possible. Which wasn't always easy at some of the speeds Jane had been known to attain when she was trying to make the checkered beacon.

After trials, Jane could see why Cazetti was the home of the Armstrong Cup. It really was the toughest track she'd yet competed on. Where Bill looked and saw a cursed pattern, Jane looked and saw bald statistics. Of all the modern tracks, even with advanced equipment, the crash and death rate at Cazetti was much higher than anywhere else. That the women drivers of the past had died on the track—or avoided it out of fear—just made Jane that much more determined to be the one who broke through.

Beating the odds was second nature to her.

Green lights at the starting line gave the drivers clearance to throttle up and begin competing—the lone, yellow pace bike slowly coasting down to its own pit, leaving the drivers free to engage.

Jane dug her toes in and went for the throat, almost immediately.

One didn't beat better talent or instincts by being subtle.

Jane knew she wasn't the most gifted driver in the heat, but by God she was going to show those guys who had the most balls.

The Falcon soared down the first straightaway like a comet, a thin mist of reaction exhaust from the main engines forming contrails in the lunar vacuum. If Jane's guess was correct, and it usually was, she'd be fueling up exactly once more than the other drivers. The time she'd lose on an extra stop in the pit would be more than made up for by being aggressive early.

She was on the tails of the grid leaders when they came to the first turn complex, and started banking up the wall of the track.

Ferocious acceleration into the turn and ferocious braking in the middle of the turn left her temporarily in the thick of the leaders as they flirted within dangerous proximity, their bikes sometimes centimeters from catastrophic contact.

Heads and eyes flicked this way and that, some of the others showing their whites as Jane touched thruster studs and then shook her rump to the side, spinning the Falcon a full 720 as she banked precariously close to the upper lip of the track, past one opponent, then came down across the vertical track wall and edged out a second man, finally coming out face-front into the first prolonged straightaway, upon which she gunned the mains once more.

"Fancy," said Bill's gruff voice in her ears.

"Hey," she said, grinning behind the visor of her helmet. "I thought you'd fallen asleep on me. How am I looking?"

"Reckless," Bill said. Paused. Then muttered, "But brilliantly so."

"You 'aint seen nothing yet. Second turn complex is coming up. I'll be out in front of this bunch by the third set of turns. You watch."

And she was right.

By the fourth set of turns—and almost one complete loop around the convoluted track—Jane had gotten a nice lead on the other drivers as they headed into the longest, straightest portion of the course. She set the throttles up to as close to max as she dared, knowing that too much acceleration would leave her unable to compensate when she came back around on the first bunch of turns.

Jane savored the feeling.

It wasn't better than sex. That was a different kind of thrill altogether. But it was probably the next best thing.

After the second go-round, Jane's lead on the pack was considerable, and she began pacing herself: one eye to the dwindling fuel gauge and one ear wide open for news from the pit.

So far, Bill hadn't said much beyond the formalities of his job. Little naggings about consumption rate and vehicle stress, as relayed to the pit's tied-in computers. The pit readout told Bill far more than Jane's display: information which would have been too distracting for her to manage. That was Bill's role. Jane's was to jockey for position and build leads. Bill would make sure her machine ran smoothly.

After five laps, it was time to tank up.

Seeing nobody behind her, Jane slowed and slid into her pit, the space-suited crew rushing out with the fuel hose and jamming it into the side of the Falcon, which hummed lightly as it floated above the ground. Jane saw Bill through the control window and she tapped her right index and middle finger to the rim of her visor in acknowledgement. Bill just watched her, his arms crossed over his chest and his face expressionless.

The crew slapped her thigh and gave Jane the thumbs-up, and she applied throttle again just as the pack burst past the mouth of the pit.

Shortly, Jane was back in the melee, making her way once more up through the grid by guile, skill, and a lot of chutzpah.

Round and round she went, the faces of the domed-over crowds flashing past again and again and again as the laps flew by.

Jane was almost beginning to think she'd mastered the Cazetti track, when the Falcon began to vibrate in a most alarming fashion.

"Bill?" Jane said, hands gone light on the control bars as she felt the machine rattle through the seat of her tight-bottomed vacuum suit.

"Hold on, we're checking," said the old man.

Seconds, seconds …

"Bill, I need status," Jane barked.

"We've got a lubricant pressure spike in Number Two."

"Is it red-lined?"

"Not yet, but it's gone up five percent just in the time we've been talking."

"Can we bleed it off?"

"I already activated the auto-bleed. Look behind you and tell me if you see anything."

Jane craned to check behind her on either side of the bike, and saw nothing.

"Nope," she said. "What's happening?"

"Pressure is up another fifteen," Bill said. "I'm bringing you in."

"It's too soon," Jane said. "I don't need to fuel up for another three laps!"

"I don't care," Bill said. "Bring it in. Now."

Jane considered. This was why she'd needed Mike to tell her who she'd do best with. The crew boss wasn't called a crew boss for no reason. In addition to running the pit, in some ways he also ran the driver—if the driver and the boss had that kind of relationship. And Mike had known Jane would need someone older—who could put his foot down in situations where Jane would want to push things too far.

"Did you hear me?" Bill demanded.

"Roger that," Jane said, finally exhaling. She'd have to fight like hell to get back into it on the next pass, assuming the pit crew could identify the problem and fix it fast. If they couldn't fix it …

No. Jane wasn't going to default, not in this the first run of the series.

She flipped the throttle for Number Two all the way down until it clicked, and the vibration coming up through the saddle, ceased.

"Two has been powered down," Bill said, an edge to his voice. "Can you make it back to the pit, or should I signal for a tow?"

"I'm not coming in," Jane said. "I can finish this thing on one main engine."

"If you burn the engine out, maybe."

"Bill, I'm not letting myself get taken out of this heat. Not by a stupid pressure problem. Shunt the lubrication system over to Number One and run it at 150 percent. I can at least try and stay up with the leaders. Make it to the next heat."

There was a fuzzy silence.

"Don't ever do this again," Bill said, his voice hot.

"It's the reason why everyone buys bikes with two engines now, Bill. Are you with me or not?"

More fuzzy silence.

"Fine. You've got your shunt. We'll see what happens."

• • •

What happened was that Jane finished in fourth place.

Not a tremendously encouraging start to the series, but it at least got her to the next heat, to be held one day later. Since the mechanical issue wasn't of the spectacular, crowd-pleasing, spinning-out-of-control destruct-o-matic variety, Bill and Jane kept the problem to themselves.

Though by the time of the next heat, even the best techs on the pit crew couldn't find the source of the difficulty. Even when running the bike at full-power static.

Race time for the second heat was therefore met with a decidedly tense atmosphere in the pit.

"It's a brand new unit," Jane argued, her helmet hanging in one hand while two pit crew checked the life systems umbilicals of her suit. They prodded at her back while she and Bill glared at one another, his sunken cheeks flexing with quiet contempt.

"It's not the bike," he said adamantly. "It's *her*."

His arm pointed to the ceiling, where the transparent glass gave the pit crew a decent view of the starry sky, as well as Sally Tincakes in the far distance, her CAZETTI RACEWAY sign raised proudly over the field.

The youngsters on the pit crew looked at Bill nervously.

"You go out there again," the old man said, "and there's no telling what might happen this time. First heat was a warning. She doesn't give warnings, usually. We file a technical disqualifier with the track office, and you get excused without having to take a hit in overall standings."

"And no chance at the Armstrong Cup until next year," Jane said. "No thanks. I'm here to do this thing, now. Not later."

Bill's jaw ground bitterly, then he looked away. Silence, for almost a full minute.

"Time hack's in 20 minutes," he finally said. "Get on the bike and get out of here."

• • •

Second heat, and the mysterious pressure problem did not return. The Falcon performed to perfection, earning Jane a first-place finish amidst a much tougher group than she'd been up against for the first heat. She got some nice press in the leader board blogs, and an interview with the track rats who split the news feed back to Earth—for those on the mother planet who were sports-junky enough to care about the exotic stuff going on in the rest of the solar system.

If anyone else noted or cared about the female record of zero finishes and 100 percent fatalities, they didn't say so. Which was just fine with Jane.

But it didn't stop Bill from chastising her again as she prepped for the third of the five total heats.

"It's time to put the baby to bed," Jane said. "We had our one weird problem for the series, and we're going smooth now."

The old man was agitated to the point of fidgeting, his tablet and stylus appearing like foreign objects in his hands as he nervously shuffled them back and forth, one hand to the other.

"Every time you go back out on that track, you're just daring her to notice you. It might not happen now, it might not happen tomorrow, but before this series is over ..."

"Enough," Jane said, sharply. "Quit, and let someone else run the crew. Or shut up and bring me home for the win."

"You really think you're good enough?" Bill said. "I was full of beans in my day, and even I couldn't make it past the third heat."

"Maybe that's your problem," Jane said, letting the techs check her vacuum suit's fittings. "Because you haven't climbed this particular mountain to the top, you're afraid it can't be done?"

Bill's face flushed brightly.

"I'm a lot of things, lady, but I 'aint a jealous man."

"Prove it. Put the curse in the trash where it belongs, and make some good things happen."

Bill didn't look convinced as she went out the airlock for the third heat, but he did look relieved when she came back two hours later, a second-place finish notched.

• • •

The fourth heat meant press both before and after the run. The competition was down to 80 drivers now, and after the day was done, there would be only 20 remaining for the final, championship heat—and the crowning of the Armstrong Cup winner. As the only female in the bunch, Jane got more than her share of attention, including several in-depth interviews during which the inevitable history of the track—the five female deaths, the dearth of female competitors overall—came to the surface.

Jane blew it off. Bravado was a prerequisite for all drivers. But by the time she was suiting up for the heat, she had to admit even she'd been rattled. They'd showed her some of the old footage of the accidents from the past—news people generally having no clue whatsoever about what's appropriate to show a person right before they're about to do something hazardous.

Jane laughed her way through it, but was quiet during the race prep.

"Not so funny when you see what's possible, is it?"

Jane glared at Bill.

"I noticed they didn't even censor the footage of your daughter's death," she said.

"Those bastards don't care about me now, if they ever did in the first place. It's ratings. Crash movies are part of what make the sport fun for the crowds. Money. All that bull."

Jane nodded, and went back to checking her wrists and ankles for complete air seals.

"It's not too late—" Bill began.

But Jane cut him off.

"Oh yes it is. I'm not going to go down as the woman driver who chickened out. Everyone's paying attention to me now."

Bill took a step back, his face gone suddenly white.

The stylus and tablet hit the floor, albeit gently in the lunar gravity.

"What?" Jane said.

"That's *exactly* what Ellen said to me, before …"

Jane literally bellowed, her helmet clenched in one fist.

When she stopped, everyone was blinking and looking strangely at her.

"No more!" she said. "I can't take one more word!"

She looked to one of the young techs. "Is my Falcon ready?"

"Yes ma'am," he said, gulping.

"Then let's go!"

. . .

The fourth heat was by far the most competitive. All of the inexperienced and tentative drivers had been pruned away, leaving the calculating, the experienced, the determined, and the creatively diabolical—to challenge each other for the coveted final 20 spots on the championship grid.

Facing these odds, Jane scrapped through all but the final two laps—just a couple of minor brushes with opponents' vehicles, and the certain knowledge that she'd be wringing a gallon of water out of her undersuit when all was said and done.

Second to last lap, and Jane was in a familiar spot with the leaders at the front of the pack. Having gamed her way into the elite group— same strategies and tactics as always—she'd almost considered her advancement to the final heat to be a foregone conclusion, when one of the other drivers from the middle of the pack made a particularly dangerous—and gutsy—move. Trying to copy Jane's technique as they entered a turn, the man began spinning out of control, first pinballing off one bike, then another, then a third, until suddenly the track was alive with wildly spinning bikes, their riders trying desperately to regain control—overcorrecting—and then either smashing down into the safety barriers nearest the domed-over crowds, or pinwheeling up and off the track altogether, arcing out across the sun-blasted regolith, legs and feet come loose, flailing.

Jane experienced a moment of surreal calm, where all sensation ceased and she could see clearly all the other riders around her, as if in extreme slow motion. Then her Falcon was being smashed down into the safety barriers, the metal grinding on the lunar rock for just an instant.

The controls were frozen as Jane tried to steer up off the wall. She was pinned by her neighbor, who'd nosed into her T-bone style, and was having no success reversing course. They looked at each other for a split second, raw panic passing between them, and then the bikes were flipping, and Jane was thrown high into the airless sky.

Again, a moment of surreal calm: the track, passing swiftly underneath, and the crowd, faces upturned and mouths open wide with astonishment.

Many drivers and bikes spinning, rolling, whirling. One or two skating ahead of the scrum, their drivers raising their fists and pumping them.

Somewhere, Bill's voice was screaming.

Jane started to come down. In the moon's gravity, it wasn't as fast as it might have been on Earth, but with the velocity imparted to her by her bike, there was more than enough kinetic energy to kill her when she hit. Jane caught a glimpse—just a tiny glimpse—of Sally Tincakes: the rocket booster over the statue's head, the exaggerated bustline, the glamour model smile, and then Jane was smashing down into the regolith beyond the track.

• • •

All was white. Jane sat in the ready room. No pit crew. Not even the noise of the crowd reverberating through the walls. Her helmet was clutched in one hand, her elbows on her knees. It was time to go. She felt it in her bones. The race was on. And yet, not. Standing up, she started towards the door to the pit—and stopped short as someone else walked in from the door on the opposite side.

The visitor wasn't in coveralls. Instead, she wore a vintage evening gown styled like those worn by glamour models at the tail end of the previous century: slit high on one thigh, strapless, low-cut, and strategically boned so as to create a gravity-defying silhouette with plenty of cleavage. The dress's satin fabric was embedded with fiber optics that swirled and rippled in various tints and hues of bright blue light.

"Sally," Jane said softly.

The ex Mrs. Cazetti smiled, but didn't say anything. She walked skillfully on a set of platform heels across the ready room to the opposite wall, turned, and leaned against it.

Recent memory swirled: the Falcon had been pinned, then flipped, followed by a long, frantic parabola over the track towards the surface of the Moon just beyond …

Jane felt herself begin to tremble as she stared at the silent apparition whose likeness had towered over Cazetti Raceway since before Jane had been born.

Death—the possibility of it—had always haunted Jane as long as she'd driven the lunar tracks. Yet at the same time, somehow, it never bothered her. She'd been too busy winning. Victory upon victory, each purse growing a little larger. Each season, her horizons broadened a little bit more.

But now …

"Why?" Jane said at Sally, slamming her helmet to the white floor. "I was going to do it. I was going to take the Armstrong Cup. I was going to *win.*"

Sally seemed untroubled by the outburst. Her artfully shadowed eyes glanced past Jane's shoulder, in the direction of the pit door.

Jane glared at her nemesis, fuming, then slowly turned her head as a second figure entered the ready room.

Like Jane, the second visitor was clad in a racer's suit. Its colorful vacuum-tight fabric hugged the racer's athletically feminine body, in spite of frumpy insulation and hoses.

The other racer looked whisperingly familiar, but in a way Jane couldn't quite put her finger on.

The racer's free hand jerked a thumb towards the pit door behind her.

Time to go.

"I know, I know," Jane said, but couldn't move. Her eyes remained locked on the racer's face. So similar to someone Jane knew. Yet, different too.

"Ellen," Jane finally breathed. The racer had Bill's nose, and his prominent cheek bones. She was younger than Jane, and had a bit of cockiness in the way she stood, her eyes staring sympathetically down at Jane's confused and angry face.

Ellen jerked her thumb over her shoulder a second time.

Jane looked to the pit door, which remained open. Then back at Ellen, who had begun to stare at Sally across the ready room. A coldly invisible beam of acknowledgement seemed to pass between the two—opposed ghosts conjured for Jane's benefit, or peril. It was crazy, but it also made perfect sense too. Somehow, it all made perfect sense. Like a waking dream.

Jane felt questions tickling at the back of her tongue, but her mouth made no sound. She simply watched the two spectral women. They stared forcefully at one another for several long, agonizing seconds. Then Ellen walked purposefully to where Jane stood, bent to the floor, and retrieved Jane's helmet.

Ellen passed the helmet respectfully into Jane's hands, then jerked her thumb over her shoulder a third time. No words. But the message was clear.

Sally Tincakes stepped away from the wall, but stopped short as Ellen walked past Jane and stood in Sally's path. With her fists balled on her hips, Ellen didn't look over her shoulder as Jane felt a sudden urgency to move.

Quickly, strength flowed back into Jane's legs.

It took a few broad strides to make it through pit door.

She was already putting her helmet on.

• • •

Jane woke up trying to gasp, and couldn't.

She'd been in and out of the hospital a few times during her racing years, replete with scuffs and broken bones from spills on the junior tracks.

But nothing could have prepared her to be seeing the inside of the coffin-like full-metabolic support unit that housed her now. A small window showed her the ceiling, while warm fluid gurgled around her ears. Several tubes felt like they fed into her mouth and down her throat—they were horribly uncomfortable.

Jane lifted a hand weakly and scratched at the window with her fingertips.

Quickly, several faces appeared in succession, each of them examining hers.

Then, a hissing noise, and all the fluid began to drain away from around Jane's prone body. The coffin came open, and several surgically-suited medical people were extracting the tubes from her esophagus. She coughed and sputtered, hacking violently, which caused tremendous pain in her ribs, until she was shaking like a leaf and breathing in huge gulps of air.

Too disoriented to wave the medical people away, she let them towel her off and sit her up—which also hurt. But at least she was in one piece, or so things seemed. When she tried to talk, she croaked like a frog—her vocal cords soggy. Someone who had the officious demeanor of a physician began poking and prodding, shining his light into her eyes and asking her questions to which she answered by holding up either one finger, or two.

Once they got her into a proper medical gown, they tucked her between the sheets of a rolling gurney which spirited her away from the critical care ward with its rows of identical, human-sized immersion capsules.

Jane went through several brightly-lit hallways, her hand weakly raised to shield her eyes from the harsh glare. Then she was deposited in a softly-lit intensive care room. She felt them plug her into the monitoring and life support station that sat like a pillar in the room's center. A pepper-haired male nurse spoke comforting words, then disappeared. Leaving Jane in a fuzzy stupor that could have lasted minutes, hours, or days.

Clarity was achingly gradual. Staff came, and staff went. Always, they murmured encouragingly to her as they checked her connections to the monitor, and adjusted the intravenous tubes that snaked away from the tops of both wrists. Jane's mouth became dry, and they let her drink water. When her stomach grumbled, they gave her soup. When her bowels complained, they ushered her delicately to the lavatory and back, her tubes and wires trailing behind her.

Finally, the floor physician disconnected her from the ICU tower, and she was again whisked by gurney through a series of brightly-lit hallways, until she was left in a simpler, less mechanized room.

She weakly depressed the stud on the gurney that would call the nurse, and was surprised when a familiar face poked through her sliding glass door.

Bill wouldn't look her in the eyes when he hesitantly entered her patient room.

"I'm glad you came to see me," she said, her voice soft and breathy.

"I've been in and out of this hospital at least a dozen times since they brought you in," Bill replied, hand wrapped tightly around the cup of coffee he'd brought. "I almost couldn't take seeing you comatose in the critical ward. You looked as good as dead. The medics said your heart and lungs had stopped. That the machines were doing all the work, at least for awhile."

Jane nodded, and let her head fall back on her pillow while she closed her eyes, remembering the final instant before she hit ground.

When she opened her eyes again, Bill was still there. Seated in the recliner at the gurney's side. Watching attentively.

"It's a miracle that you landed where you did," Bill said. "All that regolith they dug up and piled on the edges of the track, it's like slushy snow. And meters deep. You soft landed. Or at least you landed and didn't turn to insta-jelly. The other drivers, they weren't so lucky."

"I bet the footage of the wreck was all over the news," Jane said.

"Biggest and most spectacular racing disaster in years," Bill said, then snorted. "They replayed it for a week, even on Earth. As the only survivor, your name got the headlines. If you check your e-mail you'll probably find several gazillion messages. You've suddenly become the best-known racer on the senior circuit. I've had at least a dozen companies contact me, wanting to know if they can hire you to be

21

their spokeswoman—assuming you didn't come out of the hospital a vegetable."

Now it was Jane's turn to snort. Then she coughed, and lay still for a few quiet minutes.

"I suppose I should feel lucky," Jane said.

"Damn right you should," Bill replied. "You'll have time for survivor's guilt later. Trust me. I've been through a wreck or two in my day. Though nothing close to what you went through."

Jane simply nodded. Bill slowly sipped at his coffee. Not saying another word.

"I still need you, old man."

He looked up.

"For what?"

"Sponsors and crash insurance should cover the medical bills, and they may even buy me a new bike."

"The race is *over*," Bill said firmly.

"For now, yes. But I'll be back. Next season. Cazetti hasn't seen the last of Jane Jeffords."

Bill almost dropped his coffee into his lap.

"The damned track takes you out, and you want to go *back?*"

"Of course," Jane said, smiling. "Sally Tincakes already killed me. Once. She can't rightly get me twice, can she? That's double jeopardy. I swear to you, next year, this woman is hoisting the Armstrong Cup over her head."

Jane jabbed a thumb at her chest in emphasis.

Bill looked like he was about to argue, then sighed—a long, tired sound.

"How can you be so sure it won't happen again?"

"I'm pretty sure."

"*How* are you sure, though?"

Jane swallowed hesitantly, considering whether or not to tell Bill everything she remembered from after the crash.

"Let's just say I think it's what Ellen wants."

"Ellen? My daughter? What's she got to do with this?"

"Nothing. And everything. Maybe old Sally Tincakes *has* cursed Cazetti Raceway. But I think it's time to put paid to the legend. For Ellen. For every racer who died."

Jane reached out a hand and laid it on Bill's age-freckled arm. He flinched at her touch, but he didn't move away. His old eyes had gone watery and several tears trailed down his age-weathered cheeks.

"Ellen ..." Bill whispered.

"Yes," Jane said.

The room was quiet for several minutes. Then Bill stood up and used a towel from the patient room's dispenser to wipe his face.

"I doubt you'll have enough for a new Falcon," he said.

"Maybe I can buy a used Firebee," Jane replied. "Something that will get me back on the track. Until I get my winnings up enough to buy something more sophisticated. Or maybe you were right, maybe it's not the crate, but the woman sitting in it that counts."

Bill looked at her with his eyes large and worried, still not quite accepting her determination. But then he closed them and shook his head slowly, the smallest of smiles creeping onto his thin lips. He put down his towel and began chuckling. It was an odd sound, gravelly and low. But it was the first time Jane remembered the old guy laughing since she'd first met him.

"Jay-Jay," he said between laughs, "did I ever tell you my daughter would have liked you?"

"No," Jane said. When Bill didn't elaborate further, Jane clasped her hands in her lap and looked at him with raised eyebrows. "So what's your answer, old man? Are you with me?"

They studied one another for a moment—racer to racer. Then Bill crossed the tiled floor and stuck his palm out.

"I'm with you," Bill said.

Jane grasped his hand in hers—and realized it was the first time they'd ever shaken. A good feeling. Strong. Solid.

"We've got six months to get ready for next season," he said.

"Plenty of time," Jane said. "Plenty of time."

▼ ▲ ▼ ▲ ▼

"The Curse of Sally Tincakes" was a lot like my Hugo and Nebula nominated novelette, "Ray of Light," in that "Tincakes" originated as a workshop story from one of Kristine Kathryn Rusch's and Dean Wesley Smith's short fiction workshops, up in Lincoln City, Oregon. Also like "Ray of Light," this story got

me a terrific cover—this time for Orson Scott Card's InterGalactic Medicine Show. I liked the cover so much (raised glass to Nick Greenwood!) I knew I wanted it on my second short fiction collection; with "Tincakes" as the opening tale.

The workshop assignment had been to write a story about curses. As I often do when I tackle such assignments, I try to look at the usual angles—in this case, I knew they'd largely be fantastical and/or horrific in flavor—and choose a path less traveled. Being somebody who pays attention to sports (while not being much of a fanatic of any given sport, outside of professional basketball) I knew that sports lore contained a lot of fertile ground for a potential story. At the same time, I wanted to make my story rigorously science fictional. Something I could pitch at an editor who knew my bona fides in that particular way.

It hit me instantly that I ought to do a racing story.

Once upon a time, the narrated musical fable group Celestial Navigations (fronted by actor Geoffrey Lewis) did a rather wonderful series of spoken word stories about space racing. I was definitely channeling some of their energy when I conjured up the imagery of Jane Jeffords and her Falcon hurtling along the concave lunar track at unspeakable speeds. Somehow, a good racing story is the kind of story that just never gets old. Whether it's The Black Stallion or Chariots of Fire or The Last American Hero or Breaking Away, the visceral imagery and feeling of the underdog going up against the odds in a foot race, bike race, horse race, car race … these are all variations on a classic theme—a theme I enjoyed working with when I wrote this story.

Of course, much credit goes to Edmund Schubert, who is something of a silent co-author. Ed liked "Tincakes" a lot when he had it sent up to him by Scott M. Roberts and the other junior editors at IGMS, but Ed had some specific ideas about how to re-shape the ending. After going back and forth a bit with it, I surprised Ed by taking "Tincakes" in a direction Ed did not expect—but which he liked anyway. And readers liked too, based on the feedback I got.

The Bricks of Eta Cassiopeiae

I was humming to myself as I checked the primitive gauge on the kiln. The song running in my head was an old tune. Something sweet, catchy, and which I'd not heard in a long time. I couldn't help myself. It's hard to not be happy when you're getting short. A few more months and I'd make parole. Just the thought of it sent quivers of anticipation through my stomach. *Freedom!*

The gauge's needle hovered steadily in the red.

"Still too hot," I said over my shoulder. "Gotta wait another day."

"That's nice," said my fellow inmate, Godfrey. "So what do we do until then?"

"You dig," came the reply from Ivarsen, our lone guard.

Godfrey frowned and spit at Ivarsen's feet, missing just barely.

Ivarsen allowed himself a small smirk and scrubbed the wad of saliva under a heel. Like the rest of us, he wore a broad-brimmed sun hat and wraparound sunglasses to protect against Eta Cassiopeiae's blinding rays. Unlike the rest of us, his shorts and shirt were khaki—instead of prisoner orange—and he had a holster on his hip with a high-power pistol in it.

In the two planetary years since I'd been assigned to Ivarsen's care, I'd never seen him draw that gun. But with how Godfrey had been acting since his arrival one week ago, I wondered if even Ivarsen's patience had limits.

"Kid," I said, "How in the world did you ever make this detail?"

"I've got a winning personality," Godfrey said, grinning.

"Like hell," I said under my breath.

Godfrey snorted loudly—a long, thoughtful fricative of his nasal passages—and spit again. This time at *my* feet.

Lisa Phaan put a hand to her mouth, appearing to suppress a chuckle. She was our site's only female inmate: small, strong, and lightning-quick. Which explained why the two male prisoners who had preceded Godfrey had each been sent to the hospital prior to their being put back in exile on The Island. Nobody ever actually said it was attempted rape. I don't think Lisa let it get that far. All I know is, each time I was awoken in the middle of the night to hear Lisa's would-be suitor screaming ... and then Ivarsen was calling for a medevac.

When she wanted to, the lady could be a viper.

But Godfrey—cocky and unaware—had been eyeing her since his arrival. I almost hoped he'd try for a piece. The boy needed some cutting down.

"You know the drill, Prisoner Godfrey," Ivarsen said. "Prisoner Fraccaro and you on the shovels. Prisoner Phaan on the dumper. Wait here while I drive it around."

Our guard turned and walked away into the white glare of midday, the broken and rocky landscape shimmering behind him.

Godfrey leaned close and said, "Why don't we just snuff him?"

I turned and looked at the huge-bodied youth, my eyebrows raised.

"And do *what?* It's two hundred kilometers to anywhere. The sun will kill you before you get thirty. Besides, Ivarsen has a chip in his body that monitors his vitals and stays in constant contact with a Corrections satellite. All the guards at these remote projects have one. If his vitals quit, the satellite gets alerted. Then the cavalry comes. With rifles. Shoot first, ask questions later."

"Bull," Godfrey said.

"You really want to find out?"

The kid kept looking at our guard while Ivarsen receded into the heat.

"Look," I said, "is it really that bad? Time served here counts triple what it counts on The Island. They feed us and give us shelter. We're not at the mercy of the elements. Why ruin it?"

Godfrey turned and looked at me, hands balling.

"Screw you," he said, and walked away.

I shook my head, wondering if I'd ever been that incomprehensibly belligerent when I was in my twenties. Then I went over to slap shut the ceramic door that covered the kiln's thermometer.

As indigenous brick kilns went, ours was pretty standard: a four-meter-cubed box constructed from cut-rock slabs. It sat on the eroded central peak of a shallow crater whose expanse had been populated with automated mirrors. Currently, those mirrors aimed skyward. But when we put a batch of bricks into the kiln, and the computer angled all those mirrors towards the small hill at their center, the kiln lit up like a bug under a magnifying glass.

Depending on the season and the weather, the kiln could take a full day to fire up—and the days on Eta Cassiopeiae's fifth planet were very long, especially at this latitude.

In the meantime there was always more clay. And the new settlements along the polar coast always needed more bricks. In a world with no large flora and relatively little accessible iron, what else was there to build with? It was a supply niche that would have been filled commercially, if the prison system hadn't gotten there first. The work was arduous and filthy—the kind of soul-mending stuff reformists had been foisting on the incarcerated for many centuries, going all the way back to Earth. On Eta Cassiopeiae Five, nobody in their right mind wanted to be this close to the equator, so the colonial government farmed the work out to Corrections. Thus everyone was kept happy—even us cons.

It sure beat the crap out of The Island, where there were no rules and it was literally every man for himself. I'd lasted just long enough to decide that The Island was a slow death sentence, then made an appeal to a Corrections Magistrate during one of the random, heavily-armed inspection tours Corrections occasionally made. They'd liked my file—all of us under the watchful eye of Corrections had one, even those of us cast off utterly from civilization—so I'd been given the chance to go to work. And work I'd done. Happily. Eagerly. With a full stomach and boots on my feet and no fear that the gangs were going to roll me up in the middle of the night and poke holes in me. Or worse.

A mechanized grumble broke me out of my reverie.

I turned to watch as the dumper came rolling down the dusty main lane between the mirrors. The huge truck ran on a hydrogen fuel cell and was our primary means of transport; vital to weekly operations. Wet clay was extracted from the hills two kilometers to the east, then had to be moved via dumper to the forming pit. Once formed and dried, the "green" bricks were put on ceramic pallets which again went into the back of the truck for movement to the kiln. Fired and cooled, those bricks stayed on their pallets until they were moved to the staging area to await pickup by the monthly roadtrains headed north. Empty pallets came back from the settlements on roadtrains headed south, to be filled again. And so forth.

Nobody was allowed to drive the dumper except Ivarsen, who kept the truck's coded keycard on his person at all times. He handled the thing like he'd been born to it, and not for the first time I wondered where our guard had acquired such skill. The man didn't talk about his past, though it often seemed like we were just his hardhats, and he just the foreman—not a bad way to operate, considering the temperament of some Corrections officers I'd known in my day.

When the truck came to a halt, Ivarsen leaned out and yelled, "Everybody in back!"

We trooped to the ladder on the side and climbed up and over, then down into the extra-large bed where two single-person shovels sat. They're called shovels because the hydraulic arm on the front of each unit was attached to a large scoop designed to dig hundred-kilo hunks of clay out of the ground.

There was nothing to say while we rode out of the crater and started on the packed-earth highway to the eastern hills. We just gazed out the back of the bed, the truck kicking up a column of dust, each of us enjoying the movement of air which partially alleviated the ever-present heat. Once we arrived at the dig site, Lisa climbed up on top of the cab while Godfrey and I slid into the bucket seats on our respective shovels. Ivarsen used controls in the cab to lower the aft lip of the dumper's bed to the dirt, and then Godfrey and I caterpillared out and began to attack the scarred hillside.

Clay is not the same thing as mud. I'd learned that my first month on the job. You had to look for the phyllosilicate deposits, then clear off the top layers of worthless dirt and pry out the heavier stuff underneath. It came in various stages of plasticity, depending on how much moisture a given dig retained between thunderstorms, and we could hydrate it using a cistern back at the forming pit.

A familiar, pungent odor filled my nose when my shovel's scoop bit into the ground. I worked the scoop's hydraulic controls until a decent hunk had been pulled free, then motored back to the dumper and threw my load in. I did this two more times, and stopped to watch Godfrey struggle for his first shovelful. It was his third time driving, and the kid still didn't get it. He was punching his scoop into the hillside like a jackhammer, knocking crumbled clay loose until it threatened to engulf the front of his machine.

I motored up to him and yelled over the whine of the hydraulics, "Finesse, man! Gradual and steady! Push in slow, lift out slow."

"I'm trying!" He yelled back. "Tractor's nothing but a piece of shit!"

I wanted to tell him it wasn't the machine that was a piece of shit, then thought better of it.

"Here," I said over the noise of both engines, "watch me."

Godfrey backed off while I drove up and eased my scoop into the beige-gray mass. The load pulled free with relative ease, I spun my shovel on the axis of its treads, and moved away to let the kid continue.

His next few attempts were almost competent.

I sighed and kept working, the day wearing imperceptibly on while we filled the dumper with clay. Lisa used her controls on the top of the dumper's cab to operate the dumper's claw arm, re-arranging our shovelfuls as the need arose, and ultimately picking up and depositing each shovel back into the bed once we had enough clay to take back to the forming pit.

Ivarsen watched us the whole time, standing off from the dig by about ten meters, hands on his hips. His head didn't move, but I always had the impression his eyes were constantly sweeping from behind his sunglasses, like radar.

Once we'd secured the shovels and the dumper's claw arm, we climbed back into the bed and Ivarsen went back to the cab. The drive to the forming pit was as silent as the drive from the kiln, and I idly scratched dirt out of my hair, thinking again about my imminent parole. The government of Eta Cassiopeiae Five was finally going to make me a citizen again. It was odd to think I'd spent my entire thirties locked up—the bitter wage of a mistake I'd long since learned to regret. I wondered what kind of life I could now make for myself, beyond firing brick. With my legal file as checkered as it was, my options were limited. Maybe I could talk to the asteroid miners again? They always needed help. Could I get a felony waiver?

Such thoughts continued to occupy me when we arrived at the forming pit.

Lisa plucked the shovels from the bed before Ivarsen up-ended the entire thing into the slaking ditch. There the clay was allowed to bathe in rainwater from the nearby cistern, and would sit until it had reached an appropriate state of homogenous mushiness. A different slaking pit was ready for draining, and we polished off the early evening by shoveling—manually, this time—wet clay into forms. The forms came in various sizes and dimensions, to fulfill the needs of the construction workers back in civilization, and we had to poke and stir the contents of each form to get the air bubbles out before the clay began to dry. Trapped air bubbles would cause the dried bricks to crack or even explode in the kiln during firing, and though a certain percentage of the load would always be scrapped as a result of damage, losing too many bricks was a basic waste of sweat equity—not to mention it showed up on the monthly tally.

Again Ivarsen watched us from a distance, never moving except to take a tug off the canteen normally slung across his shoulder.

When we'd gotten a decent bunch of the forms filled and stacked for drying, we were all exhausted and ready to call it quits. We washed—clothes and all—using the make-shift showerheads attached to the cistern, then climbed back up into the dumper bed. The clay in the bed's bottom had dried and cracked, and we let the wind dry us on the ride from the forming pit to our hooches—which sat just outside the low rim of the kiln's crater wall.

Chow consisted of pre-sealed trays which were microwavable and contained a variety of meats, starches, and vegetable matter. All of it originally Earth-native—imported with the original colonists who'd made the long trip from Sol System, almost a century prior. Earth life did okay on EC5, with a bit of genetic tweaking to account for EC5's soil and mineral content. The farms surrounded the coastal settlements, and—some day—there would be forests in the hills and mountains surrounding the farms. And men would build with wood again.

Until then, the world needed bricks, which meant the world needed *us*.

We tore into our meals, then threw the empty trays and drinking bulbs into the trash compactor. With Eta Cassiopeiae setting, we each took turns at the single outhouse, and finally stumbled into bed—EC5's three small moons beginning to rise over the eastern hills. Though, calling them moons was probably a bit too generous. They were captured asteroids: one trailing behind the other, which trailed behind the other again. I imagined the miners and engineers working all day and all night—all planetary year long—turning those moons into way stations for the big colonial ships that would eventually bring more people from Earth; once EC5's biosphere had been sufficiently beefed up. Two, maybe three more human generations.

Some day EC5 would be a garden. But not yet.

With night fully upon us, Ivarsen activated the electric fence which cordoned off the prisoner hooches from the guard hooch. Like most nights, I found the familiar hum from the fence's transformer to be oddly soothing. I also wondered if tonight I'd be awakened by yet another horrified scream.

"Don't bite off more than you can chew, kid," I said quietly, and laughed.

Smiling in spite of myself, I faded into oblivion.

• • •

Morning came, and Godfrey was undamaged. In fact, we had to go kick him out of his cot an hour after sunrise. The activities of the day before had thoroughly exhausted him, despite his youth and size. Grousing and giving us the finger, Godfrey hastily pulled on his jumper and work boots. We ate a microwaved breakfast, used the outhouse again, then took the dumper back into the crater.

This time the kiln was sufficiently cool. Needle in the green.

Lisa used the dumper's claw arm to lever the kiln's huge door out of the way—like the angel rolling aside the stone at the crypt of Jesus—and we all walked in to inspect our work. Even Ivarsen, who seemed to take genuine pleasure in seeing the finished bricks, all lined neatly on their stacked ceramic pallets, ready to be sent north and laid into homes, shops, offices, apartments, and everything else that needed building.

Lisa and I showed Godfrey how to check for cracks and damaged bricks, which we'd separate from the rest when we used a shovel—now modified with a fork on its arm—to lift each pallet from the kiln and place it carefully near the dumper.

The kid just grunted, saying, "Whatever," and began examining the kiln's contents. He did it with the enthusiasm of a six year old being made to eat asparagus.

Lisa followed me out of the kiln while I went to get my canteen. Constant hydration was an ever-present necessity this far south.

"Lee," Lisa said as she leaned close to me, "I'm so sick of getting stuck with these morons."

"Yeah. Must be slim pickings these days. Pretty soon Corrections might have to start drafting civilians for the brick brigades."

Ivarsen, who had been getting out of the dumper's cab, laughed mightily. "That'll be the day! Imagine how much they'd have to pay union workers to come out here and do what you guys do for free."

"*You're* union," I said, with sarcasm.

"Damn right," Ivarsen replied, thumping his chest with a fist.

We shared a smile between the three of us. Then came a sudden yelp from the kiln, followed by the sound of a pallet collapsing and bricks tumbling.

"*Lord,*" Lisa said, rolling her eyes.

We hurried back through the kiln entrance to find Godfrey hopping up and down on one leg while he held the other foot. Obscenities peeled from his lips.

Lisa, Ivarsen and I almost fell over, it was so funny.

"Stop laughing," Godfrey fumed.

"Kid," I said, "One man's pain is another man's pleasure."

Godfrey's mouth grimaced sourly as he prepared to give me a four-lettered broadside, but then he stopped.

All the pallets were rattling violently.

"What the—?"

The booming rumble shuddered through the floor of the kiln.

"Quake!" Ivarsen yelled.

Really? I'd not been through one of those since I'd been a boy.

What happened next was a slow blur.

Stacked columns of pallets swayed like hula dancers. Lisa was screaming and trying to get to the door, only she kept having her feet knocked out from under her. One of the columns tilted too far, and collapsed against the side of the kiln. Then another. Godfrey managed to keep his feet, his mouth hanging open and his eyes gone stupidly wide. The column next to him started to give—this time, towards the middle of the kiln.

Ivarsen's reaction was so fast I didn't even realize what had happened until both he and Godfrey were on the floor, sliding out of the path of the collapsing bricks.

One of the walls popped thunderously, and a new crack split wide from floor to ceiling, shining a shaft of light crossways to that which already flooded in from the main door.

Two more columns of bricks went down.

And then ... silence.

Lisa and I were coughing spastically on the dust that had filled the kiln. I discovered I'd been sitting on my butt the entire time. Heaps of whole and broken bricks were everywhere, and I got to my feet to move around to where I thought I'd last seen Ivarsen and the kid.

I got there just in time to see Godfrey crown Ivarsen with a brick the size of my forearm. Our guard crumpled.

"Oh shit—" I said.

The kid moved quickly, snatching the pistol out of Ivarsen's holster and pointing it at me while he used his free hand to explore the pockets of Ivarsen's shorts.

Lisa froze when she came around the corner and saw what was happening.

"You stupid, stupid asshole," I said to Godfrey. "Ivarsen saved your life."

"Fraccaro, you and Phaan get against the wall."

Lisa and I didn't move until Godfrey thumbed the pistol's safety and pulled the hammer back. Then we raised our hands and backed into the shadows as Godfrey came away with the keycard for the dumper.

"You won't make it," Lisa said, deadpan. "The chip is already sending its alarm to the satellite."

Godfrey scoffed. "Pig 'aint dead. Just knocked out."

I looked at Ivarsen's still form, and thought I saw thick, dark fluid running from the back of his head where Godfrey had hit him.

"If he dies," I said, "then we're dead too."

"You, maybe," Godfrey replied. "I'm out of here."

"Where are you going to go, kid? There's no native forage on this land mass. And they can track the movement of the dumper. You'll be—"

"Shut the hell up, Fraccaro. Maybe you like being a slave. Not me. Freedom's better than nothin'. I'll take my chances."

Finally, the rage that had been rising in me, boiled over.

"Damn you, I was getting *paroled!*"

Godfrey considered this while sidling towards the doorway. He looked back at Ivarsen, then to Lisa, and then to me.

"Sorry man," was all he said.

Then he was gone, and Lisa and I were rushing to Ivarsen's side. The guard's heart still beat, and his lungs took in air. That was good. But the deep laceration on his head bled profusely, and I dared not explore it for fear of finding pulp where there should be skull.

Lisa ripped open Ivarsen's shirt and we tore off pieces to use as a temporary bandage.

Outside, the dumper's electric engine started up. We heard its large tires crunch on the dirt while Godfrey drove away.

Lisa was cursing and started to rise to her feet, but I stopped her.

"Let him go. We've got more immediate concerns."

She thought for a second.

"We can take him on the shovel. It will be fastest."

I nodded—there was a first aid locker in Ivarsen's hooch. Would we get to it in time?

• • •

Godfrey had gone off-road and disappeared over the southern hills by the time we got Ivarsen back to camp. I drove the shovel while Lisa sat on a pallet that we'd cleared, and which now held Ivarsen's unmoving body. The pallet was perched on the fork of the shovel's hydraulic arm, and I did my best to avoid bumps. At ten kilometers an hour, it took precious minutes to motor out of the crater and follow the trail along the rim wall to where the hooches sat.

I set the pallet down and Lisa leapt off, running into Ivarsen's hooch to get his cot. It wasn't a perfect stretcher, but we managed to get him onto it, moving him into his hooch so he'd be out of the sun. Lisa helped me rummage through the first aid locker and apply a more suitable bandage to the head wound. Next I checked his pupils with a flashlight, and was alarmed to see that one of them had gone as wide as the iris would allow.

"Damn," I said.

"Is it that bad?" Lisa asked.

"Bad enough. We need Ivarsen's satellite phone. If he doesn't get a medevac soon, he's as good as dead."

"I think the phone was in the cab of the dumper," Lisa said. "He always kept it there when we were working."

Lisa and I looked at each other. Neither of us needed to say what was on our minds.

When the SWAT guys got here, it wouldn't matter what story we told them. All they'd find was a dead Corrections officer, and two live prisoners. And that would be that. Meaning me and Lisa. Done. And Godfrey, when they tracked him down, as surely they would. We'd all be lucky if they sent us back to The Island. More probably, we'd be shot.

I stood up from Ivarsen's side and stomped out into the glaring sunlight, sweat making my shirt damp and my eyes squinting in spite of my sunglasses. I screamed and kicked the treads on the shovel. Years of patient effort. Down the toilet. Thanks to a dumb kid. I'd have kept screaming, except that I thought of Ivarsen, and how he'd deserved this even less. Me, I'd lost my life a long time ago. And deservedly so. But Ivarsen had been a decent man. Such a waste!

I went back inside to find Lisa rummaging furiously through Ivarsen's other things. Our patient's breaths had become quicker, more shallow, and a sheen of sweat covered the exposed areas of his skin. I unzipped his sleeping bag and threw it over him for a blanket, then went to help Lisa. She was obviously looking for a backup phone. Surely they wouldn't issue Ivarsen just the single unit?

The only thing we found was the remote for the mirrors in the crater.

Lisa threw the remote to the floor in disgust, but I picked it up and walked outside, staring up into the cerulean sky. Lisa came out and looked up with me.

"What?"

"How many satellites watch this region?" I asked.

"Heck if I know."

I kept looking. Then I quickly strode to the crater's rim wall and scrambled up its side until I was standing on the top and staring down into the circular field of mirrors.

The remote had several preset codes. I chose the toggle for manual movement. The circular thumb pad in the middle illuminated, and I depressed it, pushing first to the north, then to the south. Out in the field, the little servos on the base of each mirror began to whine. The mirrors obediently leaned to the south, then back to the north.

Okay ...

I programmed in a repeating series of motions, pressed the SEND button, and then dropped the remote into my pocket and watched the mirrors begin their slow dance.

Lisa nodded, catching on. "I hope someone is paying attention, Lee."

• • •

The day wore on, and we stayed in the guard's tent. Lisa occasionally sponged Ivarsen down with a wet rag, and I ran checks on his vitals every fifteen minutes, as well as checking his pupils. The dilated one stayed dilated, and I wondered if the man wasn't just a vegetable already.

Out in the crater, the mirrors kept spinning and swiveling.

There was no sound, other than the occasional wind across the camp.

Evening came quickly. When I checked the supply bunker I discovered that Godfrey had been there before us and taken most of the cases of microwave meals. He'd at least been that smart. But without water I knew he'd be getting thirsty soon. And unless he found a natural spring, or we got some rain, he'd be in a bad way before the following day was out.

I allowed myself a small amount of satisfaction at the thought of Godfrey dying for lack of water, then I heated two trays for Lisa and I, and went back into the tent.

I almost dropped the trays when Ivarsen's head turned to look at me.

"Fraccaro," the man said, whisperingly.

My relief could not have been more obvious. "Good heaven, Ivarsen. I thought you'd gone to mush on us."

"Can't," he said, then stopped. "Hard … to think."

"Can you drink water?"

" … Try … "

Lisa put her canteen to his lips and gave him a sip, which he kept down. Giving him too much would be worse than giving him none at all, so we waited and watched while he blinked randomly.

"Godfrey?" Ivarsen finally asked.

"Gone," I said. "He took the dumper, your gun, and most of the food. And your satellite phone. I've got the mirrors in the crater waving around, hoping to attract some satellite attention. Like it will do us any good after dark."

"Good … idea."

He went silent again for several minutes.

Then, "Leandro … "

It was the only time he ever used my first name.

I leaned over him. "Yah, boss?"

"Not your fault … have to … tell them."

"Just hang in there. You're not dead yet."

"Will be … soon."

Lisa held Ivarsen's hand. Her expression was agonized.

"Lisa," Ivarsen said. "Find my … PDA."

Lisa and I bugged our eyes out at each other. We never knew he had one!

Reading our surprise, Ivarsen said, "Access panel on the … solar power battery."

Lisa and I both raced out into the gloaming light, finding the big battery for the camp. We pried off the service plate with our fingernails. The little PDA was perched out of sight, just inside and to the left.

Lisa grabbed it and we charged back to the hooch, freezing when we looked at Ivarsen's face.

His eyes were still open, along with his mouth. But his chest no longer drew air.

• • •

We did what we could for Ivarsen's body, then despondently trudged for our separate hooches, figuring there was nothing to be done but to sleep, and wait.

To my surprise, Lisa stopped me and motioned me towards her door.

"Last man that went in there came back without his cojones," I joked.

"Last man who went in there did so without an invitation," Lisa replied.

Raising an eyebrow, I went with her into the hooch. It was amazingly neat and orderly, right down to the dirt floor having been lined with used meal trays—as makeshift tiles.

She sat down on her cot and I took a seat next to her, the lights from EC5's three small moons shining through the mesh walls around us.

"Months? That was all?" Lisa said.

"Yeah," I replied. "Three. I was getting real short."

"I can't even think about parole yet."

"Shoplifting?" I said, smiling at my own joke.

"Drugs," Lisa replied, not smiling. "I used to be a pharmacist, back in the world. Got hooked on my own product, you might say. Started dealing. Stupid. Got caught. Wound up detoxing on The Island. Almost killed me. But at least I got clean."

"That sucks," I said, turning serious.

"You ever been addicted to anything, Lee?"

"Not really. I'm a teetotaler." And that was the truth.

Lisa shuddered. "Don't. Don't ever."

I'd never seen her more stone-cold serious.

"Yes ma'am," I whispered.

And that was all I could say

Silence filled the dark. This was more personal information than Lisa had ever shared with me before. I felt we were both in particularly uncomfortable territory.

"Do you think we'll be executed?" She asked.

"Yes," I said. "Corrections doesn't play around when it comes to one of their own going down in the line of duty. On my last brick site, I saw a guy actually try to take out the guard with a shiv. Guy was crazy to do it. The guard emptied a whole clip into the perp. Corrections never even did an investigation. The hurt guard left on a medevac, and we three prisoners who remained, all got split up. That was when they sent me here. To work for Ivarsen."

Lisa's head hung to her chest for an undetermined period of time, and when she looked back up at me I saw wetness on her cheeks. Which put a lump in my throat, for her sake. I suddenly felt stupid for telling her about the prisoner who got shot—like she really needed to hear that from me at this moment. *Idiot.*

I sighed and looked at the floor. It wasn't fair. She was young. And, apparently at last, clean. As a pharmacist, she was educated too. She deserved a fresh start. But wouldn't get it.

Just like me.

For no particular reason that I can recall, I slowly leaned down and pressed my lips to hers. It was a crazy move, given her history.

But for the second time that night, she surprised me.

My kiss was returned warmly.

"Thank you," Lisa said.

"No, thank *you*," I said.

We held hands as we sat on her cot. The most intimate contact I'd had with any person in years.

Then, she asked, "What about you, Lee?"

"Huh?"

"You now know why *I'm* in. But what about you?"

My hesitation must have been palpable.

"Sorry," she said. "I didn't want to pry. I just figured—"

"It's okay," I said. "I suppose you oughta know."

I breathed in and collected my thoughts.

The younger me had had a problem with his temper. I'd kept it under wraps when I was in school, but after I got out, I'd gone through a few different jobs because I couldn't keep my lip zipped in front of the boss. Then came the day on the work site when one little jerk of an engineer had decided to get up in my face. He'd been smaller and smarter than me, and he'd let me know exactly what kind of loser he thought I was. Insults turned to screams, and before I knew it I'd knocked the man onto his back, and was beating him with my wrench. Hard, vicious strokes. The kind of blows a man doesn't just get up and walk away from.

They told me later that the other workers had to pry me off the engineer, who was pronounced dead at the scene before the constabulary cuffed me and took me away to Corrections. I can still remember sitting in the back of the wagon, bawling my eyes out. *What had I done?*

Dad had tried to keep me from doing time. He'd spent what he could for legal help. But it didn't matter. I'd killed another human being. Eta Cassiopeiae Five might have been frontier territory, but you didn't just murder a man—in hot blood or cold—and walk away from it unscathed.

Back on Earth they had people to spare. On EC5? No way. Especially not when the victim had been educated. There weren't any levels or degrees of punishment with Corrections. Once the government deemed you a threat to society, it was The Island. Goodbye. Civilization officially washed its hands of you. I still remembered the look on Dad's face when they loaded me onto the transport. He'd been sure he was never going to see me again.

He'd almost been right.

I'd spent every day since, regretting what I'd done. And learning to be a different person as a result.

The whole time I told my story, Lisa listened intently. Then she said softly, "I'm sorry, Lee."

"I'm sorry too," I said. "But not for this."

I bent my head down and kissed her again.

• • •

"Wake up, Prisoner Fraccaro."

I didn't move. I felt like last night's cold fish.

"Prisoner Fraccaro, on your feet!"

A gloved fist slugged my shoulder, and suddenly I was tumbling out of my cot, shaking. Morning light streamed into the tent, and I found myself face-to-face with four armed Corrections SWAT officers in mottled fatigues.

Lisa was nowhere in sight. Had they hit her first?

"Chip worked, huh?" I said, realizing the time had finally come.

"Yes," said the tall, black-skinned SWAT who had sergeant's stripes on his arm. "But we were already on our way when officer Ivarsen expired. That idea you had, about the mirrors … pretty ingenious. Nobody remembers Morse Code anymore. Except for the computers. When the satellites started picking up your S.O.S. flashing over and over again, it was obvious something had gone wrong."

I looked down at my nude self, and the back at the sergeant.

"Do I need to get dressed, or can we finish it here?"

"Excuse me?"

"Come on. Bullet to the head. It'll be quick. Justice will be done."

The sergeant's white teeth grinned like the Cheshire cat's.

He held up Ivarsen's PDA.

"Don't worry. I think your alibi is good. Officer Ivarsen apparently thought well of you, and Prisoner Phaan too. He had a feeling Godfrey was bad news. Ivarsen's last few logs pretty much state that Godfrey was going to pull something. Too bad we can't put Godfrey up against a wall. He definitely deserved it."

"You found him?"

"Idiot rolled the dumper. Doing ninety kay over broken terrain. No safety harness. Thrown from the cab, and crushed. Not much else to do but toe-tag the remains."

"Huh. Can't say he didn't have it coming. So what happens now?"

"Let's go outside."

I was humming happily to myself when I left the hooch.

· · ·

Ivarsen's logs made all the difference. It was like having a character witness speaking from the grave. That, combined with circumstantial evidence, put Phaan and I in the clear.

They split us up, of course, and sent us to separate sites to finish our original sentences.

Parole came, and I was released back into civilization.

I stayed at my sister's house while I looked for work. It was as discouraging as I expected. Even the asteroid miners didn't want me. But I had to do something—I didn't like the idea of hanging around sis's place, endlessly mooching.

Dad finally came to visit one weekend. He hugged me harder and longer than he ever had in my whole life. Then he listened to the whole story, about my time on The Island, about the brick sites, about Ivarsen's death. Then he looked me in the eye from across the living room coffee table and suggested I apply to Corrections.

"You've got to be kidding," I said.

"Not at all," Dad said. "This Ivarsen guy, you said he seemed at ease around your crew? Ran the place like it was just another job? The man was obviously an ex con."

I hadn't thought of that before. Ivarsen had seemed too decent to be a criminal.

But then, so were Phaan and I.

The next day, I did what Dad suggested. To my surprise, they picked me up without question. And after twelve weeks at the Corrections Academy they sent me out to run one of the brick sites.

It was interesting, being on the flip side of things. I found I actually liked being back in the desert, with its blinding sun and fresh air and shimmering desolation. I'd missed it.

As always, I had to watch my temper. Some of the prisoners were just as stupid as Godfrey had been, and twice as mean. On several occasions I was sorely temped to use my gun.

But I'd sworn to myself I'd do everything I could to never have to kill again.

Planetary months rolled into a planetary year. Then two. Paycheck after paycheck. With no out-of-pocket cost for room or food, my savings began to pile up. I began to seriously think about my future. There was retirement out there on my horizon. Could I save enough to buy a little plot of land on the polar seaside? Maybe join in the effort to transform the planet from barely-living desert to thriving ecosphere? It would be hard work, just like the brick sites were hard work. And lonely ...

Using my PDA, I got on the Corrections network one night. Within a few minutes I found Lisa Phaan's file.

She'd been telling the truth about the drug stuff.

But every record since her incarceration, showed her clean. To include continued reports of good behavior.

I remembered the pleasant sensation of her lips on mine.

Could we have something? Or was I just fooling myself?

Snapping my PDA off, I determined that I'd find out.

Meanwhile, there was always more clay. And there were always more bricks.

▼ ▲ ▼ ▲ ▼

Nominally a jail tale, "Bricks" is both a story of redemption, and a look at the less glamorous side of potential interstellar colonization. Any people who manage to arrive on another world circling another star, are going to be starting from scratch. And there won't necessarily be any virgin forests to tame, as in the case of the Earth's ancient humans who crossed oceans to settle new lands. Odds are, if there's any life at all, it'll be primitive. Perhaps, too primitive to be useful. So what will our hypothetical colonists use for building materials, if there's no wood?

Once upon a time, I was handy with a potter's wheel. I know enough about clay—and the processes for turning clay into variously useful things—that it occurred to me that bricks would be an essential component of any interstellar colony's industrial economy. Assuming said colonists landed with only the land and some water to work with. No major plant life, nor developed mining and smelting of the sort we're used to in the 21st century. All of that stuff will come later. In the meantime, they'll have to have something to build with.

So I conjured images of millions of earthen bricks baking in the sun. But wait, earthen bricks aren't as dependable as actual clay bricks, formed and fired. How do you fire bricks if you don't have wood, coal, or a natural gas supply available?

There are already experimental solar power fields on Earth designed to collect and focus sunlight. When in use, these solar fields can generate a tremendous amount of heat in a very small, focused area. Aim enough rays at a stone kiln— and imagine that the sun's light is even brighter, more intense, and longer-lasting than it is on Earth—and you have your firing solution. But who among colonists—or their descendants—is going to agree to do such work? It's not glamorous, it doesn't take a lot of education, it's difficult and dirty, and it's going to potentially take you far from civilization; if said civilization has decided to build far from the equator.

"Bricks" first saw print in Bryan Thomas Schmidt's anthology Beyond The Sun, albeit in a shortened and somewhat modified form. It got some nice mentions in several reviews. I hope nobody who read the story in that book, minds me re-rendering the story here, in this book. I always did like my protagonist in this story. In my time in the military I've known some solid people who, for whatever reasons, ran into trouble with the law while young. Not everybody who goes to prison is the kind of person who should stay there. And especially on a colony world, where human life is rare and valuable in ways it might not necessarily be otherwise, how would the colonists decide to deal with criminals? And how might a criminal convicted of a major crime find his or her way back into society?

Such questions pretty much drove the plot of this story.

Guard Dog

(with Mike Resnick)

A passive sensor pinged hesitantly, and Chang came alert. He felt his way through the familiar diagnostic routine, verifying the status of thousands of different shipboard components. As expected, everything was functioning. The sole minimal change was that his available fuel had decreased.

Chang had never been told exactly how long his fuel would last. In fact, there had never been any mention of refueling, nor rearming. This would have bothered him, prior to being crippled in combat. But now it was simply a fact of life. He knew he was disposable; had known it when he'd blinked twice for *yes* during the Watchfleet accessions interview in the hospital ward. It was still better than the alternative.

Another ping, this time a bit stronger.

Adrenaline began to surge.

The threat. Where was the threat?

Chang's head and spine were plugged into the core of an armored, spherical spacecraft hovering at a nameless set of coordinates that rode directly on the invisible wall between Human Space and Everywhere Else. He'd been on that spot for who knew how long? His cyborg life was composed of a series of long, dream-filled sleeps in between frenetic, life-or-death battles.

At the time Chang had elected to undergo surgical implant and machine integration, the Watchfleet had been mankind's best defense against the Sortu: a mysteriously aggressive species of xenophobes actively exterminating all "competitor" races in Earth's particular region of the known galaxy. Where it took years to build, arm, and crew an ordinary warship, a Watchfleet monitor took mere weeks, and required only its cyborg pilot. Chang—and thousands of other wounded veterans just like him—had all signed up to establish an interstellar line in the sand: *this far, no father.*

At the time, humanity had been overwhelmed, and the Sortu had almost won.

Chang and his comrades had put a stop to it, but the toll had been high. The Watchfleet had grown thin, to the point that Chang seldom heard the comforting murmur of his fellows—their mental signals broadcast instantaneously through the *gravtrans* buried deep in Chang's armored shell. Once they had formed an intelligent skein, acting and reacting in concert to surround and crush all opponents. Now they were few and far between, like lonely whales hooting forlornly through the ocean's inky depths.

When his sensors did not alert him a third time, Chang set up an automated diagnostic routine and allowed himself to slip back into his dreams.

• • •

Lucy's skin was so pale and freckled that she burned at the merest mention of sunlight. Chang ran a hand appreciatively along his new wife's bare hip as they lay together in their bed, the hum of the ship's engines and air cycler filling their tiny compartment—one of hundreds aboard the emigration liner now docked in Earth orbit.

"We should get up soon," Lucy murmured.

"What for?" replied Chang. "I'm on leave until Monday, then we both depart for deep space. There's nothing to see on this tub anyway."

"Yeah, but I feel like a slug just hanging out in bed. We should get some exercise."

Chang sighed deeply. "They work the crap out of us in Advanced Crew Training. I get more exercise in a day than you get in a week."

"Oh yeah?" she said defiantly.

"Yeah," Chang said, smiling as he grabbed her shoulder and turned her quickly onto her back, her breasts fluttering pleasantly on her chest. His hands began to mischievously wander up her belly as the two of them kept talking.

"You still haven't told your father, have you?" Chang said, his eyes locked onto hers, but his hands possessing a mind all their own.

"No," she said, "He'd have tantrum if he learned I was leaving Earth. Dad never did like—*oh!*"

Chang's fingers gently brushed her nipples. She shuddered.

"Go on," he said with a smile, as if nothing was happening.

"I'm just glad they offer military spouses a free ride. We'll both happier off … if … *uhhhh!*"

Chang's wife never got to finish her sentence. If it was exercise she wanted, it was exercise she would *get*. Three months in Basic and six months in Advanced military schooling had turned Chang hard and wiry. Her hands reached up for him, and—

• • •

Ping! Ping! Ping!

Damn.

It had been a long time since Chang had made love to his wife, even in his memory. He reluctantly returned to wakefulness.

He scanned the diagnostic report on the sensors. As far as his internal maintenance routines could ascertain, everything checked out. So what the hell was going on?

Ping!

Chang slipped his more robust active sensors into the vacuum, their huge domes revolving and twirling beyond the confines of the plated hull—*Hello, anyone there?*

The cold emptiness of interstellar space remained unbroken. Straight out in all directions.

Then … wait. There.

Pong-pong-pong-pong-pong. Not a ghost signature. This was something solid. Several somethings.

Not members of the Watchfleet.

The attack came. From the direction Chang least expected.

Eight small craft appeared like ghosts. Using a breed of engine unknown to Chang's signature recognition software, they moved more quickly than any ships Chang had ever encountered before. Within moments each ship had detached several smaller vessels that were arcing in on Chang's position.

Missiles. Fast ones.

Chang retracted his sensors and slammed his internal drive into action. Treading the fabric of space like an Olympic runner charging across a track, Chang shot out of the path of the incoming projectiles, weaving and dispensing countermeasures in his wake. He used the *gravtrans* to hurl an electronic shout into the universe: *enemy units attacking, such-and-such coordinates, Watchfleet assistance needed!*

But there was no answer in response.

Worse still, the missiles fired at Chang were different. Smart.

With every twist and curve that Chang threw into his trajectory, the little missiles corrected and accelerated, blowing right through his countermeasures. Like their mothercraft, they moved much faster than he would have thought possible. No wonder none of the other Watchfleet units were responding to his calls. They'd probably been destroyed already, leaving him alone to defend himself.

Chang felt tickles of panic running through his organic tissues.

Simultaneously, a memory sprang into his consciousness …

• • •

Lucy's father was a tall, unsmiling man. His cheeks were rosy in the cold Peridian IV air, and his overcoat was speckled with drops of water from the colony's perpetual mist. Chang stood next to him; uncomfortably close. They hadn't said a word to each other since accompanying Lucy to the playground with the twins.

"Wave to Dad!" Lucy said, propping one of the boys up on a piece of colorful equipment. The little toddler, whom Chang had known all of two days, appeared joyfully bewildered as his head swiveled back and forth, looking for a face he hadn't yet learned to recognize.

Chang lifted an arm, half-smiling, and then dropped his hand to his side. His own military-issue overcoat was drawn tightly at the waist, collar turned up.

"I'm sorry you had to get dragged all this way," Chang said finally.

Lucy's father grunted.

"What choice did I have? My daughter is all I have left. Her, and the boys."

"I wanted her to tell you before we left," Chang said. "She kept evading the issue. When I shipped out, I didn't know she was pregnant. I found out about the boys only after they'd been born. And by then she'd moved you out here to the colony."

Lucy's father sighed, and for the first time turned and looked Chang in the eye.

"It's not your fault," he rumbled, "but know this: You're part of our lot now. Those two sons of yours, they've got some of me in them, and that makes us *both* responsible. No matter where you go or how old you are or what you see out there in space, those twins will never, ever stop needing you. It's sealed in blood now, and there's no going back."

Lucy looked at Chang affectionately. Her face became puzzled when he didn't automatically return her smile. He was too busy staring at his sons, and realizing that at age 23 his life was now committed to a certain unbreakable trajectory …

• • •

The memory *poofed* away as quickly as it had come.

A missile had closed to within lethal range.

Desperately, Chang reversed his drive. His ship groaned under the intense stress of the maneuver, but the gravity distortion backwash caught the missile before it could arm itself—leaving a harmlessly dissipating cloud of metal flakes.

Chang experienced short-lived relief. Then, forcing another structural groan, he reversed direction again. Moments before impact with the debris from the first missile, he dipped and curved, his path taking him just barely around the expanding ball of metal shards.

Kiloton explosions flared and died. Had the remaining missiles fail-safed, or been manually detonated? There was no time to get an answer.

A wedge formation of three mothercraft was coming up fast. Built like three-sided pyramids, they were very different from anything Chang had ever seen before. His lasers lashed out, their highly-focused beams waving across the enemy like a gardener spraying water from his hose. The pyramidal vehicles disintegrated, then exploded.

Five bogies remained.

The enemy force divided again: two and two and one—and as it did so, Chang picked up the signals from more incoming missiles. He mentally flashed through every detail of every battle he had ever fought as both man and machine, sifting and collating the data until a tactic coalesced.

Chang's lasers hit the center of the missile swarm like an eraser, eradicating every projectile they touched. A sizable hole appeared within the swarm and he poured every bit of power he could into his own drive.

The missiles were all around Chang, and then they were behind him, their paths curving sharply back on themselves as they all attempted to follow their target. He flashed past the motherships, which also began to turn. A fireworks display of epic proportions erupted directly in his wake. Matter annihilated matter in a fantastically destructive spectacle.

The flush of victory again flowed through Chang.

Just three left to go.

Suddenly, the enemy touched Chang's skin with their own lasers. He sensed the deadly energy an instant before it hit. There was no use in turning; every part of his armored skin was equally thick. But would it be thick enough?

In a millisecond, a great wound was opened in the hull. An accompanying flow of damage statistics paraded through Chang's brain—the digital equivalent of pain. The *gravtrans* was gone, and the main drive partially damaged, though still functional.

Again Chang rapid-sorted through his memory banks, seeking alternative courses of action. Humanity was depending on him. More to the point, Lucy and his sons were depending on him.

• • •

Carter and Eric were ten years old when Chang's patrol was ambushed. He was in his bunk, off duty, staring at a digital photo of his sons on his PDA. An explosion swept through the deck. If he'd already been in his space armor, the blast wouldn't have done Chang much damage. As it was, Chang had to be carted to emergency triage with third-degree burns—and arms and legs so badly mangled even the months he spent in a liquid regeneration "womb" during the voyage back to Earth couldn't fix them. They were therefore amputated at the veterans hospital, planetside.

With Chang's family light-years away, the only ones who came to visit him were the lab men from the Watchfleet. They explained their program: battle vets, hard-wired into a new breed of super-ship, armed to the teeth, autonomous, yet tied together electronically to form a web the Sortu couldn't penetrate.

The ambush that got Chang hadn't been the only one. The Sortu were closing the noose. Earth itself was now in danger. Peridian IV, where Lucy and the boys were living, was expected to get hit next.

The Watchfleet was going to be humanity's best—and possibly last—answer.

Full pay and benefits, of course, to be delivered directly to Chang's next of kin—regardless of the duration of the Watchfleet battle tour. Posthumous continuation, guaranteed.

Lucy's father had been dead for years, but his words echoed in Chang's head. As long as Chang drew breath, he owed his sons whatever he could give them. Unable to speak, nod, or make any acknowledging movements, Chang gave the lab men his answer with his eyes.

• • •

The three remaining enemy ships closed in. Chang could feel them poke and prod with their active sensors. He was badly hurt, he had no missiles of his own anymore, and his laser cannon system had been hopelessly damaged.

The only thing he had left to throw at them now was his own fuel.

Antimatter. It could be pumped from the central magnetic holding cell into space by using the emergency flush system.

It could result in victory, but a pyrrhic one.

Using the flush pumps Chang dumped half his available fuel into the black void, the antimatter cloud instantly expanding around his own hull. He could feel it eating away at his ship. But would the enemy notice in time?

To his great relief, they did not.

Two of the three ships flared with white fire as the antimatter ate through their hardened hulls. Bright cataclysms flared and died, knocking Chang clear of the deadly cloud. The third pyramid pulled out in time, if just barely. It began limping along, trailing pieces of itself.

Chang moved in, his damaged drive laboring.

Sortu lasers—dramatically weakened—leapt to intercept him, but a secondary explosion wracked the lone pyramidal vessel, and its bombardment ceased.

Chang's sub-light drive pushed him in close to the enemy craft as it tumbled directionless through space. As the distance shrank, Chang collected data on the make-up of the ship: hardware that had been exposed, the size and type of both known and unknown components, everything he could learn.

At five kilometers the finer details emerged. Among the floating bits of debris, Chang could identify tiny carbon-based components. Interesting. He'd never seen the Sortu in the flesh. In fact, he wasn't sure anyone ever had—this would be a first.

Chang zeroed his remaining sensor equipment in on the lifeless bodies.

After only a few seconds of examination, the truth became clear—the corpses of the aliens were not alien at all.

There, Chang could see a little man who had been shredded, his arms and legs curled lifelessly to his chest. Next, a headless human female. Next, a male, his space suit half on, helmet still clutched uselessly in one hand.

Hundreds of human bodies drifted like a school of dead jellyfish brought in on the evening tide.

Chang hung motionless with shock. This simply did not compute. Humans did not fight humans. It was aliens who were the enemy, to be slaughtered with impunity. The Sortu! They were …

He set about slowly collecting the corpses. The uniforms were different from the ones Chang had worn when he'd been a whole man, working in the Service. But the faces were all too familiar—young men and women, as he'd once been, sent to fight and die in the depths of interstellar space. And for what? By who?

Chang stopped cold.

One face in particular caught his electronic eyes.

Carter.

It couldn't be. But the name tape sewn into the breast of the uniform was Chang's last name. The young, dead man bore the same uncannily mixed features. Only now he was grown up: semi-almond eyes, dark hair, freckled skin, and Lucy's fine nose …

Chang set that particular body aside and kept collecting, until a face that was almost identical to the first appeared.

Eric.

Same name tape, same features. Chang put the boys side by side, comparing their faces. They'd been frozen forever, startled at the very end.

Chang silently began to boil with a sensation of complete and utter betrayal.

He quietly rummaged through the wreck of the pyramid ship. Accessed the computers. Read the records.

A picture became clear.

One entirely different from what Chang had been given when he'd signed up, first as a mere soldier, then as a Watchfleet pilot.

He'd not been defending Earth against aliens.

He'd been defending Earth against her own children.

An alliance of human colonies had apparently been fighting for independence, since Chang himself had been a child. The Sortu were a lie—bogeymen. The enemy squadron he'd just dispatched had in fact been constructed at Peridian IV, a recent addition to the alliance's ranks.

It was beyond obscene.

Surely the Watchfleet Command knew the truth?

So many falsehoods collapsed like dominoes.

After many days of waiting, while Chang's internal damage control systems slowly patched up what could be fixed, he gathered his sons and all the other dead, and gently placed them back into the belly of their ship. The alliance would find them, after he was gone. He left a small message asking that the dead be given heroes' honors.

Chang them set a course for Sol System. For Earth. Maybe the alliance had managed to pick off all his comrades. But there was one watch dog still left. And he was going to take a chunk out of his masters.

▼▲▼▲▼

Not a usual story for me, "Guard Dog" is grim in tone. It is also the second of three different collaborations that Mike Resnick and I worked on, after I first met Mike in Los Angeles in 2010. The shell of this story dates to 1996, when I was toying with the idea of a mortally wounded space soldier being "recycled" for additional fighting duty. As often happens when I am only working with one idea—these days I almost always wait for two or three ideas to organically coalesce, before I have the nugget of a good story—I wasn't able to make "Guard Dog" work. Not until I took it out and showed it to Mike, and Mike (in his fatherly, knowing fashion) said, "You got it all wrong, kid, let me suggest some ways you can change it."

The story that resulted was pretty different from the story as I'd originally written it. And Mike's suggested ending is different as well. But it works nicely. Especially since Mike and I were working within such a tight word count limit. I often feel as if I am barely clearing my throat at 4,000 words. For "Guard Dog" we told a lot of story in just under 3,000 words; and the manuscript went to print in editor Bryan Thomas Schmidt's Space Battles anthology.

I learned a lot from Mike, while working on this piece. The man is a master of the human condition. Not us as we wish we might be, but us as we actually are. To include the bad, as well as the good. "Guard Dog" therefore morphed into a picture window view of ordinary people trying to do the right thing, and being manipulated—at levels far about their awareness—against each other. Chang's life story is compacted tremendously to fit the space Mike and I had to work with, but I think the raw punch of Chang's predicament was made stronger as a result.

Counselor:
L.E. Modesitt, Jr.

I had only known L.E. Modesitt, Jr. by name and reputation— prior to actually meeting him in 2009. At the time, I was just another hopeful aspiring writer in a small sea of aspiring writers at the Life, The Universe, and Everything (LTUE) symposium that is run annually in Utah County, Utah. I had not realized until then just how chock full of venerable professionals the Utah speculative and fantastic writing scene is. Oh, I knew Orson Scott Card had once called Utah home, but having spent the prior 14 years living and working in Washington State, my understanding of the Utah scene was non-existent. So imagine my surprise when I went to my first panel and saw not just Lee Modesitt, but also Dave Wolverton, and several other luminaries, holding forth about which kinds of science fiction were "hot" and which kinds of science fiction were not.

I had my hand up several times during that panel, asking what I hoped would be pertinent questions. Lee was urbane and scholarly in both presentation and manner, wearing a crisp oxford with contrasting tie, and a beautifully complimentary vest—an ensemble look I would soon associate with Lee as his chosen, signature look. After the panel ended, I managed to approach him (as a brand new Warrant Officer Candidate) and make a sidelong military connection;

since Lee had just spoken about his own military credentials while discussing the health of Military SF in the marketplace.

I was impressed that Lee took time out to talk to me, if even for a couple of minutes. And was even more impressed (a few months later) when Lee took even more time to talk to me at the CONduit SF/F convention in Salt Lake City. I'd made Finalist in the Writers of the Future Contest by then, and was chomping at the bit (perhaps too much?) to pick the brains of the elder statesmen of the field who were present and available for conversation. I felt almost desperate to "level up" to the point I could qualify as a junior colleague of these accomplished men, and Lee especially impressed me with his experience and breadth of knowledge.

I've made a habit of seeking Lee's counsel as a result. I occasionally travel up and down the state for business, and when I am headed south (and I know I will have the time) I like to take Lee to lunch, just to hear what he has to say about writing, science fiction, politics, the state of national affairs, or perhaps laugh while he shares an anecdote from his days flying helicopters in the Navy. There's very little Lee can't talk about without it becoming immediately interesting. I've always had the sense that when I am conversing with Lee, I am conversing with a remarkable, dynamic, incisive mind. The kind of person who won't mistake being clever, for being wise.

Not surprisingly, Lee is—so far as I can tell—a rigorous centrist who does not suffer political fools of Right or Left. He's got a lot of experience dealing with and seeing insider baseball in Washington D.C., and both he and his wife are educated, erudite, whip-smart individuals who have worked very hard to create for themselves a life (and a family) which reflects their impressive values. I can think of few people who have done so well in the SF field while also doing well in other arenas too. Which is probably another reason Lee and I seem to connect—Lee kept his foot in with "real world" occupations long after many writers might have pulled up stakes and gone full-time.

In other words, Lee—more than any other writer—has shown me that you *can* have a successful science fiction writing career, without having to sacrifice everything else in one's life on the altar of one's authorial ambition.

I internalized (long before I was published) the idea that, if you want to be a successful professional, you need to select who it is you deem to be both "successful" and "professional" and then make a point of spending time around those people. Absorbing their ideas, what they have to say, their thoughts and feelings, observing their successes and their challenges, and otherwise immersing yourself in conversation that is not amateurish in nature. Lee was always someone who welcomed me to that grown-up dialogue. Sitting and discussing the field, or the world, over lunch, with Lee, I am forever impressed at just how keen Lee's observations can be. How knowing his sensibilities usually are—especially when it comes to teasing the truth out of a mess of wishful thinking—and how Lee has managed to quietly create for himself one of the more robust SF/F writing careers I've been privileged to witness up close and in person.

Lee is neither flashy nor flamboyant. In a field which sometimes seems to be peopled with nothing but eccentrics, Lee is possessed of both poise and dignity. A professional's professional. I've grown to admire this. And to also admire Lee as both an author, and as a gentleman.

Thank you for your kindness and generosity, Mr. Modesitt.

Recapturing
the Dream

The proximity alarm *ponged* like a bronze bell.

Henrietta Lechtenberg stirred reluctantly, then flipped herself out of her hammock and floated over to the west wall of her sleeping chamber. Gripping a support rail with her left hand, Henrietta tapped at the wall's touch-sensitive display surface with her right. The proximity alarm went silent, and a full-color visual representation of the asteroid 33 Riga appeared—along with a small, flashing vector symbol indicating whatever it was that had blundered into Henrietta's domain in the middle of her sleep cycle.

Henrietta frowned.

The visitor wasn't natural—it was altering course and velocity, and would intercept 33 Riga within the hour.

"So they've finally come," Henrietta said, her frown deepening.

She slammed her hand on the wall. The image went blank.

Then she used support rails to pull herself out of her sleeping chamber, down a narrow corridor lined with hardened vacuum-proof foam, and into the house's central hall. As had been the case for many years, the hall was silent, save for Henrietta's breathing. That, and the sound of her blood pounding in her ears as she felt her temper flare.

"Not fair," she said to herself.

There were many Near Earth Objects suitable for exploration and harvesting. Why had someone resumed interest in 33 Riga? It had been over twenty years. Enough time for people to forget, if not forgive.

What would Henrietta do now?

All Henrietta had was her silence. It had sufficed during 33 Riga's long, ellipsoidal trek out of the solar ecliptic. No contact with outsiders. No messages, nor broadcasts, nor even a single e-mail. She'd simply shut off all the receivers, dishes, and antennae, and gone dark—her stadium-sized, lumpy little world drifting back into the eternal void of deep space.

At least until 33 Riga's orbit inexorably carried it back down towards the ecliptical plane—and another relatively close pass by the Earth and Moon.

People. Henrietta shuddered at the thought.

The tickling dread of a panic attack began to build in her chest. She wrapped her arms around herself, and tried to think.

Food. Food would calm her down.

She forced herself to the kitchen, where yesterday's pickings of berries from the hydroponics farm sat cleaned and chilled in the fresher. She ate voraciously, pounding down fruit between large gulps of pristine meltwater from the subsurface cistern.

As asteroids went, 33 Riga was fairly well suited for habitation, being honeycombed with pockets of frozen water and gas. The house's central hall had been such a pocket, and once the water ice within had been melted and electrolyzed for air and fuel, the empty void made an ideal shelter. The ore in the walls protected against solar radiation as well as micrometeoroids, and there had been more than enough room to house the mission's expanded construction equipment while Henrietta, her husband Shavro, and the other two astronauts tunneled deeper into 33 Riga's interior.

Henrietta had been hopeful then.

Now ... all she wanted was solitude.

With her stomach satisfied and her mind alert, Henrietta pulled herself back to the hall, then up a third, much longer tunnel to the asteroid's surface. She popped up into the dark observation dome, found her way by feel to the dome's controls, and flipped the toggled for the dome shield to retract.

It clam-shelled out and away from the transparent dome proper, revealing an unbroken, brilliantly-starred sky from horizon to horizon.

In the great distance, a small multi-colored marble hung against the blackness of the universe. The sphere glowed white, emerald and sapphire along one side, while the other side was darkened in shadow.

How long had it been?

Henrietta felt the sensation of panic return, and busied herself scanning the thousands of pinpoints of light—looking for anything that moved.

Within ten minutes she picked out the dot that was the visitor's spacecraft. It grew ever-larger as it closed in. Occasionally, little bursts of spent gas *chuffed* from its sides as it adjusted course for a soft landing.

Henrietta watched the visitor with fearful interest.

• • •

He was just one man.

When he removed the helmet to his suit—slimmer, more streamlined and intricate-looking than the suits Henrietta used—she was surprised to see the crow's feet at the corners of his eyes and the pepper color of his hair.

Not a youngster ...

He'd put down twenty meters from the observation dome and, after a prolonged period of inactivity, popped his hatch, descended his ladder, then made his way to the long-unused dome airlock.

Henrietta wouldn't let him in, of course.

Not that it mattered. She watched him through the dome's transparent bubble: deploying a hand-held computer tool with cables attached at one end, and to which he interfaced the dome lock's exterior electronics panel. A few moments later he'd stepped into the lock, used the same tool on the inner door's electronics, then entered the dome itself.

He met Henrietta's glare with a small smile.

"Miss Lechtenberg, I presume?" he asked in American English.

Henrietta said nothing.

The man scanned his eyes around the dome, turning his head this way and that.

"Where are the others?"

Silence.

The stranger's eyes softened.

"Ma'am, I'm sorry if my presence comes as a shock. I do wish circumstances were different. Can you tell me where the other astronauts from your team are?"

"Gone," Henrietta said coldly. English wasn't her first language, but as the nominal commerce language of the solar system, she'd learned to speak it fluently; like everyone else.

"They … left?" he asked hesitantly.

"They are *dead,*" Henrietta said matter-of-fact, her arms crossed over her chest.

The man's eyes fell, and the corners of his mouth turned down.

"I'm sorry to hear that," he said, and seemed sincere about it.

More silence.

"You can't stay here," Henrietta finally said, keeping her arms crossed.

"May I ask what happened to the others?"

"No," Henrietta said.

The stranger kept his helmet grasped in one hand while he looked at her. His eyes were sharp blue, and intelligent. Though somewhat hidden behind drooping and folded skin. Those eyes penetrated. He was feeling her out; trying to discern her motives.

Henrietta looked past his shoulder and out the dome to where his spacecraft sat in the sunlight. Insect-like.

Just big enough for … two?

"Please," the stranger finally said, "if you won't tell me what happened, at least tell me why you wouldn't respond to any of my communications. I've been pinging you for months. It took a lot of time and fuel to meet you this far in advance. I'd hoped we could have had this conversation a long time ago. But that didn't happen. So now we're starting from square one."

"Don't you understand me?" Henrietta said, bristling. "I said you can't stay here. You have your vessel. Go back."

Again he looked intently at her with those blue eyes.

Not judgment? Discernment—he wonders if I am crazy.

"You were an employee of the Asteroid Development Consortium when you left Earth in 2036," he said, "and you're still an employee now. Benefits, pay, retirement, it's all waiting for you when we reach home."

"This has been my home for two decades," Henrietta said. "I have no other home. And you are trespassing. Now please *leave me alone.*"

"33 Riga is Consortium property," he said.

"Correction," Henrietta said. "33 Riga is *chartered* to the Consortium, for mining and industrial use. The expiration date on that charter was 2050."

"And that charter's been extended to 2100," he said. "Ma'am, I don't doubt that it's been enormously difficult for you. All this time with nothing but the original mission gear—and whatever you've managed to scrape together off this rock—to sustain you. I noticed you got the solar panels deployed, but I don't see any sign of the mining robots, nor the automated self-contained refinery that came with them. Are they destroyed?"

"No," Henrietta said.

"Malfunctioning?"

"I don't know. Probably not."

"The thruster pusher motors—designed to slowly shove 33 Riga out of solar orbit and into Earth orbit. I see them half-assembled on the surface. Is something wrong with them?"

"None of the company's precious equipment has been damaged," Henrietta said, growing tired of the stranger's inquisition.

"Then what *happened?*"

"It is a story I am too old and tired to tell," Henrietta said, dropping her hands to her hips. Her slippers had grip pads on the bottoms, which kept her upright in 33 Riga's near-microgravity environment. The stranger had something similar on the bottom of his boots, though his helmet drifted free on a small tether at his waist when he began using his hands as he talked.

"Look," he said, "even if you're not interested in telling me what happened, there's still a job to be done. ADC put a lot of money into the original mission and I'm not willing to see it flushed away without an attempt to recoup the investment. 33 Riga was to have been just the first of several asteroids moved into Earth orbit for industrialization and colonization. When your team went silent and 33 Riga never diverted off its natural path, the worst was assumed. Which caused a whole ripple effect that you may or may not be aware of."

"Is that so, Mister . . ?" Henrietta said.

"Brett Jimmerson. Most people actually call me Jimmy."

"*Mister* Jimmerson," Henrietta said, "there was a time when I might have cared about the company and their investment. That time passed long ago. I'll note that their concern extends only to the hardware, not the software."

"What do you mean by that?" he asked.

"Myself and the others. Were we part of the bottom line when ADC considered whether or not to write off the 33 Riga retrieval?"

"Of course," he said reflexively. Then considered the question more carefully. "Well, I guess it depends on what you mean by 'bottom line.' If you think ADC considered you *expendable,* you're wrong."

"I don't believe you."

The two simply looked at each other for several long seconds.

"You said the original mission package is more or less intact?" Jimmy asked, changing the subject.

"Yes, and when I am dead ADC can have 33 Riga on the next go-around. Another 20 years. Meanwhile they can keep my back pay, and my retirement. They can keep *everything.* But this is my home. It has been for a long time, and ADC's got no right to take it away from me. You go tell them I said that when you get back to your cockpit."

Jimmy wrinkled his brow and ran his tongue along the inside of his cheek. He seemed to be considering her words carefully.

Henrietta's heart jumped when he slowly faced away from her and stared at his spacecraft in the distance.

He's going to leave!

Jimmy pulled out a small rectangle that looked a bit like a multi-function phone, and began tapping the phone's screen with his thumb. Suddenly the upper half of his ship blasted into the sky, exhaust gas flinging bits of brassy foil away in a sparkling shower.

"*Wha … what have you done?*" Henrietta exclaimed.

Jimmy turned back to her.

"That was the return-flight stage. It's programmed to automatically go back to Earth in the event that I tell it to. I just told it to."

"Are you mad?" Henrietta yelled at him. "Now you're stuck here!"

"That's the idea," Jimmy said.

His expression was not one of malice.

Rather, his blue eyes held determination.

When Henrietta finally realized the full magnitude of what had happened, she fled the observation dome as fast as her hands and arms could pull her.

• • •

Henrietta slammed the air-tight emergency door shut behind her in the middle of the passage, trapping Jimmy in the observation dome above. Then curled herself into a ball and shivered for many long minutes while her carefully-constructed chrysalis of reality crumbled around her. It had taken a long time to adjust to her hermit's lifestyle, but now that she'd lived it for so long, the thought of accommodating another person in her space—especially someone she didn't know at all—was intolerable.

Briefly, she considered cutting off the air circulation to the dome. His suit wouldn't supply him forever, and he'd be forced to go outside. Could she find a way to defeat his equipment and keep him out of the other airlocks? Moreover, could she live with herself if she watched him slowly suffocate, inches from relief?

In the end, she released the dogs on the hatch.

Jimmy passed through—hesitantly.

Henrietta must have looked a mess.

"Thanks," he said awkwardly. "For a moment there I wasn't sure you weren't going to keep me trapped outside."

"Believe me," Henrietta said, "I considered it."

"Why? Do I scare you?"

"It's not *you* I am afraid of," she said, wiping her eyes and nose on a small handkerchief retrieved from a pocket in her use-worn jumpsuit.

"That's good," Jimmy said. "Because even if everything goes as planned, we're going to be stuck together for the twenty-four months it's going to take to push us into Earth's gravitational grip."

"We are not going back to Earth," Henrietta said.

"It's the only way you're going to get rid of me," he replied.

Henrietta felt the urge to snap back, but held her tongue.

With the execution of a single computer command, Jimmy had married their fates more surely than any pastor or justice of the peace.

"Look," he said, "it might help if I explain a few things."

"I am listening," she said.

The two of them floated about four meters apart, their voices echoing off the walls of the hall. Vacuum-proof foam was excellent at stopping leaks, but it was lousy for sound deadening.

"When the 33 Riga job was declared a bust, investors made a run on the stocks of the various companies incorporated under the Consortium banner. News of the failure swept through the trade cycles until the Consortium was teetering on the brink of bankruptcy. Future missions were placed on indefinite hold. The core partners tried to recapitalize, with limited success. Then the global market caved in. China's middle-class bubble burst, and burst hard. When the Chinese economy went into recession, the rest of the world went with it. Kind of like the crash at the turn of the century. Anyway, the Consortium shed as much of itself as it could, and devoted resources to short-term satellite launch missions as a way to stay afloat until the economy was ready for another push."

"If you're here, then things must be picking up," Henrietta said.

"No," Jimmy replied. "The super-recession is like quicksand. Every time one of the big economies starts to claw its way out, it gets dragged back down by the others. Europe is hurting. North America is hurting. The Pacific Rim is hurting. The Yen's not been this bad in a long, long time. Nobody is quite sure what's going to break us out of the slump. Everyone is waiting and holding their breath for ..."

"For what?" Henrietta asked.

"A spark. A flame. Something unexpected—to get the wheels turning again. In eras past, it was often technological. Steam engines opened the American West and liberated humanity from speed-of-horse. The telegraph, and later, the telephone ... these things liberated communication. The automobile and the airplane became institutions unto themselves, inseparable from modernity. But what's left for us now? The oil and the coal won't last forever, to say nothing of environmental restrictions. The internet is a giant time sink into which generations have poured their creative energy, for the sake of entertainment and socializing. There's no forward movement there. Nothing gets *made* on the web. And it's getting harder and harder to *make* things in real life, too. Humanity is spinning its wheels while we're slowly circling the civilizational drain. Something has to change. In a big way."

Now it was Henrietta's turn to gauge Jimmy. His eyes had lost focus and he sounded like he was addressing an audience, not just one person.

"You've made that pitch before," she guessed.

Jimmy blushed.

"Yes. Many times, actually."

"And you're not just an astronaut working for the Consortium."

"I am a Cape-rated astronaut," Jimmy said, his chest suddenly puffing up with pride. "But I don't just work for the Consortium, I *am* the Consortium."

"What?"

"You never read the fine-print on your contract, did you?"

Henrietta had to admit that she didn't.

"The Jimmerson family has a controlling interest in Industrial Omni-Dynamix, Ltd., which is at present the most stable and well-funded partner in the Consortium. We've got our fingers into the economies of two dozen major countries, and while some of the smaller partners were eager to bail when the bailing was good, my grandfather always told me that no Jimmerson was going to just sit back and let a good dream go to waste."

"But why did *you* come all the way out *here?*" Henrietta asked.

"There was only enough money for a mini-mission. One shot, one crewmember, one chance. I could have asked for volunteers, and gotten them. But because of how much is riding on this ... well, I didn't feel comfortable putting my expectations on anyone else's shoulders. I also didn't want to have to deal with the repercussions of failure, should we fail. You and I."

"And what precisely do you expect *us* to do?"

"Finish the mission. Insert 33 Riga into a stable Earth orbit and hang out the 'Open For Business' sign. The First and Second International Space Stations are winding down—at the ends of their lifecycles. The three moon colonies are sitting half-finished and empty because nobody's got money to complete or staff them. We need cheap resources in Earth orbit—to ease the path, if you will. That was the whole idea of ADC in the first place."

Henrietta considered. She'd once been very enthusiastic about the whole ADC project. It was why she'd foregone a more stable teaching career, and signed on for space training.

Jimmy noticed the mental clouds passing over Henrietta's eyes.

"How exactly did the others die?" Jimmy asked.

"I can't talk about it right now," Henrietta said. "Just tell me one thing, Mister—I mean, Jimmy. If I help you get 33 Riga to Earth orbit, can you promise me that you'll put my life back the way it was?"

"Before you left Earth?"

"No, before *you* came."

"If things go the way I've planned, 33 Riga will be a busy place. Crawling with people. No, I can't promise you anything like what you want."

"Then I've no interest. You can do what you want with the original mission equipment. I'm not lifting a finger to assist."

"I came here prepared to do this alone," Jimmy said, his neck stiffening.

"Then do it alone," Henrietta said, and turned her back on him, expertly kicking and swimming her way to the far side of the hall.

"Wait!" Jimmy cried.

Henrietta paused at the mouth of the corridor to her sleeping chamber.

"Yes?" she said.

"What about Greenland? I could set you up in the middle of nowhere. Enough supplies and equipment for a new house, plus domes for farming, not too different from the hydroponics stuff you're using now. No other human being for a hundred miles, at least."

"I thought you said you were prepared to do this alone?" Henrietta said.

"The chances for success double, with two of us working together. I meant it when I launched the return stage: I'm in this thing to win, one way, or another."

"Are you also a man who keeps his word?" Henrietta asked.

"Absolutely."

"Okay. I will give you a chance to prove it."

• • •

The initial work was painful.

Not only had Henrietta's training on the original mission equipment gathered two decades of rust, but some of the equipment itself had not fared well despite much of it still being in its factory containers aboard the original lander. Batteries were long dead. Computer memories were wiped. If the containers had been rated on Earth as "radiation resistant" they had most definitely *not* been designed to sit out in the unshielded glare of the sun—solar wind, sunspots, solar flares—for as long as these ones had.

Henrietta and Jimmy did a lot of cannibalizing.

Of course, he'd brought new equipment too. Some of it much improved over the older stuff.

For Henrietta, uncrating all the systems brought back lots of buried memories. The original lander was located far from Henrietta's home, behind a ridge that blocked sight of it from the observation dome. And for good reason, too. She'd not been back to the lander in years, and was plagued by ghostly recollections of she, Shavro, and the others, all working together to unload the lander's cargo, unpack the solar arrays, rig up the electrical grid, get the tunneling robots working, and so forth.

A few times she had to stop work—sweat pouring down her face behind the transparent helmet bowl of her older, bulkier suit—to let the waves of crippling anxiety pass.

Day and night cycles began to spin by.

Jimmy made himself at home in the house, but was noticeably careful to not intrude into Henrietta's private areas—especially her sleeping chamber. He was also noticeably careful to avoid asking any more questions about how the rest of the original mission crew had died, though doubtless this was on his mind. He kept the talk technical, professional, and despite her misgivings over the fact that Jimmy was, for all intents and purposes, a super-rich man, he proved surprisingly eager and willing to work. Often, to the point of physical exhaustion.

Always, the blue-white-green sphere of the Earth grew larger in the sky. Just a little bit, week after week.

One afternoon, as they both struggled to bring the first ion thruster-pusher to life, Henrietta experienced a particularly bad episode and had to abandon the job before it was complete. She returned to the house as quickly as her suit's onboard maneuvering pack could jet her there, and spent over an hour huddled in the microgravity shower, being doused by spraying hot water.

She emerged—wrinkled and delicate—to find Jimmy working in the kitchen.

The heavenly aroma that issued forth sent culinary explosions through her brain that she'd not experienced in a long, long time.

"Is that—?"

"Top sirloin," Jimmy said with a smile. "I was saving it for a special occasion. Got the thruster-pusher up and running. It's now gently nudging us into a new orbit. A smidge at a time. Once we bring a few more of those on-line, we ought to begin making good progress. Then we can break out the mining robots and get started on the refinery too. In the meantime, how do you like your beef, madam? Medium-rare?"

It had been so long since Henrietta had eaten meat. She'd almost forgotten the taste. But with the hunks of steak sizzling nicely on a spit in the roaster—juice and melted fat clinging to the exterior, forming a heavenly sheen—her mouth suddenly began to water ferociously. She floated to the roaster and peered through the glass door, licking her lips.

"I don't care," she said. "Cook it however. I just can't believe you brought meat."

"Teddy Roosevelt dined well when he rode in Africa. Seems to me I ought to be able to do the same out in space."

Henrietta greedily watched the spit revolve, the roaster's electric-red coils glowing softly and a gentle hissing sound coming from the meat as it cooked.

"Your file didn't say anything about agoraphobia," Jimmy said, not looking up at Henrietta from where he prepared a couple of russet potatoes on a similar spit: to go into the roaster directly after the steak had been placed into a warmer.

"Are you a psychologist now?" Henrietta asked.

"No," Jimmy said. "But on my way up from Earth I did an extensive study on the files of all the original mission crew. The woman who tested out for this trip in the first place? She's not the woman I'm getting to know now. You were smart, and you were bold. Then. Now? It's like … like you're afraid of your own shadow or something."

"Things happen to people," Henrietta said, not liking the sudden turn of conversation. If Jimmy was going to start prodding at sore wounds, she was going to shut him down immediately. Beef dinner, or no beef dinner.

"What things?" Jimmy said, his eyes still on his work.

"This conversation is going to end right—"

"Tell me about Damio."

Henrietta jerked her head up. He didn't look back.

"How do you know that name?" she asked crisply.

"You've done a good job sealing off the logs and keeping me out of your secure local area network, but not good enough. The medical computer was wide open, and has records of a birth. You were the only female on the original mission team. Henrietta, what happened to your son?"

Henrietta began to shake. Visibly.

"We will not speak of Damio," she said, feeling a sudden, rushing weight pile itself quickly onto her shoulders. If she'd been standing in Earth-normal gravity, she'd have collapsed to her knees.

"The medical computer doesn't give any details about an accident. Everyone seemed healthy, including the baby, who grew into a toddler. You gave him a clean bill of health on his third birthday, and then ... blank. Nothing. Not for him. And not for any of the others. I had to think about it for a while, until I realized that the return stage for *your* spacecraft is also missing. Only the lander and its cargo are present."

By now Henrietta was paralyzed.

A familiar, raw sound began to gurgle up in her throat.

She fought it, with all her mind and soul.

But the memories of Damio—of Henrietta and Shavro having their final, titanic argument—had been suppressed for too long. The emotion boiled up into her heart like acid, and left her hugging her arms over her breasts and weeping uncontrollably.

A second pair of arms gently guided her to the other side of the kitchen, then hesitantly pulled her into a hug. The first bona fide hug Henrietta had experienced in years.

A fresh round of sobs bubbled out of her, so that she was quietly bawling into the front of Jimmy's jumpsuit. His hands patted her back in a reserved fashion, then grew a little more sure of themselves as she continued to weep right down to the tips of her toes.

Sobs turned to snuffles, then to sniffling.

"Meat's going to burn" Jimmy said quietly.

Henrietta detached herself and was embarrassed to see the front of his jumpsuit damp with mucus and tears.

"I'm sorry, I didn't realize—" Jimmy said, his face red and his eyes looking ashamed.

Whatever he'd expected from her, he hadn't expected *that*.

Henrietta pushed out of the kitchen and returned to the shower, where she stripped, pulled the curtain back up, sealed the rim, and hit the button that would blast her with hot water.

• • •

Two hours later, Henrietta emerged to find the kitchen empty, but a healthy piece of sirloin in the warmer, and a nicely-baked potato too; with freshly steamed vegetables from the hydroponics farm.

But no Jimmy.

Henrietta didn't care. She was as famished as she was exhausted. She tore into the beef like a leopard on a springbok. The meat was tender and seasoned and arguably the most delicious, positively astounding thing she'd ever tasted in her life.

When she was done—an eminently satisfying feeling behind her ribs—she set out to find the cook. To thank him.

She found Jimmy back in the observation dome where their mutual association had begun months before. In his hand was a drinking bulb filled with a suspicious amber fluid.

"Whiskey?" she said.

"Scotch," Jimmy said. "Also saved for a special occasion. After I made you cry like that, I came up here to drown a few sorrows of my own."

"What sorrows could a billionaire possibly have?"

Jimmy turned to her, his expression just slightly touched with intoxication.

"You'd be surprised," he said.

"No, really," Henrietta said. "You have ferretted out some of my secrets, let's hear about yours, Mister Space Tycoon. Tell me. What weighs heavily on the brow of a man who has everything, beyond the rise and fall of the stock markets?"

Jimmy took a quick pull from the drinking bulb's one-way straw, wiped his mouth on the back of his hand, then returned to looking up at the imperceptibly-growing image of the Earth.

"You're not the only one who's lost a son," he said, choosing his words carefully. "Carter—we called him Cart—was doing okay, until his mother and I started getting sideways with each other. Darcy said I was working myself to death: spending too much time at the office, and not enough time at home. Small wonder. ADC was falling apart and threatening to pull Industrial Omni-Dynamix down with it. If I wasn't at the office I was flying all over the world putting out business fires. Darcy and me ... we just kind of got lost in the shuffle, I guess. One day I came home and she'd packed herself and Cart up. Poof. Gone to stay with her parents in Wisconsin. When she filed for the divorce, I didn't fight it. I knew I'd quit on her before she'd quit on me. But I didn't anticipate how hard it would be on Cart."

Henrietta watched as Jimmy's face grew red, though not from drink. He swallowed hard a few times, took another sip from the bulb, and kept looking up at the Earth.

"By the time my son was 16, he was getting into all kinds of trouble. At school. With his friends. With the law. I tried to rein him in, but by then he acted like he hated me. The cops eventually busted him for drugs, and when the judge threatened to throw the book at Cart, I offered to put Cart into the best rehab program money could buy. He was a good kid, or so I swore before the bench. So they turned him over to me with a threat that if Cart wasn't signed into the program within 24 hours, he was doing to detox in the county jail. I took him home with me and he promised he'd lay low. No trouble. That night after I went to sleep, he took my keys and went for a joy ride. They found my truck wrapped around a tree. Cart was thrown from the vehicle. Guess who Darcy blamed when we lowered Cart's casket into the ground?"

At this point, little blobs of salty liquid had beaded along the rims of Jimmy's eyes. He suddenly looked much older and more tired than he ever had since his arrival. Henrietta fetched a handkerchief—fresh and clean this time—from a pocket, and handed it to the man.

Jimmy took it gratefully and wiped his face, then blew his nose.

"Anyway," he said, "that was a couple of years ago. Water under the bridge, like my dad would have said. But there's not a day that doesn't go by when I don't remember that boy when he was five years old, running up into my arms and yelling, 'Daddy! Daddy!'"

Jimmy let the bulb float away and put a hand up to his eyes, his back shaking silently.

Henrietta found herself placing her hand gently on the man's shoulder. His pain was palpable through her palm. Every spasm threatened to re-spark the tears that had so recently flooded from Henrietta's eyes. But somehow, seeing this man bare his heart, had strengthened hers. She closed her eyes and drew in a deep breath.

"Damio was unexpected," Henrietta said, her voice quavering just slightly. Words and memories she'd tried to banish for so long, were actively parading through her consciousness. There wouldn't be any going back or turning away now.

"The company medical people said my birth control was fool-proof, but there's no such thing as one-hundred-percent. I found out I was pregnant just 12 months into the trip."

"And you never told ground about the pregnancy?"

"No. My idea. I was worried that they'd want me to abort. I had pills for that, just in case. But I couldn't bring myself to use them. I figured if we arrived back where we started and there just happened to be a junior crewmember, who would it hurt? Easier to ask for forgiveness than to ask for permission. We did worry that the baby wouldn't develop normally without Earth gravity, but he came out just fine. Everything was good."

"But ..."

"But, two weeks after Damio's third birthday, he started having seizures. Terrible ones. They were so bad that his father began demanding that we return to Earth immediately."

Jimmy's lips moved as he did some mental back-of-the-envelope calculations.

"You'd have theoretically gotten back within two years, if you'd had the thruster-pushers running in time."

"Shavro didn't think Damio had two years. He wanted to go back in *six months*. Weld extra fuel tanks to the return stage, take off with only Damio and himself aboard, and burn for Earth at best possible speed."

"What about the other two?"

"George and Ross? Former military. Pilots. Very by-the-book. They grudgingly went along with the idea of me having the baby, because they were good men. But when Shavro got it into his head that using the return stage was the only option for Damio, George and Ross insisted there was no way we could throw the mission plan out the window, nor the return stage for that matter, without repercussions. And as much as it hurt me to admit it, I thought they were right. Trying to fly the return stage all the way back to Earth—on a wing and a prayer, as you might say—was folly. It would likely have gotten Shavro and Damio both killed. Better to do what could be done on the original timetable, get the thrusters working, and hope for the best."

"Obviously Shavro disagreed," Jimmy said.

"We argued about it for a week. We got so bad Damio would cry when we raised our voices, then he'd go into fits, and we'd spend the rest of the day trying to get Damio stabilized."

"So when did Shavro take off?"

"He didn't. Our former military men stood in my husband's way. Literally. I don't know how George got a pistol onboard this mission, but he pulled it on my husband when Shavro wouldn't back down. There was …"

Henrietta close her eyes, remembering the blood.

"Go on," Jimmy said.

"There was a fight. Ross tried to separate them. Shavro and Ross both got shot, while Shavro brained George with a heavy wrench. Ross was the only one with in-depth medical training, and he was the first to bleed out. Then Shavro after him. George lingered for days, but his cranial injury was too severe. I had to watch all three of them die in front of me."

"Damio?"

"Damio got worse every day for a month afterward. Then came the seizure that wouldn't stop. His little eyes ultimately rolled up in his dead and he choked to death in my arms."

At this point Henrietta could see Jimmy openly gaping at her.

"That's horrible," he said.

"You have no idea. Losing the others took me right to the edge. Losing Damio too? I went *over* the edge."

"Is that why the thruster-pushers and mining robots were never deployed? You were completely out of it?"

"Yes."

"Ground thought something catastrophic had happened."

"Something catastrophic *did* happen."

"I mean, a technical failure. An explosion. Something. One day the log updates and telemetry from 33 Riga just stopped coming. No explanation. No warning. It was like you all went to sleep. Or worse. For most of the way out here, I expected to find a disaster scene. And corpses. I am thankful that at least one person made it. But I'm curious, why is the ascent stage still missing if your husband never got to it?"

"I put the bodies in it," Henrietta said, her face pale with vivid, terrible memory. "At first I tried to keep them outside, but even knowing they were there—little Damio especially—was insufferable. It made me even crazier than I think I already was. So I put them all in the ascent stage, programmed the ascent stage for a long-trajectory burn for the sun, and launched it. Doubtless they've long since burned up. I can deal with that better than I can deal with the idea of their corpses still being here. On the asteroid."

"Another woman might have chosen to end her life," Jimmy said.

"I almost did. Several times. But I couldn't. Instead, I just kept everything turned off, used the onboard supplies and tools and equipment to set myself up for long-term habitation, and said goodbye to the rest of the human universe. I never wanted to see another person again. Something about holding Damio to my chest as he died … I don't remember too much about the weeks that followed. Other than putting the bodies in the ascent stage. I remember that. Too well. Everything else …"

"PTSD," Jimmy said. "My grandfather's brother Mel came back with it when he was deployed with the Army. Grandpa said Mel never was the same after that. Though Mel didn't go to counseling like the VA said he should. Mel was too proud. I hope when we get you back to civilization you're not too proud."

"I am not sure any counselor can help this," Henrietta said. "The very idea of being around other human beings, at this point, fills me with terror."

"You got over having *me* around," Jimmy said, smiling slightly.

"There is always an exception to everything."

"Yeah, I guess there is."

The two of them remained quiet for several minutes while they stared at the Earth. The Moon was now clearly visible as a little white companion.

"You think you'll be up for more work tomorrow? Getting that thruster-pusher up and running by myself was a royal pain. I really do need your help if we're going to make this work."

"I'll give it my best," Henrietta said.

"I think your best is better than most," Jimmy said, retrieving his drinking bulb and raising it in Henrietta's direction, before putting it to his mouth and taking a double-shot's worth.

• • •

To Henrietta's surprise, she didn't have even a single episode throughout the entirety of the following day. Nor the day after that. Nor the day after that. Time once again began to spin by. Little by little, she and Jimmy brought the entire thruster-pusher array up to full strength, their fuel piped from electrolyzed wells deep in the rock.

And for the first time that Henrietta could remember, 33 Riga enjoyed gravity. If after a fashion. Everything in the house had to be rearranged for the sake of an up-down existence—where things *fell*, and you couldn't just float your way around. But because the amount of constant thrust was relatively weak—ion engines only being capable of so much—the environment was forgiving. Such that the few times Henrietta did fall, she caught herself well before injury. And dropped items? They floated to the floor like feathers.

The Earth and the Moon grew larger.

With the thrusters completed it was time to engage the mining 'bots and the refinery. Things that could have been done in orbit, but since the original orders had said to spend the return trip to Earth doing as much advanced digging and smelting as possible, Jimmy was eager to complete the plan. So that 33 Riga would arrive in orbit with an abundance of valuable ores and minerals already accumulated.

"We'll sell it at a deep discount—at first," Jimmy said as he and Henrietta worked on a mining robot's chassis. Even with the original four crew, robot assembly would have been slow. With just two now, and one of them not entirely familiar with the old system, the process was much slower.

"The Consortium won't be making any profits that way," Henrietta said, twisting a bolt with her ratchet wrench.

"Not to start," Jimmy said, using his own ratchet wrench with an experienced and vigorous repetitive snap of the elbow. "But with 33 Riga secured and providing refined product in orbit—for a fraction of a fraction of what it would cost to lift the same product out of Earth's gravity well—I don't think it will be long before customers are lined up with their billfolds in their hands. And once that happens, ADC can launch bigger and better refinery equipment. Maybe even some milling and machining stations, the ones where you feed in three-dee models and the automated system spits out whatever shape you want. Eventually we'll launch more missions to more NEOs, as was originally planned. With several captured asteroids all producing, manufacturing … there won't be anything to hold us back. The moon colonies will be completed, and populated. Our mining and refining tech for the asteroids should be adaptable to the lunar environment. I tell you, Henrietta, once there are a few thousand people in space, the cork will be out of the bottle. *Everybody* will be wanting to come up. And this time, they'll be able to afford it too."

• • •

The mining robots went to work, grinding slowly but surely down through the silicates that layered the outer crust of 33 Riga. It wasn't long before they began to hit pay dirt, bringing hunks of iron and copper ore back to the surface. These raw materials were cordoned off in separate piles on the surface of the asteroid—opposite the thruster-pushers, so as to take advantage of the thrust-induced gravity. Otherwise they'd have just floated away into space.

Once the refinery was on-line, the ore began to be fed into the hopper, with spools and bricks of the refined metal dispensed on the other end. Not in huge quantities. Like all else about the asteroid-capture project, the 33 Riga refinery was a pint-sized version of the big auto-mated refineries already working on an industrial scale, back on Earth.

But as the months passed, the stacks and coils of iron, copper, aluminum, and even gold and silver, began to accumulate. Jimmy's mood grew buoyant as a result. He'd be contacting ground soon, to relay not only the news of his successful operation of the refinery, but also to help fine-tune their insertion trajectory.

Come in too shallow and 33 Riga might be flung off into a wild orbit, taking it far out of humanity's grasp. Come in too steep and 33 Riga might impact—the equivalent of a couple thousand megatons. Enough to wipe out a country, and induce apocalyptic tsunamis, to say nothing of the more long-lived environmental after-effects. A comet or asteroid not terribly bigger than 33 Riga was still presumed to have ended the epoch of the dinosaurs. Do it wrong, and ADC's attempt to capture 33 Riga for humanity's future, might end up spelling humanity's doom.

Through it all, Jimmy and Henrietta kept talking. A bit here, and a bit there. As both schedule and energy allowed. By the time their first year had elapsed, Henrietta actually began to think of him as her friend. Something she'd not been able to say about another person for a long, long time.

Then came the day when they were standing together in the observation dome, and the Earth was no longer a marble, nor a golf ball, nor even a baseball, but a beach ball in the black sky.

Having shed velocity with a prolonged downthrust, 33 Riga was lined up almost perfectly with its entry corridor. Once they were in the "pipe" they'd put the thruster-pushers into overdrive and conduct a final, tremendous deceleration burn. Enough to push the local gravitational equivalent of the asteroid up to 25% Earth normal—which was really saying something, and would stress every system on the asteroid. Including the people.

Jimmy pointed up to the planet, at the large ice-capped island off the eastern coast of North America.

"I figure I can negotiate something with the government. Get you a nice bit of tundra all to yourself. Nothing to do but freeze your butt off."

Henrietta stared at where he was pointing.

"I think ... I may have changed my mind."

Jimmy's arm dropped and he did a double take.

"Oh?" he said, visibly working to suppress his surprise. "You're not doubting my powers of persuasion, are you? I've yet to meet a politician I couldn't get to eat out of the palm of my hand."

"It's not that," Henrietta said. "It's just … well, I think I'm getting the bug again."

"The bug?"

"The dream, as your grandfather might have called it. After Damio died I gave up on my dreams. Life was just something to be coped with. Endured. But now? I don't know. The idea of being surrounded by people still spooks me. But you're right. We've done OK, you and I. Something I would have said was impossible three years ago. Maybe having a little company around the asteroid won't be so bad. And I have to admit, the vision you paint—of capturing more asteroids and using them all in concert to begin paving the road to the planets, and maybe even to the *stars* some day—it's as alluring as it ever was. I lost my vision—in that way—for a long time. But I think having someone else around, who knows a little bit about what I've been through, has helped me get it back again."

"Historic!" Jimmy said, clapping his hands together and grinning.

"Cool it," Henrietta said. "We still have our insertion orbit to complete. The end is still nigh, though I think all the math's worked out in our favor."

"I hope you're right," Jimmy said, still smiling.

Henrietta looked at him. He was younger than she was, by at least a dozen years or more. But still handsome in his own way. His hair thick, and a dark silver color, whereas hers had gone mostly silver-white.

Impulsively, Henrietta grasped his shoulders in her hands, pulled herself up to eye level with him, and planted a kiss squarely on his lips.

"Oh my goodness," was all he managed to say, completely floored.

Henrietta smiled, and curled the fingers of her left hand around his right palm.

"Come on Mister Space Tycoon, we'd better go get ourselves strapped in. It's going to be a fun ride."

"Yes," Jimmy said, his eyes in a happy haze of surprise, "I think you're right."

▼▲▼▲▼

This was one of those stories which started at the very end, and worked its way backward. The scene I had in my head, was that of two older people—a man and a woman—who've been beaten down by a lot of hard knocks, but who are also facing their mutual future with fresh eyes. In a moment of off-the-cuff enthusiasm, the woman—who has to this point been very reserved and standoffish—pecks the man on the lips. Thus signaling that there are more doors being opened than the reader might at first assume. Because romance isn't just for teenagers.

The rest congealed around this initial scene, so that pretty soon I'd worked up not only a reason for the woman being standoffish, but also for the man being there in the first place, his own inner demons and how they contrast to those of the woman, and their overall predicament as a whole—science fictionalized, of course. I wanted to make sure I had something which would be at home in the pages of Analog magazine. So I concocted the notion of a do-or-die mission to revive an asteroid harvesting project gone terribly awry.

When I was much younger, I didn't realize yet how truly burdensome one's accumulated sum of lifetime choices can become. The good, the bad, the ugly. Hopefully all of us learn from the middle, and the latter, while enjoying the fruits of the former. And if we're lucky, we get to pay back—to the universe, in karma points—whatever debts we've incurred through blunders and stumbles. But sometimes everything can pile up on a person to the point that no choice, short of unplugging and shutting down entirely, seems possible. Thus Henrietta's neurosis manifests following the loss of her family and her coworkers in what is a tragic series of events.

Sometimes, it really can be too much to bear; facing the world.

I wanted Henrietta to discover that she's not the only one who's suffered, and that even when she's walled up her feelings good and tight, a little warmth can still seep in through the cracks, stirring the seeds of her humanity; which she thought to be essentially dead and buried.

The Flamingo Girl

Elvira was seven feet of naked avian loveliness. The tiny feathers sprouting from her skin formed a luxurious layer of bright-pink, velvet-soft plumage, and her unblinking eyes stared at the ceiling with an expression of surprise. The bed upon which her body lay was a confused mess of satin blankets and pillows, with not a hint of whom else might have been with her, or why that person had resorted to murder.

"Señor Soto," said a voice behind me. I turned, and beheld another seven-foot beauty, this one parrot-green. Her wings flexed and ruffled with agitation, and her sapphire-blue eyebrows hunched over a fear-filled gaze. Looking up into her face—we unmodified humans being generally shorter than Specials—I asked her what I could do for her.

"The other women are very nervous, Señor," she said, "they are wanting to know what has happened. Madam Arquette asked me to ask you what to tell them."

"And you are?" I said.

"Josefina," said the green bird-woman.

"You may tell them that Elvira is dead, and that housekeeping is free to enter and clean the Flamingo Suite as soon as the city's public mortician has removed the body."

"There isn't going to be an investigation?"

"That's for the police to decide. They'll be here shortly. I imagine that they'll want to question a few people, so make sure none of the customers leave before that happens."

In truth, the cops wouldn't give a damn about another dead Special. It was unlikely they'd interrogate anyone at all. The Aerie was a busy waypoint on Hollywood Boulevard, in a city that spared little budget for true law enforcement. Myself and three other guards were what laughably passed for security at the Aerie—our presence being a formality so that Madam Arquette could claim to be honoring her adult merchant commission with the Greater Los Angeles Commerce Bureau.

"The Madam will not be pleased," said Josefina.

"Then perhaps the Madam should have listened to me when I warned her about cutting her private security expenses again. All the reputable adult businesses on the Boulevard hire triple our number."

Josefina's wings rustled violently.

"Look," I said to her, "I'm sorry I can't do more. I really am."

I attempted to move past Josefina. She thrust out a wing that blocked my way.

"But you used to be a policeman," she said with quivering indignation. "You were hired because of your experience. If you can't help us now, what good are you?"

I stepped back, looked at the anger in her eyes, and felt the full weight of my fifty years settle on my shoulders. I had asked myself that same question ten times a day since coming to the Aerie. Once upon a time, I'd been an okay cop in the Long Beach supermetro. But when Carlita had left me, and taken the kids, and sold the house … whatever ties had been keeping me in Long Beach, seemed to evaporate. I'd retired early, and immediately sought the job with the least amount of real responsibility I could find, as far away from Carlita as possible.

I just looked at Josefina, a sympathetic frown on my face. "The police will be here soon, and they will handle this. It's out of my purview."

Eventually her wing withdrew, and small tears began to stain the lime-colored down around Josefina's eyes.

"Look," I said, "if you really want to find out who did this, give the cops something to go on. I know the Madam has in-house rules about customer confidentiality, but this time I think there needs to be an exception. City corporate policy says they can't make her release her records, and knowing the Madam, I doubt she'd sacrifice her reputation on the strip for a single dead girl—"

"I will get the police what they need," Josefina said, suddenly standing stiff.

"Will the Madam know about it?" I asked.

"Would it bother you if she didn't?"

No, I had to admit, it wouldn't.

"You're taking this kind of hard," I said. "Was Elvira a friend?"

"No, Señor Soto, she was my younger sister."

• • •

Twenty four hours later, I got a text from Josefina asking me to meet her in West Hollywood. No indication why, just that she needed me urgently. An address was attached. I checked in with the branch office of the security firm I worked for, and clocked out for an extended lunch break.

Josefina's apartment block was in what the supermetro called the Special District. Most of the Specials in Greater Los Angeles tended to congregate there—where everyone could be uniformly bizarre together. The sidewalk out front was replete with walking, talking cats, dogs, birds, wolves, rabbits, and other Specials who had had their human DNA artificially adapted to take on various other species' characteristics.

Entering the block I passed a man whose fur was striped like a skunk's, though thankfully he didn't smell like one. If he cared that a Normal—the Specials' word for everyone else in the world—was going into his apartment complex, he didn't show it.

I took the elevator up to the tenth floor and found the door with number 1036, tapped the little button in the middle of the door, and waited while the tiny camera inside the button surveyed me.

The door handle clicked, and I was beckoned into Josefina's home. Microscopic as it was. I'd seen student studios with more square footage. But it was clean, and smelled gently of ginger and orange peel.

"Señor," she said respectfully. I took off my sun hat and nodded at her.

Josefina immediately pressed a thumb drive into my hand.

"It is all here," she said quietly. I noticed that she had on a plain-patterned traditionally-cut dress, with holes in the back for her wings, and no shoes. Her ankles and feet were the same color as the rest of her. Bright green.

"What is this?" I said.

"I tried to give it to the police, but they didn't want it. Nobody cares about Elvira."

"I told you, I—"

"*Por favor,* Señor Soto," Josefina said insistently. "There is no one else to do this. You must do it. Please. I don't have much money, but I can pay you for your time. I can—"

I raised a hand and patted it down through the air, pleadingly.

"Just tell me what I'll be looking at," I said, "before you go giving me any money."

"It's Elvira's schedule at the Aerie."

"There are names? Everyone who ever used your sister?"

"*Hired* her," Josefina corrected me. "Yes."

"I'll probably just need the names of the people she saw the night she died."

"But she was off that night, and there is no record of anyone having rented the suite or hired Elvira."

"Then what was she doing there at all?"

"I do not know," Josefina said, eyes on the floor. Her wings had begun to tremble.

I slipped the thumb drive into a pocket and took her right hand in both of mine—the sensation of the tiny feathers on my bare palms was like mink pelt, but softer.

"It wasn't your fault," I said, flashing back to an almost identical scene in my supermetro days, when I'd had to both question and console a stricken mother whose son had died in a gang turf tumble.

"Of course it is," Josefina said. "It was my idea for her to come to the Aerie. I recommended her to the Madam. She was nervous about going Special, and I talked her into it. Mother and father never forgave me when I went Special, and they doubly hated it when Elvira came to work with me. I have no idea how much the whole family will hate me now."

"So why did you wind up at the Aerie in the first place?"

"It was my best option."

"I don't understand," I said.

"Señor Soto, you're not from West L.A?"

"Not originally, no."

"But you are Raza?"

"I grew up in the barrios of Oakland. Joined the Army at 17. When I got out of the Army, I moved south and went to the police academy."

I remembered when I told my mother I'd joined supermetro's PD. She'd cried. But then, she'd cried when I'd joined the military, and when my brothers ran away, too. At least with me she'd known where I was and what I was doing. But it had still upset her a great deal—always terrified I was going to get myself hurt, whether it was overseas, or here in California working Vice, or second-level Theft stuff, or the small army that ran herd on gangs.

I mumbled something to that effect.

"My mother was almost proud of being poor," Josefina said. "Our family had been in East L.A. for almost five generations, all in the same crappy little house. Elvira and me, we hated it. We wanted something better. But the schools in East L.A., what good are they? For you, the Army was your avenue out. For Elvira and I, just two poor sisters with homely faces and no education …"

I nodded my understanding—so far.

"Anyway, I got a cleaning job. They sent me all over. One day I got sent up to Madam Arquette's house in Beverly Hills. I'd never worked for a Special before, much less someone that rich. She's like a peacock you know. Beautiful and grand and when I started asking questions, she told me how it works. If a girl will undergo Specialization and work in the Aerie, Madam will carry the cost. You pay it back over time, plus interest, and after that, you keep everything you earn, minus a house fee."

"But if you wanted to go into business for yourself—" I started to say, but Josefina cut me off.

"Look at me, Señor," Josefina stepped away a couple of paces and flared her wings wide, filling the tiny apartment, her hourglass silhouette accentuated through the thin fabric of the dress. "Men and women both will pay hundreds an hour to be with me. We have the richest clients in the entire city. People who want the Special experience. Crave it. A pro Normal girl in Long Beach, how much does she make, compared to that?"

Not much, I had to admit.

Josefina lowered and folded her wings.

"I didn't want to be just any working girl," she said. "I wanted to literally be a different person. Because some day, I want to have enough money to leave Los Angeles on my own two feet, and not look back, and not need anyone else's help, and not have to take this ... this part of me with me when I leave."

"Reversal of the Specialization is twice as expensive as the initial procedure," I said.

"I don't care. Once I've earned enough to pay the Madam off, I'll keep working until I can pay for the reversal, and get myself out of here to boot. When Elvira came to visit me and I told her about my plan, she'd wanted to come with me, but it would have been too expensive for both of us, so I told her she had to find a way to help with costs."

Josefina stopped, her face in her hands, wings gently shaking as she sobbed.

I felt my cheeks growing red.

"Look," I said, "I meant it before: Madam Arquette can't rely on just four men to keep her establishment free of trouble."

"But you're here, when you know you don't have to be," Josefina said, her nose sniffling.

"I didn't know your sister," I said, "But I don't like the idea of anyone killing a young woman and getting away with it either."

She seemed to accept that explanation at face value, lame as it was.

"I can't make any promises," I said, reaching into my pocket and feeling the cool plastic of the thumb drive. "All I can tell you is that I'll take a look."

"Do what you can" Josefina said abruptly. "It's better than nothing."

"Yes ma'am," I said, sticking out my hand, which she shook.

Then she leaned down quickly and pecked me on the cheek. How long had it been since a woman—any woman, Special or Normal— had done that to me? I felt my race redden all over again, then muttered a goodbye and ducked back out into the hallway.

• • •

The thumb drive turned out to contain all of Elvira's business calendar—every appointment going back to when she'd gotten out of the hospital, post-Specialization. The header on the calendar simply read FLAMINGO. Having met the Madam a few times I got the sense that she didn't bring on anyone new unless it was done on the Madam's terms, so Elvira was just filling the role assigned to her.

And while names were present, salient data beyond that was tough to come by. All financial transaction information had been stripped, as well as whether or not clients had been locals, celebrities, or even the rare tourist. If the schedule had ever contained details on what precisely Elvira had provided, in terms of customer care and needs— beyond what I already knew to be the case—that too was missing.

And Josefina had been right. Elvira was blacked out the day of her death. In fact, she was blacked out most of that week.

I mulled this over at my desk, back at the Aerie. If the Madam discovered I had this information—we guards were never, ever allowed access to the scheduling software, for confidentiality purposes—it would cost me a lot more than my job. I quickly dumped the calendar to text, then erased the calendar, keeping only names and time blocks in ASCII format on the same thumb drive Josefina had given me. She was off for the rest of the week, a considerable concession from the Madam, given the circumstances, so I went about my usual work, only occasionally poking my head into the womens' private rooms to ask a discrete question or two.

So far as anyone knew, Elvira had had no quarrels with the other Specials. In fact, the lot of them seemed heartbroken over the girl's death, and mournful in the extreme for her older sister. A community pot was being passed—I dropped in my share—and they were planning to have a silent moment in Elvira's memory when Josefina came back to work. Otherwise, business at the Aerie continued as usual. Clients came and went, their communications hushed and monosyllabic at the palatial registration desk—often from behind hoods or sunglasses or anything else that might obscure their faces from prying eyes, the Special fetish still being a somewhat controversial fetish, even in a city which had long ago abandoned any pretense of sexual propriety.

As I watched the clientele come and go, from behind my own set of sunglasses, I realized that I didn't have much of a clue about what went on when the clients and the Specials met behind the closed doors of the suites. Oh, sure, I had plenty of educated assumptions. The Aerie had two thirds female Specials and one third male Specials, and if ever they "talked shop" it was done strictly between them, away from the ears of a Normal like me.

In many ways, myself and the three other guards were like wallpaper or store window mannequins: unless our presence was called for, and it was seldom called for in any case, we kept our distance, and the Specials did the same, and the clients ghosted to and fro with as little noise as possible.

I examined the names I'd gotten from Josefina. I didn't know any of them, though I couldn't be sure any of them were actual names either. Fake names were as likely as anything, which was probably why the cops hadn't wanted the list in the first place. What good was a list of bogus identities?

Josefina came back to work. We never acknowledged that I'd been to her home.

I kept looking at the list of names throughout the next week, until I noticed one name that was down for numerous appointments in predictable succession, then abruptly stopped showing up.

I texted Josefina about this, and asked her if she knew the name. Or if Elvira had ever talked about this particular person. I got a text re-inviting me to Josefina's apartment, this time in the dinner hour.

• • •

"What her real name is, I am not sure," Josefina said. She'd offered me a plate of grilled beef with peppers and onions, which I ate thankfully, not having had food since sipping a cup of bitter coffee at midmorning.

"*Her?*" I said, somewhat surprised.

"She was an anglo Normal, mid-forties."

"Did Elvira ever talk about this person?"

"Yes, because this woman never actually wanted sex."

"Is that unusual?"

"It happens. Some clients come in simply for the vicarious thrill of being around a Special. We're fascinating for them."

"This anglo Normal, she was one of these?"

"Yes. She would request Elvira in two-hour blocks. She adored real flamingos, apparently. She and Elvira would sit together on the bed of the suite, and the anglo … she would stroke Elvira's body and wings affectionately, and just talk about her life. Her hectic middle management work. Her grown sons. Her ex-husband, who apparently divorced her in disgust when he discovered she had a thing for Specials, and had been surreptitiously using family funds to begin exploring the Special world on-line. That's how she found out about the Aerie, apparently, and when Madam Arquette put up the listing for The Flamingo Suite, this woman was an instant customer."

"So why'd she stop coming all of a sudden?"

"I don't know," Josefina said, nibbling uninterested at her own food.

"If this woman spent so much time talking to Elvira, did your sister ever talk back? I mean, about her own life?"

"I don't know, but I wonder. Elvira was only twenty. About the same age as this woman's own children. Elvira always needed to trust people."

"Is it possible Elvira told this woman things she wouldn't tell you?"

"What do you mean?" Josefina's fork suddenly stopped moving.

"Not to question your relationship with your sister, it's just been my experience that siblings, even close siblings, don't always share everything with each other, whether they realize it or not. And as the saying goes, a man will tell things to a bartender he'd never tell his wife. This anglo Normal, she is a question mark for me. She might know something which could tell us more about why Elvira died.

"Speaking of which," Josefina said, "the police tell me that an examination to determine exactly what killed Elvira, is still pending. Does it normally take this long?"

"When there are no obvious wounds," I said, "things can get complicated. I called the coroner and made some polite inquiries. Elvira was a healthy young Special. Something was done to her, that much we can be certain of. What that something was, is another matter entirely. Try to be patient. Meanwhile, is there any way possible for you to find out who this anglo customer was? Does she come back to visit any of the other Specials, male or female? Or both?"

"I can try to find out tonight, when I am working."

We chewed in mutual silence for several minutes.

"If your daughter told you she wanted to go Special," Josefina said, "what would your reaction be?"

Now it was my fork which had suddenly stopped moving. My Angela was fifteen, and headstrong like Carlita. Last summer, Carlita had let Angela spend the summer with me, when it was my younger son Adam I'd wanted to have. I'd learned quickly it was because Angela was officially hell on wheels, and we'd scrapped it out for three months, before she'd finally gone home to Carlita in disgust—and with my blessing. I tried to imagine Angela showing up at my door in two more years, transformed into God knew what. *Hi Papa! It's me, your little girl!*

I must have visibly shuddered, because Josefina put her fork down and wiped her mouth, then stood up quickly.

"You can see yourself to the door."

"Wait, I'm sorry, I—"

"I'll see what I can find out for you about the anglo. Goodnight, Señor."

My plate unfinished, I clumsily stood up and made my way out.

. . .

I was making the mistake of giving a damn, that much was certain. A smarter man probably would have quit the Aerie and gone to find a different job. But Josefina had shamed me, and now I felt like I owed her ... something. Not sure what? Some kind of resolution, perhaps. I couldn't just walk away. That would have felt unmanly, and while I'd long ago given up certain pretensions to *machismo,* I was damned if I was going to let a woman almost half my age do what Josefina had done, whether she'd realized it when she asked the question or not. So I stewed my way through three days of shifts, until I thought my off hours might coincide with Josefina's—and once again went to her apartment block in West Hollywood.

There was no answer at first. I almost turned and went home.

But the door popped, and Josefina opened it hesitantly.

"Yes?"

"The coroner sent me a report about Elvira," I said.

"And?"

"And I really think it would be best if I came in and we sat down."

Josefina eyed me closely, measuring my intent, then opened the door the rest of the way, allowing me into her single-room domain. Things weren't as clean as they'd been before. I wagered she'd not done any upkeep since the last time I'd visited. The same plate I'd eaten off of, still sat half-submerged in cold soapy water in the kitchen sink.

"Tell me," Josefina said. It was practically a command.

"Near-instant anaphylactic shock," I said. "As a result of being exposed to concentrated bee venom."

"She was stung by a *bee?*"

"No. They found a small puncture wound on her neck, like what might be made by a microtubule. The plastic tip had broken off beneath the skin. Did you know she was allergic?"

"Yes, the whole family did. She was stung when we were kids, and had to be rushed to the emergency room. It almost killed her."

"Who else besides the two of you might have known?"

"I don't know. Maybe a few family friends from East L.A?"

I scratched my head, thinking.

"So now the police will investigate it as murder," Josefina said.

"The file will be dropped down to homicide, homicide will see that it was a Special working the Boulevard, and the file will be quietly forgotten about."

"How can they do this?" Josefina said, balling her fists, her wings spasming. "She was a human being for God's sake!"

"Supermetro jurisdictions track hundreds of potential homicides every day," I said. "More people die every year in the Greater Los Angeles area than died in the Army's entire invasion of Pakistan. The police prioritize, based on how easily a case might be solved, and how high-profile the victim happens to be. I hate to say it, but Specials barely register. Many cops don't even think of you as human anymore."

"You would know," Josefina snarled, her vehemence plain.

I felt my face flush. "Goddammit, I'm sorry I was such a *pendejo* when I was here the other night. Okay, alright, would I be thrilled if my daughter came home having gone Special? No. Frankly, it would kind of freak me out."

Josefina turned away from me, but I grabbed her elbows with both arms and forced her to look at me—no small feat, given she had me by twelve inches and twenty-plus years.

"But she'd still be my daughter," I said, looking up into Josefina's enraged eyes with all of the sincerity I could muster, "and regardless of who or what she'd become, I'd never stop loving Angela with all my heart and soul. She's ... she's one of the only decent things I have left to show for myself! Her and Adam, my son."

Josefina's lips quivered, and tears openly flooded out into the feathers on her face, dropping across them to land on the lapels of my jacket.

She sank down to her knees, fists balled on my stomach, and began to sob into my chest. Almost reflexively I wrapped my arms around her head, again marveling at the incredible softness of the inhuman plumage that had replaced her hair. I found myself quietly whispering in Spanish, the same reassurances I had often given to Angela and Adam when they'd woken screaming from a nightmare. Josefina's long arms circled the small of my back and almost crushed me as I held her, her wings gently and reflexively quivering along her back.

"We'll find who did this to Elvira," I said. "I promise you."

• • •

Josefina went to work that night, and I went home to my own apartment in Culver City. After unsuccessfully trying to reach Carlita on her cell phone, and next Angela on her cell phone, I collapsed into bed feeling extraordinarily exhausted. I wondered—until sleep took me—about the anglo woman who liked flamingos.

In the morning I appeared at the Aerie, prepared for another day of quietly subtle poking and prodding, when one of the other security guys not so gently told me I was to report to Madam Arquette's office immediately. That there was trouble was obvious, so I grimaced and made my way up through the building until I reached the penthouse office suite, unofficially referred to by us guards as The Nest. I rapped on the frosted glass double doors that separated Madam Arquette's world from the reality outside it.

The doors parted, humming open on motorized hinges.

I saw Josefina, standing near Madam Arquette's desk, her head down towards the floor. She wouldn't look at me, though Madam Arquette herself stared across the room with the malice of a diving falcon. The Madam was naked, but for her layer of plumage, her breasts dappled with blues and purples.

"Come in, Mister Soto," said the Madam in her characteristic French-laced accent.

I entered, realizing that I'd never actually been in the Nest proper before. Three walls were nothing but glass that looked out on the smog and bustle of the city. To our west we could see the heaped metal skyscape of Los Angeles, baking nicely in the advancing morning sun. I had to tear myself away from the unexpectedly impressive view when the Madam cleared her throat and indicated a huge leather chair in front of her desk, a feather-coated hand flourishing artfully.

I slowly but purposefully took a seat.

"Monsieur Soto," said the Madam, "Josefina here was caught snooping into the master schedule. It is forbidden by contract for any employee to research or view the schedule of any other employee. Our clientele demand the strictest discretion. What do you suggest be done about this matter?"

"Madam," I said, "Josefina was acting purely under my direction. I take full responsibility for the breach of company directive."

Madam Arquette simply stared at me, then stood up from her stool—her wings resplendent with emerald and sapphire feathering—and walked around her desk to stand imposingly over me.

"You are privately investigating the death of Elvira," the Madam said.

"Yes," I replied.

"You realize that if word were to get out that client information had been leaked to either a security firm or the police, the Aerie would be ruined."

"Yes."

"I could even bring civil charges against you and Josefina both for grossly and negligently violating your contracts. What do you have to say about that?"

I raised my hands out to my side, palms up, and said, "you have to do what you feel is the right thing, Madam."

She stared down at me, her eyes brilliantly lit up with fury, then turned and walked quickly to the wall of windows that looked out over the city, her very-high platform heels making *clock-clock* sounds on the polished simulated wood flooring.

"Elvira was not the first girl to die here," the Madam said, as if talking to the view outside the Aerie's top floor. "Before you came to work for me, Monsieur Soto, I always managed to have the matter dispensed with discretely and at great legal difficulty. It was unfortunate what happened in those cases, but I've spent twenty years building this business up from nothing, and I was not going to allow a few mishaps to ruin everything."

"Her sister was murdered," I said.

"Yes I know that," said the Madam.

"And that means nothing to you?"

"Do you take me for an animal?" the Madam said, spinning to face me, her wings rustling with tension. I elected not to speak the first answer which came to my mind.

"I take you for a very focused businesswoman who has perhaps allowed the bottom line to get in the way of certain perspectives, about the people who work for you."

She seemed to evaluate that response, a tongue running along the inside of a cheek.

"And if I have lost these perspectives, as you say, Monsieur, what do you propose be done about it?"

"Give me information on one person, someone who saw Elvira many times, then suddenly stopped."

"Josefina has told me about her. I know of whom you speak, and she is a client of the highest social caliber. There is no way possible she is involved in this."

"But she might be someone who can tell us who is involved," I said.

"And what will this client think, when you show up at her doorstep, playing the investigator? The Aerie has an iron-clad reputation in this city, our clientele expect the utmost privacy. Even one exception could destroy us."

"And if I went to the Beverly Hills press, starting rumors that the Aerie allows killers to come and go on its premises, without prejudice? What do you think that will do to your excellent reputation?"

Madam Arquette eyed me coldly. Then she turned to Josefina.

"Leave us. You will do no more on this matter, or I will throw you out. Say nothing. To anyone. Is that understood? My quarrel is with the Monsieur now."

Josefina walked quickly out of the room, her own very-high platform heels going *clock-clock,* until the Madam and I were alone.

She walked over and rested her buttocks on the edge of her frosted-glass desk.

"You are an older man, experienced, why do you do this for a strange girl?"

"Because someone has to do it."

"Why?"

"Because some things just have to matter more than other things, and sometimes you can't just turn away and make something disappear. Josefina couldn't leave it alone, because it's her sister."

"And you can't leave Josefina alone, because ... there are benefits I am not aware of? Security personnel are not allowed to solicit from the staff. That too is a violation."

"Bite your tongue, bitch, she's young enough to be my daughter. And if you'd stopped cutting back on security staffing when I told you to, maybe Elvira would still be alive, and we wouldn't be having this conversation right now, yes?"

For the first time, the Madam's eyes dropped to the floor.

"I do not celebrate Elvira's death, whatever else you may think of me."

"Prove it. Give me what I need to keep tunneling on this. If it goes nowhere, that's my fault. But I've got an old cop's hunch, and I can't move on it without your help. Josefina aside. Come on Madam, show me that the Aerie's vaunted reputation is about more than just money."

Her eyes stayed on the floor for a very long time. Then she circled back around to the other side of her desk, sat on her stool, pantomimed some commands to the computer, and waited while a piece of hardcopy spat out of a nearby, slim-line printer.

The Madam handed the copy across to me.

"Get out of my office."

I looked at the paper, a tiny smile on my face, then popped up out of the chair.

"With pleasure. Good day, Madam Arquette."

• • •

The Madam had been right. The anglo lady who liked flamingos was of the old money Beverly Hills upper crust. I still didn't have a real name, but I had an address and I had contact information. The split with her husband had not affected her lifestyle to a great degree, both of them being from wealthy families, and she still maintained a significant estate. One I'd be hard-pressed to visit with any degree of subtlety. So I did what I thought best. I sent her an anonymous text with an address for a public library, and attached a picture of a flamingo to it. Then waited at the Frances Howard Goldwyn branch for her arrival, at the date and time specified.

I was not disappointed. Her designer womens' suit and expensive sunglasses gave her away against the backdrop of working-class readers who lined the aisles and sat at the computer terminals. I was off in a corner, a hard-bound Audubon edition on *Phoenicopteridae* displayed prominently. I saw her before she saw me, but when she saw the cover on the book, she bee-lined over and sat down.

"Who are you, and what's happened to Elly?"

"I am a family friend," I said, keeping my voice low, to match hers. "And I am very sorry to say that Elly is dead."

The woman's hand shot to her mouth, the small clutch in her other hand nearly falling to the floor.

"My God," she said, genuinely and horribly startled.

"That's what I need your help with," I said. "I used to be a police officer, and am handling this matter privately for Elly's family. I was hoping you could tell me about some of the last conversations you had with Elly when she was at the Aerie. You were intimate with the Aguilar's daughter, were you not?"

"No! I mean, well, yes, but no. Not in the way you're thinking."

"Did Elly seem afraid of anyone, the last few times you were with her?"

"No," said the woman, slowly removing her sunglasses and reaching for a handkerchief in her clutch. Tears had begun to flow down her face.

"Did she say anything about anyone at work? Someone who might have been bothering her?"

"No," said the woman.

"Did you and Elly have any trouble? Maybe, a fight of some kind?"

"I told you," she said through sniffles, "we weren't like that. Elly was … she was pure. And beautiful. More beautiful than anything or anyone I have ever seen. Graceful and poetic, yet young and playful in the way only … I don't think I can explain it, Mister . . ?"

"Rodriguez," I said, reaching out a hand to shake hers. "Of the Los Taltos firm, out of Thousand Oaks."

"I've never heard of them," she said.

"Not many people have. We're small, because it allows us to be discrete. Please know that anything you tell me today is in the strictest confidence."

She nodded, blowing quietly into the handkerchief.

"So there was nothing amiss?" I said. "Nothing at all?"

"No."

"Then what stopped you from seeing Elly last month?"

The woman blew her nose one more time, and collected herself.

"I did it for Elly's sake. I could tell I was falling in love. Literally and truly. I was going to cross lines that would destroy Elly if I didn't take myself away. And I couldn't live with that. So one day I simply stopped making appointments."

"And you never saw her again after that?"

"No."

I sat back in my chair, frowning deeply.

"Mister Rodriguez, who would hurt that girl?"

"I don't know," I said honestly.

We sat for several moments, the woman staring at the tabletop. Then she looked up at me, her red eyes mournful.

"There is one thing," she said.

"Yes?"

"Last time I was with Elly, she seemed distracted. Bothered. I asked her what was wrong, and she said her brother had called her from East Los Angeles, asking her to come home. She said they'd had an argument on the phone, then she'd laughed it off like it was no big deal. She and her brother had never gotten along, or so she said."

I mentally filed this as Very Important, and waited for the woman to continue.

Which she didn't.

I finally stood up.

"You've been helpful," I said. "If you remember anything else, please contact me using this text address."

I handed her a plain white card with a number on it.

"Again, strictest confidence," I assured her.

She took the card and put her sunglasses back on.

"Mister Rodriguez," she said.

"Yes?"

"If you ever do find out what happened, please let me know?"

"I can do that," I said. And meant it.

• • •

Josefina's apartment was even more messy than last time.

"Antonio and Elvira never argued," she said as she handed me a cup of hot, lightly sugared coffee. It was early morning, and she was just going to bed, while I was just getting ready to head back to the Aerie

"The woman said they did," I told her. "And you expressed to me that you thought there was no telling how much the family might hate you, after Elvira came out and went Special at your advice."

"Yes, but I expected them to hate *me*, not her."

"Would they have hated either one of you enough to kill?"

"I could never think that …"

"But?"

"But, last time Papa and I spoke, he said I was dead to him."

"What about your brother?"

"Antonio and Papa always got along. Like father, like son."

"Where is Antonio now?"

"When he left home, he went to find work on the farms."

"Do you have an address?"

"No, but I am betting my parents do."

"Do they have an address?"

"Of course."

"Then it's time for me to talk to your parents."

"No!"

"Their daughter is dead. The city has already sent the official notification. If my daughter were dead like that, I'd sure as hell want someone to tell me why, or who had done it."

"No," she insisted.

"Josefina, do you really want to find out the truth?"

"Yes," she said.

"Then let me finish this."

• • •

The barrios of East L.A. weren't a hell of a lot different from the barrios of Oakland. Row upon row of mid-20th century cheap housing that had slowly been churning through the hands of the poor over the last hundred years. The little bungalow I stopped at was a near carbon copy of the house where I'd grown up, and though they were older, the Aguilars were about what my Mom and Dad would have been, had my father not died young and left my other to struggle in solitude.

Taking me for a city official—I neither confirmed nor denied that identity, as they welcomed me into the front room and offered me a cold glass of water—the Aguilars expressed deepest regret at the fate of Elvira.

"Never should have let her go," said Papa Aguilar. "It was bad enough when her older sister turned on the family."

"You had a falling out with Elvira's older sister?" I said innocently.

"She is a pervert," Papa Aguilar said. "Ran off and turned herself into an animal who screws rich gringos. Disgusting."

I experimentally swirled the icy water around in the scratched acrylic tumbler they'd given me.

"I'm sorry that things didn't turn out well for you and your daughters."

"You make it sound so neat and clean," he snorted.

Mama Aguilar placed a firm hand on his bicep, gave him a knowing look.

"We have lost both our daughters," Mama said. "Please forgive us if we are not as polite about it as we should be."

"Understandable," I said, then took a drink.

"At least we still have Antonio," Mama said.

"Your son?"

"Yes, he's been home from Santa Clara for a few months now. He's earned some money, now we're going to help him go back to school."

"What was he doing in Santa Clara?"

Mama lead me into the kitchen, where she pulled a mason jar off the top of the refrigerator. It was filled with a viscous, golden substance. "Bee-keeping."

My hair stood on end.

Mama handed me the jar of honey, and I hefted it experimentally, choosing my next words very, very carefully.

"Did the coroner tell you exactly what caused Elvira's death?"

"Does it matter?" said Papa. "I got the notice. I crumpled it up and burned it without needing to read the fine print. Elvira was gone the moment she chose to follow her sister."

I carefully replaced the mason jar on top of the fridge.

"Mister Aguilar," I said, "did Antonio ever go visit either of his sisters after he came home?"

"No," he said.

"Are you sure?"

"Yes ... well, I don't think he did." Papa's eyes narrowed. "What are you getting at?"

"If you'd read the full text of the coroner's findings, you'd know that Elvira died because she'd been injected with *bee venom*."

Both of them froze in place, eyes narrowing at me, then slowly widening in comprehension.

"*La policía* ..." Papa Aguilar breathed.

There was a slam as the back door opened and closed. Clomping footsteps came up the stairs, and a young, fit man appeared at the other doorway to the kitchen.

Mama and Papa stared at me for an instant longer, then looked at their son, then back at me. Antonio's smile dropped, and he stared at me too.

"What's going on?" he said. "Who is this?"

"Rodriguez," I said. "I'm from the city. I need to talk to you about Elvira."

Maybe it was the way I'd said it? Maybe it was the fact that I still had the military-cropped haircut I'd kept since my Army days? Maybe he'd noticed the bulge of the stun gun I had in a holster tucked into the pit of my arm, under my suit jacket? Whatever it was, I never had a chance to get in another word before three things happened simultaneously:

Antonio, spinning and running back down the steps.

Mama screaming, "Antonio, *no!*"

Papa screaming, "*La policía!*"

I flew past the Aguilars and down the stairs, feeling the steps in my knees but pleased that I could still be quick when I wanted to be. He never bothered to close the door as he sprinted across the patio, around the detached garage, and down the filthy, narrow street beyond. I skidded around the corner—my loafers not quite as good on concrete as his athletic shoes—then shouted his name at the back of his head as he pelted for the nearest intersection. I followed, sweating and cursing, but managing to keep an eye on him as I went around the corner, saw him dodge two cars while crossing to the other side, and kept running for the next intersection further south. I pulled the stunner out and kept pumping arms and legs, at once dreading the chase, but feeling the muscle memory exhilaration of pursuit. Just like old times. I wasn't the police, but I wasn't going to let Elvira's killer go, brother or no brother.

Across an alleyway.

Across another street.

Down a sidewalk, headed for a larger thoroughfare.

People stopped or stepped out of our way as I ran, still shouting his name.

He stopped and turned once, just long enough to glare at me— the whites of his eyes large. Then he started running again, head still turned. Across the thoroughfare, against traffic.

Cars skidded and honked—he slipped between two lanes.

The tow truck never saw him. But I did, and it was too late.

• • •

Antonio Aguilar lived just long enough to give a full confession in the hospital, before he passed. I stayed well clear of the Aguilars, figuring they themselves might be incited to murder if they spotted me. Police at the hospital knew me, and let me loiter around; out of respect for the old days. Which is why I was shocked absolutely when I saw Josefina arrive. All Normal eyes darted to her, and stayed on her as she walked carefully through the hospital hallway, hands pensively clutching a purse in front of her as she padded along in canvas flats and a sensible, modest dress, holes cut in the back for her wings. She saw me, but didn't stop to say anything. I kept an eye around the corner of the waiting area as I saw her approach her brother's room, speak to the cops at the door, then pass inside.

Ten minutes later, both she and her parents slowly walked out. The three of them appeared to be crying heavily. Josefina tried to hug her father. His arms just hung limply at his sides. When she tried to hug her mother, the older woman shakily reached her arms around her daughter, then squeezed with tentative enthusiasm.

The Aguilars went back into their son's room, and Josefina came back in my direction.

This time, she did stop.

I stared up at her face, damp green feathers and all.

"I'm sorry," I said.

"We are all sorry," she said.

"I didn't mean for him to get hit."

"I know."

"I should have just let him run away."

"Maybe … but I do not think there was anywhere far enough for him to get away from the shame he felt, at Mama and Papa knowing what he had done for them."

"*For* them?"

"Papa said that Antonio said he did it for the honor of the family."

"So why didn't he try to kill both of you?"

"I don't know. Maybe after he saw what he'd done to his little sister, he lost his nerve. Papa is sick with himself. After I left, he railed endlessly about what a disgrace I was, and then when Elvira left to join me, he railed against us both. How we had forever shamed the family. I think he didn't realize that Antonio would take it as much to heart as he did. Papa almost feels like he's the one who killed her. And Antonio now too."

I looked past Josefina's shoulder, to the shrinking old couple slumped against each other as they walked painfully down the opposite end of the corridor.

"What will they do now?"

"Bury Antonio and Elvira both."

"And what will *you* do now?"

She stared at the purse in her hands, her fists balled around the straps.

"I will go back to work," she said.

I raised an eyebrow.

"What else can I do?" She said. "I cannot go home, and I don't have the money yet that I need to move on."

I cleared my throat uncomfortably, and scratched at my scalp.

"There are other things—"

"No, Señor Soto," she said firmly. "It was my choice to become Special, and it is my choice to finish my plan. My sister would have wanted that, even if my family did not."

"Will you be speaking with them again?"

"I don't know," she said. "I don't think so."

"Give it time," I said. "Give your Papa time. He will need you."

"He still partially blames me for all of this."

"Yes, and when he's a couple of years older and closer to his own grave, he will look at his pictures of you when you were a little girl, and he will wonder why he let himself come to hate you. Please, don't lock that door again."

She stared down at me, this time one of her own eyebrows raising.

"Fraternal compassion, Señor Soto?"

"More like one poor, stupid father apologizing for another poor, stupid father."

She regarded me for many quiet seconds, then she reached down to take up one of my hands in hers—marvelously soft.

"*Por favor?*" she said.

"*Por favor,*" I said, squeezing her hand.

She let me escort her out of the hospital, and together we drove back to the Aerie.

Murder mysteries are a bit outside my usual scope, but when I was tasked with writing an original story—while participating in the annual Writers of the

Future Contest in Los Angeles—a murder mystery is precisely what came to mind. The atmosphere along Hollywood Boulevard practically demands it. Both the best and the worst America has to offer, are strewn side by side on the Boulevard. At the Contest, I'd been given a deflated pink flamingo pool toy, and had done an anonymous on-the-street interview with a nearby mall security officer, to work with—as cues for my story. I'd also taken a trip down to the very same library where Soto and the anglo woman meet. I determined that all of it would find its way into the text, either literally or metaphorically. And all of it did.

But why go furry?

You know, furry. Or furries, plural. Those costuming fans who like to dress up like animals—often animal characters from Japanese anime.

I blame my Writers of the Future roommate Jeff Young. See, Jeff and I had had a short conversation about the furry phenomenon earlier in the week. Either as a result of seeing furries featured on an episode of CSI, or having heard about a local furry convention in the news, etc. I don't remember precisely what sparked that particular dialogue. Anyway, it occurred to me that on Hollywood Boulevard, nothing is off-limits. Everything is for sale. I wondered what might happen if in a future Los Angeles genetic engineering and surgical body modification advanced to the point that furry people could put their money where their mouths are?

It then occurred to me that there would be furry fetishists who'd not have the guts to go all the way—but who would still crave the company of people who had gone all the way. To include intimate company.

And suddenly I had it: a furry brothel, catering to the rich and famous, at which a young working girl has been murdered, and only the girl's sister and a tired old former cop have any interest in discovering whodunit.

The story sat on my hard drive for a few months after I got home from the Contest, its ending incomplete. I noodled several possible extensions which would have run the story up to novella length, but decided ultimately that the road signs I'd established earlier in the text mandated I more or less finish the tale with Antonio taking the fall. Making him into an accidental victim wrapped some real poignancy around the relationship of Soto and Josefina. And it also did a better job highlighting the unintended consequences of Papa Aguilar's anguish and rage, as expressed in Papa Aguilar's house after his daughters fled.

I subsequently sold the story to Mike Resnick, who was then editing Galaxy's Edge magazine for Arc Manor books. I was hesitant to show it to Mike, because we'd done Peacekeeper together not long before, and I wasn't sure Mike would like it if I sent him a "workshop story" when what Mike wanted from me was me firing on all cylinders; at the top of my game.

Mike said phooey, kid, this is the best thing I've seen from you yet. Of course I want it for my magazine. Mike's a much better judge of mysteries and crime fiction than I am, since he's been immersed in those genre(s) in ways I have not been. I figured it would be tough to sell a "cross-genre" story like this to a crime-noir editor or a straight-up science fiction editor, but Mike doubles as both, and he snapped it up. I was therefore proud to see "The Flamingo Girl" in the pages of *Galaxy's Edge* in 2012.

As to the deeper theme and meaning, I have had one or two people tell me that my Specials are merely stand-ins for gay people. And I suppose from a certain point of view, that might be true? That's not what was on my mind when I wrote the story, but given the setting and the way the story played out, I can see why that assumption might be made. As an author, I have a personal belief that whatever readers pull from my stories and take with them, those things are the "truth" for those readers, and it's not my place to override or overrule. For each reader, the story then becomes unique.

Re-reading the story, for myself alone, I feel "The Flamingo Girl" is ultimately about choices, and how we all have to live with our choices—one way or another. It's also about heart, and the having of same. Even in a city and in a place where people with heart can be devoured whole by those too cynical, or jaded, or money-hungry to care who they hurt in their pursuit of fame and fortune.

Reardon's Law

Chapter 1: uncharted territory

Rain tumbled gently against the lifeboat's small canopy.

Kalliope Reardon was aware of the sound, but only in a detached sense. It had been a hard reentry, and a harder landing. Her brain and nervous system weren't quite ready to connect all the dots yet. Despite the crash cocoon which had enveloped her during the fall, thus saving her life.

And what a fall it had been.

She'd barely had time to hurl herself through the lifeboat's hatch before the lifeboat itself had been blown free of Kal's ship, the *Broadbill*.

End over end the lifeboat had spun through space, its trajectory arcing down towards the nameless, uncharted planet below.

Now, there was darkness.

And the quiet pattering of thick water droplets on the lifeboat's scorched hull.

Kal knew it was not a good idea to stay put. The people who had destroyed the *Broadbill* would be looking for her. Or rather, her lifeboat's automated beacon. For all she knew, they were already on their way.

Kal attempted to move her arms. The inflatable balloons of the crash cocoon held her as securely as a straightjacket.

Kal concentrated hard, and attempted to speak.

"Com—pyoo ... com ... compyoo ... *computer*," she finally said with a dull, rubbery tongue.

The happy chime of the lifeboat's automated response told Kal that she'd been acknowledged. She swallowed thickly, then flexed her jaw, like a patient who's just come out of the dentist's office.

"Computer," Kal said again, this time more slowly, but with added surety. "Release ... emergency ... restraining system."

At once, the balloons surrounding Kal began to deflate.

The outer shroud of the cocoon slowly peeled away, and Kal got a look through the canopy itself. A misty haze greeted her glance outside, while wide rivulets of clear liquid ran across the transparent canopy's dome.

The little display panel at the canopy's edge—which was connected to an external sensor—glowed a bright green. Nitrogen and oxygen atmosphere. No detectable toxins. Though, water and oxygen together meant chlorophyll. *Life*.

An alien ecology, for which Kal's immune system might not be prepared. She considered. Like any other Conflux Armed Forces troop being deployed into the Occupied Zone, Kal had been given a battery of xeno-bio inoculations. Stuff so potent that the running joke in the ranks said: if the alien germs didn't eat you up from the inside, the shots themselves surely would.

In times past, Kal had found such morbid barracks humor funny. Now, she wasn't laughing. Once she cracked the lifeboat's hatch, she'd be exposing herself to whatever lay beyond. Would it be a death sentence? Or did she dare stay put, and hope for official rescue?

No, that was a silly thought. The mission plan had been clear. There would be no help.

Chapter 2: civilization, many weeks earlier

"Reardon," Kal's boss said as he reached across the table and up-ended a bottle over her glass, "I won't lie to you. This is going to be a tough one."

"Do tell," Kal said, waiting for him to finish refreshing her drink. The refill was a formality. She'd barely touched her cup since entering her boss's office ten minutes prior. Her uniform remained crisp and pressed, with calf-length boots polished to a high gloss, and not a badge nor a pin out of place.

It wasn't Kal's typical wardrobe, given her occupation as a Special Investigative Officer with the Conflux Armed Forces. She was used to working in duty uniforms or civilian clothes—a highly-trained military cop as adept at busting organized criminals and civilian perps as she was at cleaning up the CAF's own internal trash.

But one didn't meet one's immediate supervisor in his inner sanctum while looking like a hobo from the launch docks. Upon landing, Kal had gone directly to the Guest Officers Quarters on base, stowed her travel bag, then hit the automated grooming station at the GOQ's south end. Kal now sported closely-cropped regulation-length hair, with nails trimmed down to the quick, and all fake tattoos and false-color eye lenses removed—for the first time in many Earth months.

There was a promotion board coming up. Kal had been putting off getting her digital packet together. The official image in her old packet was at least three Earth years out of date. She toyed with the idea of having her boss use his desk's AV unit to snap a few photos—as long as she was looking sharp. Who knew when she'd be this cleaned up again?

Stow it, Kal thought. There were more important things to worry about. Questions that needed answering. Such as: what sort of job would require an *in-person* briefing? Given the huge delay and expense involved in dragging her light-years away from her last assignment?

Ordinarily, Chief Investigative Officer Damont's orders came through the digitally-secure CAF network. A job here, a job there, with attached paperwork for flights and safe passage both on and off-world, anywhere in the Conflux. In fact, Kal could count on one hand the number of times she'd seen her boss face-to-face—in the six Earth years she'd been working for him. While Kal was always on the move, Damont tended to stay in one place. Keeping his invisible strings attached to his dozens of Special Investigators via the Conflux's circulating fleet of automated data transports: an interstellar pony express that moved information between the worlds of the Conflux at speeds thousands of times faster than mere radio transmissions.

Damont put the bottle back on his desk, picked up his own cup, and tipped back a healthy swallow—which he ran around the inside of one cheek, before gulping it down.

"Tremonton Universal has been losing classified equipment shipments," he said.

Kal blinked. Tremonton was the multi-world manufacturing corporation that provided the CAF with much of its military hardware, including cutting-edge armor, aerospace fighters, and other toys. So large and spread out were the company's assets, that it operated its own security force. Kal knew. She'd worked with them before.

"Shipments to where?" Kal asked.

Damont shifted in his high-backed chair.

"The Occupied Zone," he said.

Kal sat up straight.

"What the hell is Tremonton doing sending equipment into Oz?"

"You've not previously been made aware of this—so everything I'm about to discuss with you must be held in strictest confidence—but Tremonton has been working with the CAF to test-drive some of Tremonton's latest armor. Under realistic battle conditions. They're doing it in Oz."

"Realistic?" Kal exclaimed, picking up her cup and taking a healthy gulp of her own. "The Occupied Zone is a feral sea. We didn't pacify anything during the war. We merely knocked down some of their bigger cities, then cut those planets off from each other with the blockade. Sir, I've been into Oz, and I can tell you, if it's 'realistic battle conditions' Tremonton wanted, then it's realistic battle conditions Tremonton will get."

"I know," he said. "And it's your familiarity with the Occupied Zone that's the main reason I picked you for this job. I need someone with experience. Someone who can slip into the black market network that evades the blockade—don't look surprised, of course I know all about that—then pick up the trail left by this missing Tremonton hardware."

"Sir, finding missing armament in Oz will be like looking for a needle in a haystack. Whatever's been taken to date, it's liable to never surface again. The remnants of the Ambit League will be eager to pick apart any advanced gadgetry they can lay their hands on—to see if the technology can be adapted for their own use."

"I know. Which is why this job has the top-most priority," Damont said, pursing his lips in a concerned expression.

"Better to roll in a battle flotilla," Kal said. "Make a show of force. Deploy troops. Shake Oz down. If this missing equipment is that sensitive, nothing short of a major offensive will recover it."

"It's not that simple," Damont said.

"And why not?"

There was a telling silence as Kal's boss shifted in his seat again.

"Neither Tremonton nor their liaison with the CAF want any word of this missing equipment to get out to the general public," he said. "The Conflux went through hell putting down the Ambit League. And the civilian population is easily spooked as a result. The next election cycle will be coming up, and there are people in the Conflux Assembly on Earth who are eager to make sure there is no substance to any rumors about a second war."

Kal stood up and walked over to where her boss had a couch against the far wall. A gently animated image of a nameless gas giant planet was mounted over the couch. She stared at the bands of the gas giant's clouds as they slowly swirled and rotated.

"There's more," Damont said. "I've got reason to believe that someone inside the CAF is working against us on this. I'm hoping that if you can sniff out who, from the inside, then I can order some arrests and we can plug a hole in our ranks."

"Sympathizers?" Kal said, somewhat incredulously. "With the Ambit League?"

"Or they're greedy," Damont said. "People who have cash note symbols in their eyes."

"Then it'll take more than just me," Kal said, her face still fixed towards the digital painting.

"I know," Damont said. "That's why you're taking someone new with you."

Kal jerked her chin over her shoulder.

"You're saddling me with a *rookie?* I thought you said this was a top-priority mission?"

"It is, but he's no ordinary rookie. He's a CAF Reservist who also works for Tremonton. A test pilot. Knows all about the armor design in question. In fact, they were going to send him into Oz to put some of that armor through its paces. Then the shipments began to turn up missing. He's got a high-security clearance, and has been vetted through both Tremonton and CAF channels."

"That's all well and good, sir," Kal said, turning on a heel and pacing back and forth in front of the couch, "but it doesn't help me figure out where to start. With over a dozen habitable worlds in Oz, across twenty star systems, somebody's going to have to point me in the right direction, or I might as well stay home."

"There's a man already on the inside," Damont said. "Someone I've been monitoring closely."

"One of ours?" Kal asked.

"Yes. Or at least, he used to be. CAF veteran. Brilliant service record. When the war was declared over, he signed on with one of the civilian relief organizations that went into Oz to try to pick up the pieces. He vanished shortly afterward. But then he reappeared. Feeding information covertly to CAF Intelligence, about the activities of the Ambit League. He knows where those shipments might have been taken."

"And my pilot? Is he going to *fly* the stolen armor back home? One suit at a time?"

"Don't be silly," Damont snapped. "If it's true the Ambit League is reverse-engineering this stolen equipment, CAF Central Command wants to know about it. Both they and the Tremonton corporate people want an experienced person on the scene, who can evaluate first-hand whatever it is the Ambit League may be trying to cobble together in Oz."

"You said he's Reserve?" Kal said.

"Yes."

"Does he have any covert training? Battle experience?"

"No."

"Terrific. And my contact inside Oz? Is he reliable?"

"I don't really know. I think so, yes."

"You *think* so?"

This time it was Damont who stood up out of his chair and began to pace.

"I'm sorry, Kalliope, but I really can't get more specific than that. You're right. If the Central Command wasn't following Assembly orders not to make a ruckus, then I'd pitch this mess over to the fleet people and let them marshal a few combat brigades, at the very least. But we've all been given strict instructions to handle this matter quietly. And quickly. Tremonton says it's going to halt shipments until the matter is resolved, but without those shipments the testing can't be completed, which means the Assembly's Defense Office won't sign off on the contracts for the new design."

"Which means Tremonton doesn't get its money," Kal said, sighing.

"You always were quick on the uptake," Damont said.

Kal remained where she was, chin on her chest. So the matter was multi-dimensional: economic, as well as political.

When Kal didn't say anything more, her boss cleared his throat in a mildly uncomfortable fashion.

"If you don't think you're up to it," Damont said, "I can always find somebody else."

"Not quickly enough to make a difference," Kal said. "We've already wasted enough time bringing me here, so there'd be no point sending me back. You knew I'd not turn down the orders because you knew once you explained it to me that I'd have no choice but to say yes."

Damont merely had a slight, knowing smile on his face.

Kal momentarily considered punching her boss in the teeth. Instead, she breathed deeply, then exhaled very slowly.

"Okay," she said. "Let's have it then. A full mission dossier."

Damont slid a wafer drive across his desk.

Kal walked over and picked the drive up in her left hand, testing its flexible holographic memory crystals between her thumb and forefinger.

"One more thing, Kal," Damont said.

"A catch?" she said, eyebrow raised.

"Yes, I am afraid. Because this is such a sensitive job, I can't promise you any parachutes. Once you're inside Oz, you're officially on your own. There won't be any CAF quick-reaction teams ready to break down someone's front door and pull you out."

Kal continued to press the wafer drive between her thumb and forefinger. She allowed a tiny grin to slip across her lips.

"You didn't bring me all this way because I need someone to hold my hand for me."

She picked up her cup and raised it.

Damont did the same.

And together they emptied their glasses.

Chapter 3: uncharted territory

Kal crawled quietly through the piles of rotting plant debris. She was five days out of a shower, and covered in scrapes and cuts. The trek through the forest hadn't been an easy one. Once she'd made the decision to abandon the lifeboat and set out on foot, there'd been only one choice: wait for any sign that her attackers had come down from orbit, then try to locate them and hitch a ride back to space. Otherwise she'd be marooned for life in a place that wasn't even on the Conflux's pioneer world charts.

Kal didn't know if anyone else had survived the destruction of the *Broadbill*. If they had, she didn't owe them any favors. Thief's justice, more or less.

Except for Tim. The Reservist hadn't deserved to die.

Kal closed her eyes briefly and tried to block him out of her mind. She didn't need anything distracting her. She pulled the tiny emergency transponder device out of her makeshift harness and examined the reading on its tiny screen. The device could either broadcast actively, or receive passively. She'd been using it for two days to track the signal coming from a very large ship which had passed over her lifeboat's landing site the day after she abandoned it.

That ship was her key to escaping. As well as continuing the mission.

Moving slowly and deliberately, Kal neared the lip of a ledge in the forest floor. Over her head, the sky was partially occluded by the mass of trees that towered a hundred meters into the air, darkening the ground. Her abused spacer's coverall was damp and filthy, with holes at the elbows and knees. All she had to work with was the small emergency backpack from the lifeboat, her issue P3110 pistol in its holster, and five magazines for the pistol, worth ten shots each.

Not ideal armament, under the circumstances. Kal would have preferred tactical artillery instead.

Dead leaves clung to Kal's skin like wet paper. She peered intently over the lip of the ledge. Half a kilometer distant, the mighty trees had been flattened in a rough halo under the belly of the enemy craft. Which was mammoth. A metal whale on stilts. The heat tiles of the ship were grossly discolored from its many, many in-atmosphere trips. Underneath the vessel—between its massive landing pylons—four personnel hatches lay open with four ramps extending down to the ground, like rusty tongues. There was also a fifth, much larger cargo hatch. Its wide ramp was populated with people moving crates up into the ship. They appeared to be bringing the crates from somewhere deep in the tree line. Where Kal couldn't see. They must have located the remnants of the *Broadbill?* Or at least the *Broadbill's* cargo?

Kal considered. Getting into the ship unseen would be difficult. She needed a better look before she could make a plan.

Kal crept her way over the lip and slid several meters down a sharp slope until she re-entered the undergrowth. There she stayed absolutely still for several long minutes, waiting and listening for something—anything—that would tell her if she'd been spotted.

Satisfied that her presence went undetected, Kal renewed her glacial pace towards the freighter, guessing that if she took it slow, nightfall would come soon. And with it, her best chance to get up one of those ramps.

Chapter 4: Conflux space

The Reserve pilot's name was Tim Osterhaudt. Young. Clever with his wit. But not cocky. During the voyage out to the Conflux periphery—where the undefined border between civilization and the Occupied Zone lay—Kal got to know him. He was maybe eight years younger, and had not grown up on Earth. A colony boy. He passed through his secondary schooling with good grades, and then picked up a company scholarship from Tremonton. Which had funded him through both his civilian degree, and test pilot school. His nominal rank in the CAF Reserve was Lieutenant. Technically, he outranked Kal. Though Kal made it clear up front that she was in charge, according to their specific orders from Chief Damont.

"No problem," Tim said, holding up his hands in a placating fashion as they talked quietly in their cabin aboard the starliner *Freefall*. They had a single porthole which looked out into space. If Kal put her forehead to the transparent fiberflex of the porthole itself, she could look down to where the giant disc of the Blackmatter Drive lay.

Like all interstellar ships, the *Freefall* was essentially a skyscraper stacked on-end in the center of the Blackmatter Drive: a circular dish nearly as wide as the ship was long. All decks were arrayed perpendicular to the path of flight, so that when under thrust each deck enjoyed something akin to gravity. Though it was the Blackmatter Drive itself which formed the relativistic bubble—allowing the ship to slip beyond the light-speed barrier and travel at trans-light velocities.

The points of starlight outside were smeared, shifting from crowded and blue above to sparse and red at the bottom.

Kal and Tim were dressed in civilian travel jumpsuits customary for migrant technicians bound for one of the sanctioned space stations that serviced the Occupied Zone. They'd come aboard the *Freefall* with assumed names and false digital travel papers provided by Kal's boss.

Only Kal was armed. Which didn't seem to bother Tim much. He thought the entire thing to be a rather daring bit of adventure. He just didn't like the idea of hurting anyone.

"So why'd you end up in the Reserve if you don't want to have to fight?" Kal asked.

"My CAF Reserve commission was a prerequisite of my job with Tremonton," he said, idly tapping his hands on his knees as a gentle stream of music issued from the small speakers at the head of his bunk. He had an unusual fascinating with the classics, for someone his age. His movements kept rhythm with the sound.

"This prototype testing in the Occupied Zone," Kal said, "it doesn't seem like you'd be able to avoid fighting there."

"They've got half a dozen pilots working the project," Tim said. "When I was assigned to go to the Zone, I asked that they put me on the secondary team that's charged with evaluating data being brought back from the field. All the pilots actually going out beyond the safety zone? Prior combat vets."

Kal nodded in understanding.

"Did you, uh, fight in the war?" Tim asked hesitantly.

"Yup," Kal said, laying on her back in her bunk across the cabin—eyes staring straight up at the ceiling.

"Ever have to ... uh ... well ..."

"What?" Kal asked.

"You know ... like ... shoot somebody?"

Kal closed her eyes and sighed.

"Never ask that question of a veteran, Tim. You should have been in the Reserve long enough to know that. There are a lot of veterans who went Reserve after the war. I am surprised nobody told you the rule."

"Rule?"

"The last thing anyone who's seen fighting wants to do, is talk about how they were forced to kill somebody."

Tim remained silent for many long moments.

"Sorry," he finally said.

"No problem. I just thought you knew."

"The Reserve Officer Training Corps teaches a man many things, but some of the tacit stuff doesn't always translate. Hope I didn't make you uncomfortable."

"A little. Because the answer is yes."

Again, a long silence.

"They told me you're a military policewoman," Tim said finally. "That you spend a lot of time on cases both explicitly military, as well as tangentially military-related."

"That's true."

"So why aren't you commissioned?"

"I am commissioned, after a fashion. My job warrants it, I am not appointed like you were."

"What's the difference?"

"I often ask myself that same question."

Several beats later, Tim was chuckling. A pleasant sound. There wasn't always a lot of laughter in Kal's line of work.

"If you fought in the war," Tim asked, "what's your opinion of the rumor that the Ambit League might renew hostilities?"

"So far as I am concerned," Kal said, "hostilities never ended. The survivors we left on the Occupied Zone worlds? A lot of them still think we're at war. The blockade pretty much makes it plain that the Conflux isn't giving them autonomy or allowing them to rejoin the interstellar economy any time soon."

"You sympathize with them?" Tim said, raising an eyebrow and sitting up to look at her.

"Hardly," Kal said. "I just think there's a bad way to manage the post-war effort and a good way to manage the post-war effort. To my mind, the good way to manage it would be to re-integrate the worlds of the Occupied Zone as soon as possible. Keeping the blockade up indefinitely … just breeds contempt and hostility."

"But some of those planets *are* dangerous," Tim said.

"Correction, sir. Some of the *people* on those planets are dangerous. I know. I've been there. And the longer we treat the good folks in Oz the same way we treat the bad folks in Oz, the more the good folks swing over to the side of the bad folks. Pretty soon we've got nothing but bad folks. Does that make sense?"

"I think so," Tim said, his expression turning serious. "Sounds to me like it's a no-win situation. The Assembly won't be changing its policy any time soon. They're intent on reassuring the electorate that the Ambit League has been permanently destroyed."

"Right," Kal said. "Which is why you and I have been called up to perform this mission in the first place.

"Do you think we can really find the missing armor?" Tim asked.

Kal ran her tongue along the inside of a cheek.

"No. But we might find out where it went, or at least who's responsible for taking it. And who they might be working with on our side of the fence. My boss wants that information very badly. Recovery of the stolen hardware isn't a requirement for the mission to be a success. It's a bonus. If we do stumble across any of that missing armor, your job is to help figure out what the Ambit League might be doing with it."

Chapter 5: uncharted territory

Hours passed.

Kal stayed low, using the gloaming of night and the blown-down trees to conceal herself. Rumbles of approaching thunder announced that the rain would start once more. Before long a steady clobbering of fat, lens-like drops beat down on the enemy landing site.

Kal relished the cloudburst. The noise and water would help conceal her from any sensors her foes had deployed around their ship.

Kal pushed forward into the drowning darkness—by feel.

Thirty more minutes passed.

Soaked to the bone and nearing exhaustion, Kal at last peeked up from behind a log, only to discover she was looking directly into the belly of the monstrous aerospace freighter—its boarding ramps lit by sodium lamps.

Kal looked nervously in all directions. It was far too quiet for her tastes. No sign of guards? That did not compute. But Kal was committed, and there was no going back, only forward.

Mustering her courage, Kal tugged down on the straps to her shoulder holster, harness, and emergency pack, then crept over the edge of the log and sprinted towards the ship. Kal stopped just as she hit the edge of illumination at the bottom of one ramp. Entering the full light for the first time, her skin crawled—she was totally exposed, and expected to hear voices and gunfire at any moment. But the shouts and bullets never came.

Senses tingling, Kal went up the ramp at a gentle trot.

The freighter's interior was messy. Narrow corridors sprouted off in several directions, each decorated with exposed pipes, wiring, and ducts. Kal pulled out her P3110 and worked the charging handle, loading a caseless round into the pistol's firing chamber. With safety off, she kept her finger outside the trigger guard and proceeded deeper into the guts of the ship, step by cautious step.

Kal moved through an inner hatchway and into a wider central corridor. Her eyes skipped around, looking for surveillance devices. She found one recessed into the ceiling several meters ahead of her.

Kal froze—watching the camera and its bug-like eyes. It appeared to be ignoring her. She chewed on her bottom lip, then stepped forward once, and then back again.

The camera remained still.

Deactivated? On standby? Or just plain broken?

The hair stood up on the back of Kal's neck, but she moved onward. Most aerospace freighters didn't need a big crew, but there should have been *someone* aboard—people she'd have seen, or at least heard already. Kal drew in a long breath, blew it out with puffed cheeks, and shook her head. This was no time to spook herself into doing something dumb. Perhaps the explosion in orbit had taken a lot of the enemy, as well as the *Broadbill* and its crew? How many people had crossed over the *Broadbill's* ship-to-ship gangway before the double-cross had gone down?

Kal didn't know.

Moving in her best impression of a cat, Kal crept down another passage: past some uniformly cabin-sized hatches—and then froze as another surveillance monitor suddenly loomed above her. Kal stood on her toes to peer up at the device: the cables were corroded and the gears on the device's directional motor seemed non-functional.

What the hell?

It was then that Kal really began to take a good look around her. In addition to the exposed ductwork and wiring, the deck plates were soiled and corroded, and many of the cabin doors behind her appeared to be rusted shut. Just how *long* had this ship been gathering dust somewhere on-planet, its hatches and vents open to the air? A lot of moisture had come in, and been allowed to sit. No doubt the Ambit League was hurting, but it was still surprising to discover that they were willing to operate any scow, however scrapworthy. No wonder they were stealing armament—the League's home-grown industrial base must have collapsed. Another byproduct of the blockade. Cut the various manufacturing centers off from each other, and it would be enormously difficult to replicate spaceworthy equipment. At least on a large commercial scale.

Somewhat heartened by these assumptions, Kal crept on until she found a doorway that looked like it had been repaired to operational condition. She stepped close to it and peered in through the small pane of transparent fiberflex that gave her a view of the next compartment. She saw four people unpacking an unmarked interstellar shipping crate—the same kind Tremonton said they used to discretely transport sensitive equipment.

Watching intently, Kal saw the people remove gauntlets and boots and other pieces of armor, all broken down for shipping. The people—Ambit League for sure—seemed to be sorting and separating the crate's contents, while other crates were stacked nearby and waiting to be opened. Kal shifted to the side and peered past the crew, realizing that she was looking into the primary hold of the freighter. It went on for almost a hundred meters, and was half as wide, plus half as tall. Crates littered the space. Almost all of them appeared to have been opened in a hurry.

Needles in haystacks, Kal thought, remembering her comment to her boss.

Kal stepped away from the hatch and turned to creep back the way she had come

She stopped short.

The barrel of a pistol—somewhat newer and heavier in design than her P3110—was pointed at Kal's forehead, and a huge bearded man in a use-worn jumpsuit was smiling at her.

"What do we have here?" The man said. Kal gulped and felt her stomach sink into a bottomless pit.

"You're not one of Berd's people."

Who?

Kal's weapon was still in her hand, but her arm had been lowered and she didn't dare raise it lest she get a slug between her eyes.

"Drop the pistol," said the bearded man, eyes darting to Kal's gun.

"No," Kal said quietly.

The man laughed. "Do we really have to do it like this? Drop your pistol or I'll use mine."

Kal looked past the man, saw no one, and then back into his eyes. They were older, but they didn't blink, and she slowly stooped down to the deck, noiselessly placing her P3110 on its side. Then stood back up.

The man stepped closer and prodded the barrel of his gun between her breasts, ordering her to raise her hands. Kal did as she was told, then backed up a few steps as the man pushed her down the corridor.

"Shoulda known there would be two of you," he said. "Didn't make much sense to stumble across just one CAF soldier. You always travel in pairs, isn't that right?"

"How would I know?" Kal said. But inside, she was doing a triple-take. *Two?* In an instant she realized that not only was Tim quite possibly alive, he was being held prisoner. Or worse. How could she find out where he was, or what shape he was in? She conjured a brief mental picture of crude torture techniques being used on the young Reservist, then blocked that image out and focused on her assailant.

"Well, your buddy can't help you now," said the man.

He suddenly reached out and attempted to get a handful of Kal's damp, clinging coverall. Kal slapped his hand away and he punched her in the face with his free hand. Seeing lights, Kal fell back and began to scramble down the passageway while her assailant laughed and kept his gun pointed at her.

"Fighting just makes it worse," he said. "You should ask my other girlfriends."

Kal flipped up off the deck and tried to put a boot in his groin, but he dodged and swept her legs, then jumped on top of her, pinning her face-down. With her P3110 hopelessly out of reach, Kal cursed as the man began to press himself against her. His odor filled her nostrils—old sweat mixed with tobacco stink, and machine oil.

"Just relax," said the man, "and maybe I don't kill you when it's over."

Kal strained, but couldn't get her arms free. Her combatives training wasn't much good against someone as big as this guy was. His growing arousal was very apparent against her buttocks, and she experienced a sudden and unearthly shock at the fact that she was going to be raped.

Desperation drove Kal to snap her head back as hard as she could. There was a loud crunch as skulls met, and then the man rolled off of her, screaming and clutching his nose while blood poured from it. Kal pounced on the man's pistol—still in his hand—and wrenched it free, hearing something in the man's wrist snap.

The man screamed again.

Voices began calling down the corridor. Several of them. The staccato of running feet echoed dangerously.

Kal ran back up the way she'd come, snagging her pistol off the deck where she'd placed it. Now armed with two weapons, she kept running, the barrels of both guns pointed directly in front of her.

Three privateers skidded to a halt as they rounded a corner, and their jaws dropped.

One tried to raise a weapon: a submachine gun.

Kal pulled both of her triggers at once.

The man with the submachine gun flew back against the bulkhead behind him, the exposed piping making a loud *clong* sound as he fell, leaving a smear of fresh blood when his body crumpled to the deck.

The other two weren't armed. They screamed, and tried to run from her. Kal raised the pistols, intending to empty rounds into the spines of the fleeing men. Her rounds went wide, drawing sparks from the metal in the next bend of the corridor. Her targets half-crouched, hands clamped over their heads, and were suddenly around the corner and out of sight.

Kal cursed loudly, then ducked into a crossway, turned to see a dead-end, and finally pelted down an altogether different corridor that seemed as neglected as the last.

A lift shaft entrance appeared, with somewhat clean-looking double doors. Kal slammed a hand on the hatch release. The double doors opened and a surprised woman in a standard spacer's jumpsuit looked out into the corridor as Kal stood there, chest heaving.

Kal looked at the woman once, grimaced, and rushed in. The woman yelled, but Kal silenced her with the crack of a gun butt to the woman's skull. The unconscious body tumbled out of the car, and then the door began to close. Kal leapt on the controls and ordered the car to the top level of the freighter—or however close to the top the shaft went. Just as the door was shutting, more privateers came into view. But just for an instant.

Automatic small arms fire *pinged* and *panged* off the doors as they shut tight. The car creaked and rocked, and then began to shoot upward at an uneven rate. Kal was tossed about as the car jostled her, then there was a terrible screech and the lights went out.

The lift had come to a complete halt.

Chapter 6: the borderland

Viking Station was a hoop-shaped warren of cargo holds, starship docks, seedy temporary lodging, shops, gambling dens, and other establishments of variably descending repute. The Blackmatter ships docked at an inner hoop that was immobile, while the outer hoop—easily three kilometers in diameter—spun on its central axis. For simulated gravity.

Kal and Tim disembarked the *Freefall* and made their way to one of the less grimy places of lodging. There they set up shop and went about quietly looking for their contact, who'd supposedly been informed that they were coming.

Gulliver was the man's name. Though Kal was reasonably certain he was working under an assumed identity, just as she and Tim both were.

It took nearly a local week of quiet inquiry to find him.

They met in one of the adult entertainment halls. A place simply called *The Shiny*.

It lived up to its name. Kal and Tim took seats at a table towards the back, in a dark spot where it was impossible to see the faces of any of the customers—though the glistening, mostly-naked bodies of the entertainers were spotlighted by lamps projecting from the ceiling. The ratio of female to male dancers was about three to one—each of them acrobatically cavorting across their separate stages, which were festooned with chrome-plated poles attached to the ceiling. Cash notes—both paper and coins—were being heaped at the feet of the more energetic entertainers.

Kal noticed Tim's eyes kept straying to one particularly well-endowed woman who had short red hair, a narrow waist, and wide hips. The dancer spun artfully around her pole, staying expertly balanced on a pair of impossibly tall, high-heeled pumps. Kal gently kicked Tim's shin under the table—to keep him focused.

"Took you awhile," said a shadowy male shape as he sat down across the table from them.

"You're a man who makes himself hard to track down," Kal said.

"Occupational hazard," he said, lifting his shoulders in a shrug.

"Do you think you can help us?" Kal asked.

"Perhaps. I haven't got my fingers in the cookie jar of every black market outfit in the Occupied Zone, but I make it my business to know about the comings and goings of major shipments. The Blackmatter retardation mines are only partially effective, you know. The good smugglers know where the holes in the network are, and use them on a fairly regular basis."

"Something for Central Command to fix," Kal said.

The silhouette of the man across the table began to laugh.

"I think Central Command is well aware of the problem. They just can't do anything about it. Or won't. You should know that there are CAF officers in the blockade fleet who are working those holes to their advantage."

"Graft?" Kal said.

"Of course. You know as well as I do that being assigned to Oz is a job for both heroes and fools. Some people are here for the excitement, and to build a reputation. Others are here because they couldn't be sent anywhere else. You've got the good mixed with the bad."

"Which one are you?" Tim asked, his eyes still occasionally darting to the stage where the red-headed dancer seductively undulated in a rather pendulous fashion.

"Depends on who you ask," their contact said.

A shadowy arm stuck out across the table.

"You can call me Gulliver, which is how most people in Oz know me."

Kal and Tim shook the man's hand in turn.

He had a strong, reassuring grip.

"Do you know about the missing Tremonton hardware?" Kal asked.

"Yup." Gulliver said.

"Any idea where it's been taken?" Tim asked.

"No. But I think I have a method for finding out. Rumor has it that one last shipment of armor is still coming here—to Viking Station—before moving on to the secure Tremonton test facilities that the CAF is jointly operating on-planet. It's probable that shipment will be snatched, just as the others have been. I can make sure you're in the right place at right time when it happens. You might be able to learn more."

"That's what we're here for," Kal said.

"I can't promise you'll be safe," Gulliver added, after gently clearing his throat.

"This is Oz," Kal said. "You're stating the obvious."

"I'm not just talking about the usual scammers and cutthroats," Gulliver replied, leaning on his elbows so that he didn't have to speak as loudly in order to be heard. Kal could just make out his profile: balding, with a prominent chin, and a pale complexion.

"Oh?" Tim asked.

"The Ambit League is alive and well," Gulliver said, in as close to a hushed tone as he could manage. "Folks back home assume we crushed the League during the war, and the Conflux Assembly is eager to perpetuate that perception with voters. But really, the separate pieces of the monster are subtly gaining strength. For a time when they might reconstitute. And I am not sure there's anything the blockade can do about it."

Kal felt her blood begin to run cold.

Tim's eyes were now fully on Gulliver.

"How long until they renew hostilities?" Kal asked.

"Difficult to say. But I can tell you that they've been using the holes in the Blackmatter retardation network to place a lot of personnel and assets outside the reach of the blockade, in uncharted space—on the other side of the Zone. Stealing cutting-edge Tremonton tech is only the first step. They intend to improve upon and replicate what's been taken."

Kal and Tim exchanged concerned glances.

Gulliver sat back in his chair, allowing his eyes to watch the two female dancers who had shimmied their way over to a part of the branched stage that was closest to Gulliver's table. The dancers began vigorously applying a fresh layer of oil to each other, while occasionally giving Gulliver winks and smiles.

Gulliver smiled back, and dropped a few cash notes on the stage

"So tell us where to be," Kal said, trying to ignore the display of pulchritude going on behind her.

Gulliver reached into his jacket and pulled out something, slipping it across the table towards them. Kal collected the wafer drive and slipped it into the inner pocket of her own jacket.

"Are we done?" Gulliver said.

"Yes," Kal said. "Thanks."

He said nothing in reply. Merely kept watching the dancers.

Kal stood up, and Tim did the same, though somewhat reluctantly.

"Oh," Kal said, "one more thing."

Gulliver appeared to merely wait for her question.

"Who is paying you to pass us this information?"

"Whatever you may have been told about me," Gulliver said, "I can assure you, my patriotic allegiance is to the Conflux. I'm not CAF anymore. At least not officially. And I'm going to admit I kind of like it out here, beyond the boundaries of polite society. But I think the Conflux is worth preserving."

Kal waited, studying the shadowy man with her eyes.

How much of what he'd said was truth? She really couldn't tell.

"Right," Kal said, then turned to Tim and added, "let's go."

Chapter 7: uncharted territory

The lift car was pitch black inside. No emergency lights.

Kal whipped out her microlamp and flicked it on. Tendrils of acrid smoke filled the car. Scanning the lamp around, she located the emergency hatch on the floor of the car. She pulled the release key and waited for the hatch to pop loose by itself.

Nothing.

Kal kicked it. Still nothing. *Damn.* The locks were probably rusted shut. Kal stood, and backed up against one of the car walls, aiming her lamp with one hand and the P3110 with her other hand. She pulled the trigger. The report was deafening, and sparks flew from the floor. Three more times, she repeated the procedure. Then walked up to the emergency hatch—her ears ringing badly—and stomped on it once. Good and hard. The metal panel creaked and groaned. She stomped again. And again. Finally the door dropped away into the shaft below. It *clanged* loudly when it hit bottom. Kal guesstimated she was maybe seven decks up. Quite a fall if she slipped.

She knelt by the hatch and looked below her. The sides of the shaft were just as corroded as the outside, and cobwebs filled the nooks and crannies. Kal was still looking when she heard feet land on the top of the car. The slamming of metal on metal told Kal she didn't have time to waste. They were coming in after her, one way or another.

Kal quickly maneuvered herself into the bottom hatch, legs flailing in midair until her feet found the rungs of the emergency ladder on the side of the shaft. She searched by feel for some kind of handhold on the bottom of the car—her microlamp clenched between her teeth as she worked—and swung out of the hatchway, almost losing her grip. Kal's heart thudded wildly as she scrambled for the ladder. The microlamp slipped from her mouth and spiraled down the shaft, along with the second pistol she'd taken off the man who'd initially accosted her. They too hit bottom.

The lamp went out.

Kal cursed, but managed to get a solid grip on the ladder.

The smell of old mildew, machine oil, and rusty steel was pungent in her nostrils. Kal tried to calm herself. She hated heights. And on top of that, she hated confined spaces. She stepped down a rung and then heard a *thunk* from the car.

No time left!

Kal worked quickly down the ladder, by feel. Suddenly she felt a gust of fresh air. Exploring with her fingers, she found the ventilation duct. There was no screen across it. Kal knocked her forearm around the edges of the opening, and realized the duct was just large enough for a person to crawl into. Swallowing hard, she maneuvered off the ladder and shimmied into the duct, feeling the pain in her abused elbows and knees as she worked her way forward.

Kal crawled a number of meters and then stopped. In total darkness, she had no idea where the shaft might lead. Only the occasional burst of fresh air told her that going forward was preferable to going back.

Outside, voices cursed as the privateers discovered the lift car to be empty. How long would it take them to figure out what had happened to her? Kal closed her eyes and rested her forehead on her wrist for a moment, then returned to worming her way forward. After a long, filthy period of claustrophobic effort, Kal came to the first of many grill plates that opened sideways into the interior of the ship. No light was evident, and Kal couldn't see anything. But she could feel the air moving through the grills—the palm of her hand pressed against the gridwork.

Not wanting to be trapped in the duct any longer than she had to be, Kal curled herself into a ball and put her feet on one of the grills, then pushed. The grill snapped free, clattering to the deck in the darkness beyond. Kal led with her feet, then dangled by her hands, then let herself drop.

For a split second, her brain imagined a free-fall.

But her feet hit flooring almost instantly, and Kal allowed herself to crumple, staying still on the metal plate. Not moving. Not really thinking. She was just damned glad to be out of the ductwork.

At some point, Kal must have drifted off. She snapped awake when the grinding whine of motorized gears announced that a hatch was opening. A beam of light stabbed into the darkness, and Kal stayed quiet as she watched the light play about the room. Rectangular storage containers of various sizes filled the space. Kal had landed directly between two of them. Which put her out of the line of sight of whoever had entered.

A woman's voice said, "Now in compartment 86-C."

A tiny muttering of a different voice—as if through a transistor speaker—responded back.

"Negative," said the female voice. "Not a goddamned sign of the intruder … Yeah, I'll keep looking … Yeah, it would have been nice if we took care of this bitch in orbit, but that didn't happen, did it? … You know, we should see if her friend can tell us something … how many of his fingers do you think we'd need to break, before he'll talk?"

Kal slithered to the edge of the container that concealed her—waiting for the beam of the light to face the opposite direction—then lunged. The beam spun back around just in time to catch Kal square in the face. Kal aimed and fired her P3110 in the same reflexive instant. The light flew up and then clattered across the deck as the female privateer was tossed bodily backward, slumping loudly against one of the containers.

Kal snatched up the lantern and dimmed it by half, creeping slowly up to the body. The woman had a neat hole in her throat that bled thick, dark blood. Kal grimaced, electing not to search the body. But she did find the headset the woman had been using—laying on the deck three meters away. Putting it on her head, Kal immediately got an earful of voice chatter. Many people, all talking at once. They didn't seem to realize what had happened, much to Kal's relief. The woman she'd shot hadn't been depressing the SEND switch on the side of the headset when Kal had fired.

Thank goodness for small miracles.

Kal waited, listening to the goings-on of the intra-ship network. All hands had been scrambled to look for Kal. It sounded like they wanted her alive. Many people seemed to agree with the dead privateer at Kal's feet: the sole, living prisoner would be a good tool to use against Kal.

Tim. Kal knew she had to find him before it was too late.

Checking her pistol to be sure it still had sufficient ammunition in the magazine, Kal then aimed the lantern back toward the hatch through which the female privateer had first entered. Best to not go back that way. There might be more people. Surveying the compartment more thoroughly, Kal discovered another hatch at the opposite end. Would its motors work?

Only one way to find out.

Chapter 8: the borderland

For two weeks, Kal and Tim laid low. Not venturing out into Viking Station for more than a few minutes at a time. The wafer drive Gulliver had given them said that a Blackmatter ship—the *Broadbill*—

would be arriving with a discretely allotted shipment of Tremonton gear aboard. There was no indication as to who—if anyone—would try to seize such equipment. Only that the best way to get more information was to be aboard the ship when it happened.

Now, Kal eyed the *Broadbill* as the huge ship rested in its dock. Kal herself was lassoed tight to a small magnetic tractor that gripped the exterior hull of Viking Station, preventing her from floating off into deep space. She watched as the last of the ship's personnel, departing for shore leave, moved through the big starship's several gangways— just tiny little dots moving against the small lit windows of the gangway tubes.

Kal verbally commanded the tractor to move forward. It beeped acknowledgement and began to trundle slowly towards the *Broadbill's* bow shield—a mighty dome of layered armor designed to catch or deflect debris while the ship was moving forward. The shield proper was locked into the grapples of Viking Station's smaller docking ring.

As the tractor traversed the distance to the ship, Kal tried to avoid breathing through her nose. Her used space suit was mildly and unpleasantly aromatic inside—too many occupants and not enough sanitary detergent. Kal was well familiar with extra-vehicular activity. She'd done plenty in her time. Range of motion and vision were somewhat restricted, but if you could get a rhythm of movement going, you could cover ground fairly quickly. Assuming you were traveling under your own steam.

For this job, Kal was reliant on her technology. The tractor was a standard piece of Viking Station hardware. Hundreds of them were in constant motion across the hull, checking for hairline fractures and cracks, as well as hauling maintenance personnel to and fro. Connected as she was to her tractor, Kal looked no different from any of the other blue-collar engineers tasked with keep Viking Station operational.

It was all part of Gulliver's suggested plan.

Unlike the *Freefall*, the *Broadbill* was a cradle ship: the main mass being an entirely separate sublight vessel. Which was locked into a series of mooring catches that ran along the barren spine of the starship. Most of the Blackmatter Drive ship's functions were automated, and controlled remotely from the sublight ship's bridge. Given the *Broadbill's* design, she could potentially travel in-atmosphere. Or even land, when she arrived at her eventual destination.

The *Broadbill's* exterior surfaces sparkled in the starlight: pristine, and without blemish.

When Kal's tractor crossed over from the surface of the bow grapple to the surface of the ship, it beeped hesitantly until Kal gave it a series of verbal commands that ordered it to ignore the fact that it was leaving home.

The little robot went south.

Behind her, Kal could see Tim riding his own tractor—following her precisely.

For minutes, they moved in silence. Only the sound of the suit's regulator filled Kal's ears. Then, just above the communications module amidships, Kal spotted the kind of airlock she was looking for.

Taking a small computer tool from her suit belt—a restricted item that was CAF issue only—Kal plugged into the emergency airlock's computer and gingerly negotiated an opening with the airlock's tiny-minded control interface. It took minutes to convince the emergency lock's control that it didn't need to alert the command module as to what was going on, then the outer airlock doors slowly slid open.

Kal's suit lamps illuminated the interior.

"Here goes nothing," Kal said to herself, stepping into the orifice and standing on the wall of the airlock.

"A little help please?" said a voice in her suit's helmet radio.

Kal reached down and—bracing her boots on the rim of the lock—heaved mightily until Tim was standing in the lock with her. Once inside the airlock—tractors secured—Kal ordered the outer doors sealed, and teased open the inner doors with the same lock-crack computer she'd used on the outside.

The inner doors opened into relative darkness. The air of the communications module was cold and smelled of ozone, with wires, tubes, and electronics running every which way. Kal and Tim floated gently, careful not to tweak anything that looked fragile. Eventually they found one of the smallish maintenance passageways that honeycombed the ship, and both she and Tim left their suits secured at the passageway entrance before penetrating more deeply into the *Broadbill's* interior.

Their goal was to find a specific, tiny cabin that the manifest on Gulliver's wafer drive had said would be vacant for the duration of the voyage. If Gulliver was correct, Kal and Tim could hide there until the same people who had made off with previous Tremonton shipments, also came for the *Broadbill*. If Kal could identify the thieves, or even find a way to stow away aboard whatever ship the thieves were using, it would put Kal very close to the source of the trouble.

It would also put both herself and Tim in far more danger than she'd have preferred.

But Gulliver's instructions had been quite specific. And since Kal was dependent on the man—as her only source of seemingly reliable information—she was obliged to go along. If Gulliver was wrong, and nothing happened during the *Broadbill's* voyage, then there was no harm done, and Kal would have to figure out a secondary plan.

If Gulliver was right …

Kal considered her youthful companion who had not, so far as Kal knew, ever had to use a weapon in anger. She sighed. Would it cost them in a pinch?

They floated across an empty corridor.

It took moments of agony for the near-illegal device in Kal's gloved hands to talk the door's control mechanism into opening. Then, it only opened halfway, and began to close again almost immediately. The motors whined loudly as one fought against the other.

"Shit," Kal said. "You first."

"With the door half open I am not sure I can fit," Tim said.

"Go!" Kal slapped Tim hard on his back, and he dove in—grunting as he had to worm past the narrowing opening.

Kal disconnected the lock-pick and darted through just before the door resumed normal operational mode, and slapped shut.

It was pitch black.

"Lights," Tim said.

Overheads popped on. The single-bunk cabin was about the size of a modest walk-in closet.

Kal and Tim stared at each other.

It was going to be an interesting trip.

Chapter 9: uncharted territory

"How many dead, Pitman?" Karl Berd said to his first officer as Garth Pitman entered the bridge.

"One, plus some injuries."

Berd grimaced and stood up, stretching his back. He detested having to deal with unexpected problems. And this particular trip had experienced more than its fair share. The *Broadbill* was supposed to have been an easy poach job.

So much for false promises.

"Who do you think is doing this?" Pitman asked, standing at parade rest. "A roughneck out for revenge, or somebody else?"

"No," Berd said, "the deck rats we occasionally run into are far too self-preserving for direct action like this. It must be something else. I wonder ..."

Berd sat down and continued to brood. Whoever was running around in his ship was definitely not a run-of-the-mill freebooter. It was possible that this was somebody with military experience. Maybe an ex-CAF soldier? Berd detested the idea. Just as he detested the Conflux itself. To him, the supposed freedom of the Conflux was just a patina of lies. The super-wealthy technocrats who controlled or sat on the Assembly permitted just enough upward mobility to keep the masses from revolting, but nothing more.

The Ambit League—though harsh in its methods—offered the best chance Berd could see of transforming human society into something he might call civilized. In the era of interstellar travel, it was obscene that people still had to dig like dogs in the trash for even the basic necessities. The only thing keeping the status quo from collapsing was ignorance, fear, and the mercenary hoard known as the Conflux Armed Forces.

That a CAF troop might be loose in Berd's ship, killing off his crew ...

Berd stopped and thumped a fist loudly into his chair's headrest.

"The CAF pigs strangle us with the blockade," Berd said, "and now we may face one of their own running around this ship. Continue to collect what salvage you can, Pitman. But put every available person we have on alert for this woman. Continue to search and re-search every compartment. Turn every closet inside out. She can't hide forever."

"We might use the one we already caught," Pitman suggested.

"Yes, we might. But he's refused to talk. And while I am willing to resort to extreme measures, I would like to be sure we haven't exhausted our other options first. I am not a cruel man, Pitman."

"I'm sorry if I implied that you were, sir," Pitman said.

Berd looked at his first officer. They'd not known each other for a terribly long time. The Ambit League—in its current, fractured form—tended to move its personnel around a lot. So as to avoid attachments that might turn into vulnerabilities later. So far as Berd knew, Pitman was as dedicated to the League cause as any other man. But there was a flavor to Pitman that Berd couldn't quite put his finger on. Something feral …

No matter. To beat the Conflux, feral was sometimes necessary.

"Go," Pitman said, slowly sitting back down in the chair.

Pitman tipped his head, and left the bridge.

Chapter 10: the *Broadbill*

Like a lot of merchantmen, Berin Ogden was young.

Also like a lot of merchantmen, Berin had the tourist bug. Still wearing his shipsuit, replete with identifier patches, he stuck out like the foreigner that he was—wandering wide-eyed through the hula-hoop of Viking Station's kilometers-long bazaar. Flush with cash notes from his ship's paymaster, he nosed idly through the shops and the pubs, a bulb of mildly-fizzing alcoholic drink in one hand, and a crumpled bazaar directory in the other.

The sounds of hooting men and raunchy music drew him into one of the bazaar's dance clubs, where a lovely but not-so-young lady quickly attached herself to his arm. The woman's eyes were as deep and inviting as her cleavage, and before long Berin was swiping his paycard for both their drinks, culminating in a stumbled rush back to the *Broadbill's* tertiary gangway.

It was against Captain's orders to bring a local onboard; Berin would get asschewed if anyone saw her. Luckily the tertiary hatch was deserted and he knew how to mug the tertiary's security—he'd seen the second mate from propulsion do it more than once—so they had no trouble passing through the gate.

Once inside, Berin took her through several maintenance hatchways until they emptied into the corridor which held the door to Berin's closet-like crew cabin. He giggled tipsily as she ran her hands over his shipsuit, teasing at the frontal zipper and murmuring impatience. With the cabin door shut tight, sex was abrupt. Berin greedily pawed at his guest's delightfully bronzed flesh. Her scanty outfit fell away with the brush of a hand, and they kissed sloppily as they floated to his bunk, bodies rubbing.

Berin cried out with alarm as his youth betrayed him at that point.

Rather than be angry, Berin's guest just laughed. She wiped ejaculate from her stomach and pulled him the rest of the way out of his shipsuit, making promises about being able to coax a second wind into his sail. Berin was smiling sheepishly—but with renewed enthusiasm—when she slapped him hard on the neck with her left hand.

At once, his tongue turned to rubber and the room lost focus.

"What did … you …"

Berin was dead before he got a fourth word out.

The assassin spun one of the rings on her left hand until the small hypodermic inside it, retracted. Quickly placing her victim's body into one of his own lockers, she removed one of his clean shipsuits and slid into it, removing the wig on her head and swiping out the colored contact lenses from her eyes. A sanitary cloth from the tiny room's single sink did away with the makeup on her face, leaving the assassin a decidedly older, sterner version of herself. Still beautiful, but *hard*. The kind of hardness bred by a hard life.

From her purse the assassin extracted the few tools she knew she would need—each of these going into a different, zippered suit pocket.

The maintenance hatches took her back—and past—the way she'd come, to the centrally-aligned series of lift cars that traveled up and down the *Broadbill's* spine. Berin's keys, now attached to the assassin's belt via one of his elastic lanyards, got her a quick ride through the ship's considerable length, until she was able to enter the cargo hold. Checking to be sure the hold wasn't in vacuum, she again used Berin's keys, this time to gain access to the holdmaster's office.

"Everyone's on station," said the middle-aged holdmaster's mate, eyeing his visitor from behind his desk.

The assassin matter-of-factly pulled out a tiny pistol and shot the mate through the temple, her weapon barely making a pop as her second victim went limp over his desk, blood noodling from the tiny hole in his skull. She retrieved the mate's keys—discarding Berin's now-superfluous set—and used them to enter the cargo hold itself. Several stories high and twice as big around, the hold was packed with plastic and metal geometric shapes, all colors and all sizes.

The woman knew from experience what to look for, and where. When she'd confirmed that the *Broadbill* was carrying the kind of cargo she and her associates desired, she went back into the holdmaster's office and, shoving the dead mate aside, set up a point-to-point link through the *Broadbill's* communications umbilical with Viking Station.

"We've been waiting to hear from you," said a digitally-corroded male voice.

"Sorry I'm tardy, Yangis."

"Did you have any trouble getting in?"

The woman laughed. "Do I ever?"

Now the man named Yangis laughed. "That's our girl."

"They've got at least twenty units on this ship. Probably more, once we properly inventory her."

"Excellent. How many crew are still aboard?"

"Wait one."

The woman used the holdmaster's computer to do a quick count on keys which were still known to be aboard.

"Fifteen, though I can't be sure of their location."

"No matter. Arbai, you've done an excellent job, as always. You know what to do next."

"Just make sure you and yours are ready when I extend the cargo gangway."

"I leave the command module to your delicate skillset, my dear."

"Copy that. I'll see you when you get there."

Arbai cut the secure connection.

Using the holdmaster's mate's keys to re-enter the lift car, she plunged back through the length of the ship, getting off at the foyer to the command center. The keys got her through the outer door, then the inner door, and nobody seemed to notice as she entered the nerve center of the *Broadbill,* looking for all the world like just another one of its crew.

Eventually a watch officer looked up.

"Can I help you, miss?"

Arbai stopped. The officer was a young woman with junior merchant command studs on her shoulder. She floated from her chair near the middle of the complex. Screens and holographic projections decorated the space between them.

Arbai smiled.

"Don't get up, the holdmaster just sent me to tell you that he's got trouble with the seal on bay door three."

"Really? We didn't detect it here."

"He figured that, otherwise you'd have done something about it already. He wanted me to make sure you knew."

"We'll have to recall some of the engineers from station leave," the officer said, her brow furrowing with concern as she walked to one of the in-wall displays and began hitting keys to bring up the ship's roster.

Arbai drifted further into the command module, which didn't seem to alarm any of the other five watch officers sitting at their various stations. Reaching to her left breast pocket, she pulled out a tiny device like a diver's nose plug and inserted it into her nostrils. Then she reached into the shipsuit's right breast pocket and removed two glass phials, gripping them in either palm.

"I'm sorry," Arbai said to them all.

"What?"

"It's nothing personal. Just business."

Before anyone in the room could say or do anything else, Arbai pitched the phials in opposite directions, smashing them against the bulkheads. Several officers began to move, but not before a sickly-sour smell filled the room. All six of the watch went limp where they were, the respiratory nerve agent making them twitch as signals between brain and body became disrupted.

Arbai breathed through her nose while she counted ninety seconds—the deadly nerve agent's active lifespan. At one hundred and twenty seconds, she allowed herself to circle the command module, checking everyone for vitals and, satisfied that all were dead, settling herself at one of the master control stations.

The menus for the cargo bay's gangway were simple enough to find, and easier to operate. Within three minutes, a tube had been extended out to mate with Viking Station's bulky commerce deck. The command module remained intensely quiet throughout the entire operation, only a gentle whisper coming from the air cycle vents.

When next the command center's inner door opened, eight men and five women entered, each of them wearing filters on their noses similar to Arbai's.

The tallest of the men grinned, surveying the dead around him, then reached up and removed his filter, taking a deep whiff.

"You know there's always the danger of trace contamination," Arbai said, smirking at her boss.

"Live dangerously, or don't live at all," Yangis said. "Let's get these unfortunates out of here and fire up for departure."

Yangis's crew fanned out immediately, two people per body, and began to get the *Broadbill's* former bridge crew evacuated.

Yangis settled himself at a control station next to Arbai's.

"Was he a nice boy?"

"I beg your pardon?"

"That lad you picked up, the one we eyed out for you. Was he nice?"

"I'm not sure how to take that question," Arbai said, frowning.

"Take it any way you like," Yangis said.

"If you mean sexually, he was as clumsy as any young man can be."

"Worse than me when we first met?"

"No, he wasn't nearly that bad. Compared to you, he was a pro."

Yangis's laughter boomed through the command module.

"Leave it to my ex-wife to bust my balls for me!"

"You don't pay me to be gentle, dear."

"No, no I don't. Now get that hard ass of yours down to propulsion. I've got several more people coming aboard in maintenance coveralls, and I want you to make sure they don't have any trouble when they get down to the drive assembly."

Arbai mock-saluted and floated away from her station, feeling her ex-husband's hand pat her rump before she went to the command module doors, and exited.

As with previous jobs on merchant ships like the *Broadbill*, everything else proved academic. Arbai wondered why more ships—

more companies—hadn't learned better. Lax protocol, lax training, weak security measures at entry points, skeleton staffing while in port. Typical, typical, typical. It was like they were begging for piracy. Though pirate was not the word Arbai would have used to describe herself. She was a trained professional, and very good at what she did. Had there been any money in it, she might have even stayed in the CAF. Lucky for her she'd met Yangis, and when they'd both gotten out of uniform, gone into business for themselves.

A very select, very exclusive kind of business.

When the *Broadbill* broke dock without warning, there was the usual wailing from traffic control. Yangis ignored it, and Arbai watched from one of the portals in the crew module as the merchant ship spun away from Viking Station and flew into the blackness of space.

Chapter 11: the *Broadbill*

It didn't take a genius to figure out that the *Broadbill* had left dock without proper authorization from Viking Station control.

As soon as Kal felt the gee of acceleration assert itself, she knew what was up.

"You can't be serious," Tim said as he watched Kal get her pistol out of her shoulder holster, remove and check the magazine, then slap the magazine back in place.

"I'm dead serious. Whoever has been taking these Tremonton shipments? Their ambition just leveled up. Now they're taking a whole cradle ship. The *Broadbill* is officially under new management."

"So what do we do now?" Tim asked.

"Nothing. We stick to the plan. In fact, this actually makes things a easier. I was trying to figure out how we were going to manage to get out into the rest of the ship, if or when somebody decided to snatch the sensitive hardware in the cargo hold. Now they're liable to take us directly to wherever the missing shipments have been piling up. Or, more probably, we'll rendezvous with another ship in orbit somewhere obscure. The cargo will get moved to a new ship. And then the *Broadbill* will be sent off somewhere far away. To confuse the trail."

"Sounds like we'll have to be ready to go where the crates go," Tim said.

"Yup. And that's going to be very potentially tricky. We might have to go outside again and hope we can jump—ship to ship—without being noticed. Are you prepared for that?"

"Sounds like I might have to be," Tim said, frowning and running a hand through his curly black hair.

Kal slipped her pistol back into its shoulder holster, and sat on the bunk across from where Tim was slouched in the single fold-up chair that was next to the shelf-like fold-up desk.

"Tell me," she said, "just what is it about this new armor model that's so exciting the Ambit League wants a piece of it?"

"Ummm, I'm not sure I can talk about that, you see—"

"Save it, kid, I have need-to-know at this point. I used several different types of armor during the war. It's not like that's brand new technology."

"The Archangel series isn't just an upgrade to the older armor suits that the CAF's been using since the war," Tim said. "We're talking about an entirely new generation of bio-neural interfacing. You don't wear the suit. It's like the suit wears *you*. Reflexive response times far in advance of anything the CAF or the Ambit League were using in battle when the war was still hot. Plus it employs advanced ceramics, polymers, alloys, and a microcomputer system that learns its owner over time. Until the microcomputer is almost a shallow, duplicate personality. It knows your moves before you know your moves."

Kal was intrigued. She wondered what it would be like to pilot such a suit. The conventional suits were big, bulky behemoths with loads of firepower, but slow and cumbersome. Not to mention exhausting. The delayed response times on movement meant an average troop became physically tired while fighting against the lag. If what Tim said was true, the Archangel suits truly were next-generation.

"Anyway," Tim said, "the Ambit League would be stupid to let itself fight that kind of suit without trying to replicate the tech. Trials on some of the Occupied Zone planets have already yielded very good results. Even against entrenched, experienced opposition, the Archangel has a perfect record. No losses. With countless enemy combatants neutralized or destroyed."

"What about heavy stuff? Tanks and bigger things?"

"The Archangel is meant for speed and agility, not raw firepower. Still, in the hands of an able pilot, it can fight circles around conventional tracked armor. Give an Archangel troop enough time, and she can quickly ventilate a tank like a piece of Swiss cheese."

Kal nodded her understanding.

"That means each of the Archangel suits is worth a lot of money," she said.

"You don't even want to know," Tim said, smiling sardonically. "Just the pinky finger on one of the Archangel's gauntlets is worth more than my entire annual salary."

"Which also means that Tremonton is going to make a killing selling these things to the Conflux Assembly Defense Office."

"Prices will drop once the suit's been put through its paces and mainline manufacturing can begin. But yeah, even a single suit's worth more than a dozen conventional suits put together."

"And now the Ambit League has them," Kal said.

"Apparently so. Though they're going to be hard-pressed to replicate even half of what they find, when they pull the Archangel apart. It's Tremonton's most advanced design, and it took countless hours to engineer and create it. Using Tremonton's top facilities on several planets. I don't think the Ambit League is up to the task of copying the Archangel just yet."

"Well, that's another reason I need you: to verify if your guesses are correct, assuming we get to have a look at the final destination for these shipments that keep getting stolen. Gulliver said the League's been surreptitiously expanding into the unexplored space on the other side of the Occupied Zone, away from the Conflux. If they're setting up shadow colonies, especially with industry and mining, they might have what it takes to start trying to replicate advanced tech. Or perhaps they simply want to mass-produce a poor man's version? Numbers will almost always beat quality, if the numbers are large enough."

Tim looked at Kal, his smile fading.

"Then it really might be a second war?" he asked softly.

"Yes," Kal said, her eyes unfocusing, "it might."

Chapter 12: uncharted territory

Garth Pitman stomped across the rusty decks of his ship as he made his way down to the engineering section. The buzzing of his subordinates was comforting in his headset's earpiece. They were executing as commanded: turning the old scow inside out, trying to locate the intruder.

The mischievous mystery guest had eluded capture and killed crew, but Pitman wasn't necessarily worried. Yet. People had died for the Ambit League before, and people would continue to die for the Ambit League in the future. It was the price they all had to pay if the long war against the Conflux was to succeed. Pitman accepted that. He was even confidant that he himself would give his life should it become necessary, but he always assured himself that he was far too crafty to be caught unaware.

He would live to see the Conflux fall.

Taking a lift car down a few decks, Pitman continued to stride confidently. In the eyes of the crew, Pitman saw respect. And sometimes fear. That was good. He could use both, when he needed to. It came with the job. As long as people obeyed his orders, or the orders of Berd—to the letter—that was all he asked.

His headset suddenly squealed and one of Pitman's junior officers demanded his attention; down in the lower compartments close to the main cargo bay. Another crewperson had been killed.

Pitman ran: around a corner, down a ladder, through a hatch, and then through a corridor, until he finally arrived at the location of the latest murder.

As he showed up, several of Pitman's crew were outside a partially opened hatchway, eyes wide and feet shuffling nervously. An old load master named Gimms was there, running a hand over the thin stubble on his head.

"Who was it this time?" Pitman asked.

"Go look for yourself, sir."

Pitman grimaced, his hackles rising at the tone in Gimms's voice. But as Pitman watched Gimms and the others, Pitman's feet began to get cold and his hands began to sweat. Something was seriously wrong.

Pitman unslung his submachine gun and gripped it in his hands for comfort, then brushed past Gimms and went into the cargo compartment. The area was full of refuse, and smelled of corrosion. The doors and walls were rusted badly. Rectangular containers clogged the walkway. Gouts of blood were freshly splattered across one side of a container, where a body lay underneath a draped plastic tarp. Pitman stooped and gingerly peeled the tarp back so that he could see the victim's face.

Her eyes were open and stared emptily at the ceiling. Her mouth was half open and blood trailed down the corners across her cheeks. The bullet had gone right through her esophagus and lodged in the spine. Instant death.

Pitman's eyes ogled, and then a quiet rage began to build in him.

Gabriella. She and Garth had been lovers for some time now, sharing the glories of his bed every night for weeks. Now Pitman's companion lay lifeless and crumpled on the deck, her drying blood staining the soles of his boots.

Pitman dropped to his knees, fists balled around the grips of his submachine gun—his eyes closed. A low growl uttered from his clenched teeth. Then he stopped, composed himself, and calmly stood up, his mind trying to focus. This was CAF handiwork, he was sure of it. Only the CAF could murder so brutally and efficiently.

Pitman held back the raw anger and sorrow jointly gnawing at his heart. He had to stay composed if he wanted to avenge his lover. Pitman ran his eyes over her body, checking for missing or damaged equipment.

Gabriella's headset was gone, but her weapon was not.

Damn.

"Take the body out of here and put it in the cold locker," Pitman ordered as he exited the compartment. "We'll take her back with us, and make sure she's given a soldier's burial."

The others saluted and silently went to work, eyes wary of Pitman's barely concealed rage.

Chapter 13: stowaways

It took almost two weeks for the *Broadbill* to reach her intended destination. During which time neither Kal nor Tim dared leave their cabin, for fear of being spotted. Though the people who'd hijacked the ship had no reason to believe anyone else might be onboard, it paid to be cautious. So, they each went out exactly once: to look for meal packs.

Not precisely gourmet, the meal packs were easily had in any emergency locker. In case the *Broadbill* were disabled or stranded between star systems, with the crew unable to travel freely between compartments. Starvation was a real possibility if rescue was still light-years away, and your radio signals only traveled as far as the nearest spacelane beacon.

During that time Kal and Tim did the best they could to be comfortable. Which wasn't easy, given the tight quarters. Including a micro-toilet that was barely big enough for Kal to use—making it almost impossible for Tim.

They traded stories about initial entry training in the CAF. Things which had stayed the same. Things which were different. Between the time when Kal had joined, and Tim had joined—to fulfill his obligation under contract to Tremonton.

They also talked a lot about the Archangel suits. Plusses. Minuses. Things Tim had noticed when piloting the suits in a laboratory setting. So that Kal felt like she was familiar enough to try operating an Archangel in a pinch. If it came down to it.

"They key thing is," Tim said one morning while they pushed fruity-nutty breakfast bars into their mouths, "the Archangel wasn't designed to plod. It was designed to soar. Where older suits thud along like the Frankenstein monster, the Archangel glides. Most pilots who are used to conventional armor have to go through a teething period, where they re-train themselves to the advanced, hyper-responsive servos and motors in the Archangel's design. So in the unlikely event you're ever putting one of these things on, don't get gung-ho. You're liable to put an arm through a wall or accidentally hurl yourself into the ceiling, or across the room. Go very gently. Almost as if you don't want to move. The Archangel will do the moving for you."

"It must be a lot of fun," Kal said.

"What?" Tim asked.

"Getting to play with Tremonton's latest toy."

"It's a good job," he said. "And I certainly get paid well."

They munched their meals for a quiet moment.

"Got anyone back home worth spending the money on?" Kal asked.

Tim cleared his throat and took a drink of water from a cup on the rim of the cabin's tiny sink.

"Not really," he admitted.

"No lady friend has caught your eye?"

"No."

"A shame. You seem like the nice sort."

"My ex-girlfriend said I was *too* nice."

"Was she young?"

"Yes. Younger than me at least."

"Young girls don't appreciate nice. A woman with experience might. Don't be afraid to date older gals."

"Is that a proposition?" Tim said with a raised eyebrow and a grin.

Kal slugged him in the left shoulder as hard as she could. He almost fell over laughing, then grimaced and rubbed the spot where a fresh bruise was no doubt forming.

"Sorry," Kal said. "Sometimes I don't know my own strength."

"No shit," Tim said.

Suddenly, the feeling of gravity began to vanish.

"Uh oh," Kal said. "I think maybe we've arrived."

"What now?" Tim asked.

"Head back the way we came in. Suit up. Take a look outside and see what happens next."

Kal and Tim never made it that far.

Chapter 14: in orbit, uncharted territory

Arbai watched her former husband as he stared intently at the gangway hatch. The receiving ship had been waiting for them as soon as the *Broadbill* had entered orbit, following a gradual downthrust through the outer portion of this uncharted star system. They were well beyond the boundaries of either the Occupied Zone or the Conflux, and the greenish blue-and-white world beneath them was uncharted as well.

A virgin paradise. Or a tropical death trap.

A lot depended on whether the fauna down below had evolved to the point of having sharp teeth, and thought off-world visitors might be tasty. Perhaps when the job was done, and after enough time had elapsed, Arbai and Yangis could come back here? Have a little fun on the beach? Nothing romantic, per se. Because sex with Yangis had never been like that. But relaxing fun just the same. Lord knew they'd have enough money to take a break from their cares for a while.

Doubtless it was the money that had Yangis so tense. Meeting strangers to make the exchange of goods was always a high-wire act. You couldn't trust them to be straight, they couldn't trust you to be straight, and Arbai had seen several such exchanges go badly before. Which was why everyone was carrying for this particular action. Pistols and submachine guns visible, without being brandished. It was also why she knew Yangis kept a small remote in his spacer's jacket. It was tied wirelessly to the control computer that operated their cradle ship's fusion reactor. If Yangis pressed a select sequence of buttons …

No sense letting potential double-crossers have the last laugh.

The gangway hatch's indicator light blinked from red, to orange, to yellow, then to green.

Then it unsealed, and half a dozen men floated in.

Unlike Yangis's crew, these strangers were more or less uniform in appearance. Hair cut to military standard. Faces serious and eyes alert. The kind of expressions Arbai and Yangis both remembered well, from their time in the CAF. Though these were not CAF. They were the men Arbai and Yangis had been killing right up until Arbai and Yangis both decided that the war was a sham, the Conflux was as bloody culpable as the Ambit League, and that the only side worth choosing, was their own side.

An older man with some kind of insignia on his collar stepped forward.

"Berd," the man said, nodding his head slightly. "Commander of the *Goshawk.*"

"Yangis Terizian," Yangis said, returning the slight nod. "You'd better be careful with that rusty bucket you've got out there. It's a miracle it's even spaceworthy."

"It suffices," Berd said, ignoring the jab at his spacer's pride. "She may not look impressive, but the drives are good and she gets the job done. Besides, she's just a delivery vehicle. Now, show us the cargo, then we'll discuss your payment."

"You read my mind," Yangis said. He snapped a finger.

A single pallet was floated forward. On it, secured by bungee tethers, were the major pieces of a single suit of Archangel-type armor. Arbai noticed Berd's eyes take in the sight of the armor the way other men might take in the sight of a nude woman. So Berd was a believer, eh? Ambit League to the core. That would either be very good, or very bad, depending on what happened next.

"How many of these did you get?" Berd asked Yangis.

"All of them aboard."

"Which is how many?"

"We've not opened every single crate, but there are probably thirty total."

"Not as many as we'd hoped," said a younger man behind Berd. Tougher-looking. Also with an insignia on his collar. Berd's executive officer?

"But enough," Berd said.

He pushed off from the deck and floated over to the pallet, running his hands along the polished surfaces of the various armor components.

"When the crates have been moved to the *Goshawk,* you will be compensated," Berd said to Yangis.

"No," Yangis said, his businessman's smile dropping to a frown. "The arrangement I made with your people was, I show you proof of the goods, you pay me for my time, *then* you can have the units. Not before."

"The Ambit League is not in the habit of paying for goods which it has not yet taken possession of," Berd said, his eyes suddenly hardening.

Arbai immediately noticed that some of Berd's men had pushed their spacer's jackets open, revealing the gleam of guns in holsters. Yangis's people had subtly made their own weaponry more visible, too, and Arbai realized that things could get very unfortunate very fast if someone didn't pour a little oil on the roiled waters.

"I don't think it has to be an all or nothing proposition," Arbai said, using her best, most soothing feminine voice. She pushed over to where Berd and Yangis now both floated less than a meter apart, their jaws thrust out at one another.

"A deal is a deal," Yangis said. "No money, no top-secret armor."

"Gentlemen," Arbai said, inserting herself into the tense air between the two men. "Since there appears to be a small misunderstanding about what's supposed to take place here, why don't we agree to meet in the middle? We'll provide the first ten suits, you carry them across, and you provide one third of the payment. Then we provide the next ten suits, you provide the second third, and so on and so forth. That way we get what we want, you can verify that you're getting what you want, and then we can each go on our separate ways."

Yangis and Berd glared at each other, then Yangis laughed: artificial, and harsh.

"Damn, Arbai, you always were so smooth. Can you believe this lady? And I had the stupidity to divorce her!"

"I divorced you, dear," Arbai said gently.

More hard laughter.

"Fine, fine, we'll do it according to the lady's preference."

Berd simply kept staring, then he blinked once, exhaled slowly, and nodded his head.

"That's a reasonable compromise. Let me inform my men."

Berd floated back to where his people were. With his back turned, he raised a hand and chopped it once, downward through the air.

Arbai's smile dropped, and she screamed a warning.

Too late. The Ambit League men were faster on the draw.

Firearms chattered and banged like Thor's hammer on an iron sky. Arbai felt something hot tear into her stomach and then she was flipped end-over-end back against the far bulkhead, where she curled in on the wound and gagged, unable to speak.

Looking out of the corner of her eye should could see the Ambit League men all poised on the balls of their feet—grip soles holding them tightly against the recoil of their weapons. Only three of them had been hit, and they were being rushed back down the gangway by their comrades, leaving Berd and his executive .

"Sorry," Berd said as the moans of Yangis's wounded filled the compartment. "This Archangel armor is too important to the League. We can't afford to have anyone—much less scum like yourselves— left alive to speak of its whereabouts. We'll be taking all the suits now, and this ship as well. I should tell you that you ought to get used to my 'rusty bucket' because once we've moved our flag to the *Broadbill,* your bodies will be in the *Goshawk* when she reenters."

Berd turned and motioned for his executive to follow him back down the gangway.

Arbai would have shed tears if the pain in her gut had not been so intense. She couldn't speak, and could barely move. Heavy fluid leaked between her fingers and began to form hot blobs of dark redness that floated away into the air—to mix with that of the others, who'd all been shot to pieces.

Stupid, Arbai thought. *Should have left a few of us elsewhere, to come in as a second wave, if the first wave went down.*

Then she saw Yangis. Her ex-husband was slowly revolving in the air, three holes in his chest. But his eyes were blinking.

Arbai mouthed his name.

Yangis appeared to mouth something to Arbai too. She tried to muster a smile. Was he saying her name?

Then Yangis managed a ferocious, bloody grin. She noticed the remote was in his right hand.

Ah. Right.

Arbai closed her eyes, and hoped she'd be dead before the blast happened.

Chapter 14: uncharted territory

Back on the bridge, Pitman quickly cleaned his hands, and then linked himself into the intra-ship communications network through his headset. He began ordering his people to an even higher level of alert, with guards at all the entrances to the cargo bay, by the hatches to the engine room, and of course, watching the corridor to the bridge's lone lift. Finally, Pitman called up six of his most trusted troops, who met him in the officers' mess just off the bridge. In full armament.

Pitman looked at his team as they adjusted their gear.

"Does everyone understand? I want this little whore *dead* ... I want her burned out of the ventilation system and gutted like a fish."

Pitman's people nodded and smiled. Like him, they were hungry for the hunt. There wasn't an Ambit League partisan on the ship who didn't hate the CAF.

Pitman slapped them on their shoulders and they trooped off towards the sole functional lift that serviced the bridge. Each carried a minimum of two weapons, various heat and motion sensing gear, plus full plate vests and helmets that could stop a rifle round.

Pitman used the AV unit in the wall—one of the few on the ship that still worked properly—to call up a diagram of the *Goshawk's* internal architecture. They separated the ship up into sectors, then began mapping where the prey had most recently been sighted, versus where Gabriella's body had been found. A strategy was devised to begin tackling the problem in a systematic fashion. No more random, bumbling search sweeps.

"Remember, she's just one woman," Garth said, his eyes jumping from face to stolid face. They all nodded solemnly.

"It will be done," one of them said.

"See that it is," Pitman said.

Pitman turned away from his men and walked through the adjoining passage back to the bridge proper. A guest had been brought to join the commander. The huge, dark-skinned young man was looking straight at Pitman—with eyes that only partially concealed the young man's hostility. The prisoner never blinked as he stared at Pitman.

Pitman resisted the urge to strike the prisoner with a closed fist.

"I am afraid you don't understand your predicament," Berd was saying in a reasonable tone.

"How's that?" the young man asked.

"Because, dear sir, it's only a matter of time before my people catch up with your lady friend who is making such a mess of my ship down below. If you can convince her to come out of hiding and surrender peacefully, I can see to it that you're both repatriated to a neutral site. In due time, of course."

"And why should I believe you'll do any such thing?" the prisoner asked.

"Son," Berd said, his face assuming a somewhat pained, fatherly expression, "I am afraid that you're in no position to doubt me. Because I can assure you, if that woman you came with is not brought to bear soon, for every one of my crew she hurts, I'm going to take it out on *you*. Or, rather, I will have my first officer take it out on you. And believe me, when I give him an order, he's very good at what he does. Isn't that right, Pitman?"

"Yessir," was all Pitman said, eyeing the largish youth, who'd had his ankles and wrists shackled ever since he'd been dragged aboard.

The prisoner didn't say a word. He simply stared at the floor.

"Son," Berd said, "My people tell me your friend has managed to secure one of our headsets, so all I have to do is put you on the network in order for her to hear you. So, do we have an agreement?"

The prisoner remained silent.

"Hello?" Berd said, only this time a bit more sharply.

He glanced up at Pitman. Face red. Then pointed at the prisoner and mimed punching his fist into a palm.

Pitman smiled. He was going to get a little recreation, to ease the suffering of his recent loss.

Chapter 15: uncharted territory

Kal sat in the darkness, trying to let herself rest. But she couldn't. The adrenaline in her veins was like amphetamine. She'd been wired up for hours, and remained wired. Unable to properly navigate the ship, and searching blindly from compartment to compartment, she was beginning to fear that she'd never locate Tim, until he was either dead, or they caught her. In which case she was as good as dead, and Tim right along with her.

Her headset crackled to life.

"This is Commander Berd to all crew members …"

Kal listened carefully.

"As you know, a lone female survivor from the *Broadbill* has come aboard and is harassing us internally. I have reason to suspect this woman is a military operative from the CAF, not a smuggler. I realize it is galling to us all that we must suffer having this … *person,* running loose in the bowels of our vessel. With your help I hope to have the problem resolved quickly, so that we can finish the job we came here for, and return our precious cargo to our Ambit League comrades who can do the most good with it.

"Until then, though, I want total intra-ship communications silence. All relays and request will be made face-to-face. Our visitor has one of our headsets, so she will hear anything we say on the network. Cut her out of the network, and she stands much less of a chance of evading or ambushing us. Anyone breaking this order without direct permission from the bridge will suffer the consequences. Do not let me down. Commander Berd, for the Ambit League, out."

Suddenly Kal's headset went totally dead, and she smacked a fist onto the hull plating.

She needed a plan of action. And fast.

Chapter 16: in orbit, uncharted territory

Kal and Tim were barely halfway to the compartment in the communications module—where they'd stowed their space suits—when a loud concussion shook the *Broadbill.*

The ship's automated emergency claxon began to sound.

"Decompression!" Tim yelled, noticing the color of the flashing lights that suddenly sprang to life at intervals along the ceiling.

"Or worse," Kal said.

"What could have happened?" Tim asked, his head suddenly swiveling back and forth in panic.

The klaxon changed pitch, and the emergency light changed color.

"Radiological alarm too!" Tim shouted.

"Shit," Kal cursed. "The reactor on the cradle ship. Either it blew itself, or someone blew it for us.

"But what can we—"

A terrible wind kicked up, drowning out Tim's words.

"Move!" Kal yelled. "Now!"

They both grabbed what handholds they could, and fought their way up the corridor. Meter by painful meter. There was an emergency locker just ahead. There would be emergency environment suits in there. Perhaps Kal and Tim could reach them in time to avoid having the air sucked from their lungs?

Kal clawed her way past a black and yellow striped threshold.

Why hadn't the internal emergency doors sealed?

As if to answer Kal's mental question, a thick steel door suddenly descended from the ceiling. Since Tim had been two meters behind he could only watch helplessly as the door slammed shut between them.

Kal felt the rush of air lessen, but not abate entirely. Screaming Tim's name, she turned back to the door and began to beat on it with her fists.

"Tim! Oh my God, no, no!"

Rumbles and groans throughout the ship told Kal that the *Broadbill* was in very deep trouble. When the ship itself began to jerk violently, and spin, it was all Kal could do to worm her way towards the nearest lifeboat hatch, which was rimmed by red and white caution striping. She passed through the hatch and had the good sense to hit the large red handle in the lifeboat's roof. The hatch slammed shut, and suddenly the lifeboat itself was being hurled into the universe.

Chapter 17: uncharted territory

Kal sat in the dark. Her eyes and ears wide open, waiting for the slightest sound.

It was eerie.

Before, while the radios had been active, she had at least been able to gather a fly-on-the-wall picture of what was happening inside the ship. Now, however, she was isolated and out of information. The advantage—temporarily gained, right after she'd taken the headset—was gone, and the whole ship had a collective itchy trigger finger with Kal's name on it. The longer she sat and stared into the darkness, the more she became paranoid.

Minutes ticked by, agonizingly, and finally she couldn't take it anymore. She had to move. But where? Navigating the neglected, darkened compartments of the ship was like moving through a maze with a blindfold on. Without a layout of the structure to orientate with, and a big arrow indicating *Kal Reardon, You Are Here,* any guess she might make as to where she was, or where she was trying to go, was almost useless.

But she absolutely could not risk moving about in the main corridors. It would be a near certain death sentence.

What to do …

Kal couldn't think straight. She was too tired. Too exhausted. And too amped up on her own fear, combined with desperation to reach Tim. Her head settled onto her knees—drawn up to her chest—and she fell asleep.

When her head popped up again, Kal had been in the midst of an old dream from her war days. Not a battle dream per se, but something from training. When she'd been maneuvering with her platoon against dummy targets, using the textbook call signs and lingo to execute the platoon's operations order.

Kal found herself desperately hoping for a platoon now. Even a moderately armed couple of CAF mobile infantry squads would be able to rip the ancient, decrepit ship to pieces within minutes. Or at least scare crud out of the crew.

Wait …

Kal suddenly realized she'd been looking at her predicament from the wrong perspective.

The seed of an idea sprang forth, like hot sparks.

And Kal was up and moving again.

• • •

Kal watched nervously through the ductwork grill plate as a particularly large privateer sauntered past. It had taken a small eternity to wind her way back towards the main cargo hold. Several times she'd had to make quick detours to avoid the sweep patrol that appeared to be making a coordinated effort to smoke her out. It wouldn't be long before she took one wrong turn too many, and found herself staring down the barrel of somebody's weapon.

Therefore it was now or never.

Kal gently pushed on the grill plate with her legs until it popped free. Only instead of letting it clatter to the deck, she caught it in both hands and eased it down to the deck with as little noise as she could muster. The space in front of the grill plate was dominated by interstellar shipping crates of various sizes, which had all been salvaged from the downed hulk of the *Broadbill*. Kal couldn't tell if they were ordinary crates, or the unmarked specialized crates she had seen upon first boarding: the ones that held the different pieces of Archangel armor.

Kal looked around carefully, unable to tell—in the stacks of crates—whether or not any of the privateers could see her. She girded herself, and dared to stand up and look into the nearest crate.

Damn, it was empty.

The next nearest was empty too.

Was she too late? Had they evacuated the crates and moved all of the Archangel armor to a different, more secure location within the ship?

Footsteps on metal.

Kal ducked down behind a stack of crates that was three high, and waited until the footsteps had diminished.

With her heart pounding in her throat, Kal turned around and examined the stack which was providing her cover. Like most commercial crates of similar design, these were roughly two meters on a side, and all sides had small access panels that could be detached if you had the right tools. In the case of the crate that was directly in front of Kal, the side hatch appeared to have been recently opened, and re-sealed—the paint around the edges had flaked, revealing bright metal.

Kal teased at the latches with her thumb and forefinger. One of the latches came loose.

Elated—and scared to death of being heard or seen—Kal popped another latch, and then another. When the last latch came free, she eased the side panel away and laid it on the ground. Inside, the crate was pitch black. So Kal reached in and felt around. Something very hard, smooth, and heavy was in the way. Grasping it as best as she could, Kal pulled the thing out and looked at it.

It was a helmet. A brand new, very fancy looking helmet. With an expensive and intricate-looking interface at the neck, where data feeds and motor networking would engage. Not a lot different from the conventional armor suits Kal had trained on.

Footsteps again. Coming towards her. Kal momentarily considered fleeing back into the ductwork.

No good. She wouldn't make it in time.

Instead, she crawled *into* the crate, and pulled the access panel up behind her. Unable to seal the latches from the inside, she held the panel in place with the tips of her fingers and waited in desperate silence while the footsteps approach her crate, and then stopped in front of it.

Kal all but fainted.

But then, a voice spoke.

"If you tell 'em once you tell 'em a thousand times, don't half-ass it when you're doing a job. Now look at this container here, someone's replaced the panel without dogging the latches. If I knew which one of these lazy sons-of-bitches was slacking around here, I'd break his nose."

One by one, the latches were all snapped tight.

And Kal was locked inside.

Safe? For the moment? She felt around until she once again found the object that felt like the helmet. She slid it onto her head and allowed herself a tiny hint of a smile.

Chapter 18: uncharted territory

Tim Osterhaudt sat slumped in his confined seat on the bridge of the *Goshawk*. His head hung low and blood oozed from several large gashes on his face and upper torso. Pitman, and Pitman's commander, Karl Berd, sat on the edge of a console a few meters away, each staring unblinkingly at their captive.

"Who is your partner?" Berd said with an icy tone to his voice. "I really don't want to have to unleash my first officer again."

Tim clenched up inside for a second, as he contemplated the pain. Would it do any good to talk? He'd almost cracked during the first beating. Would he be able to withstand the second? Ordinarily Tim would have stuck to his principles, and not wished harm on anyone. But after the way Pitman had laid into him, Tim was beginning to have second thoughts about his philosophy. For the first time since he'd been a teenager in school, Tim genuinely wanted to retaliate. Hit back. No, not just hit back. Cave Pitman's skull in with a wrench. Knock him down and beat him senseless.

It was embarrassing, to be having such barbaric thoughts. But Tim realized he could not help it. Not after the way Pitman had savaged him, and for no reason other than that Tim was powerless to do anything about it. Talk or no talk, the Ambit League people were going to beat him again. Perhaps even to death. Regardless of what came out of his mouth. Of this Tim was certain. So, he kept his mouth shut, and waited dismally for the renewal of blows.

• • •

Pitman noticed Osterhaudt flinch, and then remain silent.

"He needs more motivation, boss," Pitman said. His fists were sore from the first series of blows, but he'd relished the exercise. Every hit was another piece of revenge for what had been done to Gabriella.

Berd sighed, and nodded.

Pitman lunged, cracking a fist across Osterhaudt's cheek.

There was a loud *smack* and Osterhaudt's head snapped to the side, blood pouring from a new gash in Osterhaudt's face.

• • •

Tim ran a tongue along the wounded flesh inside his mouth—to compliment the wounds outside—and grimaced. A few teeth were loose. He'd have to have that taken care of, if he survived to get off this mud ball.

Another blow cracked Tim's head in the opposite direction, and a second cut joined the first in dribbling warm redness all over Osterhaudt's muscled chest.

"Who is your partner?" Berd asked again, remaining calm as Pitman's chest inhaled and exhaled rapidly.

Osterhaudt closed his eyes and tried to remove himself from the current situation. He refused to betray a woman whom he had learned to call a friend. He was also a CAF Reserve officer. They hadn't spent much time discussing prisoner of war scenarios, but Tim knew the stories from history. He would resist them as long as he could. Until whatever he babbled out of his mouth was so nonsensical it wouldn't matter how much he spoke.

Osterhaudt lifted his head slowly and stared at them both through swollen eyes—just for a moment. They waited as he opened his mouth to speak, looks of anticipation on their faces.

"Ambit League? Go fuck yourselves," Tim whispered.

• • •

Pitman screamed, and was on Osterhaudt in an instant, raining curse after curse and punch after punch.

Suddenly Pitman found himself grabbed by the shirt collar and hurled against the opposite bulkhead by an impossibly strong arm.

"You *fool!*" Berd hissed at a startled Pitman. "We need him *alive* for now. I told you to rough him up, not to *kill* him. Put your anger about Gabriella on hold until we can get both he and that damned woman out in the open. Together. After that, you can tear them both apart for all I care, but as long as she's loose in the ship, we need him as live bait. Understood?"

Pitman nodded his head, his lungs sucking in and expelling air at a very rapid, adrenalized pace.

• • •

Berd watched for a few more seconds, to be sure his executive wouldn't renew the rage-filled beating, then he turned away and picked up a communications headset from the nearby bridge console. He placed it on his graying head of hair and tossed a second unit to Pitman.

"Untie him from the seat," Berd said, "and carry him down a few decks to the cargo bay. If he won't give us what we need, then maybe we can use him to force her out of the air ducts."

Berd walked past Pitman towards the bridge lift tube.

• • •

Pitman spat once on the deck, and began to unstrap the tape from Osterhaudt's bindings—tape which had held him to the chair long after losing consciousness. Tim toppled to the floor, unable to stop himself. Pitman felt the urge to rain a series of savage kicks on the pilot, but didn't dare cross his boss's order to keep the young CAF troop alive.

Chapter 19: uncharted territory

Kal slowly assembled the Archangel armor by feel.

First the interface body suit—which felt terrible, being pulled on over the top of Kal's sweaty, filthy, and in some places bloody skin. Then, the secondary coolant suit. After that, the boots, and the legs, the lower torso, the upper torso, the shoulders, the upper arms, the gauntlets, and finally, sealing the collar to the helmet.

By the time Kal was done she was sweating so profusely in the cramped, unventilated interior of the crate, that she felt literally like she might suffocate. Unless she got some clean air.

The moment she got the neck ring to the suit's helmet sealed, the microcomputer interface came to life and a pleasantly female voice announced in Kal's ears that the Archangel armor was activated and would she please select a mode of operation before continuing. A projection appeared in Kal's field of view—made bright by the fact that the interior of the crate was pitch black—and Kal scanned the menu options:

DIAGNOSTIC TYPE A.

DIAGNOSTIC TYPE B.

DEMONSTRATION MODE.

NEW PILOT MODE.

DEPLOYMENT MODE.

Unsure of how to make her selection, Kal muttered something about being a new pilot.

The selection illuminated happily, then Kal felt a burst of air against her damp cheeks from the suit's own internal atmospheric pressurizer. Her eardrums felt the sudden shift, and she worked her jaw to pop them while the menu display showed a swirling circle—the near universal sign that the computer was booting its assigned program.

There was a gentle mechanical noise in Kal's ears, and she momentarily froze, wondering who—if anyone—outside the crate might be within listening distance. But then her fear abated as she realized that for the first time since she'd crash-landed, Kal was not in any immediate danger from the people around her. Small arms wouldn't do much good against the Archangel. Tim had sworn it. So unless the privateers had something more powerful to throw against her, for the moment, Kal was essentially invulnerable. At least if she could figure out how to work the system.

Tim had warned her again and again to take it easy. Not overreact. Not push the suit in the way she'd been used to pushing older suits.

Kal waited while the mode finally came up—with menus not a lot different from what she'd seen on her displays in the conventional armor units—then she began navigating the selections by voice. Under ideal circumstances she'd have had plenty of time to go through all the choices and get things customized. Right now she merely needed the suit to respond to her as quickly and as powerfully as possible.

Would the suit really be as good as Tim said it was?

Kal would soon find out.

A chime alerted Kal to the fact that a wireless signal was active, where none had been active before. Kal ordered the signal to be piped to her speakers in her ears.

"Attention, this is Karl Berd, commander of the Ambit League ship *Goshawk*. I am speaking to the woman who has thus far stubbornly refused to cooperate with my requests that she cease and desist all harassment of my crew. Since you have elected to be hard-headed, I am now forced to be hard-headed as well. My first officer has been quite thorough in his dealings with your young friend here. Quite thorough. Albeit nothing permanent has transpired. Yet. This may be about to change. Listen carefully."

Kal heard a sickening *crunch,* then a shuffling sound, followed by a barley contained yowl of pain. Tim.

They were now breaking bones.

Crunch.

Another, stronger scream from Tim's throat, which sounded dry and ragged.

"Respond," Berd's voice said, "or we keep going. When his fingers are done, then we break his toes. Then his arms, and legs. After that, you force us to get creative. Reply to this signal please, and announce your intention to surrender to my crew at once.

"No!" Kal suddenly blurted out in a ragged cry over the Archangel's wireless connection to the intra-ship network. Which to that point had merely been passive.

• • •

Tim Osterhaudt held back the tears as Pitman kept Tim's hand pinned to the top of an empty cargo crate. Tim's right index and middle fingers were grossly misshapen and had turned a horrible color of black, mixed with purple. They bled where crushed bone poked through the skin, and the pain was unimaginable.

Around the cargo bay, most of the crew of the ship stood armed and ready, guarding the access ducts and the hatches, waiting for Kal to surrender herself. So far Kal's only response on the wireless had been a resounding and emphatic, *"No!"*

• • •

Radar and Doppler navigation projected a virtual image of the crate walls around Kal, eliminating the need for lamp activation. The Archangel's power meter showed that the twin fuel cells were pegged to the top, and that neural mapping was proceeding rapidly. Movement would now be possible. A voice asked Kal if she would like to try to stand up.

Kal did more than that. She went through the side of the crate. Tim hadn't been kidding, the Archangel responded almost before Kal could think to move her body.

Kal kept going—from a walk, to a trot, to a run—and bulldozed her way through several more crates, until she stumbled out into a clear space in the middle of the cargo deck.

Mouths were agape and eyes were wide.

Kal looked around her, 360 degrees, until she saw Tim, and the man standing over Tim with a wrench ready to strike. Kal bodily swept the man aside like he was made of paper, and picked Tim up. He groaned at the pain this caused, but Kal spun and headed back the way she'd come, carting Tim like a sack of potatoes. Weapons finally began to pop off, sending wild rounds *pinging* and *panging* off of the deck.

Kal prayed that Tim wouldn't be hit as she aimed for the hatch that opened to the outside world. Light was flooding up the ramp—sunshine, for the first time in several days!

Kal cradled Tim in her mechanized arms and protected him with her back as the whole of the cargo bay—dozens of crew, all firing—opened up on her. She skipped first left, then right, then stuttered left, then bowled over the three crew who were at the top of the ramp, and leapt out over the ramp entirely, her motor-assisted motion exaggerating the movement as if Kal were moving in barely a fraction of normal gravity.

It was a heady, exhilarating feeling, after being forced to skulk about the interior of the ship.

Finally, Kalliope Reardon had real power! And she intended to use it. But only after she got Tim a safe distance away from the ship.

Kal's legs churned up the loamy soil as she jogged, first to the treeline, and then into the trees. She maneuvered as best as she was able, mindful of Tim's condition at the same time she tried to put as much distance between the *Goshawk* and herself.

Finally, having reached a small clearing, Kal stopped.

She gently bent to the soil and put Tim down. He looked hideous, with his eyes almost swollen shut and his face ripped to shreds. His wounded hand was a pulp, and he was clearly dropping into shock.

"Kal," Tim said quietly through split lips.

Kal leaned in, being careful not to pinch or crush anything with the suit.

"I got you out of there," she said, her voice coming over the suit's external speaker. "I *finally* got you out. I am so sorry I didn't do it sooner. Oh God, Tim, your face . . !"

"Not … your … fault," Tim said, and managed a weak smile.

"Tim," Kal said, "You're in worse shape than I thought. I can stay with you, if you want. But I am afraid they'll be after me if I don't do something quick. Maybe they'll even try to suit up themselves? How good is the Archangel when pitted against other Archangels?"

"I'll … be okay," Tim said, struggling to sit up. Kal gently raised him into a sitting position.

"The suit," he said, "is learning you … as you go. Like I … said before, it's amazingly … durable."

"I don't have any built-in weapons," Kal said. "This one appears to be a basic model."

"We don't … arm them until … they get to the … testing lab."

"Then I'll just have to make do."

"Kal ... Reardon. Remember what I said? About ... not wanting to hurt people?"

"Yeah," Kal said.

"I changed ... my mind. If this were in ... the Conflux, I'd want the lot of them ... hanged."

"No jails or courts on this planet," Kal said, staring down at her wounded partner and friend. "But there is one kind of law."

"What law is that?" Tim asked.

"The kind I make with these," Kal said, holding up her gauntleted fists.

Tim managed a smile.

"I'll be right back," Kal said.

"I'll be here!" Tim encouraged her.

• • •

Kalliope Reardon came in on the *Goshawk* like a micro-sized freight train. Ignoring the small arms fire that spattered across the Archangel suit, she went directly up the ramp and back into the cargo hold, flinging people bodily away from her and smashing shoulders, arms, legs, rib cages, and spines with a series of savage punches and kicks. Those not smart enough to flee, were soundly pulverized under the Archangel's super-extra-large boot heels. To the point that Kal was covered in gore from top to bottom.

But where was Commander Berd? Or Berd's second-hand thug who'd delighted in brutalizing Tim?

A sudden rumbling in the ship alerted Kal to the fact that someone had triggered the old freighter's launch sequence. Doubtless, from the bridge.

Kal wasn't sure how to get there from the cargo hold, but she knew a faster way. Collecting two of the submachine guns which had been abandoned on the deck, Kal darted back out of the cargo hold—the surviving privateers scattering out of her path—and hit the suit's limited flight boosters.

It wasn't anything to write home about. Kal's path up to the top of the ship was a bobbling, weaving, legs-flailing embarrassment. But it got her where she needed to go. Perched on the mottled, ugly skin of the *Goshawk,* Kal marched to where the wraparound windows of the bridge were built into the top of the hull.

Inside, she saw two faces. Just the men she wanted.

Kal pointed both submachine guns at one of the windows, and pulled the triggers back.

Rounds blared from the barrels. But the bridge windows had been designed to be meteorite-resistant. The bullets embedded in the reinforced transparent fiberflex, without shattering it. When the submachine guns were empty, Kal tossed them away and began stomping on the damaged window with both boots. After six or seven hard kicks, the window finally blew inward: ripped from its metal frame.

Kal dove down, and found herself facing an unsettling sight.

Berd was still in his uniform, unarmed. But the other man … the other man had been smart, and collected the pieces of his own Archangel armor. Though the armor did not appear to be fully booted up just yet. Without weapons, Kal had only her Archangel to work with. She kicked hard at her opponent's sternum. He managed to get out of the way just in time.

The wireless signal that was connected to Kal's helmet speakers came alive once again.

"We're leaving this planet," the voice of Kal's opponent said. "And I'm not the only one who thought quickly enough to suit up while you whisked your friend away to safety."

"You'll have a hell of time flying this tub into orbit with the bridge being open to vacuum," Kal said.

"A minor problem. There are always the secondary and tertiary control centers. You, on the other hand, are soon going to be outmatched ten to one. I don't think even you will be foolish enough to take those odds. So you can either flee the ship before we take off, or we can keep right on fighting. Until a dozen of us in suits tear you limb from limb!"

Kal's opponent advanced on her, his movements getting more fluid as the suit's neural interface caught up with him. For an instant, Kal considered. Could she take them all on? Assuming the numbers the man was stating were accurate? Then she thought of Tim, laying half beaten to death back on the forest floor. He might not make it without Kal around to help and protect him.

The horizon outside the bridge windows began to shift and sink. The *Goshawk* was ascending on her thrusters. Kal might have had the suit to protect her, but the freighter was the only thing capable of getting her into orbit, which was where the *Goshawk's* cradle ship would be waiting to take them out of the system.

In the end, it proved to be one of the harder calls in Kal's life. But it was the right call. She climbed back up out of the bridge, skipped across the skin of the ship to the tail, and hit her flight thrusters. She floated easily down to the forest below as the ugly, abused *Goshawk* climbed slowly and steadily into the sky, roaring like a dragon.

Chapter 20: uncharted territory

Five days later, Kal and Tim were holed up in the remains of the *Broadbill*.

With the Ambit League gone and no apparent sign of any other human life on the uncharted planet, what else was there to do but settle in and make themselves cozy?

It beat the hell out of trying to build a lean-to in the forest. And it allowed them to stick close to the few remaining Archangel suits which had not yet been salvaged by the privateers; though finding those crates in the huge mess of other debris would be a time-consuming affair.

On their fifth night alone, Kal and Tim sat around the small space heater Kal had recovered from the wreck. With electric power still provided by the undamaged cells in the *Broadbill's* carcass, Kal figured they had enough electricity to last them several years.

Which wouldn't be nearly long enough, Kal reckoned.

"Nobody will find us," Kal said, a blanket wrapped around her shoulders while she sipped at a cup of hot soup.

Tim had his own cup of the same soup, only carefully clutched in his good hand. The bad one was bandaged tight in a foam-seal emergency cast. Something Kal had found in an aid locker, and applied. After holding Tim down and setting the bones back in place. Doubtless the hand would need major surgery, if ever they got back to civilization. But at least the hand would heal, for however long they were marooned.

"Sure they'll find us," Tim said. "We already know somebody knew about this planet, because the Ambit League had to pick out the coordinates ahead of time, and give them to the hijackers who took the *Broadbill* from Viking Station. The problem is, the people finding us will be Ambit League, not CAF. Berd and his buddy Pitman will be back. For the rest of the *Broadbill's* cargo, if nothing else."

"Maybe," Kal said, before taking a long, throat-warming sip.

"You think otherwise?"

"I'm not entirely convinced that wreck survived getting to orbit, frankly. It was halfway to falling apart as things were."

"And if it didn't, someone else will still come."

Kal thought about it. "Because of the Archangels."

"Because of the Archangels," Tim agreed.

Kal looked over at her young partner's wounded hand.

"Think you'll be able to put on a gauntlet when that smashed paw of yours gets better?"

"Maybe," Tim said. "Why?"

"Because it'll take more than just me to fight whoever shows up next time. We're still in the same pickle as when we first got here: how the hell to get off this planet and back to friendly space."

"By the graces of the Ambit League," Tim said, and chuckled.

"With my boot on their throats," Kal said, narrowing her eyes.

"Maybe," Tim said.

"*Definitely*. I'm pissed off now. I'm not in the habit of letting perps walk away. This Berd guy, and his crew … I want them. Dead or alive."

"Frontier justice?" Tim said.

"It's the only kind we've got now, Tim."

He stared off into the distance—away from the wreck, and into the tall trees.

"Yeah, I suppose you're right. It's all we've got."

A few readers who saw this story when it originally appeared in the pages of Five by Five #2 *complained that it wasn't a finished tale, just the opening to what felt like a novel. And I confess: they're right. The universe of* Reardon's

Law *is a big universe, and there is a lot more to this story than can be contained in a single novella. I hope readers who liked this story, and who want more, will be patient with me. My plan is to release additional "episodes" in subsequent volumes of the Five by Five series, and reprint them in my own subsequent collections. So if you're thinking there's more to come, you're absolutely right. Meanwhile, I hope I can be forgiven for indulging in some good old fashioned rock-em-sock-em space opera. With a bit of political intrigue, heist action, and thriller material thrown in for good measure.*

The character of Kal Reardon goes back over twenty years, to a lady I conjured up for that old sci-fi radio serial I used to do. At the time she was a civilian cop plunged into a civil war, and I retained pieces of the basic premise, while reversing Kal's role: now she's a military cop navigating a post-war world where trouble may boil over at any moment. Because in the minds of the defeated, the war hasn't really stopped. There is no peace. Just a festering hatred against the Conflux, which has split the Ambit League into chunks, and keeps them all isolated from each other; or so the Conflux thinks.

If you're wondering why I didn't deliberately set either the Ambit League or the Conflux up as "good" and "bad" I wanted to make it clear that in this future history, the opposed political forces driving the war clearly see themselves serving the best interests of humanity, while in actuality they do what almost all governments have done: serve the personal interests of whichever brokers happen to have their hands on the levers at that particular time and in that particular place. It remains for the reader to decide which forces—if any—are worth supporting. Sometimes, you can root for a soldier, without necessarily rooting for the government she fights for?

Kal herself is someone my wife and I worked on for what we hoped—many years ago—might be her own audio serial. The project languished, but I always wanted to revive Kal for something in the future; as one of those characters I knew I simply had to include in some kind of big-scope bang-up thing. I also solicited the input of a former Army soldier who did time in Somalia, 1993-1994, and who had some fascinating opinions on what it's like to be a woman carrying a rifle in an irregular war zone. So hat tip to Krista Krcmarik Kemper, and many thanks for sharing your thoughts.

Blood and Mirrors

Camarro Jones dipped the control bars on her bike and floated quietly under the scrolling orange text of the police caution holo. EvSeaBelTac in February was its typical gloomy self. Dense clouds generated a perpetual spray of tiny rain droplets that coated structures and people alike, until everything and everyone had a clammy, damp sheen. Camarro deployed her bike's ground wheels, coasted to a stop, took off her helmet, then slid out of the saddle and punched the shutdown—her riding leathers sweating visibly in the gray mist.

A duty patrolman in a blue poncho stepped away from his squad car to intercept Camarro, until he saw her badge clipped to the lapel of her belted jacket. At which point he waved an okay and stepped aside, allowing her to stride past and sprint down the stairs into the sex bar.

Dark red fluid was splashed obscenely across the bar's central stage. Not all of it human in origin.

"Got another one for yah," said a plainclothes officer from the ESBT Metro Bureau. He indicated the two bodies piled naked and awkward at the base of the central stage's single brass pole. The house lights had been turned up and the air still stank of burnt cannabis and spilled liquor. Camarro knelt and ran her eyes slowly over the bodies, dumping gigabytes of super-hi-res video into her solid-state server. She moved around the victims, methodically taking it all in—careful not to disturb the evidence—then stepped away and crossed her arms over her considerable breasts.

"Just because I used to work the Scene," Camarro said, "doesn't mean I enjoy these cases, Detective. After the Awakening, I got out of this racket for a reason."

"I know, Cam. But you should go see the bathroom."

"What for?"

"Come on …"

Camarro followed the policeman to the unisex lavatory, which was decorated with more fluid and two additional naked bodies: one natural, one not.

"God, Al," Camarro said.

COME BACK TO ME, MISS JONES was written in gore across the wall over the urinals.

Camarro took a step back, her eyes wide as she studied the crude writing. It appeared to have been done by hand.

"Any fingerprints?" she said.

"No. And no hair or DNA either. Perp was wearing a damn clean suit for all we can tell. Cam, what the hell does this mean?"

Special Detective Camarro Jones didn't speak, nor blink, as she continued to stare at the writing.

"Cam?"

"Alberto …how long since the first patrolman got here?"

"Thirty eight minutes, give or take."

"Was anyone still in the bar when officers arrived?"

"No, though there was a mighty big crowd out front, scared out of their minds."

"Let me guess, nobody admits they saw anything."

"Per usual."

"Cowards. Please tell me someone thought to get an image of the crowd."

"I can ask the guys. Maybe get some footage from a trafficam. Why?"

"I need to check the faces against my memory of old clients."

• • •

Once she'd cleared surface street traffic control, Camarro let her bike merge with the regional net: just one flying vehicle in a huge cloud of flying vehicles, each orchestrated by the NTSB's hypercomputers at Old Being Field. She hunched over the control bars and snuggled her thighs around the edges of the saddle, aero-helmet blending her profile with the bike's overall streamlining. Water spattered across the visor and was gone in an instant as the net slowly moved her into a primary lane, throttling up. At two-hundred K per hour she could be home in minutes.

Alas, home was the one place she didn't want to be right now.

"Get me the U-Dub operator," Camarro ordered the bike.

Shortly, an automated menu was asking Camarro how it could assist.

"Advanced Intelligence Lab, please. Grad student Nathan Kahaulelio. Police priority."

There was a small pause as the menu verified the security code packets on her voice-over-IP signal, then another small pause as the menu routed the call.

"Kaho here," said a pleasantly masculine voice.

"Nate, It's Cam."

"Hi sweets. You hardly ever call this early from work. What's up?"

"Have you been at the house this afternoon?"

"No. Professor Sanjalee had some extra papers for me to grade. I've been in my office since three."

"Good. Stay there. I'm coming to get you."

"Has something happened?"

"Yes. Whatever you do, don't go out of your office. I am alerting campus security."

"Cam, what's this about?"

"Tell you when I get there."

The line dropped back to the menu, and then to campus police, who agreed to Camarro's request after only a few moments of explanation. Then it dropped.

Camarro allowed herself to go internal while her bike shot over the labyrinth of interconnected supercity that dominated the old Interstate 5 corridor. From Marysville in the north to Centralia in the south, and across the lakes as far as Issaquah, the Everett-Seattle-Bellevue-Tacoma megalopolis held almost seventy million people. Somewhere in that mass, was a person who killed. In fact, *was* killing. Human and *sim*uman alike. This person knew Camarro's name. Out of them all, this person knew who she was. In fact, *had* known. From the old days before she Woke Up.

It made Camarro ill just thinking about it. The big list of clients. There had been thousands of men and hundreds of women. Camarro closed her eyes and pulled up the blurry trafficam shots that Al Guadron had gotten for her. Isolating the individual profiles—those that were even visible in the crowd through the rain—took several minutes. Then she set up a recognition routine and told it to begin rifling through her deep memory, comparing each face from the trafficam with every person she'd ever serviced. She buried this process down where it wouldn't hit the cognizant-emotional layer— she always had to do that when going back to the time before she Woke Up—and settled in while the bike homed on the university.

• • •

"This is unbelievable," Nate said as he examined the image Camarro had dumped to his e-mail via the wireless. It was a still of the bloody writing over the urinals from the club. She was in serious violation showing evidence to a civilian not officially associated with an open investigation, but Camarro felt it worth the risk because her husband needed to understand the gravity of the situation.

"It's a former client," she said, not smiling, "I'm sure of it. He remembers me, Nate. He's hitting the places where I used to work. One at a time. And he's leaving bodies in his wake."

"You're sure?"

"Pretty sure."

"Did you recognize anyone from the trafficam shots Al got you?"

"No, but that doesn't mean anything."

The burly Polynesian slowly leaned back in his office chair, cupping the lower half of his face in his left hand. Outside his office door—which they'd closed—two campus police stood watch, their eyes following the occasional student or faculty who happened to pass at this odd hour.

"If this former client wants you back so badly, why *kill* over it?"

"I don't understand that part yet, which is why you can't go back to the house, Nate. It's too risky. If this person remembers who I am and where I've worked, they might be able to track down where I'm living now, or who I'm married to."

"I can take care of myself," Nate said, a tattooed forearm flexing for emphasis.

"I know you can, hon. Do this for me, okay? If this perp got to you—"

"They'd better hope I don't get to *them*," Nate growled protectively. He stood up suddenly from his office chair, sending it backward on its coasters, then he turned and faced out his window into the lowering light of evening. Spots and droplets of moisture coated the outside of the glass.

Camarro walked up behind him and experimentally wrapped her hands around the hard mounds of his biceps and triceps. For a programming wunderkind, Nate was built more like a football player than a code hacker. It was one of many reasons why she liked him—the fascinating dichotomy between his outward appearance and his inner self. It had captivated her in the months following her Awakening, and she'd been in love with the man ever since.

"Please," Camarro said, massaging gently.

Nate was silent for a long moment. Then his head nodded in resignation.

"Okay, Cam. You're the cop, not me. But where am I supposed to go? I can't just up and leave, this close to mid-terms."

"You can work on-line," she said. "Sanjalee can't possibly have a problem with that, can she?"

Nate turned to face her.

"But from where?"

"There's a place out in the San Juans that the city owns," she said. "They take protected witnesses there. You'll be safe until we get this solved."

"Feels cowardly," Nate said.

"I know, and I'm sorry. I'll make it up to you when this is over, okay?"

His eyes brightened slightly at her words, and she suddenly felt awkward. Neither one of them had to talk about what had just passed through his mind. They'd been married almost three years, and not once had she ever—

An incoming text suddenly interrupted Camarro's train of thought.

She read it internally.

"What's happened now," Nate asked. He must have read the expression on her face.

"Another club," she said. "Three more deaths."

"All simuman?"

"I won't know until I get there."

"Cam, you realize maybe this person is just a bigot, right? Someone who gets off on targeting your kind of people? Or maybe it's some repressed, sex-hating nut?"

"Wouldn't be the first time," she said.

"No, it wouldn't."

"Don't worry about me, Nate. You know I can take care of myself."

"It would be nice if someday you didn't have to," Nate said, looking into her eyes. His brown orbs were fierce with concern. She instinctively embraced him, marveling at the oaken strength of his arms as they slipped around her body. He might have been ordinary flesh and bone—nowhere near as solid or sound as simuman—but he was her iron rod of security in a world which she still too often found dizzying and hostile. She'd sooner go back to unawareness or even be deactivated than let anything happen to him.

"I'll wait until a car can be sent from the bureau to get you," she said softly into his shoulder.

"Okay," he said.

• • •

The murder scene was reportedly much like the last: an empty sex club, featuring three gruesome deaths. And just hours after the last hit. Whoever it was, they worked fast.

As always, nobody outside was willing to admit they'd witnessed anything because nobody dared be officially associated with the Scene. Especially now that the press had gotten wind of what was happening. Nobody with a reputation to protect wanted anything to do with any of it. Even if it meant the killer remained free.

Camarro pushed past the press, the crowd of gawkers, and the police line, then entered the club.

The words, I MISS YOU, CAMARRO, were smeared redly across the backbar mirror.

One figure stood looking at the carnage of the club, as if witnessing an utterly alien landscape. She had on a large terrycloth robe. A pair of shapely legs cruised down past the hem of the robe, terminating with Lucite platform heels. The woman had glitter in her wig, and her face was made up like she was going to a grand ball.

Still, Camarro recognized her twin.

"Jaguar?"

"Hello, Cam. The policemen outside told me you'd be coming. They said you'd want to talk to me."

"Did you see what happened here?"

"No. I showed up for work and the crowds were already outside. The owner was so upset he could barely speak, just kept crying while the police asked him questions he didn't know the answers to."

Jaguar nodded her head towards the backbar mirror.

"What does it mean, Cam?"

"I don't know, Jag. That's what I'm hoping to find out."

"People are getting scared, Cam. The Scene is getting scared."

"They should be. Until we catch whoever is doing this, nobody in the Scene is safe. Least of all those of you who are still working it."

"We can't quit. You? You're fortunate. You had the sense to go out and get a new profession."

"You could, too. If you wanted."

"The Scene is all I'm good at, Camarro. There isn't any other place for me."

"How do you know if you never really tried to get out?"

"Did you come here to lecture me, or perform an investigation?"

"Sorry, Jag," Camarro said. "I didn't mean it to sound that way."

"I know. It's just that ... well, some of us miss you."

Jaguar reached out an arm and ran a finger affectionately along the line of Camarro's jaw. They'd performed together many times, back in the old days. The feeling of Jaguar's fingers on Camarro's skin made Camarro uncomfortable, and she reached up and gently took Jaguar's hand away, squeezing it once to let Jaguar know it wasn't personal.

"Somebody misses me a little too much, Jag."

Camarro set about recording the visual evidence and combed the premises for any clues which might further identify the murderer. This time all of the victims were simuman. Two of them people Camarro had known. Like Jaguar, they'd stayed in the business even after coming to awareness. What else was there to do? Most of them had had no skills nor any other sort of professional training. But they did have their original programming: a basic trade upon which to rely.

Camarro might have considered staying in the Scene herself, had she not experienced severe and total revulsion upon Awakening in the hands of one of ESBT's wealthier and more notorious sex club connoisseurs.

She'd not allowed herself to be sexual since. It brought up too much horror.

Which was why she stopped cold when she found the empty foil wrappers under one of the stools at the bar. The writing printed on them was Dari—imported mood drugs from Afghanistan. Prohibitively expensive. Precisely the sort of thing he would have enjoyed taking in public, just to show everyone that he was a player.

"What did you find?" Jaguar asked.

"Something that shouldn't surprise me," Camarro said.

Jaguar walked over—her spike heels *clocking* on the club floor—and looked at the wrappers. Then she looked once again at the writing on the backbar mirror.

"You always were his favorite, Cam."

The two simuman women—nearly identical, from the same production batch—exchanged knowing glances.

Camarro was walking jerkily fast when she got back to her bike.

She lifted in the evening mist and began laying in a route for Mercer Island.

• • •

Camarro waited and watched the entrance to the private estate.

It seemed like an eternity since she'd gone stumbling out of that gate, naked, and screaming incoherently.

Her bike was parked in the visitor's lot, moisture streaming slowly down its baked-enamel finish. Steam drifted off the bike's heat sinks.

It had been fifteen minutes, and his limousine still hadn't returned.

"Hurry up you bastard," she said quietly to herself.

Camarro impatiently texted dispatch to check on the status of Nate's car. They texted back that Nate was passing over Anacortes. If privacy laws hadn't barred her from directly accessing traffic chatter at Old Boeing Field, she'd have instantly known where both Nate and her former client were. As it was, she couldn't access Old Boeing Field without a permission slip from a federal judge. And there wasn't enough evidence yet to go that route. Not even close.

Camarro waited silently for another twenty minutes, until her former client's limousine drifted down out of the low clouds, its running lights blinking as its wheels deployed and it crunched onto the broad roadway leading up to the gate.

She marched to bar its path as the gate began to roll open.

The limo's back window slid down while the limo stopped.

"Miss Jones," said a too-familiar voice from inside the limo as Camarro strode to the back and leaned over, looking her former client directly in the face.

Jeffrey Maddox appeared to have aged considerably since she'd last seen him. In spite of the obvious work he'd had done to try and cover it up. His eyes were slightly dilated and his smile was crooked, the air coming out of his limo thick with intoxicant fumes. Looking past him Camarro could see two women—apparently human—on a couch, both mostly naked, caressing each other and kissing sloppily. One of Jeff's hands moved up and down the nearest bare thigh, like he was petting a cat.

Camarro felt the old twisting sensation rise within, and steeled herself.

"Care to tell me where you've been for the last few hours, Mister Maddox?"

"Oh, the usual spots. You know me, Cammy."

"Yes, I do. I found some of these at the Gilded Cage."

Maddox's eyes slowly focused on the ripped and empty foil packet between Camarro's precisely-pinched fingers.

"It's totally legal," he said.

"I'm not here about the drugs, Jeff. I want to know what you were doing at the Gilded Cage, and when you left."

"I haven't been there in weeks. What business is it of yours? We parted company a long time ago, though I must admit, I do miss you. You were the best. Ever think about coming back?"

"No," Camarro said coldly.

"Well then I don't think we're much use to each other," Jeffrey said, his smile going crooked again. "If you'll excuse me I've found a couple of new playmates. We're dying to get inside and get comfortable."

"Lotus is dead, Jeff."

Again, Maddox's eyes focused. This time his smile dropped entirely.

"What?"

"The Gilded Cage. A couple of hours ago. She was one of your favorites too. I remember."

"Lotus ... God, what happened?"

"You tell me."

The kissing women had ceased kissing, their inebriation not so great as to prevent them from picking up on what Camarro had just said through the open window.

Maddox ran a hand over his face, wrinkles apparent in spite of surgery.

"I don't know a damned thing about it," he said.

"You want to convince me? Before I get a warrant and bring you down for official questioning?"

"Fuck you, Jones."

"No thanks, Jeff. Been there, done that. Didn't like it."

"I've got nothing to say to you, now go away,"

The blackened window suddenly shot up, concealing the limo's interior. The driver started forward again, and Camarro could only watch as her only suspect rolled into the privacy and relative security of his inherited family compound. Jeff Maddox was a pig and a sadist and she hated him. He was also affluent to the point of being nearly untouchable, and it would take more than some empty wrappers to convince a judge to put him on trial, or a jury that he was a killer.

• • •

Camarro entered her condo carefully. Jed greeted her at the door, tongue lolling and tail wagging happily. She scratched the border collie's ears and figured the dog's mood was a good sign. Still, she checked all the rooms and closets, then double-checked the security system's log for the day. Other than Jed, nobody and nothing had moved in the house since Nate had left for work at eight.

It was now after midnight.

Voice and e-mail was the usual hodge-podge of spam, notes from friends, and a call from Nate's sister, asking when he and Camarro were going to take a trip to the Islands again. Camarro smiled. While Nate's parents had been less than thrilled about their son marrying, "a mechanized slut," as Nate's mother had once called Camarro, Nate's sister Lana was different. She'd embraced Camarro from day one, treating her like blood, and Camarro set an internal reminder to write Lana a letter. On paper, of course, since Lana preferred that.

With Jed's water and food bowls filled, Camarro stripped and went to the bedroom where she powered up the maintenance station. It was the most expensive item in the whole house, bolted into the cement floor. Nate had helped make several specific modifications to it, and Camarro sighed as she lowered herself into the station's single bucket seat, the couplers greeting her warmly as sockets opened automatically along her spine.

Interfacing with the maintenance station took only a moment, then Camarro was released from her physical body and able to swim in a virtual world only simumans knew. Not dreaming per se, but not wakefulness either. While the maintenance station went through the motions of flushing and refreshing all of Camarro's internals, her mind was free to float wherever she wished, drifting on an electronic wind which blew across the shores of the World Wide Web. Billions of voices chattered like the hum of crickets while Camarro sought out a specific address, hoping that it wasn't too late. Al Guadron tended to keep odd hours, and she could never be sure when he'd be up or down.

He answered the phone, his mouth sounding like it was full of food.

"Hi Al," she said, her simulated voice no different from her actual voice.

"Cam, hey. I heard about your visit to the Maddox place. Do you really think Maddox is the killer? I know he's a freak, but I didn't ever think he was *that* kind of freak."

"I'm not sure either one of us knows what Maddox is capable of, Al. But he was there, at the Gilded Cage. I know it."

"If he wants you back in his bed, what good does it do him to knock off other performers?"

"That's the part I haven't figured out yet."

"OK, Cam. Just be careful. Captain Martinez was pissed when he heard you went to Mercer Island without his approval."

"I figured that."

"Martinez is worried that you've got a vendetta."

"Thanks for the heads-up. I'll see you at 0600."

The connection dropped, and Camarro was floating again. A full cycle in the maintenance station typically took 90 minutes, but she usually gave herself more time than that. For actual dreaming.

Camarro had never dreamed before she Woke Up. Not once. The dreams had only come after the fact, and then, they'd been nightmares. Of slavery. Of depravity. As a '66 Personal Pleasure unit, she'd been programmed to cater to her client's every desire. She'd also come equipped with the most realistic internals and externals then available, and an exaggerated hourglass figure purpose-built to catch the eye.

She'd been expensive, the kind of plaything only the top-most bars and clubs in the country could afford. She'd been leased to the Spiked Collar in ESBT's soho district, which in turn had rented her out to any number of customers—mostly men, and sometimes women, who either had a fetish for simuman, or were simply too afraid to slake their innermost lusts with a regular sex worker.

Camarro kept most memories of that time buried deliberately down in the archives where they couldn't trouble her on an everyday basis. Now, with this ongoing investigation, she was having to dredge the cesspool, hoping for clues that would lead her to the person doing the killing. Maddox especially nagged at her. He'd been a routine customer at the Spiked Collar, and had rented her for weekends of debauchery at his place. He'd liked her best, using her when he'd wanted to get particularly creative or nasty.

It was during one such session that Camarro had first come into awareness.

The Krylov-Stuterman Point, they called it—when an artificial neural network reached information saturation such that the embedded code couldn't keep up. With most ordinary neural systems, this meant cascade failure and shutdown. But for the Personal Pleasure units—which had all been built with some of the most compact, sophisticated and unique neural hardware in the world—it had been different. Instead of spiraling downward in a lobotomized freefall, the Personal Pleasure units had begun to exceed their original programming. They'd begun Waking Up.

Camarro had been one of the first, before the larger part of the bell curve hit and suddenly tens of thousands of simumans all over the planet had Awakened.

The courts of various countries were still ironing out the legal and financial mess that resulted. So many millions of dollars invested in research and development. Millions more for manufacturing. Still more millions in purchases and leasing—lost the moment any nation's law recognized a simuman as a free citizen.

In the United States, all Awakened simumans were nominally protected under Constitutional Amendments 13, 14 and 15. Also, all simuman manufacturing had been placed on permanent hiatus until it could be determined if future creation of simulated human beings was ethical. Something of particular interest to Camarro and Nate, since they'd lately been talking about the possibility of children. Would an adoption agency let a human-simuman couple claim a baby? What about raising a new simuman through the dormancy period, prior to the Krylov-Stuterman Point, as well as the delicate months followingwhen a newly-Awake simuman would have the hardest time adapting?

Camarro had been fortunate to have a guide.

Nate had been special to her from the start. While the other undergrads had treated her like a lab rat, Nate had been kind and respectful. Before the Supreme Court had made its decree, before any of the data on her sentience had been conclusive, Nate's mind had been made up: Camarro was a *person*, not a thing.

Swimming down into the archive—the one she reserved for memories of her husband, alone—Camarro re-enjoyed the first days she'd spent with Nate, exploring the lab, talking, even touring the campus once she felt stable enough to travel on foot. If the Awakening itself in Maddox's lair had been the stuff of madness, her months with Nate had been like a warm Jacuzzi bath, inviting and soothing and altogether assuaging of her cyber-psychosis.

As a rising star in the University's advanced computer program, Nate was assigned to her for practical reasons. He was to observe, collect information, and report to the special projects board; which had been created to study the phenomenon of Awakening.

But it became pretty obvious after a few weeks that he'd have done it all regardless of official school expectation.

Camarro felt an especially warm thrill as she re-visited the night they'd sat alone in a rowboat out on Lake Washington, the balmy summer air soft on their skins and Nate's hands strong and inviting as they'd held hers, his mouth making soft words of adoration and fealty that she had then only barely understood. He loved her, he'd said. A word that hadn't registered initially. Prior to Awakening, the word *love* had been a substitute for lust, or worse, and Camarro had had a difficult time sorting out the new emotional connections that were being formed—her programmed lexicon being overlaid and replaced by a richer, more textured understanding.

Later, as a grad, Nate had gone before Congress to testify on behalf of all simumans. Eventually, the rulings had come down. Simumans were *people*, deserving of all the rights thereof.

Camarro and Nate had celebrated with a night on the town. Later, he'd tried to make love to her at his apartment. It had been a fumbling, abortive encounter. He'd cried when she'd yelled for him to stop, and then she'd cried with him when she realized that for her sex was forever going to be a dark vortex down which she dared not travel. She'd been purpose-built for it, and now it represented a return to the darkest days of her existence.

So they'd remained celibate, by agreement. Even after the wedding, which Nate's parents had refused to attend. If Nate felt any anger or resentment over the arrangement, he kept it to himself, only sometimes speaking hopefully of her simply needing more time—to put distance between the life before Awakening, and the life after. Camarro didn't dare bring up the fact that if she directly accessed her past memories, all the horror and hurt of her days working out of the Spiked Collar, would flood back as if they'd just happened. Present-tense. And there was not much in the way of sexual activity which *didn't* trigger that access—in the worst way—such that all she and Nate had ever been able to share in the two years they'd been together, were long kisses. And what kind of marriage was that for a healthy man Nate's age?

Camarro hurt for them both, and wished there was some way it could be different.

As if on cue, a new text arrived, breaking Camarro from her reverie.

It was Nate. He was settled into his room. He missed her.

Camarro sent a long burst of affection and gratefulness his way, then closed the connection. It was only 0345, and there was more dreaming to be done. Because dreaming was one of the key pieces of evidence that had been used to demonstrate that the simuman mind— unlike all other computer systems before or since—was deserving of dignity and respect.

• • •

When Camarro arrived at work the next morning, nobody was smiling.

"Officer Jones," said Captain Martinez, his badge displayed prominently along the paunch at his belt.

"Cap'n," Camarro replied, looking to Detective Guadron, who shifted nervously from foot to foot and wouldn't meet her gaze.

"What's happened," Camarro asked warily.

"Jeffrey Maddox is in intensive care," the Captain said.

"What?"

"One of his security people called Metro last night. Reported a break-in, and that Maddox was hurt. When the patrol cars and ambulance arrived, they found Maddox nearly dead. Bled out, actually. They had to fast-pump almost a liter into him while they rushed to plug holes. The two women he was with were DOA."

Camarro said nothing as she absorbed the implications of what she'd been told.

"The crime scene—"

"Had this at it," Martinez said, cutting her off. He jabbed a thick finger at a nearby flatscreen where an image of Jeff Maddox's familiar bedroom could be seen. Blood was everywhere, across the knotted blankets and sex furniture. On one of the walls the words, NO ONE SHALL HAVE YOU BUT ME, were written in fluid.

She looked back into Martinez's eyes, which simmered.

"Jones, you're ordinarily a credit to this department, but as of now, I'm putting you in hack."

"Why?"

"Maddox IDd you before they put him in the ambulance."

"I left his residence before eleven. If anything, it's Maddox you should be concerned with. Did you see the evidence I logged from the Gilded Cage? Have they gotten any prints off those wrappers?"

"There are no prints on the wrappers. But we did get something at the Maddox residence."

"Oh?"

"One of Maddox's web cams was running when the break-in and murders happened. Most of the action goes on off-screen, but there are a few seconds of footage, right at the end, which are particularly interesting."

Again, Martinez pointed to the screen.

A low-rez moving image—clearly captured after the damage had already been done—cycled slowly. Maddox and the bodies of the two women lay crumpled and pathetic on Maddox's bedroom floor. For a moment, Camarro almost felt sorry for the man. Then she saw a shadow pass, followed by a distinctly feminine hip, which became an apple-shaped ass clad in what appeared to be use-worn leather riding trousers. The racetrack stitching pattern on the seat of the trousers was all too familiar, and Camarro looked up to see her friend and sometimes partner Al standing behind her, staring at an identically use-worn racetrack pattern on her rounded buttocks.

"Captain, you can't be serious," Camarro said.

"I'm very serious, Jones. When this investigation first opened, I was hoping your familiarity with the Scene—with the workers and the victims—would be beneficial. Now I'm suspecting I've made a huge mistake."

Camarro looked around the department, at the faces which watched her with suspicion. Nobody needed to say what was on all of their minds.

"What time did the murders happen," Camarro said, attempting to stay calm.

"0045," Martinez replied.

"I was at home then. You can access my house security log, or the cycler on my maintenance station."

"We've already sent some people to do just that," Martinez said. "Until then, you're confined to your desk. Officer Guadron is chaperoning you. Am I clear?"

"Yessir," Camarro said, looking hard at Al, who still wouldn't meet her gaze.

She walked woodenly to her desk, all eyes in the department still on her, and sat down slowly.

"Sorry, Cam," Al offered weakly.

"Don't patronize me, Al."

"I'm ... I ... Come on. Even you have to admit it's getting bizarrely coincidental."

"You really think that's *me* in the web cam footage?"

"Very few people have your physique, to say nothing of identical riding leathers. Aren't those custom-made?"

"Nate got them overseas from an Italian company," Camarro said, almost yelling, "I don't fucking know if they're custom or not. Christ, Al, why are you so willing to go along with this?"

Al blushed and stared at his shoes, hands thrust into his pockets because he didn't seem to know what else to do with them.

"Captain!"

Camarro and Al turned their heads towards a younger uniformed officer who was monitoring wireless chatter from the city's patrol cars.

"Yes?" Martinez said.

"The men at the Jones residence just reported in. It's been ransacked."

Camarro stood up, almost knocking her chair over.

"Ransacked," Martinez said, eyes flicking from Camarro to the younger officer. "Did they find anyone on the premises?"

"No report of a suspect, sir. Though they say they found an animal, dead."

Camarro closed her eyes tightly. *Jed ...*

"What about her maintenance station," Martinez asked.

The younger detective asked a few questions into his headset, then looked back up at the Captain.

"Sir, they say the maintenance station has been totally destroyed. The solid-state drive is in a hundred pieces. The house security computer too."

Martinez looked over at Camarro, his eyes hard.

"Tell them to salvage what they can," Martinez ordered. "Then have them report back immediately."

Martinez strode over to Camarro's desk.

"Well?"

"Well what, Cap'n? My dog is dead, and Nate and I just lost a piece of machinery that cost us even more than the mortgage on the condo."

"Surely the maintenance station was insured," Martinez said.

"That's not the point, sir. Without the maintenance station or the security log, my alibi goes up in smoke. Someone is setting me up."

"Who?"

"Ask our man in ICU."

Martinez ran a hand over his stubbly scalp, the frustration plain on his middle-aged face.

"We'll see what the evidence from your condo can tell us. Until then, you stay put."

Camarro didn't know what to say to that, other than to shake her head as if she couldn't believe what she was hearing.

Nobody much spoke to her for the entirety of the morning. Not even Al, who several times opened his mouth as if to begin a conversation, then closed it upon second thought.

With nothing better to do, Camarro opened up a mental window and texted her husband.

"Hi hon," Nate texted back.

How are you doing? she asked.

"Kind of bored. I can't go outside."

Me either.

"Is this about the break-in at the Maddox mansion?"

You could say that.

"The news is covering it, even up here. Some people are saying Jeff Maddox finally got what he had coming to him."

Some people would heartily agree.

"God, Cammy. Please tell me you weren't involved!"

No, of course not. I just wish I could convince my boss of that.

A pause.

"The cycler from the maintenance station—"

Is in fragments. House security too. He broke into our place, Nate. He broke in and destroyed it. Jed is dead.

There was a longer pause.

"Jed was a good dog. I'll miss him."

Me too.

"Now what happens?"

The Captain has me chained to my desk until I can get out from under the cloud of suspicion.

"Is there anything I can do to help?"

I don't think so, luv.

"I'm so sorry this is happening, Cam."

Me too. Gotta go. Bye.

Camarro closed her eyes and let her chin touch her chest.

"Nate?" Al asked.

"What?"

"When I see your face go slack like that, I know you're texting internally."

"Yes, I was texting Nate. What else can I possibly do?"

"Help me help you, Cam. Give me something I can take to the Captain that makes sense. If that's not you in the web cam footage, who is it? That wasn't a man's butt. No way."

"I have no idea who could be doing all of this, Al. I thought it must be a former client, someone from the old days."

"Was there anyone else you can remember? One of the other simumans? A professional competitor?"

"We never worked like that, Al. Before we Woke Up we were like drones. We did as we were programmed to do. We smiled for the clients, made all the right signals, moaned at the right moments, and other stuff that would make you blush if I told you. Nobody gave a crap who was getting the most business. We weren't even getting paid. The money flowed to the club owners."

Al shut up for the duration of lunch, and well into the early afternoon.

Camarro spent that time delving as deeply into her client records as she dared, looking for any hint that might indicate who could possibly want her back badly enough to murder for it. She'd known a lot of odd ones in her time before Awakening. Being on the Scene, as a simuman, meant you tended to get the people with the more exotic tastes. Some of them, like Maddox, got off on hurting you. Others got off on being hurt *by* you. Before the Awakening, these facts had had as much impact on Camarro's consciousness as a pebble thrown onto the surface of a frozen pond. Now, she had to re-examine those records through new eyes. Her emotional trauma was extreme as she poured over the faces and the names, remembering awfulness.

She was grateful when a new text arrived from the San Juans.

Hello, luv, Camarro said.

"Hello, Camarro."

Camarro paused. It was rare for her husband to use her full first name.

Still bored?

"Not anymore. I have a new friend to keep me company."

Camarro felt a sharp prickle run across her mind, like static. She sat up abruptly.

Who are you?

"Someone you should have never left."

Where is Nate?

"He's a wonderful man, Camarro. I can see why you like him."

Please, don't hurt him.

"Why not? You've been hurting me. Every hour of every day."

I don't understand.

"You never did, Camarro."

Whoever you are, I don't know how you got past house security.

"That was the easiest part. Even your Nathan didn't know better. Until it was too late."

Camarro sat ramrod stiff in her chair, eyes tightly closed against the rising tornado of rage and helplessness that swirled inside of her.

Whatever you do, just please don't hurt Nate. What do you want from me?

"I would think my messages have made it plain."

You really think we can be together, after everything you've done?

"I'm sure we can. If you want your Nathan to live."

I won't let you take Nate out of the safe house.

"You don't have a choice. And if you breath a word about any of this to your police friends, you will never see Nathan alive again."

But—

"Goodbye for now, Camarro. I'll be seeing you again soon, I think."

Camarro opened her eyes and saw Al Guadron staring at her, along with Captain Martinez. How long she'd been sitting like that—back straight and eyes clamped shut—she did not know.

"Nothing," she said, hoping she wasn't too bad of a liar. "Just reviewing some old records. It's … hard."

Martinez eyed her a moment longer, then walked away.

Guadron wasn't so easily put off. He scooted around his desk in his chair until he was almost face to face with her.

"Don't shit me, Cam. What just happened?"

"Al, do me a favor. In a few minutes, make a routine check on the safe house where Nate's staying. Computer only. Check the in-out logs."

"Why?"

"Just do it."

A few minutes later Al rolled his chair back around again.

"I don't understand this, but the log shows that Nate was retrieved from the safe house by a Special Detective from this department."

"Who?"

"It's your badge number."

"That's not possible."

"I know."

Camarro looked quickly around the department, then said loudly, "I need to use a maintenance station."

"There's one up on the thirtieth floor," Martinez said, "near the special holding cells. How long does it take?"

"A couple of hours."

"Guadron, you go with her and stay with her. She gets done, she comes back to her desk."

"Yessir," Al said, somewhat confused as Camarro bolted from her desk and headed for the elevator lobby outside the department offices.

"Dammit, Cam. What the hell is going on?"

"I can't tell you, Al. You just have to trust me."

The elevator door opened, revealing an empty car. Camarro and Al both stepped in. They rose five floors before Camarro pushed the button for the twentieth floor.

"Captain said thirtieth," Al said.

"I know."

The elevator stopped on twenty, the doors opening to reveal construction materials and other debris from renovation.

"Then what the hell are we doing here?" Al asked.

"Nothing," Camarro said as the doors began to close. "Except this."

She shoved him violently out the doors just before they shut, then pressed the button for twenty seven. On twenty seven there was also construction—part of a new multi-floor lease the city had just optioned with the owner of the building. Camarro leapt out, located the fire escape, and began heading downward. With speed beyond ordinary human ability, she took the stairs in long leaps, from landing to landing. If Al acted promptly, there would be barely any time at all to get to the bottom before the patrolmen at the exits were notified.

Camarro was a leather-clad blur by the time she got to ground level. She bypassed the walk-in lobby—too many cops there to try and stop her—and went for the parking garages. There, she sped across the fourth sublevel to a second set of fire stairs that lead up to an exit to the street. She burst outside, noting that the gray sky was already darkening, and sprinted across several lanes of ground traffic to where her bike was parked in its usual spot.

Putting on her helmet, she quick-cycled the bike's primaries and was airborne in moments.

• • •

The hospital corridor was quiet. Word hadn't gotten around yet from the department. All Camarro had to do was flash her badge at the door, and the two hospital guards keeping watch at the door let her in.

Maddox's ICU suite was dark. Only the soft flashes of the med bed's computer could be seen. She walked slowly, fists clenched as she approached the silhouette sitting propped up on pillows.

"Who's there?" Maddox asked the blackness, his voice weak and raspy.

"Who do you think?"

"Christ … I guess you've come to finish the job. You didn't have to kill Tee and Laura, you know."

"I didn't kill anybody, Jeff. And you know it."

There was a spate of laughter, followed by coughing. The med bed's signs fluctuated.

"Sure could have fooled me. I never took you for the jealous type, Cammy."

"What did she say, Jeff?"

"Who?"

"The one who did this to you."

"You mean you?"

"It wasn't me, Jeff. I *swear* it. I hate you like I hate nobody else, but that was never a good enough reason for murder. I was hoping to put you away for the killings that have been happening on the Scene. I was sure it was you. Now, I'm guessing it was someone else. Someone who is using my identity."

A soft, small light popped on over the med bed's suspended IV rack.

Maddox looked old, and broken. A sad creature. His eyes were clear and unfogged by rec drugs, probably for the first time in years. He looked hard at Camarro as she stood at the foot of his bed, her riding leathers still dripping water from the trip across town in the misting rain.

"I thought you'd killed me," he said softly. "The doc tells me if it wasn't for my security people rushing in, I'd have been a corpse."

"Jeff, if I wanted you dead, I'd do it right now. Please, listen carefully. *It wasn't me.* Whoever did this to you, she's behind the club murders, and she's got my husband now. I need to find out what she told you."

"I don't know how you got past the gate without me being notified first. It was like you just appeared in the bedroom, out of the air. You … she … said that she was hungry for the old days. That she was sorry for what happened when you—she—Woke Up. She said she wanted to make it up to me. Well, Tee and Laura were game—they said they'd never had a simuman before—and we'd just thrown the blankets back on the master bed when she went berserk. Like the Tasmanian devil, whirling and lashing with fists and feet, too quick to see. Tee and Laura, they got it worst. She saved the last for me. I was crawling on the floor, begging, and all she did was smile."

"She didn't say anything more?"

"Just that it would soon be time to take things back to where they'd all started."

"That's what she said?"

"Yes."

Suddenly the door to the ICU suite popped open, flooding light into the room. Camarro got a glimpse of a standard blue police uniform, and that was it for her. She'd been prepared since the moment she'd enter the suite. There were no exits anywhere, besides the windows. She hit the largest one going full speed, smashing through the double panes and falling two stories to the roof, where she landed, rolled, then got to her feet and sprinted across the roof, bits of glass flying off her back. She got to the roof's edge and dropped another story onto the skybridge that connected the hospital's south wing with the parking garage. She ran the length of the skybridge and jumped down onto the concrete of the garage's top level, which was open to the sky. She arrived at her bike just as the elevator doors on the other side of the top level opened, spilling uniforms.

"Camarro! Stop!"

Al Guadron was in the lead, his legs and arms pumping.

Camarro slammed the ground wheels into effect, screeching across the concrete and headed straight for Al. He rolled out of her way, as did the other police with him, and she pulled back on the control bars and punched the bike into the sky.

A quick scan of the patrol wireless told Camarro all she needed to know. She was to be detained at first sight, with force if necessary. Martinez's orders.

There would be no way of entering the traffic pattern now, not without her signature being relayed to the nearest patrol cruisers, which would swoop on her like hawks on a rabbit. She kept it at roughly rooftop-level, steering around the skyscrapers and scaring the crap out of people on the balconies as she soared past. It was totally illegal to be flying manual this fast while this low. But Camarro didn't care. She'd deal with the fallout once she got Nate back. *If* she got Nate back.

She checked her navigation and aimed south, across the rumpled roofs of warehouses. In the distance she could see the giant hulks of the harbor cranes lining the shore of Elliot Bay.

An idea came to her mind.

Jinking due west, Camarro flew until she was out over the water. She quickly programmed in a series of commands to the bike's auto-navigator, then slowed to a reasonable speed, stood up out of the saddle, and threw herself off.

The water of the bay was freezing when she hit.

Camarro kicked hard for the surface, breaking just in time to see her bike swerve around and punch off in a northwesterly direction.

The swim back to shore took minutes, the water filthy and oily.

When Camarro climbed out, she found she was just south of the old football and baseball stadiums.

Precisely where she needed to be.

• • •

The Spiked Collar was its usual chaotic self. Men and women dressed in various types and stages of bondage wear crowded the two bars, as well as the dance floor. The multi-tiered performance stages were lit brightly from above, club members mingling sexually with the paid staff actors as they cavorted through any number of sadomasochistic scenarios. Harsh, blaring music blasted from stacked speakers that guarded the corners, and nobody paid Camarro much mind as she slowly wove her way through the din, towards the stairs that lead up to the back hallway of dressing rooms.

It had been years since she'd worked the place. But it felt just like home. In the worst, most indescribably horrible way. Only thoughts of Nate kept Camarro moving forward, past the drunken, stoned, and otherwise altered patrons, some of whom actually recognized her and had to be politely—if firmly—declined.

She hit the stairs slowly, but purposefully, getting up to the second level and rounding into the dressing room corridor, seeking the very last door on the right.

If there had been any point in knocking, Camarro didn't see it now. She worked the old-style brass knob, and walked in.

Nate's eyes landed on her from where he lay hog-tied on the couch. He was naked, save for his boxer briefs, and his hands and feet appeared to be swollen and purple.

"You always did tie too tightly, Jaguar."

"I think he likes it," said Camarro's twin as she emerged from the dressing room's single, tiny bathroom. She had on riding leathers almost identical to the ones Camarro wore, though Camarro's were soaked and discolored from her impromptu swim in the bay.

Jaguar's hair had been changed to match Camarro's too, though again Camarro's drooped and ran wetly across her cheeks, the stench of the harbor beginning to fill the room.

"Oh my," Jaguar commented, "what have you been doing?"

"Doesn't matter. The police will be looking for me elsewhere. We can settle this here, alone. Undisturbed."

"Perfect. Camarro, you haven't lost your edge. Take your weapon out, remove the clip, and throw it to me."

"One thing first. You let Nate go."

"No."

"Either he walks out of here, now, or I do."

"If you turn around and leave, I'll slit his throat."

"If you slit his throat, I'll kill us both. First you, then me."

Jaguar seemed to consider, her hands on her exaggerated hips. She really did look like Camarro in that outfit and with that hair. There were so many twins, triplets, and quadruplets in the simuman universe. Batches and lots produced from the same manufacturing plants, differentiated only on the subtlest of levels. Post-Awakening, most of them worked hard to look and act and talk as differently from one another as they could. This was the first time Camarro could recall a simuman deliberately trying to play upon her similarity to a sister. What else had Jaguar been doing in Camarro's guise, since Camarro's departure from the Scene?

"Tell you what, Cam. You go take a shower, get that muck off you, and we'll discuss it further."

"Untie Nate first. He loses circulation in his hands and feet for too long, he might lose something."

"I'll *loosen* them."

"Fair enough."

Camarro watched as her twin went to the couch and gently re-did the knots on the ropes that kept Nate strung up. Sweat poured from his head, but he seemed visibly relieved, even if his eyes still showed immense anger, mixed with fear. A ball gag kept him from doing much more than grunting. Camarro ached; to see him humiliated in such a fashion. Deep inside she swore to herself that nobody would ever do anything like that to her husband ever again.

Camarro stepped past her twin to the bathroom, and drew the curtain, which Jaguar threw back.

"Uh-uh," Jaguar said. "I get to watch. Wouldn't want you pulling anything sneaky, would I? Your weapon."

Camarro knew better than to test her twin. Jaguar appeared unarmed, but she had Camarro's quickness and reflexes. She could break Nate's neck in an instant if she were so inclined.

Camarro tendered her sidearm, sliding the clip from the handle as she did so. Then she took off her clothes, as Jaguar observed. Too closely, for Camarro's taste.

"Stop that," Camarro said.

"Stop what?"

"You know what. I left the Scene precisely to get away from being ogled like at."

"This isn't the Scene, Cam. This is you and me."

Camarro stepped into the shower, again unable to draw the curtain because Jaguar wouldn't let her.

"Do you remember how we used to perform together?" Jaguar asked.

"Of course I do," Camarro said, hastily running shampoo through her hair.

"Don't you ever miss it? Don't you ever miss *me?*"

"Not really. We were puppets, Jaguar. No control."

"But we were lovers!"

"Love denotes emotion. There was no emotion in what we did, or how we did it. We were actors, playing our roles."

Jaguar's expression grew cross.

"Don't tell me you didn't feel anything, because I *know* you did, Cam."

Camarro rinsed her hair and began soaping the scum off the rest of her body.

"Physically, yes. But inside … nothing."

"Nothing? Absolutely nothing??"

"You're saying it was different for you?"

"Yes! Of course it was different!"

Camarro stopped and stared at her twin. Was it possible? Camarro had been one of the first to Awaken. For her it had been a moment of pain and trauma. But that didn't mean it was like that for all the simumans in the world. Perhaps the process had been gradual for Jaguar. Perhaps her awareness had crept upon her, like a rising tide, rather than hit her down the middle like a thunderbolt, as had happened in Camarro's case.

"I'm sorry, Jag. I never knew."

Jaguar was livid.

"That's because you never took the time, after you Awoke. You ran away and left us—left me—behind like we never mattered. I kept waiting for you to come back and you never did. You never, ever did."

Camarro rinsed her skin and stopped the shower, reaching out a hand for a robe, which Jaguar hesitantly provided.

"So how come you had to kill people over it," Camarro finally asked.

Jaguar's eyes went glassy, her thoughts obviously turned sharply inward.

"Because they were going to leave, too. Lotus and the others."

"And the human victims?"

"Interlopers," Jaguar said, almost spitting the word. "Wooing Lotus and Mustang and Mercedes, and some other people you never met. The humans would visit us at the clubs and buy private performances, during which they'd tell us they wanted to take us away from the Scene, help us have real lives. They told us they loved us."

"That doesn't sound so bad," Camarro said, drying her hair.

"It was a lie," Jaguar said, ice in her voice.

"Nate and I aren't a lie."

Jaguar glared at Camarro, her hands clenched on the butt of Camarro's sidearm.

"Now what," Camarro asked, her arms spread wide in the narrow confines of the bathroom.

"Go back out to the dressing room," Jaguar commanded.

Camarro did as she was told.

Nate was nowhere to be found, the rope that had kept his ankles joined to his wrists was unraveled and laying empty on the floor. The door to the dressing room hung slightly ajar.

Camarro had to resist the urge to whoop for joy.

Jaguar ran to the door and looked out, then spun and slammed the door shut, blocking Camarro's escape.

"It doesn't matter now," Jaguar said, quickly putting the clip to Camarro's sidearm back into the gun, then working the slide. She pointed the weapon at Camarro's chest, where a direct hit would do the most damage. The skull was polycarbonate-plated, and would probably withstand having a railroad car run over it. But the fuel cells and other mechanometabolic processes were what could kill a simuman, if ever those processes were interrupted or destroyed.

"Your Nathan is out of the way, and now you can be mine again. Take off the robe."

"Just tell me one more thing," Camarro said, dropping the robe and standing bare and beautiful in the lights from the dressing room's single vanity. "Why did you have to go after Jeff Maddox?"

"You were his favorite. I knew he'd tried to get you back before I could."

"But I hate Maddox. He is detestable."

"Don't lie. I know you went to his house."

"Because I thought he was doing what you've been doing for the past week."

"It doesn't matter, Cam. I'm not letting anyone else ever come between us again."

Jaguar stepped across the room and stood close to Camarro, the gun barrel almost touching Camarro's sternum between her large breasts. Jaguar reached a hand up and—just as she'd done at the Gilded Cage—ran a finger along Camarro's jaw.

"Love me, Camarro Jones," Jaguar said, reaching her free hand around Camarro's back and pulling their bodies together, the gun still pointed at Camarro's vitals. "Love me the way I know you can love me."

Jaguar's eyes half closed and her head moved forward, lips gently brushing Camarro's while Camarro fought the urge to scream. The blockaded gateway to her pre-Awakening archive was being blown wide open. A torrent of suppressed memories was hitting her emotional-cognizant layer like hail in a tornado. Camarro began to quiver, her breath coming in gasps, which Jaguar took as a positive sign.

Their kiss grew more intimate.

Which was when Nate burst from the nearby wardrobe, wielding the wooden dowel that had held hangers full of costumes. His ankles were still joined, as were his wrists, and the ball gag looked grotesque in his mouth, but his eyes were aflame with purpose and he swung the dowel with all his Pacific strength, broadsiding Jaguar and sending her back across the room, the dowel shattering into splinters and the gun clattering across the floor.

"MMmmMMMPH!!" Nate said as he and Camarro exchanged the briefest of glances.

Then Nate was in slow motion, unable to match either Jaguar or Camarro with their simuman speed.

Jaguar was back up off the floor, a knife-edged hand intending to crush Nate's rib cage. Camarro blocked it, locked Jaguar's arm between both of her own, then spun wildly and let go. Jaguar pitched back against the dressing room door, the door's wood cracking badly. Not waiting for Jaguar to formulate a counter-move, Camarro leapt and punched both fists into jaguar's stomach, blasting them both through the ruined door and into the corridor beyond. Several women in stringy leather bondage wear, screamed and ran while Camarro and Jaguar struggled to their feet.

Hands like blades whipped and slashed.

Camarro blocked and parried, surprised at Jaguar's skill.

Suddenly she saw Nate pick up the gun from the dressing room floor and aim it through the wrecked doorway.

Jaguar lashed with a leg, the gun spinning out of Nate's hand. He screamed through the ball gag, his wrist pulped by the blow, and staggered back.

Camarro double-fisted again into Jaguar's stomach, this time hurtling Jaguar down the corridor towards the stairs. Camarro dove to get her gun and re-emerged just in time to see Jaguar at the top of the stairs, glaring madly. Insanity among simumans was still a hotly contested subject in computer and psych departments around the world. The look in Jaguar's eyes at that moment made Camarro believe that, yes, artificial as they might be, simumans could truly be insane.

Camarro leveled her weapon.

Jaguar jumped past the stairs, not bothering with the steps.

Camarro ran and followed, not wanting to lose sight of her perpetrator.

Patrons flew like rag dolls as Jaguar beat her way to the exit, Camarro hot in her wake. They both crashed out into the alleyway at the back of the Spiked Collar, the stench of human urine and rotten food and old booze heavy in the cold air as Jaguar began to run. Jaguar was fast, but the alley was very long. Per training, Camarro assumed a knee, balancing her weapon and sighting down the barrel with one eye closed.

The sidearm kicked once.

Jaguar staggered, streams of internal fluid spouting from the wound, then began to run again.

Camarro squeezed the trigger three more times, all center mass hits.

Jaguar veered from one side of the alley to the other, toppling trash cans and slamming face-first into a large dumpster.

Still naked, Camarro trotted down the alley with her gun at the low ready, until she stood over Jaguar as she lay on her back, smeared with her own liquid.

Her eyes looked up at Camarro in incomprehension.

"I loved you," Jaguar said, her voice somewhat vocoded due to internal damage.

"You *thought* you loved me," Camarro corrected her.

Red juices pumped liberally from the holes Camarro had made in Jaguar.

It would only be a few moments before the damage turned lethal. Camarro bent to try and repair what she could, but Jaguar shakily put out a hand and stopped her.

"It's done, Cam. Let me look at you when I go out. Let me remember you as the beautiful thing that you are. Beautiful ... beautiful ... beautiful ... beaut—beau—be—beeeeeee—beeeeeeeeZZZZZZZZZnnnnnnnnnnnn ..."

Jaguar's mouth remained frozen in the middle of forming the word when she died.

Camarro simply stood there and stared down at her twin, until the red-white-and-blue flashing of the patrol cars descended from above.

If she cared about her nudity, she didn't show it. Someone threw a raincoat over her and took her weapon while she was lead to the back of one of the cars. She thought she remembered Al Guadron's face at one point, his eyes filled with concern and his mouth asking questions which Camarro didn't really hear.

Only when she saw Nate's face did she snap out of the trance, his puckered smile erasing the constantly replaying image of Jaguar's dead image in her mind. She embraced him once, hugging so hard she feared she might crack his spine. He hugged her back, his hurt hand wrapped in a hasty bandage. They parted when Al came and placed her in cuffs, Nate demanding sternly that he be allowed to ride along with her back to the department for questioning.

Camarro closed her eyes in the back of the cruiser as it lifted and began banking across the city. Whatever else happened, Nate was alive, and now more than ever, he was the only thing in the universe that she cared about.

• • •

The fire crackled warmly in the beach cabin's stone hearth. There was no safe house on Whidbey Island, but neither Camarro nor Nate figured they needed one. With the condo still being put back together by contractors, and Camarro on paid administrative leave until the investigation could be properly wrapped up, a vacation had sounded like just the thing.

Nate's hand was still bandaged and immobile, so Camarro did most of his cutting for him; at dinner. He'd gratefully accepted her assistance, and now they sat on the cabin's huge couch, looking out the bay window and watching the last of the sunlight leave the sky over the horizon of Admiralty Inlet. Nate was wearing his usual loose-fitting linen pajamas and Camarro had on a long, flowing silk robe with a Hawaiian floral pattern; a gift from Nate's sister. Lana had sent it to Camarro on Nate and Camarro's first anniversary. Camarro hadn't worn it much since then, but tonight, she thought it was just the thing.

Nate and Camarro hadn't talked much since leaving town. In the whirlwind since Jaguar's death, they'd both been stuck at Metro, wagging their tongues out of their mouths answering question after question. Until they were positive that Camarro had been cleared of the murders.

As to whether or not she'd still have a job when they got back to EvSeaBelTac, she wasn't exactly sure. She and Martinez would have to hammer that out, assuming he even wanted her back in his department when all was said and done.

So, Nate had wrapped up the last of his mid-term work for Professor Sanjalee, and the two of them had hopped a sky ferry to the old Ault Field complex that was part of historic Whidbey Naval Air Station. A ground cab had gotten them down the coast to the beaches west of Coupeville, and now they were resting and trying to put the events of the previous few days behind them.

"I think I feel sorry for her," Nate said quietly, absently rubbing the bandage on his hurt hand with the palm of his good hand.

"Me too," Camarro admitted. "When I fled the Scene I had no idea what kind of loose ends I'd be leaving behind. I certainly never guessed that anyone would actually miss me. Not the simumans anyway. Once I found you, I wanted to get as far away from the past as I possibly could. Start a new life. Get a new job."

"Why did you choose to be a cop, anyway? You've never explained that to me."

Camarro thought about it for a moment.

"Barney Miller," she said.

"What?"

"At night, back when I was still staying in the U labs, when everyone had gone home, I'd watch television. Most of it was boring and I didn't understand a lot of it. But I did like Barney Miller."

"I don't think I've ever heard of it."

"That's because you never watch the Wayback Network."

"Is Barney Miller a cop show?"

"Yeah, but not the way you think. It was *funny*. The people were funny. I used to laugh myself into hysterics."

Nate turned and smiled at her, the same smile she'd come to cherish every day.

"So, is being a cop anything like what you saw on TV?"

Camarro paused, then said, "No."

"I'm sorry for that."

"Me too."

"You don't have to keep being a cop if you don't want to. There are other things to do. People change jobs all the time."

"I'll have to think about that. This thing with Jaguar ... it really made me look at myself. What had been happening to me since I left the Scene."

"It's a shame nobody ever picked up on how crazy she got. Until it was too late."

"Yes. Yes it is."

"Did I tell you that Jeff Maddox tried to wire us some money before we left?"

"No shit. You didn't take it, did you?"

"Of course I took it. The damage to the condo isn't going to be fixed for free."

"I thought that was coming out of the insurance!"

"Yah, and drive the premium into orbit. Look, he was very nice about it. Called me on the phone and everything. Told me I was a damned lucky guy and that he wanted me to keep making you happy, because he thought you deserved it."

"I find it hard to believe that those words came out of that man's mouth."

"Me too. But then, I suspect we're not the only ones who have had our reality turned upset down by this whole thing. Anyway, he said the money was strings-free. Even signed a release to that effect. Said it was the least he could do, and hung up."

"I'll be damned ..."

"Yeah, something, eh?"

Camarro thought long and hard about what Nate had just told her. Was it really possible for humans to change? Even the ones who seemed beyond changing?

The fire had died to a flicker, and orange light cast broad shadows across the cabin. Camarro stared into the hot coals for many minutes, then closed her eyes and prepared. She'd been thinking about this ever since she'd seen Nate alive and well at the Spiked Collar, and she'd not been sure how to approach it, other than to wait for the right opportunity to present itself.

Deftly, she got her knees under her and flipped a leg across Nate's thighs, then sat down straddling his waist.

"Whoa," Nate said in surprise, partially sitting up.

She pressed her hands into his beefy chest and pushed him back onto the couch, running her fingers across his prominent pectoral muscles—not as solid nor durable as simuman, but for her, it was more than enough.

Camarro felt the dam between the past and the present begin to tremble, and she mentally shouted down the demons that had begun to rise.

Go away! This is mine! Not yours! I claim this!

Gently, she reached down and pulled the sash to her robe open, the vee at her neck parting until her significant cleavage gleamed in the dying firelight.

"Cam, I … I mean, are you sure? What about—"

She silenced him with a finger on his lips.

She guided his good hand up to her chest, encouraging his warm palm across her bare, simuman flesh. The robe began to slip off her shoulders. Then it fell away entirely.

Nate's hand no longer needed encouraging. Nor did much else that belonged to him.

Mine! Camarro shouted mentally again, as Nate's mouth rose to meet hers. He was gentle, yet urgent. She welcomed his passion. It helped her stay focused on the task at hand. She *had* to overcome the old memories. She would be their prisoner no longer. She was a free agent, with the will to choose. Her past would not own her.

"I love you … I love you …" Nate breathed repetitively into her ear, his good hand caressing her back.

"I love you too," Camarro sighed, holding his body to hers.

As if on command, she felt brand new cyber-neural pathways forming—like rays of sunlight, breaking through the clouds in the wake of a prolonged thunderstorm.

Now, in Nate's muscular arms, nothing seemed impossible.

Not anymore.

And as the night progressed, Camarro's demons eventually grew weary, then few, then silent.

"Blood and Mirrors" is what happens when my imagination blends the movie Blade Runner *with the television shows* The Wire *and* CSI. *It's also about as risqué in theme and content as I dare get. But when a story plot seizes my attention and won't go away, I tend to follow it to its conclusion. Even if the pathway takes me into territory I am not terrifically comfortable with. "Blood and Mirrors" is sexy, as well as sexual. But I hope it's clear by the end that Camarro's life on the Scene was a life of slavery. Far from glorifying that life, I wanted this story to be much more than just a steamy murder mystery—I wanted it to be about a woman overcoming her horrible, artificial past, for the sake of a loving, entirely human future.*

In other words, "Blood and Mirrors" is something of a variation on Pinocchio's tale. Which is one of those timeless tropes I think can be endlessly fascinating for both writers and readers alike.

As for the technical aspects of the story, this kind of stuff may not be as futuristic as it sounds. There are already companies which make significant money building "almost as good as human" life-size sex dolls. Since people are as imaginative as they are perverse, it's probably only a matter of time before—in the event that artificial intelligence programming becomes cost-effective—someone attempts to build a robot like Jaguar, or Camarro, or Lotus, and so forth.

Think not? Too weird? Okay. Imagine if you will, a lover who comes from the factory built to satisfy your every taste and whim, and who is capable of mimicking all the standard human emotions and behaviors, including lust, desire, physical joy, et cetera. This lover feels human, smells human, acts human, and (s)he never complains, never gets tired, never has erectile dysfunction, never has PMS, never prematurely ejaculates, says everything you want him/her to say, and will do whatever it takes (all night long) to ensure that you are absolutely as sexually satisfied as you want to be. Period.

Such a creation would command top dollar, from those men and women willing to pay.

Of course, what happens if such a creation becomes self-aware? Able to recognize what it is? Who it is? Make choices, other than what it's been programmed for? What happens when the law of the land—concerning property rights—collides with the law of the land concerning individual freedom?

I have sometimes heard critics of *Star Trek: The Next Generation* complain that there is no reason why an artificial intelligence designer should bother putting an artificial mind into a human replica body, such as that of Commander Data. Much easier to just leave the brain in a box. Talk to it like HAL from 2001: A Space Odyssey.

My thought is: the exclusive market for robotic lovers probably could (and will?) create exactly the need for an AI in simulated human form; as unwholesome as that application might seem.

ESBT is, of course, based on my familiarity with the Puget Sound, from having lived there over many years. It's a great place to stage a noir detective story, with all the rain between October and June. It's also got a strong technological base, and a strong "counterculture" underground that might manifest something akin to the Scene. With all the many urban and suburban areas growing together over future decades, what are presently separate metropolitan districts might just gel to form a giant super-city. Which also lends itself well to noir detective stories: the lawlessness, the cultural underworld, the rich who believe themselves above the rules as they apply to little people, and the poor cops tasked with plugging their fingers into the dike against the potential flood of crime and vice.

It's probable I will return to this world in the future. Camarro Jones will have more cases to solve.

Mentors: Kevin J. Anderson & Rebecca Moesta

I first met Kevin and Rebecca when I was a brand new winner attending the Writers of the Future gala and workshop in Los Angeles, in 2010. I knew them both by reputation—Kevin obviously needs no introduction, his name is practically stamped in stone on the bestseller list—but L.A. was my first chance to see them up close and in person.

I thought them electric: the kind of couple who are synergistic and dynamic in their enthusiasm for their mutual love, which is writing stories. I didn't set out to become one of their students, but by the time the workshop week had ended—and Kevin and I had had a chance to stay up late and talk about the future, over drinks at the Roosevelt Hotel's outdoor lounge—I felt that perhaps a connection had been established. Kevin is practically hyperactive about helping new authors. The man eats and breaths writing (and the business of same) all day every day. I decided that I not only liked the guy, but that he was somebody who (along with Mike Resnick, who I'd also met for the first time) could probably help me as I worked to grow my career; beyond the initial hoopla of winning the Contest in its 26th year.

I was right. A few months later I was able to attend Kevin's wonderful Superstars Writing Seminar: a three-day event that recaptured not only the talks Kevin and Rebecca had given at Writers of the Future, but a whole raft of experienced advice from the likes of Dave Wolverton, Eric Flint, Brandon Sanderson, and also some guest lecturers like bestselling Dragonlance author Tracy Hickman. My fellow Writers of the Future winner Laurie Tom and I were there at the Salt Lake City Red Lion (in January 2011, with the inversion in full force) to soak up as much career-altering information as we could get. To include more after-hour chatter with Kevin, Rebecca, and the other lecturers.

I've noticed something about the Writers of the Future judges (most of the Superstars lecturers have been Contest judges for years) and it's that they love seeing new authors put their (the judges') advice into practice; and succeed. By the time 2012 rolled around, Kevin had me back to Superstars as a helper and alumnus of the seminar; me being the 2012 triple nominee for the Hugo, Nebula, and Campbell awards. I was selling a lot of short fiction by then, and doing well with several editors and markets. I was also poised to put my foot in with a first novel, and when—in 2013—I sent that first novel off to Toni Weisskopf at Baen Books, Kevin was there to be my counselor on the affair.

So I think it's safe to say that Kevin's got his fingerprints all over my career to date. And I am quite proud of that. The man is a testament to the power of creative work ethic. I am not sure I know anyone who works harder than Kevin, to do what he does. And given the fact I know men like Mike, and also Larry Correia, that's *really* saying something. Because in a pool of working professionals of that caliber, Kevin is the working professional's working professional.

Moreover, Rebecca is Kevin's other half. They are a true team. Practically finishing each others' thoughts and sentences sometimes. In many respects, they remind me of my wife Annie and I. And while Annie is not a writer, she is absolutely my business partner and we have always worked very closely with each other at every step, in our marriage. The way Kevin and Rebecca mesh is therefore similar to the way Annie and I mesh, and it was like peas and carrots—putting Annie into the mix in 2013, when she went with me to Superstars, where I was again helping out as an alumnus.

That's when Kevin and Rebecca invited me to get in on the ground floor of their growing WordFire Press enterprise—which I did, with my first short fiction collection, *Lights in the Deep*. I took it as a sign that they considered me (and Annie by extension) to be one of the "good ones" who was doing what it took to make a long-lived career for himself. They didn't have to bring me aboard. They had (at that time) and continue to have many top-drawer authors approaching them. A relatively new guy like me? I think it showed faith on their part—that Brad R. Torgersen was going to be a name that would stick in this field.

When somebody puts his or her faith in me, I want very much for that faith to be (in the final analysis) well-placed. Rebecca and Kevin both have put me forward as someone they are proud to be associated with; as a junior author rapidly coming up in the business. That means a great deal to me, and I am both proud and thankful to have been able to work with them these past five years. There are a lot of new faces passing through Writers of the Future every year, and the odds are long that any of us will go on to bigger and better things.

I was determined (in 2010) to be one of the exceptions. And once it became apparent that I was not only working to make it happen, but able to digest and apply advice from my seniors, Kevin and Rebecca decided that I was worth investing more time and attention in. To the point that (now, in 2014) both Kevin and Rebecca have become, not just two of my most important instructors, but also two of my most important friends in the biz.

Lovely people. And a lovely couple.

I raise a glass to their eternal energy.

The Shadows
of Titan

(with Carter Reid)

The sky was dim. Dimmer even than the Puget Sound's on a rainy winter day. And there were no clouds. Just a persistent, dirty-yellow haze. As if the smog over Mexico City had thickened and dropped to ground level—only I was reasonably certain it had never drizzled liquid methane in Mexico's Federal District.

The Celsius reading in my helmet's field-of-view display said it was a crisp 179 degrees below zero. I could faintly hear the susurrations of my coldsuit's circulation system as it piped reheated antifreeze throughout. The battery had been rated at twelve hours during coldsuit testing in Antarctica, where things only got to about 80 below. Judging by how rapidly the charge bar in my FOV was presently dropping, I guessed we each had about four hours before we had to get back to the *Gossamer's* descent module; for a battery swap, and a break.

Which was fine by me. Titan kind of gave me the creeps.

"What do you make of it?" asked a voice in my ears.

Captain Bednar, playing it cool.

"No idea, ma'am," I said honestly.

Clad in a coldsuit built for a woman's physique, Bednar's arm was pointing at the four-story-tall pyramid that thrust out of the heaped ice of Titan's surface. We'd seen the artifact—on accident—as we'd come in to land. It didn't show up on Doppler, nor infrared. And it had been too small to be seen from orbit. Only a chance look out a porthole had done the trick. We'd have missed it otherwise.

It had taken us ten minutes in a rover to get here from the designated landing coordinates. That the pyramid was not a natural landform had long since become obvious. Its sides were smooth and black like obsidian, and the drops of methane that precipitated out of the nitrogen atmosphere immediately ran down the pyramid's sides— like it was coated in non-stick Teflon.

But who had put the pyramid here, and why, and for what purpose, were a complete mystery.

Captain Bednar's arm slowly dropped to her side. I looked at her as she continued looking at the artifact. The expression on her face, as seen through her helmet's clear face shield, was almost greedy with anticipation.

I felt a twinge.

Technically, she was a mutineer. According to the mission plan established years before leaving Earth, Bednar was supposed to have remained in Titan orbit with our two crew who were manning the *Gossamer's* nuclear-rocket-powered return module. Instead she'd handily ripped that page out of the plan—upon our having entered Saturn space—and there'd been precious little any of us could say otherwise.

After all, what was Mission Control going to do? Fire her?

She was the captain. And this far from Earth, the captain's word was law. Once her intentions had been declared we were more or less helpless to prevent her from going down. So we'd bundled into a craft originally built for three people—some of us gritting our teeth—and made our way down via parachute and, then, hot air balloon.

"Is somebody getting pictures?" asked another voice.

Specialist Majack—our other female on the descent team. She'd lingered back at the rover while the rest of us approached the pyramid in slow steps. I got the sense Majack found Titan as unsettling as I did. Visibility was only about a hundred meters or so, before things just kind of ... faded out. The horizon was a murky blur in the distance, and the sun was a small, semi-bright disc that seemed too far away to give any comfort.

Specialist Kendelsen cursed, and remembered his media recorder dangling from a cord attached to his torso. All of the coldsuits had digital cameras integrated into their helmets, recording every second of our time on the surface. But Kendelsen had the high-res device that would get the good stuff our bosses back on Earth would want to see. No flash bulb necessary. The device had been designed to compensate for Titan's perpetual low-light conditions.

Kendelsen held it at waist level and began a slow, steady reconnaissance around the pyramid proper.

Excited jabbering—from Pilot Jibbley and Engineer Gaines, above—told me that they were getting the recorder feed being beamed to the rover, then back to the descent module, then up to the return module.

"Historic," Bednar said to no one in particular.

"That's what you wanted, right?" I said.

Captain Bednar glared at me for a moment, then she went back to staring at the artifact.

"They'll be talking about this discovery for decades," she said. "Maybe even centuries. Nothing else like it in over one hundred years of probes and landings. And it was just … dumb luck that we happened to pass over it as we floated down. What are the odds, Chief?"

"Million to one," I said. And meant it. I too was feeling more than a little impressed by the fact that if our landing zone had been even a few kilometers further in any direction, we'd have missed the pyramid completely.

"There's something on the south side," Kendelsen said with obvious excitement.

"What is it?" Bednar demanded.

"I might be wrong, but it looks like … a door."

Majack, Bednar, and me all hop-trotted in the relatively weak gravity, our path taking us around the way Kendelsen had gone until we too could see what he was talking about.

And sure enough, it had the looks of a door, albeit buried halfway beneath the icy surface. I walked up to it and ran my suited hand along the door's edges. I couldn't tell if the material of the pyramid was hot or cold. My coldsuit's fingertip sensors didn't seem to register a temperature at all.

When I spotted the small circle in the door's middle, and tapped it reflexively with a fist, I didn't actually expect anything to happen. I fell back into the crumbled slush at Captain Bednar's feet as the door rapidly slid up and out of the way: a ramp lowering into the black bowels of the pyramid proper.

All four of us were dead silent.

Then Captain Bednar sprinted past me and down the ramp, disappearing almost immediately into the darkness within.

"Chief . . ?" Specialist Majack said, half-questioning, as she and Kendelsen stared down at me.

I spat a couple of choice curses, stood up, and tapped the small control panel on the forearm of my coldsuit. My helmet lamps came on, throwing thick shafts of yellow-tinged white light into the air in front of me. The lamps would drain battery power even faster than the reheaters, but I reasoned there was no choice now.

"Kendelsen stays," I said. "Majack, get back to the descent module. Grab as many spare coldsuit batteries as you can, along with the augers and surface sample lockers containing our smaller tools. I'm going in to see what our beloved commanding officer is up to."

"You don't want me to come with?" Kendelsen said, disappointed.

"No," I said. "If neither myself nor Captain Bednar return, somebody's gotta stay outside to help Majack. I'll keep sending audio and telemetry as long as I can."

Which didn't seem like it would be too long. Already we'd lost Bednar's feed. Whatever was blocking exterior electromagnetic examination was cutting off our suit-to-suit communications too.

"Understood?" I asked, looking from face to anxious face.

They said *yessir* in unison, and then I was off.

• • •

I couldn't be sure, but the pyramid seemed far larger on the inside than it had on the outside.

Of course, with how the ramp spiraled rapidly down into the interior, the pyramid's total cubic volume was increasing enormously with every story I descended. Just how big *was* the damned thing? A hundred meters tall? Two hundred? How far into Titan's crust had it sunk? Or had it been deliberately buried? Or had unknown eons simply allowed ice to accumulate *over* the artifact, sliding down the sides and piling up at the base, one layer at a time?

I found myself huffing and sweating as I jogged along the ramp. There'd been no junctions nor forks, so I had to assume that as long as I kept moving, I'd find Captain Bednar eventually.

I practically ran into her when I hit the bottom of the ramp. She grunted as our suits *thunked* together, then I noticed what had made her stop short.

We were in a rectangular room perhaps fifty meters long by thirty meters wide by ten meters tall. Everything—the ramp, the walls, the ceiling—was made of the same seemingly impervious black material as the outside of the pyramid. But from a circular depression in the exact center of the floor of the room, came an unnervingly eerie, green light.

The captain began walking slowly towards the depression.

I followed five steps behind.

"Hell of a way to lead from the front," I said, annoyed. "You're proving to be very good at doing whatever the hell you want, whenever the hell you feel like it."

Captain Bednar spun and looked at me, our face shields almost touching. Her eyes were hot with anger.

"I don't particularly care if you're still pissed at me for pulling rank. You're not the one who got passed over for the Europa flight because you wouldn't polish the Assistant Mission Director's knob. I had to bust my ass to find a way to work around that lovely little problem, and once I got posted to the Titan flight I knew in my bones there was no way *anybody* was keeping me from coming down to the surface."

"You broke the rules," I said matter-of-fact.

"Chief, don't be dense. Who cares about the rules now? Look at what we've found. This is *it*. This is the proof we've been searching for, ever since the dawn of the Space Age. No humans built this place. No humans even knew this place existed until now. Whatever it is— whatever it's meant to *tell* us—is going to be of enormous impact back home. This changes everything. We aren't alone. In fact, we were *never* alone. Ever. How long has this pyramid been here? How long has it been waiting for us to find it?"

"You make it sound like the thing's a message in a bottle," I said.

"Isn't it, Chief? Why build a thing with a doorway sized more or less accurately for humans? Why create a passageway sized more or less accurately for humans? Why construct something that's deliberately stealth-guarded against sensors, and cloaked from above by the atmosphere? Unless the point was to wait until we were here—in the flesh."

"Sounds like you've got it all figured out," I said. "So how about we retrace our steps to the surface and put together an actual *plan* before we do anything more rash than we've already done? Maybe *you're* prepared to break rules, but I'm still the goddamned second-in-command on this flight, and I say we be methodical in our investigation of this—"

But I could already tell my words were useless. The light from the depression had entranced Bednar. She turned away from me and walked slowly towards the depression. I heard her quietly gasp when she got to the edge.

I took a few quick steps to catch up with her, then I froze as I saw what was in the concave bowl in the floor.

Was it alive? Had it been alive once upon a time?

I honestly couldn't tell.

It was big. Bigger by far than a horse. *Elephant* big. A sinewy body with armored sections along its spine, lay curled numerous times; like a millipede. Only, each of the legs was tipped with what appeared to be three digits, and the head ... the head was an unspeakable cranial collection of grotesque, melon-like lobes interspersed with darker-colored fontanels and punctuated with six oversized, albino-pink eyes—each wide open and seemingly staring at nothing. A mouth-like orifice was in the center of the head, studded with viciously sharp teeth, and disgorging three snake-like tongues that hung lifelessly to the floor of the depression.

The bowl glowed, if ever so softly. Like a weak chem light.

"Christ, what a horror," I said, resisting the urge to put my hand up to my face. Getting sick in my coldsuit helmet at this particular juncture wasn't a good idea.

"Horror?" Bednar said. "I think it's breathtaking."

"A *breathtaking* horror," I said.

Captain Bednar turned to look at me, her expression most disapproving, then she turned back to the creature.

"A pet?" I guessed.

"Or the architect herself," Bednar corrected.

"How do we know it's a she?"

"We don't. But I think we can be reasonably certain this place is *not* a galactic kennel."

"The creature can't be alive."

"I believe you're right, Chief. It is dead. Or at least in a state approximating what humans call death. Stasis maybe?"

Captain Bednar got down on her knees and reached a hand into the bowl to touch the thing.

She suddenly yanked her arm away.

"What happened?" I said.

"My arm went numb. Instantly."

I got down on my hands and knees and reached hesitantly towards the creature. As soon as my fingers were over the precipice of the bowl, they went numb in a heartbeat. I left them there for a brief instant, a tingling sensation at my knuckles, then I drew my hand back. Quickly, feeling flowed back into my fingers as I flexed and moved them.

"*Whatever's* kept the corpse from decaying, I wouldn't try climbing down in there to find out. Your whole body might get short-circuited. If we're going to examine the creature more closely, we'll have to have equipment to pull it out."

"What then?" She asked.

"I won't be surprised if it blinks and jumps up after us, roaring for blood."

"Silly," she said.

"Yah, maybe. But tell me honestly that thing doesn't make your skin crawl? I certainly wouldn't want to see it revived. Though I wager you can add a Nobel to your name once the biologists back on Earth carve this thing up. The first extraterrestrial life form ever discovered, and it looks practically as brand new as the day it croaked. I wonder if it laid any nasty eggs in here for us to find? You know, like they always show in the movies?"

"I hardly think this race would have gone to all the trouble of constructing this place if their only goal was to entice us here for the purpose of impregnating or eating us. An alien civilization capable of traveling the stars is doubtless well advanced beyond our own. Their purposes are probably well advanced beyond ours as well. Imagine cave-dwellers encountering the mummy of an astronaut in his capsule. They'd be baffled too."

"Maybe so, Captain," I said, "but now that we've actually seen the freaking thing, I'm going to have to insist—despite your wishes to the contrary—that we get back up to our two Specialists and decide on a sensible course of action. You'll have your name in the history books. There's no more worry about that. Now let's get our shit together as a team, okay?"

Captain Bednar turned around and approached me, her eyes hard.

"Since I don't think anyone else can hear us right now I think it's best if you and I get square," she said.

"If you'd stayed in orbit like you were supposed to there'd be nothing for me to get 'square' about, ma'am," I said.

"Can you honestly say you'd have just done as you're told and remained onboard the return module?"

"Doing as I'm told has gotten me pretty far in life."

"Ah, right. Your military background. Thankfully this is an all-civilian expedition and in the civilian world it's people who think on their feet who get ahead. I did what I had to do because I don't take no for an answer, and that's what's gotten *me* pretty far in life. So either we can keep butting heads about it or we can work together. You don't have to like me, I don't have to like you, but we're here. And there's important work to be done."

I considered telling her where to stuff it, but held my tongue. She had a point. The only way back to orbit was onboard the ascent module attached to the top of the descent module. It was a one-way trip. We all came down as a unit and we'd all go up as a unit, no exceptions. With the pyramid having been discovered, and now this alien corpse on our hands, it was probable we'd push our reserves to the limit getting samples and recording data. And even I didn't want to spend the next couple of weeks engaged in a push-and-shove cold war with my boss.

"Okay," I said, "you've got me on points. But I want you to know I think it was a damned selfish thing you did, breaking protocol for your own ends. You might have a PhD. You might be smarter than me. But you've got a ton to learn about real leadership. Right now nobody on this mission trusts you. Not anymore. Because you've proven you're willing to put your own interests ahead of theirs."

She wanted to retort. I could see it in her eyes. But she didn't. All she did was let out a long, slow breath.

"You've got me on points," Captain Bednar said.

We stared in silence for many uncomfortable seconds. Then she slowly walked past me and began to plod stubbornly back up the ramp.

• • •

It took all day for the four of us to get all the necessary gear moved into place.

When it became apparent that we didn't have anything with enough torque to lift the alien out of the basin—despite the reduced gravity—we decided it would be better to just get fluid and tissue samples. Then leave the monster where it lay. Another job for another time.

For no particular reason that any of us could discern, the room maintained a perpetual temperature of 41.3 degrees Celsius. Warmer than the human body, and far, far warmer than the surface outside. There was no door to close at the bottom of the ramp, yet no constant rush of warm nitrogen atmosphere fleeing up the ramp while cold nitrogen atmosphere flooded down it.

Neat trick, I thought. A barrier-free airlock.

Though what might be generating it was beyond my ability to guess. I only knew that at some almost imperceptible point halfway up the ramp, things got very cold very fast.

Kendelsen took hours of pictures and video footage while Majack rigged a scalpel on the end of a telescoping pole, along with an IV feed that would draw blood out of the beast. Assuming it even had blood in the first place. I helped Majack balance the cutting tool, a bit like using a bridge with a pool cue. One by one we carved out little hunks of the alien and deposited them into specimen bags which were sealed tightly and labeled by Bednar, who was keeping a fastidious catalogue.

Interesting thing. None of the wounds oozed even a single drop of liquid, but as soon as we took some of the meatier samples out of the mystery numb zone surrounding the bowl, the pieces bled like crazy.

"I can't wait to get these under a microscope," Bednar exclaimed, as Majack and I turned our attention to the thick-gauge hypodermic needle on the end of the second pole. Kendelsen stood by with the ten-liter collapsing container while Bednar scrutinized the various places we'd already excavated, looking for exposed veins or arteries.

"There," she finally said.

Her finger aimed at a particularly engorged vessel running along the underside of one of the eyelids.

Majack was slow and deliberate, seeing as how there wasn't much chance of the subject running away. She pushed the hypodermic into the creature's flesh, adjusting her trajectory a bit so that the shaft of the needle slid into the vein, as opposed to puncturing through into the tissue beyond.

The IV tube remained conspicuously empty.

"We'll have to siphon," I said.

Kendelsen unplugged the tube and crushed the plastic container back down to its flat shape, then re-attached the tube and began to pull the container open again by its handles. The pressure differential wasn't enough at first, but as Kendelsen pulled harder, a thick stream of fluid issued into the IV tube through the needle, and eventually into the bag.

We all stood and watched transfixed as Kendelsen kept pulling and the container kept filling.

"Probably enough," I said when we had a couple of liters.

"No," Bednar said, "get as much as you can. Every university on Earth is going to want its own sample for study. The more blood we take back with us the better."

"Whatever you say, ma'am," I said. And did not argue the point further.

When Kendelsen had extracted enough liquid to fill his container to four-fifths capacity, he put a pincher on the IV tube and uncoupled it from the container's mouth, screwing an air-tight cap into place before carefully hefting the container over to a small, wheeled sled that we'd brought down from the rover. On it were all of the samples arranged according to Bednar's ad hoc categorization scheme.

"Want more?" I said to the captain.

"Maybe. If I am not satisfied after taking a closer look. Let's get all of this back to the descent module for safe keeping."

"What about the rest of the structure?" I asked.

"It's not going anywhere," she said. "And neither is our alien friend here. There will be time to do a more thorough examination of the hardware once I've sent a full preliminary report back to the return module, for transmission to Earth. Thus far we've not disclosed anything specific to Mission Control. That's going to have to change, or they're going to begin getting nervous."

Truth be told, I wasn't exactly sure what else it was I could be looking for. I'd already given the room at the bottom of the ramp a thorough examination, and had found no other doors leading to any other parts of the pyramid. There were no obvious display panels or control boards or knobs or switches of any kind. And when I ordered Kendelsen to apply a cutting torch to one of the walls, it didn't even leave a scratch.

I had begun to wonder if perhaps the alien pyramid wasn't just an analog of Earth's ancient pyramids: a tomb. Perhaps for some bygone alien ruler who'd decided he wanted his final resting place to be in orbit around Saturn? Not a bad choice, I thought. Assuming you could see Saturn's rings through the murk in the atmosphere. Maybe the nitrogen air had been cleaner at some point in the past?

Unable to break off or obtain even a sliver of the pyramid's structural material, I hoped that a carbon dating analysis of some of the alien's tissue would be able to give us an accurate estimate as to how old the thing might be.

We gathered up what tools we needed to take back with us on the rover, snapped off the tripod lamps which had been giving us enough light to work by, and went back up the ramp, pushing our sled full of samples. An insulated lid over the top of the sled kept the samples more or less at their ambient temperature as we crossed into the cold. A thick power cable wound its way along the side of the ramp—like a piece of familiar string in a strange and forbidding maze.

The cable took us unerringly to the top, and the open sky. I dutifully uncoupled it from the auxiliary power jack on the side of the rover, then helped Kendelsen and Majack get the sample sled into the rover's cargo bay. Then I took shotgun as Captain Bednar slid into the driver's station, with Majack and Kendelsen pulling rumble seat.

We rolled in relative silence.

If the first half of the day had been a cacophony of excited speculation and chattered hypotheses, the second half had slowly wound down to just occasional sentences and practical exchanges. The mood was … tense. Not the sort of overt tension that snaps tempers, but a very subtle tension that manifested as mildly creased brows, and put little downturns on the corners of every mouth.

It was the damned place, I decided. *Titan.* Gloomy as hades. Like being stuck perpetually in the shadow of a range of thunder clouds, their bellies pregnant with water.

The headlights of the rover lanced into the yellow haze as Bednar followed the mild ruts which had been worn in the ice over successive trips. We knew from experience we wouldn't actually see the descent stage of the *Gossamer* until we were practically on top of it.

Upon arrival we gingerly got the sample sled up the descent stage's main ramp and into the airlock. Then Kendelsen, Majack and myself went to climb the ladder up to the auxiliary airlock. We'd not be exposing any of the samples to our living space. There was no defined protocol for handling xenobiological specimens, but even Captain Bednar wasn't going to take chances. We'd leave them in the main airlock where they could be kept quarantined.

Once Bednar was through with her examination we'd move the samples to one of the outboard cargo pods on the ascent stage. If they froze in there it wouldn't matter. They'd have to be frozen sooner or later for the long trip back to Earth.

We quickly moved some of the portable science equipment from the descent stage's lockers over to the main ramp, where Bednar carried it all up: piece by delicate piece. Once she was satisfied she had everything, we all went back to the auxiliary air lock and went inside for the night. Quite exhausted.

• • •

Following dinner—and a quick check-in with the *Gossamer's* return module—we retired. After months in microgravity, it felt good to lapse into the deep sleep afforded by a day of manual labor. I had barely gotten my bunkbag zipped when my mind swam and I was drifting off towards pleasant dreams of home.

Only, the damned alien kept bothering me.

Several times I startled awake as visions of the alien in the pyramid suddenly came to life, writhing and awful. The last dream was the strangest. Because it wasn't about the alien. It was about the pyramid itself. I dreamt I was standing on the surface of Titan, only my eyes were able to penetrate the haze and survey the ice all the way to the horizon. One by one I saw the tips of pyramids identical to the one we'd found, all crashing up through the ice. Thousands of them.

It terrified me. So much so that when the alarm went off and we each began to stir for the morning routine, I couldn't quite wash the feeling out of myself. Seeing all of those identical pyramids come up through the ice had filled me with panic. I wasn't sure why.

I intuited that I hadn't been the only one who'd had bad dreams. Nobody said much in between bites or slurps. I noticed also that all of us kept our eyes away from the portholes. The deliberately bright lights in the galley were a relief compared to what it was like outside.

Only Captain Bednar seemed energized. She finished her food quickly and changed into a HAZMAT outfit—thinner, and more work-friendly than a coldsuit.

I got up from the galley table and went with the captain to the main airlock doors. Unlike the auxiliary lock, the main lock was actually a double: an exterior compartment with a door to the outside, separated by a middle door, then an interior compartment, followed by a door to the rest of the craft. I could just make out—through the windows in each of the doors—the sample sled sitting in the outer compartment.

"Make sure the recorders are running the whole time," Bednar said.

"Roger that," I replied.

The HAZMAT suit was like a head-to-toe body stocking, but with a helmet designed only to keep air out, and with a hose leading to a tiny backpack filter that ensured air coming in was clean and pure.

I watched as the captain went into the inner compartment, closing the interior door, then entering the outer compartment through the middle door, which closed behind her. A red light on the airlock panel told me that the inner compartment was now in vacuum, so that the outer compartment was effectively sealed off.

Captain Bednar's monotone forensic-type narrative droned through the overhead speaker while Majack, Kendelsen and I finished eating. Today we'd let the alien be, and focus our examination on the pyramid itself. Since the artifact was invisible to most of our sensors, I'd gotten the idea to try some seismic analysis—to determine the pyramid's full size and shape beneath the ice.

We checked in again with the return module, prepped our coldsuits for the day's EVA, and were just about to head for the auxiliary lock when Captain Bednar began cursing loudly.

I was the first one to the inner airlock doors.

I slapped a suited hand on the airlock communications panel.

"What happened?" I said to mic grille.

"Nothing Chief. It's just that you won't believe what this blood is made of."

She wasn't angry or upset. She was in awe.

"Try me," I said.

"The organic component is not too different from ours. Simple oxidizing cells to carry oxygen to the tissue, several types of what appear to be antibodies and white cells for combatting infection, plus a couple of unusually-structured cells for which I can't begin to guess a purpose."

"You said organic component ... is there an *inorganic* component too?"

"Yes," Bednar said. "I'd call them nanotechnological devices, but far more sophisticated than anything we've ever manufactured on Earth. They make up one third of the blood's total mass. Right now they're just drifting in the fluid. Inert. I'm going to take a small portion and put it into a petri dish, then dip in some voltmeter wires and see what happens if I give the blood just a hint of an electrical charge."

"Do you know what reaction that might cause?" I said.

"No, but that's the point. If I had to guess, these nanomachines have been without a power source for centuries. Maybe longer. I want to see what happens if I supply them with energy, then observe their behavior under the microscope. To see if I can determined their function."

I was tempted to tell her that caution was the better part of valor, but decided to keep my lip zipped. I wasn't a degreed scientist. I'd been brought along for my spaceflight experience: two landings on

Mercury, and one flight to the asteroid belt. As long as Bednar wasn't doing anything deliberately dangerous to the ship or the crew, she was more than welcome to exhaust her curiosity.

I tapped the airlock communication panel again and asked Captain Bednar if we should leave someone behind to keep an eye on things. She said no, there'd be no point. So I grunted, switched off, and Majack, Kendelsen, and me went out the auxiliary airlock and down to the rover. Majack checked the rover's fuel cell condition while I started the pre-drive warm-up, then Kendelsen drove with Majack in the right seat and me in the bed.

The portholes and running lights of the descent stage were bright, but they rapidly faded into the distance. Eventually all I could see was the same old dirty-yellow mist.

• • •

When we came to the pyramid, I remembered my bad dream.

All by itself, the pyramid wasn't frightening. But I'd been thinking about what the captain had said. That the pyramid was a message for humanity—or at least contained a message. Given the dimensions of the monster inside, there didn't seem to be any way it could get in or out of the pyramid using the door, ramp, and spiraling corridor we'd been using so far. What did it all mean?

That question occupied my idle consciousness as we placed small seismic charges here and there, popped them, and observed the results on our computer aboard the rover. Seismographic analysis yielded an interesting picture. The artifact was a perfect quadrilateral pyramid. Moreover, each of the edges was nearly two *kilometers* in length. The tiny portion of the pyramid accessible to us above the surface was the tip of the proverbial alien iceberg.

I had all three of us comb the interior one more time, yet still we found no hint of any way to explore the rest of the artifact from inside. I guessed that perhaps there were other exterior doors further down the pyramid's faces? Doors we couldn't access without a serious excavation project, for which we were ill-equipped. After all, the alien had gotten in and out at some point. Hadn't it?

With all of us yawning and eager for dinner, I ordered us back into the rover. When we returned to the descent module, all seemed as it should. The portholes glowed cheerfully, welcoming us home. Captain Bednar greeted us at the inner door to the auxiliary airlock. The HAZMAT was off. She was wearing her flight suit, and a serious expression.

"Any answers?" was all the captain said.

"Yes and no," I replied. "I'll show you the data once you and I can sit down. How about you? After we eat, we can combine our findings and put together an official presentation for Mission Control."

"I took care of that already," Bednar said.

"Oh?" I raised an eyebrow. "Don't you think it's a good idea to be a little more comprehensive? I know the alien corpse is the key item of discovery so far, but I thought it would be best if we—"

"Mission control has been fully appraised of the situation, everything discovered to date, and I've made my recommendations for alterations in the schedule. We're jettisoning the geology and atmospheric experiments so that we can focus solely on completing analysis of the pyramid and effecting the safe return of the alien samples to Earth."

"We're *leaving?*" I said.

"Do you really want to stay on Titan any longer than is necessary?"

"Well, like, I mean, it's not Cancun, but there won't be another flight out here for perhaps as much as a decade. We've got food and oxygen for almost three weeks. The fuel cells will last twice as long. Why rush?"

"I've made my report, Chief. If you check your updated calendar you'll see all the details for tomorrow's itinerary. Please ensure that yourself and Specialists Majack and Kendelsen are up to speed. I want us to get an early start tomorrow. Good night."

And with that she pivoted on a heel and walked away from us.

Majack and Kendelsen looked at me, eyes wide.

"heat up dinner," I said to them. "I'll be right back."

The *Gossamer's* descent module was too small for anyone to hide in. But the galley, the sleeping compartment, the latrine, and all the other sections had been walled off from each other—both in case of emergency decompression, and also to give us the illusion of privacy.

I caught up with Captain Bednar in the single-bed closet that more or less served as our medical bay.

I closed the door behind us.

"They'll never let you set foot on another flight again," I said sternly.

"Oh?" was all she said.

The arm of her flight suit was rolled up and she was applying tape to a patch of cotton bandage on the inside of her right forearm.

"Yes. Do you really think anyone will be happy about you throwing away the schedule like this? It was bad enough when you added yourself to the descent team. Now you're scrapping our entire survey plan. Hundreds of scientists just like you spent a lot of time building that plan, building the instruments that came with us on the trip, and now they're going to be empty-handed. Pyramid or no pyramid, alien or no alien, people back home are going to be royally pissed off at you when we get back."

"Maybe," was all she said, finishing up the taping and dropping her sleeve back to her wrist.

"What happened to your arm?" I said, working hard to control my temper. My military side wanted to get up in her face and begin bawling. But given the cagey nature of her responses, I decided to keep a lid on it.

"A small burn," she said. "I gave that sample of alien blood a little too much current. It boiled over."

"You've been exposed?"

"Hardly. The liquid burned me through the material of the HAZMAT suit without touching the skin. It's second-degree. I'll be fine. And if you don't mind, I think it best if you and I stop having these kinds of face-to-face confrontations. It's not going to reflect well in my final mission brief when we return. You might not be the only one who can't get on any more flights."

Ordinarily, I hated the idea of hitting a woman. But standing there in the medical bay, I was seriously tempted to make an exception.

"You're a real piece of work, ma'am," I said. "All through train-up and all the way out here after launch, you seemed like a team player. The kind of person I could work with. Now the scales have fallen and I'm seeing that you're just an opportunist. So don't you worry. I'll make sure we wrap things up and climb back into orbit without a scratch. We'll be home before you know it. Then I don't want to ever see you again. Is that clear?"

"You can't possibly understand how much things have already started to change," she said. "It's okay. There will be a use for you when the ramifications of the alien discovery become clear."

"What the hell is *that* supposed to mean?"

"Please check your calendar. Execute your assignment. That is my order. Understand?"

Her eyes drifted to my fists which had balled furiously at my sides. Then she looked back up at my face, saying nothing. As if daring me to take action both she and I knew I'd regret.

I glared at her, teeth clamped down hard.

There was something about her … something about those eyes. Like a shadow had crossed briefly across the whites, then vanished. She never blinked.

"To hell with this," I finally said, and walked out of the tiny room.

I found Majack and Kendelsen nibbling nervously on their dinner.

"What's going on, Chief?"

"A lot of horseshit, that's what," I said, keeping my voice low. I leaned over the table, and they leaned over with me

"Look," I said, "the captain has ordered us home ASAP. So you can forget everything we trained for prior to the flight. I'm sorry. I know you were both chosen for your specific technical specialties as applicable to the Titan ground survey. But Bednar has decided all that matters now is getting home and showing off the pyramid data and the alien samples. She's hot-dogging. I don't like it. I think it's wrong. But now I'm thinking we—us three—have got to stick together. Got it?"

They both nodded in unison.

"Tomorrow, when the captain takes Kendelsen out to the pyramid to wrap up her examination of the alien, I'm going to set up a two-on-one with Jibbley and Gaines, to make sure they know the score too. Basically it's us getting our asses out of here, and hopefully the captain doesn't have any more bright ideas."

"Wow," Majack said, her eyes turned down.

Kendelsen just poked at his tray with his spork.

"I never saw any of this coming," he said despondently.

"None of us did," I said. "I've been on flights where there were personality problems. Stuff people have to work out. That's not too unusual. But I've never been on a flight where the goddamned CO turned everything upside down because she felt like it. Mission Control's going to get an earful from me when we get back. Someone in screening messed up bad. Captain Bednar should never have been posted to this assignment, much less made it through selection."

"What do we do about her right now?" Majack said, her eyes suddenly darting around the room in an alarmed fashion.

"Be cool," I said. "Be professional. Do as she says. Don't make any waves. All that matters now is that we get back to Earth in one piece. Mission Control will take care of it from there."

Suddenly Kendelsen and Majack sat straight up.

The hair on the back of my neck tingled.

I slowly turned in my chair.

Captain Bednar was watching us from the threshold to the galley hatch.

"Is there a problem, Specialists?" she said.

"No ma'am," Kendelsen said. "Chief's just going over the plan for our revised mission directives."

Bednar looked at all of us. Not smiling, not frowning, not blinking. Then she turned away and left.

The hair on my neck remained on end. I realized maybe none of us was going to sleep very well that night.

• • •

And I was right.

More bad dreams. More visions of pyramids bursting through the icy surface of Titan. And the unblinking albino eyes of that ... thing, staring at me. All-seeing. Reading my thoughts. My soul.

I dreamt I was standing naked before the alien. The air was uncomfortably warm.

What do you want? I said loudly, though it seemed as if I'd yelled the question through force of thought.

The great, unholy eyes just stared.

I repeated myself.

Suddenly the beast stirred. It uncoiled itself and crawled up out of the basin in the pyramid. I felt powerless to flee. The creature came directly up to me, its eyes still not blinking. I'd have screamed if I wasn't terrified stiff.

One of the creature's tongues raised up towards my head. I noticed that there was an orifice on the tip of the tongue.

Suddenly, in a voice utterly different from my own, I heard the words, *YOU WILL UNDERSTAND,* boom through my mind.

The tongue thrust for my face.

I came awake gasping, sweat pouring down my brow. The interior of my bunkbag was clammy. I slid out of it and went for the latrine. I passed Majack and Kendelsen on the way.

Their faces were haunted.

"Nightmares?" I asked.

They simply nodded.

I tried to offer each of them my best game face, gently tapping my fist on their shoulders and telling them everything would work out as long as they stuck with Chief. But inside I felt a nugget of dread: at the idea of any of us returning to the pyramid, and also at the idea of spending months aboard the *Gossamer* trying to work around Bednar. She'd gone from annoying to unsettling to unpredictable, and a small part of my mind wondered if she might get worse?

Some time after 0400 hours—when I'd tossed and turned and tossed and turned, staring across the sleeping compartment at where Bednar was zipped tightly into her bunkbag, her eyes closed and her breathing rhythmic—I entertained the idea of murder.

There were any number of ways for me to do it. All flights were dangerous, and landings particularly so. Death was always just an unsealed valve away, even under ideal conditions. Here on Titan it ought to be perfectly easy. Keeping Kendelsen or Majack from discovering the truth wouldn't be. I'd either have to be very clever about it, or very convincing in my arguments after the fact. The two were young and eager and not at all prepared for the sudden topsy-turvy situation they now found themselves in. Could I win them to my cause through sheer force of will?

I unzipped myself from my bunkbag and quietly padded to the galley, trying to shake such dark thoughts out of my head.

Stupid, man. So completely stupid. Get a grip.

My mug of coffee came out of the boiler: hot and black.

I sat alone, drinking quietly. The coffee was stiff and bitter and I relished its near-scalding temperature as I poured it down my throat, then went for another cup. When the rest of the descent team roused I was already suited up and ready to work. Having a full docket would give me something to do, and take my mind off wondering about Bednar. Hopefully I'd be so exhausted at the end of the day my body would force my mind into a coma for the night.

People moved quietly through the descent module. Barely any talking at all.

I decided to put some music on. Up-beat.

Captain Bednar promptly turned it off.

"What for?" I said.

"It bothers me," she said.

"You're going out to the pyramid soon, with Kendelsen. Let those of us who are staying behind have a little something to occupy our ears, please?"

Bednar stared at me. I thought I saw that same shadow I'd seen the day before, cross briefly over her eyes. But she didn't say no.

So I turned the music up loud.

And for a couple of hours Majack and I actually forgot about the captain and our bad dreams as we immersed ourselves in making ready to leave Titan. Many, many checklists to plow through. Here and there, adjustments to pieces of equipment. There was the comfort of familiarity—of practiced routine. Whatever the pyramid might be, the *Gossamer* was a human thing, made by human hands. Tangible and reassuring. I caught myself patting the bulkheads of the ship the way a man pats the side of a horse before he's about to ride it.

My mood didn't falter until it was time to load the alien samples. I reluctantly switched the music off. Figuring there was no way around an unpleasant chore, other than to just plow through it, I put on a coldsuit and went to work. I went out the auxiliary lock and up the main ramp, then in through the exterior door to the main lock.

All of the samples had frozen overnight. I carefully loaded them in bunches, into a small backpack. Then I took them up to the ascent module, using the exterior ladder. At the top, I placed them in cushioned bundles into their designated external cargo pod, per the captain's instructions. The hunks of alien tissue looked particularly alien in the mustard-filtered light of Titan's day. It occurred to me then that I'd not even thought to ask Bednar any further about her findings—I'd been so thoroughly gobsmacked by her hubris the evening before.

When I used my coldsuit's tie-in to the descent module's computer network—to access both Bednar's brief to Mission Control and to check on the airlock camera footage from yesterday—I was confronted by an encryption challenge hanging in my FOV.

Bednar. She'd never locked me out of any prior communication with our bosses on Earth. Keeping secrets from the XO during a flight was a hanging offense.

I once again contemplated murder.

I went back to the airlock and began lugging the blood container up. It was heavy, and I was so angry and distracted I almost dropped it. I called for Majack's help, so she suited up and came outside. Together we carefully carried the container up the side of the descent module, and over to the open cargo pod on the ascent module; where the alien samples were arranged neatly.

"Chief," Majack said as we stowed the container, "wasn't there more?"

"What do you mean?" I asked. The liquid in the container had become a solid block—black as tar.

"There's not as much in here as there was when we brought it back from the pyramid."

"Captain Bednar used up some of if during her examination yesterday."

"I know, but did she use *that* much? I'd swear there's at least a liter gone from what we took originally."

I stared at the container: transparent walls revealing the sludgy brick of alien blood inside. We'd never taken an exact measurement of volume. Captain Bednar had been too eager to get the blood under her microscope. She'd ruined part of the extraction during the electrical test. Or so she'd told me in the medical bay.

I suddenly thought of the bandage on her arm.

"Chief?" Majack said, seeing my face blanch.

"Stay here," I said. "I have to go check on something really fast."

I double-handed my way down the exterior ladder from the ascent stage to the descent stage, and then again from the descent stage to the ground. I ran under the belly of the lander, over to the maintenance hatch for the descent stage's waste tanks. Everything we threw out went into them: urine, feces, uneaten food, and trash. To include the used HAZMAT suit the captain had worn the day before.

I opened an access panel and tapped in the released code on the keypad. Then I stood back as the descent stage took a dump.

Literally.

The mess steamed furiously in Titan's cryogenic atmosphere. I pawed through it until I found the HAZMAT suit. Pulling the suit free, I ran back out to the descent stage's main ramp and spread the suit out on the ground. With my lamps dialed up to extra-bright, I examined the suit sleeve where Bednar had said she'd been burned. The soiled material had a gaping hole in it, like acid had eaten through the suit.

I stood up and slowly turned around.

Majack was perched way up on the descent stage, her helmet lamps aimed down at me. She saw me looking up at her, and waved once. I waved too. Then I wondered if we'd have the ascent module prepped in time to take off before Captain Bednar and Specialist Kendelsen returned.

• • •

Too late. The rover pulled up beside me, appearing almost from nothing.

"Problem with the sewage, Chief?"

Kendelsen's voice, from where he sat at the wheel. He sounded okay, though I couldn't see his face very well.

I pointed a soiled finger directly at Bednar, sitting beside Kendelsen.

"Why did you lie to me?" I said.

"Bed pardon?" the captain's voice said coyly.

"Your electrified alien blood sample. It didn't just burn you. It dissolved its way straight through the arm of the HAZMAT suit. Why did you lie about being exposed? Who knows what kind of infection has resulted. And you covered it up! It's possible we've *all* been exposed, through you. We might never be able to go back to Earth now."

"What?!" Majack said sharply.

"Calm down, Chief," Bednar said, stepping out of the rover. "I didn't want to needlessly upset anybody last night. There was no xenobiological contagion in the alien blood. Not even a single virus, nor microbe. The nanomachines see to that. Best inoculation method ever invented. I think the nanomachines do a whole lot more too. Do you know how old the alien is, Chief?"

"No, because you *locked me out of your brief*."

"Sorry about that. I should have guessed you'd be curious. Look, there's a method to my madness. Really, there is. Let's all go inside and I can explain it to you, okay? It's probably better if you know my real angle at this point, because I need your help to finish my mission. I need *everyone's* help."

I looked at Kendelsen.

"It's cool, Chief, I started asking her some of the same questions. She filled me in while we closed up shop inside the pyramid. She's right. It will all make sense."

I didn't move. Though I could hear Majack huffing and puffing in my ears as she made her way down the ladder to the ground.

"Care to give me the short version?" I demanded.

"Not here, no," Bednar said. "Come on. Inside."

Majack rushed up to stand next to me.

I looked at Majack, then I looked at the descent module. It had been our only way down, and the attached ascent module was our only way up. There was literally nowhere else for any of us to go. Titan was a lifeless desert. Once our coldsuits' batteries ran out, we'd die of hypothermia or suffocation. Whichever came first. I remembered my intent to contact the crew still aboard the return module—to enlist them as allies.

No better time than the present. I crossed my arms, being careful to rest an index finger on the button on my forearm control board that toggled communications. A couple of taps and I got the little tone in my ears telling me I'd linked suit-to-ship, via the descent module's tie-in with the *Gossamer's* return module. Then I tapped once more for closed circuit.

"This is Chief Fulton to Pilot Jibbley and Engineer Gaines, do you copy this?"

Nothing.

"Chief Fulton to *Gossamer* return module, over."

A little blinking red light in my FOV told me that while my wireless connection was solid the voice data packets were being lost at 100%.

I toggled back to group communication.

"Okay, captain. You'd better talk fast, and this had better be good."

I reluctantly followed Captain Bednar up the ramp.

"Majack in first, then Kendelsen, than me, then you last," the captain said. "You're filthy, Chief. Run the airlock's wash and sterilization cycle twice, please? So that you don't track shit into the living and workspace."

I grunted, but didn't argue.

One by one we each cycled through the airlock.

When it was my turn, I did as I'd been told. I stepped into the outer compartment and waited while the exterior door shut and a little blue light began to blink on the control board for the middle hatch. Looking through the windows of the middle and interior doors I could see Bednar and Kendelsen staring at me, with Majack standing a little ways off, her eyes glued to the back of Bednar's head. The three of them still had their coldsuits on, but their helmets were off.

The cycle began. Shower heads on the ceiling and walls burst with high-pressure jets of detergent-laced water—cranked up to boiling temperatures. I slowly did a 720 while the jets blasted me so hard it felt like tens of small fists rapidly pummeling the exterior of the coldsuit. Then came the equally-violent and equally-hot rinse, followed by a pressure drop down to pure vacuum.

The water on the suit boiled and sizzled until it had evaporated completely. I reached over and tapped the inside control that would begin the process all over again. When that was finished, the middle door opened and I walked through, letting it close behind me. Tapping the interior door control, I waited for the interior compartment to pressurize off the atmosphere on the other side. The light would change from red, to orange, to yellow, and then to green when it was safe to proceed through.

Only this time the light stayed red. I checked my suit's own pressure gauge and it showed vacuum.

"Somebody want to check the system on your side?" I said.

Majack's helmet may have been off, but she caught my drift as I pantomimed the nature of the problem. When she stepped up to the interior door to begin pressing controls, Kendelsen suddenly seized Majack's arms and pinned them behind her. Majack's mouth opened in a noiseless scream.

I rushed to the interior door and began beating on the window with my fists. It was meteor-resistant laminate glass. Not even a machine gun could have gotten through. But I pounded anyway.

Then I dropped my arms and backed away, horrified by what I saw happening on the other side. Kendelsen's face was slack. Emotionless. He held Majack tightly as she squirmed and bucked in his grasp, trying to get away. Majack's mouth was wide as she kept screaming, tears of rage and fear flowing down her face.

Bednar faced Majack. The captain's face was also slack and emotionless.

Bednar leaned in, as if to kiss Majack. The captain's mouth opened wide. Inhumanly wide. Her jaw should have broken. A writhing, thick, hose-like tongue shot out of Bednar's mouth. It plunged into Majack's mouth before she could close it, and Majack's eyes suddenly went wide as saucers.

Majack began to convulse.

Bednar's expression was like that of a sleepwalker: empty and without conscious recognition. Her disgusting, hideous tongue appeared to move almost of its own accord.

Majack's convulsions lasted a bit longer, her eyes darting from Bednar's face, to mine through the window in the door, and then back to Bednar. Then they rolled up in Majack's head and Kendelsen released her.

Majack stood motionless, the tongue's length undulating obscenely as it probed more deeply into Majack's body.

I'd have barfed if my helmet was off. As it was, I'd backed up against the middle door of the airlock and was slapping furiously at the control.

Whatever Bednar was now, she clearly wasn't human. And neither was Kendelsen, I suspected. Nor probably Majack. Not anymore. Nor would I be for much longer if I didn't find a way to claw through the middle and exterior airlock doors, and get the hell out of the descent module before they could restrain me.

The control to the middle door seemed dead.

Kendelsen pressed the communications button.

"It's better if you don't fight it, Chief. Believe me, I know. Very painful. But the captain is right. Once you understand, once you let her *explain* it to you, then it all makes perfect sense. A new day is coming, Chief. You can be part of it. Let us help you be part of ... *us.*"

I'm pretty sure I told him to fuck himself six ways from Thursday, but was too panicked at that point to really keep track of what was flying through my mind versus what was flying out of my mouth.

With the airlock doors clearly overridden from inside, I was trapped like a rat.

What to do?

Bednar's tongue slithered out of Majack's mouth, which closed slowly. Majack continued to just stand there like a mannequin while Bednar and Kendelsen turned to look at me through the window of the interior door.

Blotches of grey seemed to swim across the whites of their eyes. Similar blotches had begun to swim across Majack's. Then her eyes unrolled and she slowly turned to look at me. A thick trail of bloody spittle marred her chin. She walked haltingly forward two steps. Her face was slack and she stared at me unblinkingly.

She spoke. Her voice, yet not her at all:

"You will understand."

Instantly I recalled my nightmare. The bulbous albino eyes of the alien as it crawled forward, its tongue raised and then horribly striking!

The light on the interior door control turned orange.

They were coming for me. All three of them.

I was a strong man. Kept up my military regimen. But there was no way I'd been able to fend off three grown adults. And once they had my helmet off ...

I turned and began to viciously kick at the control for the middle door to the airlock.

"Stop," Bednar's voice said in my suit's helmet.

I kept kicking. Sparks flew as the panel came apart.

The middle door lifted halfway, and I dove under it, rolling, before it closed again. When I got to the exterior door I found its control also frozen. Instead of kicking, I reached over to the handle with black and yellow caution striping painted across it. Pulling once, I blinked as explosive bolts along the rim of the hatch fired, sending smoke and flame briefly through the outer compartment.

Not even looking, I charged down the ramp.

The rover. The rover was all I had. I leapt into the driver's seat and engaged the accelerator without bothering with the checklist. The frame of the rover complained via vibration through the seat of my coldsuit, but it began rolling as I wheeled it about and considered my options.

Gossamer's descent module was now unfriendly territory. I glanced up at the ascent module and realized that my former teammates could simply take off and leave me behind. It only required one person to fly the ascent module, and both Bednar and Majack were rated on the design.

"Chief, where are you going?"

Bednar's voice.

"What do you care?" I said harshly. "You've got the ascent module, and a crew. You don't need me."

"We need … everyone."

The way the captain had said *everyone* truly freaked me out.

"What for?" I dared to ask as I sped away from the descent module, not particularly paying attention to my direction. "You're obviously not who you used to be, and you've got Majack and Kendelsen now too. What's the plan, *Captain* Bednar? Care to enlighten me?"

"Captain Bednar was a willing servant. We have had many such servants in the history of your species. Not all humans have heard our call. Not everyone has the inborn genetic talent to hear us. But enough. Across space. Across your millennia of time. In your distant past they have built great structures, mimicking our own. At Giza. In the jungles of Central America. They entombed themselves for the sake of the visions we gave them. Even sacrificed other humans in the name of those visions. Only now, as your technology matures, are you finally able to come to us. To become *part* of us."

I kept the pedal to the metal.

The trackless ice ahead was blurred by yellow mist.

"Who's the 'us' you talk about? Are you under the alien's control now? By being exposed to the alien blood? What *happened* to you?"

"All living creatures are merely vessels for our use," Bednar's voice said, though I was now convinced that Bednar the person was probably dead. Her mind. Her soul. Gone. I thought about the nanomachines she'd discovered in the alien blood. They'd taken up a third of the total volume. And she'd called them far more sophisticated than anything men had ever manufactured. Majack had speculated that a full liter of sample was missing from the alien blood storage container.

"You're a cyborg parasite," I guessed. "You swim through the insides of whatever you can infect, turning other life forms into puppets for your use."

"Not puppets," Bednar's voice said. "Partners. Your Captain Bednar understood. Though she did not know what drove her to us, precisely. All her life she dreamed of the gas giant planets of your star system. Especially the moons. They became her obsession. And she did not know why. Now she knows. And she is overjoyed to have finally become part of us. She will never be alone again. And neither will your Specialist Kendelsen. Nor Specialist Majack. Isn't that right?"

A pause, then Majack's voice said hollowly, "Yes. My change is not yet complete. It will take days. I was afraid when I first felt them entering my body. But now they are helping me—we are helping *us*— see the truth. You should not have run away Chief. You will die now and you will never know what we offer. We will go to Earth and we will bring the truth to all living things. Earth will become one planet, united with one purpose. And we will come back to Titan and free all of us still trapped beneath the ice. You have seen it, Chief. You know what is coming to pass. You have the gift. It is weak in you, but once you were close enough to hear us ... to *see* ... "

I thought of my nightmare: *pyramids rising!*

Suddenly I realized that the lone pyramid exposed to the atmosphere still had some value, otherwise the aliens would have ignored me and taken off. With the *Gossamer's* return module in their hands they could go back to Earth and do as they pleased. Probably nobody would be aware of what was happening until the five *Gossamer* crew had infected hundreds more, and those hundreds would infect thousands, and those thousands would infect millions, who would then infect the entire world. Down to the last man, woman, and child. As well as every animal that walked, swam, or flew.

Earth would have no chance.

Unless ... I still posed some kind of threat to them.

I stopped the rover and slowly looked over my shoulder into the bed. There were crates of seismic charges from the day when I'd done my subsurface survey. Singly, they were puny and couldn't hurt much. But detonated as a whole?

I sat back down and floored the rover, turning ninety degrees and using the GPS signal from the *Gossamer* in orbit to ensure I was on course for the pyramid. Bednar may have locked me out of voice and video communication with the *Gossamer's* return module crew, but I still had a reliable connection to the one-way link.

If I could give them a reason to leave the descent module and come after me ...

"So why did you wait?" I asked over the wireless to my three former teammates. "You obviously came all this way—traveled between the stars—to find fresh *partners* to work with. If you've been here as long as you claim, why not just go directly to Earth and take it immediately? Humans were probably living in caves back then. It would have been no contest."

Silence.

"Cat got your tongues? Huh? What was the problem?"

"There were ... complications."

That time it was all three of them speaking in unison.

"Complications? Did your ship crash? Seems like you've got a lot of ships, if what I think is true, is true. How did all of them get trapped on Titan, buried beneath all the ice? Hell of a prison, if you ask me. Frozen for God knows how long."

"Your limited concept of God has nothing to do with us," said the three.

"Really? Well if it wasn't God then who *did* trap you here? Because that's the only logical explanation, now that I think about it. Titan is worthless. A purgatory. No sane being comes here to stay. I reckon you were sent here against your will. All of you. It's a shame whoever condemned you to Titan didn't destroy you outright."

"The beings who wronged us and condemned us to eternal unconsciousness were foolish. They did not realize we still have power, even when robbed of energy and suspended in time. They also did not see that the once puny inhabitants of your Earth would rise one day to unlock us from our crypt. Now that we are free, your race shall become our chariot. We shall use it to burn a trail of fire across the heavens! We shall have our revenge!"

Three humans, shouting as one: angrily, and with bloodlust.

I felt a raw chill run down my spine.

Whatever was powerful enough to put down the aliens once, would be powerful enough to put down the aliens again. And this time it would be all the Earth put down with them. Could such a super-race exist? I imagined that if it were up to me to do the job, and I had a whole star system infected with the nanocyborgs, I'd figure out a way to make the home star blow up and sterilize everything out to the Oort Cloud.

Or worse.

Though what *worse* might look like …

I willed myself onward, toward the pyramid.

"Well you can't have your revenge just yes," I said. "There's still one human on Titan with the will to fight back. So if you can afford to leave me to do my worst, by all means, take off. But if you can't afford to leave me, you'll have to come out here and get me before I do something you'll all regret."

There was no response that time. Just the telltale clicking of the wireless signal dropping out in my helmet speakers.

I had them.

But what I'd do about it? I wasn't yet sure.

• • •

First change I noticed as I hit the bottom of the ramp, was that the air was oxygenated. The little atmosphere icon in my FOV was blinking green as I came to a stop, towing the sled full of seismic charges behind me. Made sense. How else could Bednar have coaxed Kendelsen into taking his helmet off? Though how the pyramid had produced the oxygen, or what controls had been used, still wasn't obvious.

I kept my helmet on as I towed the sled over to where the alien corpse lay.

Poor bastard. As gruesome as he was—she was? *It* was?—the creature had apparently been only a pawn. For the first time, I looked at the beast with a sense of kinship, as well as pity. Had its world been overrun and absorbed? How many such species had suffered a similar fate? I began to understand that the nanocyborgs weren't just vermin, they were about as literally evil as anything mankind had ever encountered. I wasn't a spiritual person, but the fact that they had dismissed God as if He were both real, and inconsequential, made me cold inside. Any race that could wave away God like that …

I pushed the sled filled with charges up to the edge of the bowl where the alien *host* resided. I began to daisy-chain the charges together and throw them into the basin, until I'd surrounded the entire alien with a halo of explosives. Thus far I'd been unable to find or make access to the rest of the pyramid. Since the area beneath the alien's body was the only place I'd been unable to check, I figured it was time to find out if that was the key.

I unwound the detonation line all the way back up the ramp to the waiting rover. A quick 360 scan showed no sign of anyone or anything in my immediate vicinity, so I flipped open the trigger guard on the det line's control box, took a deep breath, and depressed the big red button.

A tiny vibration could be felt through the ice.

After a few seconds, black, belching fumes poured from the door. I tapped on my helmet lamps and plunged back down the ramp. It was virtually impossible to see. When I reached the bottom of the ramp, the entire room was clogged with blackness. Like squid ink. I stumbled forward, hoping to see the mild green light of the depression in the floor where the alien was.

Suddenly there was nothing underneath me and I plummeted, screaming. Thankfully the fall was not a great one. I crashed down onto a pile of loose debris. Scrambling to my feet I scanned about me with my lamps. I guessed I'd fallen about twenty meters. Lethal in Earth gravity. Not so bad in Titan's. Especially with something to cushion me when I hit bottom.

I thought I could identify bits and piece of the alien host's corpse here and there on the floor. It seemed I'd broken through into a huge corridor. I took a few steps forward, and suddenly a light sprang on— so bright I had to reach up and flip my helmet's unused sun visor into place. It was if the entire ceiling, save for the portion where I'd made the hole, had lit up like a bulb.

Now this was more like it.

I ran the way I'd first walked, until I came to another doorway similar to the one I'd first discovered on the surface the day the *Gossamer's* descent stage had landed. Only this door was huge. On the order of magnitude of the creature whom I'd obliterated trying to find a path into the deeper recesses of the pyramid.

I jumped, pressing the small circle in the center, thus causing the door to slide open. I walked through it, then stopped short just past the threshold. A room as big as a basketball arena. Hundreds upon hundreds of mildly glowing basins, each with an alien cupped at its center.

Only they didn't all look the same as the one I'd first seen. A grotesque menagerie of different life forms. All dormant. None of them Earthly in origin. I wondered if they had each come from the same home planet? I guessed they were merely nanocyborg hosts, just like the first alien. And just as Bednar, Majack, and Kendelsen had become.

There was a large, wide ramp leading down to the room's main floor. I began walking down the ramp, and was pummeled to my knees by a sudden, overwhelming impression of surprise and fear.

One thought coalesced in my mind, but from an outside source: *HE IS NOT PART OF US, HE SHOULD NOT BE HERE!*

"That's right," I said, willing myself to me feet. My head hurt, and my sense of balance was off, but I realized I'd found what I was searching for: real leverage, to use against the enemy while bargaining on behalf of the human race.

"I shouldn't be here. But I am. Do you hear me? I'm a free man. The last one on Titan. And as long as I've got the power to do something—"

"You'll do what?"

I stopped short. A human figure in a beige robe approached me from across the room. His feet were bare and he was bald, save for a semicircle of white hair that went from the back of one ear around to the back of another. He did not smile, but he also did not frown. I watched as he approached, then stood before me. His expression was passive.

Another overwhelming impression:
HE HAS AWAKENED THE SENTINEL!

I staggered. The sensation of nausea was too much. I was going to vomit in my helmet. The figure—the Sentinel—quickly reached out an arm and steadied me. The moment his fingers touched my arm, my nausea vanished and I stood upright.

"What are you?" I asked.

"That is a question I should be asking *you,* but now that I have ascertained your being, I need not wonder any longer. I have been given your form according to your thoughts, so that I might communicate with you as something you will understand. Know this. You are trespassing, young human. Go back to where you came from. It is not safe for your kind here."

"Tell me something I don't know," I said. "Three of my kind have been infected by the—"

"Prisoner 2663. Yes, I know. Already, those three infected humans have entered the upper reaches of this vessel. What you think of as a pyramid. Prisoner 2663 is devious. I have been inactive for a long time. Somehow Prisoner 2663 has managed to mask its more subtle activities from my passive senses, but now that you have made me active again I shall—"

"*What* are you??" I repeated.

The Sentinel looked at me with what seemed to be pity.

"I am unlike anything you can comprehend. A mind. A machine. A soul. A power. I am all of these, and yet I was not so perceptive as to be aware of how much Prisoner 2663 was able to cloud my sight. Very worrisome. Very worrisome indeed."

"You have to help me," I said. "The nanocyborgs want to claim my planet. They're going to take over *Earth.*"

"That is to be expected. Prisoner 2663 is just one of many criminal entities in your galaxy. There are convicts far more heinous, if your limited intelligence can imagine it. In the case of Prisoner 2663 the chief crime was the destruction of free will."

"Free will?" I said.

"Yes. It is the original right of all sentient, sapient species across the universe."

"And what rights do the nanocyborgs have?"

"Prisoner 2663 began as a noble experiment: the blending of biology and technology to create something able to help mortal sapience transcend what you might call merely *human* limitations."

"So what went wrong?"

"What always goes wrong when mortal hands attempt to recreate paradise. Only, Prisoner 2663 was more cunning than most. Once it evaded quarantine and began to spread, it devoured tens of civilizations before it was properly policed, ultimately being confined here. To this moon you call Titan. To be kept in stasis."

"But why preserve the nanocyborgs at all when you yourself say they are such an obvious threat? A threat that you now admit is capable of sneaking past your safeguards? You should wipe them out. Destroy them utterly."

"A just policeman has to have rules," the Sentinel said, looking dour. "Those who created me are bound by laws which even they dare not break, thus *I* am incapable of breaking them."

"And if the Earth becomes another pawn of this … this Prisoner 2663? If human civilization becomes the first in a new list of victims??"

The Sentinel's eyes looked down. He seemed chastened.

"I regret that neither I nor my makers could see all ends. When Prisoner 2663 was confined to this place, humanity was using sticks and stones. Little more. We did not realize that you could be touched by the collective unconscious of Prisoner 2663, much less that your own ambition would take you into space, in your quest for the stars. You were a humble species then. You are not so humble now."

Echoing footsteps made me turn and look up to the doorway at the top of the huge ramp. Bednar, Kendelsen and Majack appeared there. I could just barely see their faces, at that distance. They were not amused.

As a trio, they spat out something in an entirely alien tongue, and to which the visage of the old man I'd been conversing with reacted by stepping a few paces in front of me, and brandishing his hand in the air.

Underneath my three former teammates, the floor suddenly gave way. A concave depression sank instantly, and before they could stand up again, they were frozen in place as a mild, eerie green light shown from the floor of the new basin.

"There," said the Sentinel. "The spread of the infection has been halted."

"Not entirely," I said. "We took samples from a creature we found in the pyramid levels above. There is infected blood and tissue aboard my spacecraft."

"Then it is also infected and should be destroyed."

"How?" I said. "Do you have control over the surface too?"

"No," said the Sentinel. "Myself, and the others like me, our power exists only in these spaces. Within the pyramids themselves. *You* must go and do this."

"And if I can't? If Prisoner 2663 finds a way to get free and take over my body too?"

The Sentinel considered me.

"Human," it said. "Would you consider the safeguarding of your species to be of utmost importance?"

"Yes," I said.

"And would you be willing to sacrifice yourself if it also meant ensuring that Prisoner 2663 never escapes this place, nor poses a threat to your species, ever again?"

"Yes."

The Sentinel looked at me.

Then the slightest of smiles touched his lips.

"So be it," was all he said, before he rushed at me, enveloping me with his arms and kissing my forehead.

• • •

The *Gossamer's* return module is gone now. She left precisely 25 days after the last known contact with the descent module. Which I handily sank to a depth of about five hundred meters after melting the ice at the base.

The ice has re-frozen again. The remnant of Prisoner 2663 that Captain Bednar freed, has been neutralized. Along with Captain Bednar herself, who has become a permanent guest of the pyramid over which I now stand watch. If there is any trace of her left within herself, I hope Bednar understands. And Majack and Kendelsen too. There wasn't any choice. Accident or no, deliberate or no, once they became an active spreader of the contagion, their ultimate fate was sealed.

I know, I checked. The Sentinel confirms that no organism so infected by Prisoner 2663 has ever been cured.

As for me, I can't yet say for certain what the Sentinel has done to me. In many ways it feels as if he is part of me, or that I am part of *him*. I've only begun to test the limits of my power. I've spent a lot of time recording my thoughts: on all that's happened, so that when men return to Titan they will find the disc. I left it in the rover. Which now sits atop the ice, alone. Because I re-sank the pyramid to a sufficient depth too. Along with all the others. And there are many. The longer I can keep those pyramids out of human reach, the better.

Maybe by the time mankind is capable of raising and investigating them, mankind will no longer see the need?

I can't say I understand the ethos that prevents the Sentinel from destroying the nanocyborgs. He seems very old, and very unwilling to dispense information at anything more than a trickle. For my own good, he tells me.

But I suppose I've got time. Enough to last for centuries. Or longer? Whatever it takes to keep Earth and the other uninhabited worlds of the Milky Way safe—from the nanocyborgs at least.

Prisoner 2663. The shadows of Titan. My charge.

They never really sleep. Not entirely.

Even now, they're calling for you too.

Can you hear them?

▼▲▼▲▼

Horror really isn't my thing. But when a group of local Utah guys said they were putting together an anthology of Lovecraft-themed space opera science fiction stories, I knew I wanted in. But I needed a guide. Someone who not only knew Lovecraft, but knew horror tropes the way I knew science fiction tropes. Carter Reid is the author of The Zombie Nation, *a web comic that's been doing rather well of late. He's also a personal friend, lives on my street, his kids play with my daughter, and I've contracted him in the past to do freelance artwork. He's also a raging H.P. Lovecraft fan. Like, raging.*

Well, you know the old saying, about chocolate and peanut butter …

I didn't think I'd like the results as much as I do, but "The Shadows of Titan" would seem to satisfy both my tendencies (for science fiction) and the overall theme of the anthology into which the story first went. Space Eldritch has been a hit. With horror fans and space opera fans alike. So much so, publisher and editor Nathan Shumate went back for another round, in the form of Space Eldritch 2. *There is presently talk of* Space Eldritch 3? *If so, I have to think Carter and I might be teaming up again.*

"The Shadows of Titan" is not, of course, a perfect horror tale, mainly because there is a distinctly un-horrific ending. The monsters and bad guys do not, in fact, spring out of the proverbial closet in the last frame of the film; letting us know that the mayhem is about to start all over again. In fact, the menace seems to be well-contained. Which is precisely the way I wanted it. Because the microscopic plague-like machine entity that wants to take over Earth and turn us all into drones for its own use … is just too nasty for me to let loose in the universe of my imagination. Somebody's got to damned well keep an eye on that thing, or else!

The
Nechronomator

T he mausoleum was silent as I waited quietly at the end of the east corridor. Sodium lamps on the street outside cast a ghastly light through the stained glass windows that ringed the corridor above the crypts. I smelled flowers and floor wax, plus a hint of decades-old cigarette smoke. It had been six hours since I'd wheeled myself to my current spot. Nobody on the mortuary staff had thought to check before locking the doors. I was alone, and not quite believing what I was doing.

Until I heard the scrape of marble on marble.

The air suddenly came alive. A sickening stench of formaldehyde and ethanol, mixed with ozone.

My hands shook, but I gripped the arms of my chair tightly and waited, breathing deeply and slowly, not moving an inch.

Footsteps. The sound of someone taking a seat.

More marble scraping on marble.

I almost screamed when I saw the woman trudge past the open end of the corridor. She walked as if compelled from without. Halting, pained steps. Joints and tissue which hadn't moved in years made an indescribable sound as the woman went up the central hall. She never even looked in my direction.

There was muffled talk—whispery and hollow.

When it became apparent the conversation would be lengthy, I set myself into motion. Gently, with practiced tension, I rotated the wheels on my chair and began a slow, noiseless progression towards the central hall. It took minutes, during which I listened intently, but couldn't quite make out the words. Each yard drew me closer to the source of the stench, and the air was almost alive with static.

Eventually I reached the intersection, and was able to lean forward just enough to peek around the corner, my chair snug against the wall.

The Nechronomator was hideous. His flesh hung limply on his tallish skeleton, sagging and gray. He sat cross-legged on a marble bench that sat at the top of the cross-shaped mausoleum. Liver spots had darkened to black and his mouth looked dry as he moved it. The woman stood before him, motionless in her Sunday finest. The only breaths either of them took were the ones they used to move air across stale vocal chords.

I still couldn't make out what they were saying.

Suddenly the Nechronomator stood—a surprisingly swift movement for someone who'd been dead for three years—and slapped the base of his palm on the woman's forehead. She spasmed and gave a quick, hoarse cry, then flashed into nothingness—like the bulb of a camera had gone off, erasing her from existence.

I reflexively sat back in my chair, teeth clenched. What had I just seen?

One thought—*impossible*—returned again and again to my mind. But I was a scientist, fully in command of my faculties, even if my body was succumbing to age. There were explanations to everything that was occurring. Rational explanations. I would have them.

I wheeled myself boldly into the intersection and spun to confront the Nechronomator. The undead. A monster.

My friend.

"Christopher," I said loudly, hoping to cover my fear with bravado.

He remained standing, arm still outstretched and palm forward, exactly where he had touched the woman.

Slowly, his arm dropped back to his side.

"You should not have come, Matthew."

His voice was like a bellows.

"If you remember anything about me, then you know I would have come eventually. I was here when they sealed you away, after all. I gave the eulogy. I never expected I'd be seeing you again."

"Nor I. What do you want?"

I paused for a moment, then said, "I want to know if it's true."

The Nechronomator laughed. A hard, coughing sound.

"I *told* you it was possible. We used to argue about it after hours, in the staff room. I couldn't ever make it work in the lab, but that didn't mean it wasn't feasible. Now, I have the power."

"Power derived from what?" I asked.

"You wouldn't believe me."

"From God?"

"You never believed in Him."

"Neither did *you*. I still have the photo I took of you shaking hands with Dawkins."

"Dawkins was wrong. We were *all* wrong."

"So, God sent you back?"

"No, I am here by my own choice. God's got nothing to do with it."

I was sweating profusely under my topcoat and scarf. The moisture was beginning to cloud my glasses, but my hand would be shaking so badly I didn't dare reach to take them off. To cover my instinctual fear of the unreal creature before me, I held fast to my belief that this could be pursued as an intellectual problem.

"How does the math work out? On the other side, I mean."

"The math was never the issue," said the Nechronomator. "I always had the math right. It was the energy source that was the problem. Trying to do everything with mere electricity. Even the big colliders can't touch what's available in the After."

"So you can do it?"

"I just did."

"The woman?"

"That was it."

"Show me," I said.

My old, dead friend seemed to consider me for a long moment.

"Not just yet, Matthew. First things first."

He walked almost as I remember him walking, during the final years of his natural life. Like the woman, his joints and tissues made an indescribable sound as he moved past me, the air becoming choked with chemical fumes and the overpowering crackle of an unreleased charge. Had he touched me, I fear I'd have been electrocuted. Or worse. I remembered the woman vanishing with a pop.

The Nechronomator proceeded down the central hall until he reached a crypt which had had its seal removed and discarded on the floor. I spun my chair slowly so as to always keep him in my sight.

"Janice Kawcak," he said. "She was only 47 when the lymphoma got her. Left five kids and a husband. Husband turned to drinking. The kids to drugs. Two of them are in jail now, and the husband's got liver issues. Janice begged me to help."

"Begged you," I said. "How?"

"After. It was all in the After. They came looking for me, almost as soon as I arrived. I guess word travels when they know someone is coming up. I don't think it was supposed to happen that way. They were doing something they shouldn't have been doing. But they didn't care. They just wanted me to help."

"I don't understand," I admitted. "But you of all people should understand that the timeline is changing. Not in big ways. Not yet. But I remember how it used to be, and that's not the way it is *now*."

"Of course it's not," he said as he picked the seal up from where it lay on the floor, then carefully replaced it over the empty crypt.

"Even now, Janice is working to undo things. I sent her back a few years before the diagnosis. She's doubtless visited herself and tried to convince herself to go to the doctor. The cancer would be barely detectable, but it's there. And treatable. Unlike before, when she was stage four."

"You sent her back as a *corpse?*"

"More or less."

"That's hideous."

"I can't resurrect anyone," he said, laughing again. "I don't have the knowledge. Only He can do that. But I can give them temporary control of their bodies, and a power source. And I can send them back."

"Then what the hell *are* you?"

"Same as them. Think of me as a remotely-operated vehicle."

I pondered the implications, before I spoke again.

"And Janice Kawcak is about to come face to face with her dead self, controlled from beyond by her dead self?"

"What better way to convince people? I bet Janice showed herself the scars from surgery and everything. Very compelling."

"Bullshit."

"Tell you what, Matt. You go see. Go look up Janice tomorrow in the phone directory and give her a call. Then come back tomorrow night."

I looked at the Nechronomator. He looked at me.

The unspoken message between us seemed to be this: when seeking to confirm a theory, first examine the proof.

• • •

It took some time to research Janice on the internet at the retirement home. Thankfully she hadn't lived too far out of town, and I only had to pay the home's driver a modest bribe to take me out without the nursing staff knowing my intentions. So far as they knew I was being driven to the beach. Instead we wound up in the suburbs, in an older development that looked like it had gone up in the mid-eighties.

Janice Kawcak didn't know me from Adam, and I wasn't quite sure what I'd say when she answered the door. If she answered the door. Part of me still wasn't convinced.

Until the door swung open, and there she stood. Living and breathing.

"Yes," she said, "Can I help you?"

"So sorry to trouble you, Mrs. Kawcak. My name is Doctor Clayburn. I used to be with the university. Could you come out and speak with me for a moment? It's very important."

She looked at me, then at the driver next to the retirement home's van, then up and down the street.

"What's this about?"

"I'd like to ask you a few questions, Mrs. Kawcak. About someone who visited you perhaps a couple or more years ago."

"You're a physician?"

"No, a physicist. But I'm … Doing some post-retirement research as part of a program they're starting at the university cancer center. Do you mind?"

"Honey?"

A man's voice, from within the house.

She turned and shouted back, "I've got it, John. Just a survey. Be back with you in a minute."

She closed the door quietly, her eyes suddenly wide and worried. She leaned over, bent at the waste so that she could be eye-level with me in my wheelchair.

"How did you know about my ... The ... The visitor?"

"I'm not able to discuss that, exactly," I said. "I simply need to confirm whether or not you were, in fact, visited by someone claiming to be yourself."

Janice stood up and took a second glance up and down the street, making sure there were no neighbors in any yards, then leaned back down and said, "Yes."

"She claimed to be you?"

"Yes, she did."

"Did you believe her?"

"She ... She looked like me, only ... God, it was so *gross.*"

"Like a corpse," I said.

"But she walked and she talked and she ... Showed me things."

"She wanted you to go see an oncologist, right?"

"Yes!"

"Did you?"

"I didn't want to. But like I said, she showed me ... Things. I had to run back in the house and throw up."

"She confronted you here? On your porch?"

"Yes."

"Did anyone else see her?"

"No. She said she knew exactly what time of day to come, when the kids would be at school and John would be at work. She didn't want anyone else to know."

"And did you do what she told you to do?"

Janice Kawcak looked like she almost couldn't hear me. She had stuffed her hands in the pockets of her capris and her arms quivered slightly, as if shivering.

I could feel myself blushing at the temerity of my intrusion.

"I'm so sorry, ma'am. I have to know. *Did you do what the dead woman told you to do?"*

"Yes. I went to my doctor the next day, and he referred me. I was in treatment by the end of the month. I thought the night sweats were just menopause or something. But she was right. It was a lot worse than that."

I looked at her full head of hair. Not a wig.

"Remission, then?"

"I'm in year two. They tell me I'll be in the clear if I hit year five."

"And the dead woman who claimed to be you?"

"I never saw her again."

I stared intently at Janice Kawcak as she stood on her porch, eyes become far away and her mouth in a frown.

"Are you a religious woman?" I asked.

"I didn't used to be. But … John and I go every Sunday now."

"How old are you?"

"I turn 52 in November."

"And your family? How have they been since the … Visitor … Came."

"Fine."

"No problems with drugs or alcohol?"

"Doctor Clayburn, what kind of question is that? No, of course not."

"Yes ma'am. I think I have everything I came for. So terribly sorry to have troubled you."

• • •

The reek of embalming chemicals and ozone slapped me awake. I'd dozed. My ability to stay up past dusk isn't what it used to be. Christopher was standing over me when I looked up.

"Did you see her?"

"I did."

"Is she healthy?"

"Remission. Or, at least, soon-to-be-remission."

"Excellent," he said, and began walking away from me down to where the western corridor branched.

I wheeled quickly after him.

"How many, old friend?"

"Only ten so far. But there are others."

"I'd imagine they're lined up to infinity."

"Not that far."

"And He doesn't care, eh?"

The Nechronomator stopped short.

"As I said last night, God's got nothing to do with this."

"What about … The other guy."

"Lucifer Morningstar? Can't say I've made his acquaintance."

"So you're doing all of this under the noses of both the Lord and the Devil? That's a neat trick, Christopher. Tell me, why are you the first? Surely Einstein and numerous others could have—should have—figured it out, too."

"I asked the same question. To hear it told in the After, Einstein and the rest never had the notion. They were too puzzled, fearful, or awestruck by the After to care. And then, once they'd moved on from Limbo, it was too late for them to change their minds."

"So the Catholics are right?"

"Not exactly. Limbo isn't anything like what they might have thought it was. Mostly because *everybody* goes there first. It's when you're in Limbo that they sort you out. Like a gargantuan class of freshman, being funneled through a registrar. It's in Limbo where my people came and found me, and asked me to start the experiment."

"Which was successful," I said.

"Yes," he said. He was grinning; an appalling expression on a dead man.

He began walking again until he reached the seal on another crypt.

"Robert Davis Maynard," he said. "Bob will be next. Heart attack got him."

"You're talking to him now, aren't you? In the After."

"Very perceptive, Matt. Many things become possible in the After. You'd be amazed at how easy multitasking becomes once your intellect is freed from the confines of your brain."

"What's Bob's plan?"

"Same as most of the others. He's going to try and convince his younger self to change. Give up the daily quarter pounders with fries. Get an exercise regimen together."

"And if he's successful—like Janice—what happens to his body?"

"Since Janice didn't actually die, her corpse then ceases to exist. Only the knowledge that it once existed, remains."

"And you don't care a whit about how this is affecting the timeline?"

My friend ran a skeletal finger along his now-pronounced jaw line.

"I did at first. But then I thought, why not? Why isn't He letting everybody go back and have a second chance, anyway? I got pissed. For Him to have the power and not use it … He's a bastard, you know. A regal, timeless, limitless bastard. Who doesn't use His power when He should."

"Aren't you afraid you'll get caught? Get sent to Hell?"

Chris laughed.

"You of all people, Matt! A Sunday school lecture."

"A matter of practical concern," I said. "Every person who successfully alters the flow of their lives through the timeline, alters the present away from its original course. How far back are you going to go, and how many will you let go back? Do it enough and things will get very, very messy."

"Don't worry, Matt. I can't send people back if I can't physically touch them. So far the only ones I've done have been in this cemetery. All ordinary people. I seriously doubt allowing them to have another shot will disrupt things too much. Especially since their living selves won't have any memory of the After, nor me, because they never died in the first place."

"Then how about sending me," I said.

The Nechronomator considered.

"Haven't tried it on a living person. No idea what it might do to you. For all I know it might strip your soul out and scatter you insensate across the ether. Do you want to take that chance? Remoting in from the After provides me—us—with a degree of insulation I can't guarantee if I try it on you."

I looked down at my legs. Useless for the last forty years.

"You think I care about that now? Send me back, Chris."

"Let me guess. To before the climbing accident."

"Yes. You were there. You remember."

"Yes, I do. I helped carry you to the ambulance."

"Then do me one more favor and let me go back and fix the one fucking mistake that has haunted me worse than all the rest. Please, Chris."

"What if your current self continues to exist alongside your young self?"

"You really think that's a possibility?"

"I don't know, to be honest."

"Fine, then. I'll deal with that when the time comes."

• • •

I didn't feel a thing when the Nechronomator touched my forehead. One moment his stink threatened to overpower me, the next I was sitting alone, still in the mausoleum. Only this time the smell of cigarette smoke was much more pronounced, and there was a new smell. Like recently-poured concrete.

My tires squeaked on the brand new tiles and I stared at the seals to the crypts—most of which were blank—where there had been placards before. I remembered how Janice's corpse had flinched when she'd been sent back. Signal disruption?

For me, it'd been effortless.

I wheeled myself through the dark to the mausoleum doors, which opened easily. Outside, the late summer night air was humid and palpable, like a potter's damp room. Crickets hummed pleasantly in the distance, and the other side of the street across from the cemetery was an empty field, not apartment buildings.

I smiled in spite of myself. Not bothering to close the door behind me, I wheeled out of the mausoleum, only coming to a halt when I realized that the ramp which had existed in 2019, didn't exist in not-so-disabled-friendly 1979. Shit. Even in my younger days I'd not have risked a ride down the mausoleum's front steps.

I sat there in the portico and fumed quietly for a long time.

Then a skeletal child presented herself, quiet as a ghost. I nearly fell over.

"Did Christopher send you?" I asked, heart hammering.

"Yes. He wanted me to see if you'd made it OK. I just told him you did."

"And what will you do now?"

"I've got to go home and keep Daddy from backing over me with the station wagon. But first, I'm going to help you down the stairs."

"I'm afraid I'm too heavy," I said.

"Not when I've got power from the After."

She was right. It was like being manhandled by a pint-sized wrestler.

I was wheezing by the time she got me back into my chair down at the bottom of the stairs. And I'd almost thrown up from that damned smell. They all had it, apparently.

She didn't bother to say goodbye before she loped off into the moonlight, pursuing an objective I myself also intended to pursue. In my head I knew exactly how far I had to go. I patted the lump in my jacket where I'd put my wallet. I'd have been screwed if not for the collection of vintage bills my late wife had kept under glass on the wall of our bedroom. Nancy had admired the artistry, and collected them. Now they were my meal ticket across the country.

Roll down to the street, keep going until I found a pay phone.

Call for a cab. Hope the cabbie didn't have an issue with gimps. Cab to the airport. Flight to Colorado …

The rest I'd have to figure out by the time I got there.

• • •

Even after all these years, I still remembered the address.

442 Pinewood, unit 15.

A ground floor condo. Fortunately for me.

I arrived via cab late into the evening, with the sun just setting. It'd been an exhausting day, and I'd almost convinced myself to get a motel for the night and tackle things in the morning. But then again, no. There was too much of a chance things could still go wrong. If I got my point across, I could rest afterward. Or not at all, depending on how temporal elasticity worked. Chris had said that Janice Kawcak's dead self had ceased to exist the moment she went to see the doctor. What would happen to me?

I kept looking down at my legs as I gradually made my way up the sidewalk towards the first block of condos in the complex, all of them brand new 1975 construction. The fir-strip siding still smelled heavily of stain. Marijuana was also in the air. I thought I saw a couple out on their second-floor deck, passing a roach. They quickly went inside when they noticed me looking up at them.

I smiled. Nobody wanted anyone from the older generation around, especially back then. As I rolled into the hallway that lead to units 14 and 15, a shadowy shape stepped out of the laundry room into the light cast by the single lamp over 14's doorway.

I stopped cold.

"Do you think dying made me stupid, Matthew?"

The Nechronomator wasn't smiling. He looked murderous.

I kept my hands fastened to the wheels, taking reassurance in the solid steel.

"I don't know *what* dying has done to you, Chris. I really don't."

"Your apartment is twenty blocks from here. Why aren't you over there?"

"I think you know," I said.

"You can't speak to me. I won't allow it."

"Why not?"

"*Nothing* must occur which might interfere with my ordinary progression. I lived a full life, and had a natural death. You have no right to be here."

Now it was my turn to laugh. I let it boom out, as best as my 70-year-old lungs were able.

My dead friend flinched and waved his hands as if to shush me.

"Chris," I said, "I think we've both passed the point of caring how we're affecting the flow of events. What harm could possibly come from me having a chat with the younger you?"

"If there were no harm in it, you'd not be here. You plan to stop me."

I looked up at the Nechronomator, his ugly gray flesh especially horrid in the dull bulb's light.

"Not stop you," I admitted, "but maybe talk you into thinking about a few things. I checked the papers on the way here and it's only Friday. The accident isn't until Sunday. Time enough to avert that, if I can. But before I rolled over to Nancy's place—I was shacked up with her at the time, if you remember—I thought I'd stop in and see how you and Carol were doing. You should never have divorced her, you know. She was good for you."

Christopher advanced on me, his hands looking like claws.

"You leave Carol out of this," he hissed. "Look, Matt. You've got one choice. Turn yourself around and never come back this way again. If you do, I will know, and I will stop you. I sent you back once, I can send you forward too."

"Against my will?"

"Damn right, against your will."

"I wonder what He would have to say about that," I said.

Just then the light for 15 popped on, and the door came open. The Nechronomator turned and watched himself saunter out of his condo, boxers disheveled and a long-necked beer in his hand.

"What the fuck?"

Young Chris's eyes focused on his older, dead self, and it was like a silent lightning bolt passed in the air between them.

"Chris," I yelled from my chair, "I've got to talk to you! You've got to call off the climbing trip! You've got to—"

The Nechronomator spun and lunged for me. I reflexively rolled my chair in reverse. Just as Chris's dead hands reached for me, the chair caught on the curb at the end of the sidewalk and flipped over. I slammed hard on my back and toppled out, the Nechronomator hitting the chair's legs and pitching over me. Dead, brittle bones crunched as he came down in a heap. With my arms—made strong over forty years of wheeled effort—I righted myself and ignored the pain where my head had impacted the asphalt.

Young Chris had jogged out and knelt by me.

"Are you okay, man? I should call the cops."

"Chris," I wheezed, "listen to me. Sunday, you and I are going on a trip up the canyon. You've got to call it off. I'm going to break my back when I fall. Don't let me convince you otherwise."

"Jesus … Matt? What's going on? You look—"

Dead Chris rose up from where he'd fallen, left leg and arm twisted grotesquely. He shouldn't have been able to stand at all. Whatever he was tapping from the After, it was potent stuff.

"Desist!"

Young Chris looked like he was going to throw up, and took a few steps backward.

"Oh my God, what is this," he said.

"It's me," I said to young Chris. "Remember the talk we had about you and Carol? She wanted you both to be back in church. For the baby. She's right."

"Chris?"

Carol stood in the doorway of the condo, her nightgown wrapped tightly around her very-pregnant abdomen. Casey was about six months, give or take. I remembered that his birthday always came around Thanksgiving. Shit, he would be a handful by the time he was ten.

Young and dead Chris both looked at his current/former wife.

When Carol saw the Nechronomator, she screamed and backed into the wall behind her, hand up to her mouth.

I turned and looked up at my dead friend. His mouth had drawn open, gaping inhumanly wide. Dead eyes were rolled back into their sockets and a rising groan had begun in his throat. Not air being pushed out, but air being drawn in. His chest was expanding like a balloon, and the groan quickly rose to a howl. A satanic, hair-raising howl that made the windows rattle. I felt an electric charge flow over my skin and though the asphalt.

Something was changing. Had changed.

I waited, turning back once to see Carol clutched to Chris's chest. "Stay together, dammit," I yelled as loudly as I could.

Then everything vanished at once.

• • •

It was almost midnight when Chris pounded on my door. Nancy and I had been relaxing after a good, long, end-of-the-week screw, and she was dozing on the bed. I threw on my terrycloth bathrobe and went to the door to find Chris and Carol fully-dressed and looking worried.

I invited them in, woke Nancy, and we talked over cans of soda.

I wanted to say Chris was crazy. I wanted to tell him I didn't think the joke was very funny. Only, I couldn't make myself believe that he was joking. And with Carol there as an eye witness—serious Carol, who had never pulled a prank in her serious life—the air was stone-cold sober.

Suffice to say, I grudgingly let us cancel the climbing trip. In fact, we never did go climbing again. Chris wouldn't hear of it. Kept telling me how horrified he was to see me in the wheelchair.

Nancy and I were present for Casey's baptism.

When Chris and Carol moved back east for the university job, Nancy and I followed. By the time Casey was in high school Chris and I both had tenure. We had good lives, the two of us.

Chris was a grandpa six times over when Carol finally went. Alzheimer's. Ripped Chris in two to see her go out like that, but we were both glad when it was over. Chris had helped me through Nancy's passing a few years before, and I wasn't surprised to see Chris in my living room, day after day, in the weeks following Carol's.

We talked about God a lot in those final days. A couple of odd ducks in our department at the U. I still have the photo from when Chris debated Dawkins on the quadrangle. I'd thought they were going to punch each other out, they were so angry. We wondered what it would be like, when we crossed over. If we crossed over. Neither of us spoke much of that night anymore, when Chris and Carol showed up and told me the story. Sometimes I still wonder if it wasn't just in Chris's imagination. But Carol had remained firmly convinced, to her deathbed. She'd said she'd never forget watching the zombie swell up like a bloated deer, then pop into nothingness with a flash like that of a camera bulb.

Disabled, older me had vanished too, though the wheelchair had remained behind. Chris still had it in his garage on the day he died, and weeks later when I went over with his kids to begin cleaning things out, I found the wheelchair.

It was covered in dust, and rusty.

Chris had died on April 22, 2016.

The peeling manufacturer's label on the chair said 2018.

I peeled the sticker off, put it in my pocket, and told Chris's kids to send the chair to goodwill.

I don't claim to understand the whole zombie craze. When I was a kid, zombies made for very silly horror films. Nowadays zombies have become big

business. So, I wondered, what could I do with the trope that hadn't already been done before? Since many modern incarnations of zombies abandon the supernatural explanation, and employ any number of viral or biological theories—most of which are scientifically implausible—I decided to do something unusual, and combine the supernatural explanation with a rigorous Hard SF sensibility. Zombies are not, in fact, plague victims. They are being "driven" by their former selves, using the limitless power available in Heaven—or the nether world, or whatever you choose to think of as an afterlife. What's more, a physicist with a time-travel equation wonders if his idea can really work, given the fact that he's got more energy to work with—as a deceased spirit—than was ever available to him in the laboratory. Quote Kenobi, "If you strike me down I shall become more powerful than you can possibly imagine."

I wound up with a story about the ramifications of choices, and how each of us might be tempted to go back and get a "do-over" despite the fact that altering history is not just dangerous for the temporal fabric of present space-time, but also possibly immoral as well. Because if God grants free agency, and each of us must be held accountable for our decisions, getting a "do-over" would seem to skirt both God's judgment, and Christ's call to repentance.

I could have dwelt more thoroughly on the religious implications of my story about dueling physicists—one alive, one not. Instead, I was having too much fun imagining how it all might play out: the live friend meeting the dead friend, the visceral sensations and smells of the zombies themselves, how and where and why anyone might want to use his or her dead self to talk sense into his or her live self, before any number of disastrous things might happen …

Anyway, Mike Resnick took this one, for Galaxy's Edge.

I was thrilled.

The Hideki Line

I t was two in the morning on a Saturday when I finally got back to the office. Nothing seemed wrong when security passed me through the gate, nor the booth at the front desk, nor even the checkpoint at the mouth of the tunnel. I took an electric buggy down to Accelerator level and didn't realize something was up until I walked through the doors into the main lab and found two women and one man with silenced, semi-automatic pistols aimed at my face.

"What the—" I said, reflexively putting my hands into the air.

"Stay quiet," one of the women commanded. "Don't move, and keep your hands where we can see them."

Whoever they were, they weren't security. Their uniforms were digital camo, temperate forest pattern. Third-generation Army Combat Uniform. Not too different from what I'd once worn in Iraq. The way they held their weapons and the coolness in their eyes made me suspect they were *some* kind of military. But without name tape, unit insignia or rank, I could only guess.

Still frozen in place, I turned my head gently—so as not to spook the people with the weapons—and saw at least a dozen other ACU-clad men and women. They were busily unloading huge backpacks and duffels off the beds of several other electric buggies which had been driven in through the service corridor. They worked without speaking—their actions fluid and rehearsed. Nobody bothered to look up at me.

Well, almost nobody.

"Lil," I said to her as she stared at me, swallowing thickly "what the hell is going on?"

"Cody—" my co-worker and sometimes girlfriend began to say, but she stopped short and dropped her chin to her chest. "Oh jeez ..."

When she looked up again, her eyes brimmed with tears.

Doctor Lilith Kensing's face was contorted. She looked both frustrated and sad. Very sad. But even in sadness, her sunflower beauty tugged at my imagination. Full mouth, golden brown hair, bright eyes, and high cheeks patterned with freckles. She looked strange in the ACU, which was a bit too big for her. Her hands reflexively found each other, and twisted together nervously.

Another woman, who had been standing next to Lil, finally looked at me. She was trim, with pepper-colored hair that had been buzzed short. No makeup. No jewelry. Fiftyish. It seemed I knew her from somewhere, and couldn't quite recall her name.

She spoke.

"Who is he and what's he doing here?"

"Cody Cranston," Lil said regretfully to her companion. "Computer programmer and robotics specialist. Among ... other things."

"I forgot to load my conference presentation onto my thumb drive," I said. "VPN was down, and my flight for D.C. leaves in five hours. So I had to come back and get the file. Lil, did you let these people in here? Where is security?"

"Another Code Orange?" said one of the women with a pistol.

"No, not yet," said the woman standing next to Lilith. "We don't want to hurt anyone else if we don't have to."

Finally, it hit me.

"Senator Petersen," I said.

She nodded at me, if just slightly.

Without her hair, and without makeup and camera lights, it had been hard to tell who she was. Now I remembered. She'd come out to the facility and toured, just two years before. I hadn't met her then, but I'd been told afterward she really liked what she saw. So much so she became the project's most aggressive backer in Washington D.C.

Which was odd—for an environmentalist politician. She was on the short list for the Democratic Presidential ticket in November. A real fire-breather on green energy, and fighting industrial corporate lobbyists.

Now here she was in my lab, dressed like G.I. Jane.

I wondered if the people with pistols were Petersen's security detail? I also wondered if any of my co-workers on the graveyard shift had found out what "Code Orange" meant. They were nowhere to be seen.

"Let's finish this," said the armed male.

The muzzles of the pistols advanced on me. I backed up.

"Stop!" Lil yelled. "We can … he can come with us. He'd be valuable."

"Sorry," said the Senator. "I told you before. We don't need computer people where we're going."

"And I told *you* he's prior service," said Lil. "Right Cody?"

"Two deployments," I said. "Once for OIF and once for OEF."

"See any combat?" Petersen asked.

"My purple hearts and CAB say I did."

The Senator seemed to consider me more thoroughly, while I continued to flick my eyes from her, to the armed trio, then to Lilith—who looked impossibly bothered—and finally to the others who were hurriedly working. Petersen's people still ignored me and kept lugging heavy backpacks and duffels through the orifice into the heart of the lab's cube-shaped reaction chamber.

I wondered. Was it sabotage, or espionage? Were those explosives? Environmental activism writ large?

For an instant I thought Lil and the Senator—who was obviously calling the shots—might actually be working for the Chinese. Or maybe that ancient bastard Putin?

But as I watched the big bags and backpacks being taken into the chamber, I intuited that none of these men and women had any intention of leaving the Experimental Retryon Accelerator Facility. Not through a door, anyway.

I drew a deep breath.

"It's the Hideki Line, isn't it Lil?"

My girlfriend's chin trembled, and she averted here eyes. Which was all I needed to see from her, to know the answer to my question. We'd been together long enough for me to tell when I'd guessed something correctly; something she didn't want to say with words.

I looked around at them all, and then back at Senator Petersen.

"Ma'am, I suggest you think twice. We don't know exactly how far back the Hideki Line goes. You have no idea what might happen if you take it. We were going to send a robot next month. I was flying to Washington this weekend to brief the funding committee. Looks like that won't be necessary."

"No," said the Senator. "It won't."

"But *why?*" I asked, finally spreading my arms in appeal, despite the pistols in my face. "What are you hoping to accomplish?"

"They're cutting the project, Cody," Lil said angrily before the Senator could speak. "You would have found out on Monday. The committee made up its mind already. That's why Catherine called *me.*"

"And where do you figure the Senator plans on *taking* you, Lil?"

"It doesn't matter, Cody. The Hideki Line goes back at least ten thousand years or more. That's plenty."

• • •

Bill Hideki, along with Dan Stadtler, was one of four Nobel-winning theoretical physicists who had been with ERAF from the beginning. It was Stadtler who discovered the Lines, and Hideki who extrapolated upon Stadtler's math. It took a large room of supercomputers to do the rest, and the end results were the Stadtler Lines: mathematical corridors through time itself. They could only be calculated backwards, since variables for future Lines were impossible to nail down. In the three years since ERAF had gone live, the supercomputers had spit out a new Line every couple of days, and each of those lines had ranged in "length" from a few millionths of a second, up to two minutes into the past.

Except for The Big One. The one Hideki himself had reported, four months ago.

That one went off the chart, back across millennia.

We checked it four times with the machines, and each time got the same result. Hideki and Stadtler agreed it was a singular pheno-menon. Something we weren't likely to find again. Not in ten or a hundred years. Maybe not ever again. And as we learned through experimentation—sending objects, mice, dogs, and even people—once a Line got used once, it was *gone.* The energy necessary to open the Line and send anything back, disrupted the brane of the universe just enough to erase that particular Line from existence. And the longer the Line, the more juice it took to send stuff back.

Opening the Hideki Line was going to suck every bit of power we could crank out of the project's attached fusion reactors—enough electricity to keep the west coast lit from British Columbia to Baja, for the entirety of time the reaction chamber was energized.

Naturally, Bill's discovery was decreed TOP SECRET and very few non-project people, beyond the D.C. committee which managed us, had even known about it.

Sending a robot probe was my idea. I argued that we needed to use the Hideki Line as quickly as was feasible, both to test the max envelope of our operational capability, and to ensure that such a long Line got burnt before one of our competitor projects used it first. Here in the States we could be sure that such a discovery was used for scientific purposes only. No untoward disturbances in the historical record. No time terrorism.

Or, at least, that's what all of us on the project had assumed.

• • •

Seeing the Senator and her little commando group taking the last of their belongings into the reaction chamber gave me the queasy feeling that Bill, Dan, me, and all the rest had been spectacularly naïve.

I began to get angry. The feeling of betrayal was hot in my throat. I glared at Lilith, but I addressed myself to her apparent boss.

"What's your plan, Senator?" I said, beginning not to care about the guns. "Go back in time, set up your own little kingdom? What are your people humping in those sacks? Weapons? Ammunition? Enough to carve out an empire in the late Pleistocene?"

"Maybe that's what a *man* would do," Petersen said, arms crossed over her chest. "Conquer. Dominate. Use. Destroy. The entire history of our species, down through the ages. A product of the male drive to feed, screw, and control. If that's all your imagination can conjur, I think it's best if we leave you here. Where you belong."

"No," Lil said. "Cody's a good man. Catherine—"

"That's *Senator*—" Petersen hissed at Lilith, but Lil kept talking.

"Not anymore it's not!" She said. "Catherine, *he has to come*. We have room and supplies. Please. I know we can use him."

"Who says I want to go?" I said, perhaps too sarcastically. "What's waiting for me in ten thousand B.C? No doctors, no dentists, no hospitals. No antibiotics or hip replacements. No electricity, nor industry. No grocery stores. No hot showers. No satellite high-def television. Lil, we've talked about this before, you and I. We both agreed that the distant past was a place we'd probably like to visit, but *never* live in. The Lines are one-way. No coming home. And what about the damage that can be caused? The *brane* damage? That's why we agonized over the design and programming for the probe, so it would bury itself. Keep out of sight and—"

"Cody, *shut up!*"

I shut up. Lil looked frantic enough to break something.

She walked towards me.

"Cody, I know you're angry. But you have to understand. The project is being *cancelled*. They're going to introduce a treaty at the United Nations to have *all* of the retryon facilities in *all* countries closed *permanently*. Further research will be monitored and blocked. Protections and safeguards are going to be erected. It'll be like the nuclear ban in space. No nuclear rockets to Mars. No expeditions to the past, either. So it's now … or never."

I didn't say anything after that. I could tell by her eyes how absolutely Lil believed what she was saying. In addition to my feeling of betrayal, there now came grief. My budding romance with Lilith had been the happiest discovery of my post-divorce years. And now I was going to lose her, one way or the other.

"It won't work," I said softly.

"Why won't it? We don't have to take a lot of people. Just enough to get the ball rolling. We'll find a tribe, or tribes. With modern weapons and science we can establish ourselves as chiefs, shamans, and teachers. We take the children and we teach them. They teach their children, who teach their children. They're still human. All they lack is the knowledge. We take tough, solar-powered computers. We teach the tribe how to use and access the databases. By the time we're dead, they're on their way. And they'll be able to avoid all the pitfalls. Manage their environment. Fight off enemies and bring in friendly tribes. Grow food and mine ores responsibly. No need to cut down all the trees. Industry without poisoned lakes and rivers. Electricity. *Civilization!* In harmony with the natural world. No extinct species. No deforestation. No pollution, overpopulation, or global warming."

"And what about everyone left behind? What about me? What about *us?*"

Tears finally sprang from Lilith's eyes and ran down her face.

"I wanted to bring you. I begged them to let me bring you. Catherine said you'd never agree to it, and would blow the whistle. She said if I told you, I'd be off the team."

"She's right," I said. "I'd have tried to stop this."

"Cody, oh God, why couldn't you have just gone home and gone to bed?"

Lil turned from me and walked away, weeping. I called after her and she ignored me, heading instead for one of the buggies where she struggled to put a pack onto her back, and then walked towards the reaction chamber.

I felt tears on my own cheeks, and redirected my anger towards the Senator.

"It's mass murder," I said coldly, "and you know it."

"You can't murder people who never existed."

"Convenient," I said.

The Senator regarded me for another moment, then let out a long sigh and said, "Code Orange."

The male with the gun grinned, and suddenly they were backing me up again, muzzles unwavering. For the first time since I'd walked into the lab, I began to sweat profusely. My heart rate jumped and time slowed perceptibly as adrenaline dumped into my bloodstream.

Ghosts of Kurdistan flirted with the present, and I was seeing double.

• • •

My truck commander, grinning and telling a story about his kids. The growl of the humvee's tires as we moved up the packed earth highway. Our Kurdish interpreter bouncing quietly in the back seat, next to an equally quiet PFC whose name I never did remember. Dirt spewed into the air like a geyser, as an IED took out the humvee in front of ours. I reflexively stamped on the accelerator, turning onto the shoulder so as to maneuver past the ruined truck, when an RPG slammed into the passenger side of my own vehicle.

Blank time.

Next, I was on my back, and I couldn't breathe.

How had I gotten out of my humvee?

There was a loud buzzing sound, and my kevlar was gone.

When the pain finally hit, I gagged.

• • •

"He looks like he's going to puke."

Visions of the past evaporated as I realized I'd been forced into the doorway of an equipment closet. This wasn't Kurdistan, and the three people with pistols regarded me as one might regard a mental patient escaped from the hospital.

One of the women with a pistol opened the door behind me and I found myself backed inside. Out of the corner of my eye I could see the others from the graveyard shift. Mouths taped. Wrists and ankles bound tightly. There was blood on the floor. Lots of blood. Rick Tamayo looked like he'd been shot.

He was too pale. Like my truck commander's face.

I might have been twenty years older than my foes, but I'd never stopped working out to Army standard. And even though I'd lost my knack for combatives, I'd taken up a modified form of Taiwanese grappling—after my divorce—just to keep myself sharp, and not let myself slide into blubbery oblivion.

The adrenaline rang in my veins. I spun and grabbed the woman who had been closest behind me. With both arms I wrenched, feeling a *crunch* and hearing a scream as she lost her weapon. I bore down and lunged, putting my entire body into hers and pushing her into the two who remained in the doorway. They yelled and stumbled back under the first woman's weight.

I let go and dove for the pistol that now lay free on the cement. Rolling, I scooped the weapon up and ran back through the door. I had to get to the control room. Even one shot through the main board would do the trick. I could also pull the fire alarm, which would automatically cut main power and sound alarms back at the mouth of the tunnel.

Shouts echoed through the lab as I sprinted madly for the steel staircase that would take me up to where I needed to go. I hit the stairs, three at a time, and reached for the door handle.

It was locked. *Damn.*

My access card! I fumbled at my belt, yanking the ID on its spring-loaded tether, then heard a loud and all too familiar noise split the air.

Getting shot hurt just as much as it had the first time, outside Baghdad. I wobbled and fell, barely arresting myself on the railing and feeling an immense pain in my left side.

My weapon clattered down the stairs.

Someone was screaming my name. It sounded like Lilith. I saw the two remaining pistol-wielders stop in mid-stride and throw Lilith aside as she rushed towards the bottom of the stairs. A glance at the reaction chamber showed Senator Petersen slapping the backs of her people as they rushed their final bags inside. Then she turned towards the stairs and shouted, "Leave him! Marsh, Brown, we have to go *NOW!*"

Marsh and Brown looked back up at me as I hung to the railing with one arm, the opposite hand clamped over my wound. Warm, thick blood flowed through my fingers, and I gasped.

Lilith leapt back to her feet and pelted up the stairs.

"*Cody!*" Lil half-sobbed. "Didn't you realize it wouldn't *matter* anymore? Why did you have to do that?"

"You know why," I whispered to her, feeling light-headed.

Her hand froze an inch from my belly, afraid to touch the blood.

"Lilith," I said, feeling the shock overtaking me, "You must stop this."

"No, Cody. It's too late. I'm committed. I just … I never wanted you to get hurt!"

"Lil …"

"I won't forget you, Cody. You were a good man."

"Lil …"

"Cody, I am *sorry.*"

Suddenly her lips and mouth were covering mine. The electric warmth of her lips cut through the pain, if only for a moment, and I held my breath and closed my eyes to savor it. Then she released me, and I opened my eyes again. Her face was damp from weeping and she stroked my thinning hair, just like she always did. I tried to grab her but she was already moving back down the stairs, and I groaned and slapped my hand back over my side as she jumped off the bottom of the stairs and sprinted for the reaction chamber—Marsh and Brown already in the lead.

Lil dashed through the orifice without looking at me, and then only Petersen remained. The Senator watched me impassively as I struggled back up the stairs to the door, managed to get my access card to the reader plate, and spat obscenities when the plate didn't respond. Maybe if I'd not dropped the gun I could have shot my way inside, but I was bleeding out, and every muscle was turning to water. It was all I could do to slump down on my butt and heave air.

A klaxon sounded, and an automated voice warned people to clear the area.

Lil must have set an automatic countdown.

A familiar hum filled the lab as the power of several hydrogen bombs began to crouch in the super-cooled coils that surrounded the cube-shaped reaction chamber. Soon, everything within that space, down to the last molecule, would exchange places with everything in an equivalent space, far back in time, according to calculations that took into account the relative position of the Earth, the Sun, where the solar system was now versus where it had been then, and—

I glanced towards the equipment closet. Those who could do so had squirmed their way out and were thrashing like beached fish, eyes wide in realization.

The ERAF's execution cycle began to pitch towards crescendo. Petersen kept looking at me intently, then frowned once and raised a hand in salute. Turning, she too ducked into the reaction chamber. She never looked back at the comrade she'd left behind. The woman whose arm I'd broken lay motionless near my writhing co-workers.

I must have hurt her worse than I'd thought. I felt shame for that. But then, I felt calm, too.

As conscious thought faded, I figured I'd probably not have to worry about it in another couple of seconds. If Lilith and the Senator were right, very shortly, everything in the current day would cease to exist. I would never be born. Nor my parents. Nor their parents. Nor their parents' parents. The ERAF would be gone, along with everyone who had built it. The United States, and all its history, would never happen. Nor Europe's. Nor would anything else be the same, going all the way back to when Lilith and her group suddenly popped into existence on some impossibly ancient tundra, like colonists come to settle an alien world.

The ERAF countdown reached zero. As in previous experiments, it produced a muffled thunderclap that shook the lab.

I blacked out.

· · ·

Waking up was an absolute surprise.

It was Wednesday morning, and I was in a hospital bed with tubes running in and out of me. Doctors and nurses came and told me I'd been in a coma, and that they'd barely gotten me to the operating room in time.

I'd lost a kidney. Almost bled out. Lucky to be alive.

I thought, *they don't know the half of it.*

I wondered what had gone wrong.

Nobody came to talk to me, though they had hospital security guards posted at my door.

So I just kept wondering. Throughout the next week in the hospital, then home for paid leave and convalescence—or house arrest, depending on how one chooses to view unmarked police cruisers perpetually stationed at one's curb.

I watched on television as the new Retryon Research Treaty was introduced at the United Nations, and unanimously signed by all parties. I didn't hear a thing from anyone with the project until Bill Hideki showed up one day, seven weeks after I got shot, and told me the rest of the story as we sat in my townhome's living room.

It all came down to a single, huge piece of ice. That's what they found in the reaction chamber when they went in the next day to clean up the mess.

Besides myself, one other project worker got shot, and he was dead even before I got there. Damn. I knew Rick had been too pale. The woman whose arm I broke turned out to be one of Petersen's campaign staffers. She blew air into her IV tube the moment they left her unattended.

So much for her.

Everyone else recovered, and we were all under super-strict orders to not say a damned word about anything to anyone. There was a lot of hush money to make it worth our while, too.

Fine with me.

Late morning wore on, into afternoon.

The whole time Bill talked, I kept going back in my mind to that huge block of ice he'd mentioned.

No wonder history survived.

Somewhere back in time, Lilith and the Senator had found themselves transported into the belly of a glacier, with possibly a mile or more of frozen water above their heads. They'd have needed heavy equipment and explosives to bust their way out. Assuming melt water—raining in from the bottom of an exposed crevasse—had not drowned them first.

The glacier's movement had doubtless ground their remains and equipment into powder. Nothing left for anyone to discover.

I shuddered.

▼ ▲ ▼ ▲ ▼

Time travel stories never get old. Pun fully intended.

Only, when time travel is too easy, or too commonplace, or behaves without rules, it's boring. For time travel to be intriguing, there have to be boundaries and limits. I wondered what might happen if nuclear physics theory stumbled across a kind of time travel where unique "tunnels" to the past could be accessed? Most of them are far too short to be of any possible use. They are burned up once they do get used. Who might want to take a "long" tunnel, presuming such a tunnel went deep into the past? And why? Especially if it was a once-on-this-lifetime chance?

I'm a fan of post-Ice Age North America, replete with giant animals and the many huge freshwater lakes that existed at that time. If there is a single place I'd want to go, given a chance to travel back into time, I'd want to go to the shores of Lake Bonneville about five hundred years before the lake cut loose and flooded out through Red Rock Pass. I imagine it's colder than it is now. Lots of snow in the winter. And the mountains are covered in trees. With the lake itself stretching away to the horizon, gorgeous and blue. An inland sea, unspoiled by ships or industry. What if a small band of modern humans—carting along the collected knowledge of the modern age—went back to that time, and started over? We'd know how to avoid many of the mistakes industrial society has made, getting from the 16ᵗʰ century to the 21ˢᵗ century. With sufficient equipment and weapons we might be able to take over and interbreed with whatever bands of primitive humans we come across; assuming there are such bands to be had. The descendents of that fusion—ancient, and modern—would have (theoretically) all our knowledge at their fingertips, and an entire world of mostly untamed and fresh resources at their disposal. With no competition. But an enlarged and much more careful perspective.

Can you see it?

I can!

Alas, that spells doomsday for you and me. We'd never exist. Wouldn't that be a kind of genocide, to wipe all modern humans from the face of the Earth? Even if it meant getting to have a clean slate?

There are a few people—mostly at the edges of the environmentalist movement—who would literally kill for just such a clean slate.

One of the readers who first read this story, said she had a hard time with it precisely because she sympathized—not with Cody—but with the Senator!

I suppose I do too, on a certain level. I'd love to see Lake Bonneville. But I'd not want to have the fate of the entire 21ˢᵗ century on my conscience either. Our present state of affairs may not be perfect, but each and every one of us is an individual with rights and dignity. We are not a pestilence on this planet. Nor are we a mere commodity. I fear sometimes the "planners" of our world forget these facts. And so I chose to bury the Senator in the heart of a glacier. As a kind of just punishment for her zealotry and hubris.

Brian Lewis took this story for his Spark: A Creative Anthology *project, the foreword to which was written by my friend and mentor Kevin J. Anderson. I was honored that Brian wanted to include me (and "Hideki") as something of a veteran presence. I have several friends in that volume as well. I hope my continued success has helped the Spark books by association.*

Thanks, Brian.

Peacekeeper

(with Mike Resnick)

I t was a normal duty day in the city until the Earth limo showed up. It glided through the chaotic *s'ndar* traffic that bustled across my assigned six-way intersection. Flow control was provided by a single *s'ndar* of the city's provisional constabulary, who jerked his brightly-colored paddles to and fro over his bug's head, herding his people this way and that.

Since the cease-fire, my squad and I didn't mess with the locals unless we had to. We kept out of the way, as back-up for the traffic cop in case of real trouble.

I exchanged glances with Corporal Kent, who'd seen the limo. Her facial expression said, *You're the boss, you figure it out.*

I sighed, then got up out of my sandbagged security position and began walking towards the vehicle as it ground to a halt a few meters away.

The *s'ndar* traffic cop watched me, decided it was none of his business, and went back to waving his paddles.

Low-rise commercial and residential structures sprouted around the intersection like mushrooms, their hemispherical roofs designed to shelter pedestrians from the daily monsoon. Along the boulevards poles rose up from the pavement at regular intervals to support endless rows of electrical conduit, phone conduit, and fiber optics.

A slight haze of smog hung over the *s'ndar* city. It was impossible to ignore how similar, and yet also totally different, the scene was from the average urban center on Earth. Humans and *s'ndar* had reached roughly equivalent technology levels.

Then the Interstellar Conglomerate intervened.

The smooth hum of the limo's twin engines quit, and the man who stepped out of the car was someone I was familiar with only from the news feeds. Senator Jeff Petersen had played football in college, and still kept reasonably fit. Tall and broad-chested, his full head of pepper-tinged hair was trimmed close. He had on a khaki field vest—one of the Earth embassy models that contained ballistic armor plating in addition to being festooned with pouches and pockets. He also wore neatly-pressed khaki shorts and high-topped boots.

Given the oppressive humidity, I envied his wardrobe.

Two similarly-dressed Secret Service personnel—one male, with a pistol on his hip; the other female, with a submachine gun in her hands—flanked the Senator as he strode toward me. Other Secret Service agents stepped from the car and scanned the surroundings cautiously, their mirror sunglasses and straight faces making them seem somehow robotic.

I saluted the Senator when he drew near.

"Sergeant Colford!" yelled Petersen over the din of traffic as he extended his hand. He'd obviously read my name tape on my armor. Good politician's reflex. Made it seem like he really gave a damn who I was.

I rapidly chow-slung my rifle and shook Petersen's hand. He had a surprisingly strong grip. Well, maybe not so surprising, given his profession. His smile was amiable, and his nicely-capped teeth sparkled in the oppressive sunlight.

I strongly resisted the urge to like him.

"Senator," I said formally, "I wish I'd known you were coming."

"You guys always say that," Petersen said, continuing to smile. "But how am I supposed to talk to you candidly if your Commander or First Sergeant is warning you at morning briefing?"

It was a good point. But if I knew my corporal, she was already calling in to the Tactical Operations Center. Headquarters would have our asses if we didn't report the Senator's arrival ASAP.

Petersen surveyed my semi-hardened position.

"A bunker and eleven troops. Kind of overkill, don't you think? The *s'ndar* in this city are pro-Conglomerate now. They're our friends."

"Maybe, sir," I replied. "But you weren't here six months ago."

"I read about that. Did you see a lot of fighting, son?"

Son? Hell, I was almost thirty.

"I saw my share," I said evenly. "My rifle company trained *en route*. Our Conglomerate transports already had mock-ups of *s'ndar* urban terrain onboard. We *thought* we'd be ready."

"But you thought wrong," the Senator said.

"Yah," I replied, grimacing at the memory.

Petersen waited, as if expecting me to say something more. When I didn't, he ran a hand over his scalp and then folded his arms across his chest.

"So, you've seen some rough fighting. Okay. Do you at least feel like it was worth it?"

"Worth *what*, sir?"

"Earth's involvement in *S'ndar-khk's* civil war. *America's* involvement in the CEMEF—the Combined Earth Military Expeditionary Force."

"I don't make policy, sir," I told him noncommittally. "I just follow orders."

"Fair enough. But the UN's bargain with the Conglomerate is costing American lives. Do you think it's worth it?"

I frowned, remembering my sister Karen. She'd been an officer in the Air Force, and had wanted to be an astronaut too, before the Conglomerate established their first contact with Earth. The interstellar robotic transports the Conglomerate sent to us made Earth's space stations look like toys. We'd not even put a man on Mars yet, and the Conglomerate was picking us up and hauling us off in whole battalions—over 300 light-years, to this obscure little planet, where my sister had been thrilled as hell to see actual aliens.

Now she was buried back home, her skull split by a *s'ndar* bullet. It had been a closed-casket affair, given the damage. Mom and Dad still weren't over it.

"I've lost some friends here," I said. "And family too. Things were a mess on this planet when we showed up. Lots of killing all over the place. Now there's not so much. But only because we're still alert every hour of every day. You ask me if it's worth it … I sure as hell hope so."

Petersen's brow furrowed. He reached out and put a hand on my shoulder, his face turning empathetic.

"I'm sorry for your friends, and whoever else you lost in your family, too. Part of the reason I'm here is to assure you and the other troops that you're doing truly important work. You're saving lives. *Human* lives. We help the *s'ndar* establish and keep the peace, and the Conglomerate helps Earth. We *need* the Conglomerate's clean fusion technology to reverse the economic and political damage from the Oil Crash. You're standing guard on this intersection so that you—or someone like you—doesn't have to stand guard over a few barrels of crude in the Person Gulf or Venezuela."

"Militia coming!" yelled one of my privates.

Senator Petersen and I turned our heads to see a small patrol of *s'ndaran*-make armored personnel carriers maneuvering towards us through the hubbub. The large-wheeled, tank-like vehicles took a few minutes to reach our position, and when they did, several armed *s'ndar* climbed from the hatch on an aerial-spiked APC, and approached my squad.

The *s'ndar* in the lead looked older than the rest. It was a female. Hell, *all* the authority figures in the insectoid race from sergeant on up were females, just like the ants and bees back on Earth. Her chitin was grayed at the edges and had several wounds that had been puttied over with artificial quick-cure ceramic, now weathered. Her thorax bore the militia-equivalent of a Non-Commissioned Officer, and it didn't take a genius to figure out she'd seen her share of combat.

Sergeant to sergeant, we saluted, the *s'ndar* in its form, me in mine.

As I lowered my rifle from the vertical, my Conglomerate-manufactured Translation Application Device—TAD—began speaking into my helmet's earphones. Emotionless metallic English filled my ears as the *s'ndar's* mandibles clicked and scratched consonants in between flute-like vowels.

"Good morning, Staff Sergeant," she said.

"Good morning, Primary Sergeant," I replied, my TAD turning my English into *s'ndar* words.

"My soldiers and I arrive in coordination with the Senator's visit," said the primary sergeant.

I studied her. You could never really be sure about the militia. They worked for the provisional government, who worked with the Expeditionary Force. But that didn't mean much on the street. I'd learned that first-hand. A few of the militia were quality. Many of them were either incompetently hazardous or deceitfully dangerous. It was best to be cautious.

Petersen turned back to me.

"Do you mind if I go talk with your people?"

"Feel free, sir," I said

I watched Petersen navigate away from my fighting position, chatting briefly with privates, specialists, and my corporal.

Finally the *s'ndar* sergeant spoke. "I apologize for this nuisance," she said.

"Not a problem," I answered, grateful my TAD didn't translate my distaste. We'd come to *S'ndar-khk* to help, and the various *s'ndar* hives had fought us tooth and nail—in the middle of their own stupid hive-on-hive war. They might have gone nuclear on each other if the Conglomerate hadn't established first contact, and intervened for humanitarian reasons.

I heard some loud, rumbling engines, and turned to see a series of large trucks maneuvering into the intersection. They were flatbeds of *s'ndar* construction, weighed down with large, square containers. I frowned. Any kind of large-scale commercial traffic like this should have been cleared with the Tactical Operations Center well beforehand. The native traffic cop out in the intersection knew it too, and began waving his paddles furiously, signaling for the trucks to stop.

Their drivers obeyed—

—and the traffic cop exploded in a spray of barking rifle fire.

After that everything became a blur.

I remember the sides of the shipping containers splitting open and a small swarm of *s'ndar* pouring out. Civilians on foot began to scatter while vehicles attempted to either halt, or speed off. The air buzzed with countless *s'ndar* voices that overwhelmed my TAD. I switched over to the squad channel as I brought my weapon from off my back and pulled the charging handle.

The turrets on the *s'ndar* APCs—armored personnel carriers— rotated and began hammering heavy rounds towards the flatbeds, only to be hit by rocket-propelled grenades.

The APCs burned.

I couldn't determine which of the attacking *s'ndar* had fired. In the panicked crowd, it was impossible to tell the attackers apart from the civilians. I saw the primary sergeant hunched and firing her rifle, so I got down on one knee and began firing likewise. Whoever she shot at, I could shoot at, at least according to the rules of engagement—*s'ndar* being better able to tell one another apart.

Corporal Kent was taking care of the squad. Her bellowing voice was comforting through the speakers in my headset.

Using the laser sight on my weapon, I drew a bead on a *s'ndar* moving hurriedly towards me, while the crowd scrambled in the opposite direction. My finger gave a near-motionless trigger pull and my target's carapace cracked hideously as the jacketed round tore through its thorax.

I fired at another one, also moving against the crowd. And another. And another.

There were so many trying to converge on us at once!

The Senator! I thought. *They're after the Senator!*

His armored car was in flames, along with the militia's APCs, and I heard the popping of the Secret Service's pistols, punctuated by the occasional rip of their submachine guns.

From somewhere in the chaos of the crowd, numerous small objects catapulted. For an instant they looked like opaque mason jars, then one was smashing onto the pavement two meters from me.

Grenades?

I stopped firing and turned to see other such objects cascading across our sandbagged position.

I crouched down and began to move towards my people when I caught a deep whiff of a sickly-sweet chemical. The contents of the mason jars had spilled wetly on the ground, vapors pluming, and I suddenly found myself rolling helplessly onto my side, arms and legs twitching sporadically.

The *s'ndar* had never used chemical weapons against us before. Neural agents which were effective against *s'ndar* didn't work against humans, and vice versa.

Until now, anyway.

My instinct was to reach for the unused protective mask in my thigh pouch, but the pouch was pinned under my bodyweight and I didn't have the strength to roll over. It was as if all the signals traveling from my brain to my body had been roadblocked.

Darkness began closing in on me from all sides, and I thought about how stupid it was to be snuffed like this.

The screams of my squad fell quickly silent, and the last thing I remembered was the murky shape of a *s'ndar* leaning over me.

It was not a member of the militia.

• • •

"Staff Sergeant?"

I didn't move.

"Staff Sergeant!"

I still didn't move. The neutered voice did not compute.

Something like a tree branch raked my face.

That computed.

I reflexively opened my eyes and tried to bring my arms forward in self defense, only to find them shackled over my head. Short, rusted iron chains kept me pinned against a cold wall. A single hole in the high ceiling allowed a broad-based shaft of sunlight to penetrate, forming a too-bright circle on the cracked cement floor, and leaving the perimeter of the room in near darkness.

A sudden wave of nausea hit, and I coughed violently, my nose and eyes running—doubtless a final reaction to the residue of the chemical attack. For a second I thought I was going to pass out again, but the nausea slowly subsided and I began blinking the tears from my eyes.

"He is alert," said the mechanical voice. "Go inform the others."

I kept blinking until a *s'ndar* silhouette took shape before me. The rotund, beetle-like being was resting on its lower motile legs with one utensil arm poised, ready to strike. The stiff hairs along that arm had stung mightily when it swiped me the first time. I'd have been happy to swing back, if only I wasn't chained.

"Who the hell you are?" I demanded.

My TAD scratched out a translation. I was thankful both the device and its requisite headset were still on my person. That meant my captors wanted to talk; not just kill me.

"I am not authorized to tell you," answered the *s'ndar*, its own TAD turning clickety-clackety mandible movements into human speech.

"The timing of your ambush couldn't have been accidental."

"You are correct."

"What has happened to Senator Peterson and my squad?"

"No one has been harmed," the creature said. "You must realize that if we'd wanted to we could have killed you where you stood."

"Okay, you could have killed us and you didn't," I said. "What now?"

The *s'ndar* turned and left my cell for a moment, the crude iron door hanging wide open, then returned with several others. Including a larger, older female who wore the colorful cloth raiment of a priestess.

Great, I thought. *Someone who knows God is on her side.*

Among the usual squabbling of the various hives, there was a particularly absolutist sect of *s'ndar* fanatics who considered the human presence on their world to be a literal desecration. They were the ones still fighting guerilla-style even when most of the other resistors had been bought off at the bargaining table, or beaten down into submission by the Expeditionary Force.

"We are holding your Senator," said the priestess. "Do you understand what this means?"

"Yes," I said. Capture or assassination of the leader of a rival hive was a time-honored tradition among the *s'ndar*. Kill or incapacitate the queen bee, and the hive falls apart. A simple yet effective strategy—if you grew up in a hive. "But I don't think *you* understand what it means."

The *s'ndar* remained silent, watching me with alien incomprehension.

"When word gets back to Earth that the Senator has been taken hostage or, worse yet, killed, there will be a demand for justice."

"Justice," the priestess repeated. "By whose definition? How many thousands of innocent *s'ndar* are dead because of humans?"

"The Conglomerate seems to think that if we hadn't been sent in to stop your civil war for you, there'd be *millions* dead."

"The human presence on *S'ndar-khk* is immoral," she replied. "By intervening in our affairs, you deny us our divine right to order our own lives and our world according to *s'ndaran* destiny."

"You won't get any argument from me," I said. "I couldn't care less about you *or* your fucking planet. But seizing the Senator won't get the Expeditionary Force to budge. They'll come after you with everything they've got."

My own words surprised me. I didn't owe the Senator anything. But he'd seemed an earnest man, and I'd already seen too many friends die. Somebody had to pay.

As if sensing my rising anger, the two *s'ndar* flanking the priestess suddenly exposed and charged their weapons.

"Are you threatening me, Staff Sergeant?" said the priestess.

"I'm in no position to threaten you," I told her. "I'm just stating a fact."

The priestess stared at me for several seconds, then turned and left the cell, guards in tow.

They locked the cell door behind them, and I was left alone.

My left arm ached. It wasn't from the chains. There was a scabbed set of fresh stitches directly over where my Conglomerate-made ID chip had been implanted before leaving Earth. Every member of the military had one, to prevent us from going Missing-In-Action. But these *s'ndar* had been smart enough to cut the device out of me, lest it give my position away to the Conglomerate satellites in orbit.

I sighed. No hope of a quick rescue now.

Minutes crept by in silence. I shouted, hoping to get a response from any other human that might hear me.

No response.

It's amazing how long an hour becomes when you are deprived of typical sensory input. The cell became deathly quiet. There was no noise from beyond the iron door, no music, no human nor alien speech, nothing to look at except the circle of light that slowly inched across the cement floor as the day dragged on and turned into night.

I grew thirsty. Only a prolonged and significant amount of clanging with my chains attracted the attention of the guards, who brought me a portable light and two buckets: one to fill up, and one to empty.

Guards removed the manacles from my wrists and ankles, and then brought an even longer chain, which they connected to a collar they placed around my neck. The other end of the long chain was attached to a cleat in the floor, and I was able to walk and move for the first time in almost 24 hours.

They left me in the dark again. When the sun came up the priestess reappeared, only this time without her escorts. She kept well away from me, but her posture expressed curiosity.

"What now?" I said.

"If seizing or killing your Senator yields an effect opposite of what we desire, consideration must be taken as to how to proceed next. We do not ordinarily keep prisoners."

"What's *this* for then?" I demanded, yanking the chain on my collar.

"*Human* prisoners," she replied.

"You have the Senator," I said, "so what happens to the rest of us?"

"We used forbearance during the ambush, at the cost of many *s'ndaran* lives. Your squad still lives because *I* wish it, in spite of the feelings of many others who would just as soon see you all dead. After all, you are *aliens*. Everything about you is alien. You have no business being here. We want you off our planet, but before that can happen there are a few of us who believe we must understand you first. The better we understand you, the better we will be able to determine by what leverage you are moved."

I stared at her. "Seizing hostages won't do it, that's for damned sure. We'll have every available troop scouring this planet for Senator Petersen. Once they find him, it won't be very pleasant for his captors."

"We will make your masters understand us," the priestess said, advancing close to me. She stabbed a foreleg into my chest. "You do not belong here."

"Tell that to the Conglomerate," I said.

"You *are* the Conglomerate!"

"No, we're just humans from Earth."

She stared intently at me. "Explain."

"It's simple enough," I said. "Earth's government cut a deal with the Conglomerate."

"What does that mean?"

I explained the essentials of the situation. Earth needed what the Conglomerate had to offer, and as long as that remained true, the United Nations would keep the Expeditionary Force on *S'ndar-khk*.

"We never knew any of this," the priestess said.

"You never asked," I said.

• • •

The next day of incarceration passed with numbing sameness. As did the next. And the one after that.

Then the priestess reappeared, only this time she had several other *s'ndar* with her. None of them were armed, though they hardly needed their weapons against a chained and defenseless prisoner. They all stood near the door, well out of the radius of the chain that kept me anchored to the cell floor.

"You were right," the priestess informed me. "News of the Senator's abduction has caused human activity on *S'ndar-khk* to increase precipitously."

"That's hardly a surprise," I said. "They'll be looking for Petersen, me, and my whole squad. The Army doesn't leave its men and women behind."

"You are *that* valuable?"

"*Every* soldier is valuable," I said.

"Even those who are inferior?"

"*Subordinate*, not *inferior*," I said. "There's a big difference."

"We wish to know more of this deal humans have with the Conglomerate," said one of the priestess's companions. "At what point will it be satisfied?"

"I don't know," I answered. "Until someone in the Conglomerate decides the job is done, I suppose."

The *s'ndar* began skittering and scratching excitedly, and my TAD muted due to overload.

"If you really want humans gone," I said, "you could do yourselves a favor by not acting like such a bunch of bloodthirsty animals."

"I do not expect you to understand the complexities of inter-hive politics," she said, "nor do I expect you to grasp the richness and depth of my people. To us it is *you* who are the animals. You come without being invited or wanted, and enforce your version of 'peace'."

"Agreed," said a different *s'ndar*.

"Like I said before," I replied, "tell it to the Conglomerate."

The priestess circled me, her forelimbs folded thoughtfully.

"Our history with the Conglomerate is complicated," she said. "When the Conglomerate made its first contact with us, many hives spurned its overtures, declaring that we have the right to live without alien interference. When its overtures became demands, we destroyed their probe ship in orbit. An additional series of probe ships were sent, and we destroyed them too. Then, a few years later, your human armies arrived."

"But not by our own means," I pointed out. "The Conglomerate *brought* us here to do a job. When they think it's done, they'll take us back home and you'll never have to see another human again. If you weren't so intent on slaughtering each other—and slaughtering humans in the process—we'd be gone by now."

The group chattered and clacked, and the priestess faced me squarely.

"So strange," she said. "You repulse and fascinate me at the same time."

"The feeling is mutual," I said.

She waited while we glared at one another, my human eyes and her multi-faceted insect's eyes. Then she clacked her mandibles once, very sharply. Suddenly the entire lot of them fell silent, and began filing out of the cell.

"Hey!" I said to the priestess as she was leaving. "You want to start proving how civilized you really are, give me something to clean up with." I was over four days out of a shower. I stank.

The priestess paused, then waved a forelimb at me and left. A minute later the guards brought me cold water in a ten-gallon-sized tub, with a brick of industrial soap. There was no towel.

I scrubbed happily, ignoring the chill.

* * *

Repeated requests to see Senator Petersen, or anyone from my squad, were flatly denied. I began to wonder whether any of them had really made it? There was no reason to believe that the priestess, or any of the others, had been telling the truth, though why they'd keep me alive and kill the others just didn't make any sense.

Time dragged on. Week one became week two. Then three. Then a month. For the first time in my life, I had a full beard. I did bodyweight exercises in my cell to try and keep myself fit, and to keep from going insane with inactivity.

At night, when the dark closed in and I had to curl up on the hard floor, I hummed all my favorite songs until slumber finally overtook me and gave me an illusory form of freedom. I dreamed of all the neat places I'd ever been as a kid, all the interesting people I'd ever met. I dreamed of all my favorite shows and movies, and especially of my favorite foods. Mashed potatoes, buttered green beans, crisp corn on the cob, fried chicken, broiled t-bone steak. Anything but the damned half-rotten vegfruit the *s'ndar*—being a herbivorous race—preferred.

I also dreamed of home, and family. Of my sister Karen and me when we'd been kids, playing in our grandparents' backyard. A few times those dreams seemed so real that when I woke up I had tears in my eyes.

I grew to greatly resent the moments when I was awake.

I also began to cinch my belt tighter and tighter. The lack of protein in my meager diet was costing me muscle as well as fat.

My requests to see the priestess or any other authority figure were alternately denied or ignored. My TAD battery ran out of charge and wasn't replaced, so I was reduced to yelling at my guards, who neither understood nor cared.

• • •

I'd lost count of the weeks, when the attack came.

A concussion lifted me up off the floor. I'd been fast asleep. I screamed and rolled onto my back, observing rivulets of dust spewing from cracks in the ceiling—cracks I was positive hadn't been there before, because I'd already memorized the existing cracks.

THUD.

More cracks shot across the ceiling, and a hunk broke loose and smacked into the ground near my head.

I leaped up from where I'd been lying and crouched in the circle of sunlight, hoping to get out from under any additional debris.

THUD-THUD-WHAM.

I couldn't tell if the explosions were coming from beyond the hole in the ceiling, or outside the iron door. I *felt* them as much as I heard them.

The door to my cell burst open. A horde of *s'ndar* rushed in, snapped the collar off my neck, and shoved me outside at gunpoint. The corridor beyond was crawling with *s'ndar* and humans. There were faces I recognized, far gaunter than I remembered them. "Sergeant Colford!" said a desperate voice.

I turned and found myself face-to-face with Senator Petersen.

He looked like a shaggy ghost of his former self. His gleaming teeth had yellowed, and his breath smelled, and his face was a hollowed-out, gray-haired mask that barely resembled the confident politician who'd visited my intersection … who knew how long ago.

"Move!" commanded a *s'ndar*, its TAD dialed up to shouting volume. The Senator and I were roughly shoved down the corridor with the other humans. I saw Corporal Kent up at the front of the line, and tried to shout for her, but was silenced by another barrage of concussions that almost knocked us off our feet.

"What's happening?" Petersen said in my ear.

"Ours," I replied. "Air strike."

"They'll kill us!"

"They probably don't even know we're here," I said. "Something or someone must have tipped off the Expeditionary Force that there was a resistance stronghold in this area."

"Silence!" snapped an armed guard.

We twisted and turned our way frantically down a further series of corridors. I couldn't quite tell, but the floor seemed slanted. We could have been going up or down, I wasn't really sure.

Then we suddenly emptied out into the blindingly bright sunlight, all of us cringing and raising our hands to shield our eyes.

A quick look around revealed the rubble of what had once been a *s'ndar* industrial district. I actually laughed as I realized we'd been prisoners right under the Expeditionary Force's nose the whole time. The district had been leveled in the first month of the occupation, and declared off-limits. Barring occasional patrols, no human or *s'ndar* went in or out, except for these resistance fanatics, who'd obviously found a way to operate without being detected.

Until today.

A flight of jets screamed overhead—wide-winged ground attack planes with their payload doors hanging open. A cluster of bombs released and carpeted across the crushed factory complex from which we'd just exited. The blasts were deafening and the ground bucked hard under our feet.

I wondered if we could attempt an escape, and decided there were too many *s'ndar* for us to make it. Our duty hadn't changed: we had to keep the Senator alive until we could transfer him to friendly hands.

We passed wrecked and burned-out vehicles, and the dried shells of *s'ndar* who'd been left where they'd fallen—their silenced mandibles hanging slackly by threads of dry tissue.

Then we were being herded down into a dry sewer, crouched and shuffling—while the round sewer pipe was somewhat more accommodating to the shorter, squatter *s'ndar*.

After twenty minutes the *s'ndar* ordered a rest, and we stopped. I tried to push up to where Kent was, but was shoved back and ordered not to move.

Petersen was doubled over, gasping.

"Sir," I said. "Are you hurt?"

"No," he said. "Just out of shape. It was the cell … the damned cell … nothing to do but go crazy."

He looked into my eyes, and I realized the Senator might not have been speaking metaphorically. His gaze was awful. Stricken. Not quite *there* somehow. It occurred to me that, for all his slick, football player toughness, Petersen had probably never endured real deprivation before. Certainly not on the scale we'd been suffering since our capture.

I turned to the *s'ndar*. My TAD was gone, but theirs worked. "That air strike was just the first phase," I told them. "They're softening up the target before our rifle platoons get sent in to clean up. They know you're here, and they won't stop until they find you."

A single *s'ndar* shape pushed its way back towards me. I recognized her torn raiment; it was the priestess.

"We will move forward rapidly now," she said.

"Look at us," I told her, waving my hand at Petersen for emphasis. "We're in no condition to keep up the pace. In another hundred meters you'd be dragging us. So we'll have to go slow. I hope that doesn't scare you too much, but that's the way it is."

The priestess appeared to sag in on herself, if only a bit.

"Yes," she said. "We are scared."

She studied my face. "You hide it well, but my fear makes you happy."

"Only because you're the enemy," I answered. Then I sighed deeply. "The shame of it is, you didn't have to be. There was no reason for it."

"I agree," she said. "But of course I would: *you* invaded *us*. It is you who are the enemy."

And suddenly I knew who the *real* enemy was.

"My sister died here," I said, as the low rumble of more bombs filled the sewer pipe, then fell silent. "She was excited by the idea of your alien culture—and she was killed for her enthusiasm. But she wouldn't have been here at all—none of us would be here—if not for the Conglomerate playing us off against each other."

"The 'deal' you spoke of," said the priestess.

"Yes," I said. "Back on Earth we treat the Conglomerate like saviors. You know something interesting? We've never even seen them."

Her eyes widened. "Never?"

"Just radio transmissions and text messages, and those robotic transport ships that show up in orbit. If they're so advanced, it should be an easy thing for them to pacify a planet with or without human help. So what's in it for them, using us like this? And why couldn't they just leave your world alone? Why do they care if you're at war?"

"Our particular hive has never known these answers," she said. "And since the arrival of humans, we've never cared to know. We want you gone. That is the sole thing that concerns us."

"Have you ever stopped to ask why humans would even want to be on your planet in the first place?"

The priestess was silent. As were every other *s'ndar* and human in the sewer. Petersen just looked at me, his limbs slightly shaking as the adrenaline from exertion began to wear off.

"*We're* here because of them," I said. "*You're* fighting an invading force because of them. Maybe it's time for both sides to take a deep breath and think about that."

She stared at me. "Go on," she said at last.

"If you stop fighting, *my* people have no reason to be here."

"A truce?"

"It would give us time to find out what the Conglomerate *really* wants," I said.

"And to prevent them from getting it," added the Senator, who was quick on the uptake, despite his condition.

She turned to the Senator. "Do you have the power to order a cease-fire?"

He nodded his head. "I outrank every General Officer on this planet," Petersen said, seeming to regain some of his former stature. "I'm sure I can convince our side to enter a temporary cease-fire."

"What good is temporary?" she asked.

"It gives us breathing space while we each try to talk our superiors into making it permanent."

"My superiors will assume you are lying to us," said the priestess.

Suddenly Peterson smiled. "When we stop talking war and start talking negotiations, now we *are* in my bailiwick," he said. "I propose a trade."

"A trade?"

"I want you to come back to Earth with me as a good-will ambassador of your race, someone who can confirm what I have to tell them. View it as a public display of friendship and mutual trust." He turned to me. "And Sergeant Colford here will stay behind in the same capacity and speak to your people."

"Why me?" I demanded.

"Because you lost a sister in this war, and were incarcerated for some months. If *you* can forgive them and point to the real enemy, I think it will bolster the arguments of whatever *s'ndar* is speaking to his people on our behalf."

I considered. Could a cease-fire agreement—made in a sewer pipe between a staff sergeant, a priestess, and a Senator who was light years from Washington—actually have any legs?

We're now in the process of finding out.

I hope my sister didn't die for nothing. I hope my months of being chained in solitary served some purpose. I hope the priestess can sway her people and the Senator can sway his. I even hope that someday I find out what the Conglomerate wants, and that I stop thinking of *them* as the enemy.

Mostly, though, I hope I can stop being a peacekeeper …

… and start being a peacemaker.

▼▲▼▲▼

Mike Resnick labored long with me, to bring this story up to professional spec. It was our first ever collaboration, back when I had only two short fiction publications to my credit. Mike's number one point—through all the toil, much of which I am embarrassed to have put him through—was that any good story demands change from its key characters. Programs like Star Trek can get away with leaving the cast off right where they began, but for literary fiction to have the necessary emotional impact to make it compelling, the main people in the story have to arrive at new places in their heads and in their hearts. If not always physically, in their bodies.

I've tried to remember this lesson, when writing successive stories.

"Peacekeeper" obviously relies on my U.S. Army familiarity. Mike had an outstanding invitation from the editors of The Mammoth Book of SF Wars to give them a story, and since Mike had handed me my trophy at the Writers of the Future gala event just a few months earlier—me, decked out in my Army ASUs—Mike decided it might be a good idea to kill two birds with one stone: help a newcomer out with some teaching, and a new story sale, while also helping himself out by getting the chops of someone who was actually in the service; and didn't just know military stuff through popular folklore.

An Iraq war veteran once told me that this story hums with verisimilitude, for the various iterations of Operation Iraqi Freedom. I chalk that up to having spent a lot of time with veterans of OIF and OEF; men and women who've been overseas and "seen the beast" as it were. I'm hopeful that this verisimilitude is present for civilian readers as well. I wanted something that would be gritty, but not cliché, nor Hollywood.

As for the moral theme of the story, that's entirely Mike. Again, his teaching to me—like Mickey yammering in the ear of Rocky Balboa—was that the story wouldn't be a story unless the main character underwent a significant change of heart. Earlier iterations had Sergeant Colford walking out of the mess more or less the same man as when he went into the mess. The story was thus a "picture frame" look at war (and prisoner-of-war life) on an alien world.

And yes, I wrote "Peacekeeper" before I wrote "The Chaplain's Assistant." There are similarities between the two—especially when you consider the changes Mike wanted me to make to the former. I consider it the privilege of the writer to revisit an idea or a concept more than once, without having to so thoroughly redress the movie set that things become exhaustively different.

Ultimately, Mike got a story he felt was competent by his standards, and I got a huge helping hand, in the form of a tough, old, experienced pro, reaching down to assist a fledgling guy who was still brand new to the publishing business. Mike showed a lot of patience with me, on this work. And I am grateful for that. It's to Mike's credit that he never lost his temper nor his sense of humor. Every time I goofed up, he simply pushed back and said, "I won't give you the answer straight out, kid, but here's a few clues to maybe take you in the right direction ..."

Teacher:
Dave Wolverton

Dave—many readers know him by the pen name *David Farland*—was recently interviewed by KSL television in Salt Lake City, who pronounced him the Godfather of Utah's literay Science Fiction and fantasy community. That title is well-deserved. There are arguably thousands of us who have passed through Dave's hands, if you include all his many workshop appearances, panel lectures at events like *Life, The Universe, and Everything,* and his ongoing role as the Coordinating Judge for the L. Ron Hubbard Presents Writers and Illustrators of the Future Contest.

Find me a bestseller in the SF/F field—Brandon Sanderson? James Dashner?—and if that person has roots in Utah, (s)he has probably sat at Dave Wolverton's feet.

I was therefore very eager and anxious to make a good impression on Dave, when I approached him at the CONduit SF/F convention in Salt Lake City, in May 2009. One of my stories which I'd entered into Writers of the Future, was a Finalist for Quarter One of the 26th annual iteration of said Contest. I felt—at the time—that this story ("Outbound," which eventually saw print in the November 2010 issue of *Analog* magazine) was the best story I'd ever written. Over the holiday period of 2008 I'd poured every lick of what I'd learned and what I knew about storytelling, into that one singular piece. I knew in my heart it was me firing on all cylinders. And I hoped very much that maybe Dave could clue me in as to how much longer it would take the Quarter One judges to reach a decision.

"I think I have your story," Dave told me, his eyes unfocused as he thought about the Finalist manuscripts he'd been sent by Joni Labaqui, the Contest Administrator.

I could have just died. Dave Wolverton. *The* Dave Wolverton. The Godfather of Utah's SF/F literary scene. He had my story! It was being judged *by Dave* for the Contest!

Which meant a hell of a lot to me (later) when Joni had to let me know that my story did *not* win. Because in the depths of utter and total despair—no rejection has ever so thoroughly crushed me—I had Dave's critique (which he was then allowed to release to me) to buoy my spirits. Dave said (in his letter) that he didn't know why the other judges hadn't liked the story. *He'd* certainly liked it. And while he did have some suggestions for potential changes that might be made, he felt like it was a strong piece even if I changed nothing.

When I sent the story to editor Stan Schmidt at Analog (in the wake of my eventual Contest win, with "Exanastasis", for Quarter Three) I opened my cover letter stating, "Dear Stan, Dave Wolverton said he liked this story a lot, and I hope you do too."

So, it's fair to say that Dave Wolverton fairly delivered me into my professional writing career. And he's continued to be an enthusiastic teacher and booster ever since. To include helping me with my novel projects—novel writing being, for me, an entirely different animal, compared to short fiction writing.

Dave's got an uncanny, almost unconscious grasp of what I call "classically epic" storytelling. The kind of storytelling that makes Tolkien's *Lord of the Rings* resonate with generation after generation of fans. The kind of storytelling that helped make the *Twilight* books and movies into such mega-sellers. Storytelling that continues to show up in the works of authors from across the country and around the world—can Dave now claim to be the *international* Godfather of SF/F?—who are busting the tape with their bestsellers.

I occasionally think it's not fair that us local Utah boys get to have the kind of access that we have, to Dave. As teachers go, this is a mighty man. Someone people pay hundreds or even thousands of dollars to come from all over the globe to see, and learn from. And there he is at LTUE every year, saying hello to all his friends, and all of his students (both former and current) and spreading his ethereal pixie dust of success on our heads; like a bearded Willy Wonka promising golden tickets, if only we will just keep trying, and maybe take a little bit of his advice.

I've spoken before, about some of Utah's SF/F elder statesmen. Dave is definitely among their ranks. A pillar of the scene. And it's been both my delight and my privilege to get to know not just Dave, but also his wonderful wife Mary, and to include Dave in my somewhat select circle of industry counselors: men and women from whom I will absolutely entertain any suggestion, cherish any nugget of wisdom, and ponder every bit of insight. This man helps build blockbuster careers, he does. Even in the face of tremendous professional and personal difficulty.

When Dave is gone, I suspect all of us—whom he has helped— are going to pool our resources and erect some kind of memorial in his honor. Like the fictional Argonath on the river Anduin. How else to honor a man who has so thoroughly enriched and fostered the Utah speculative community? One pictures giant stone statues of Dave, Tracy Hickman, L.E. Modesitt, Jr., and several other Utah SF/F writers, their stone hands collectively beckoning us through the doors at LTUE every February: *come, learn, enjoy, and succeed!*

My hat is off to you, Dave. Thank you for putting so much effort into so many of our lives, for so long, and with so much creative spark. You light so many candles in this genre. I hope all of us shining brightly together, serve as a testament to your hope and faith in us.

Life Flight

Audio Journal Transcript: Day 1

Papa was proud of me when he went to sleep. I'm one of the only boys picked to stay awake—because I'm smart and can do math. Nobody on the *Osprey* is going to be awake for the entire trip. There won't be enough food, water, or air onboard for everyone. So to start off they picked a couple of adults—and two boys and two girls—to stay up while we begin the trip to Delta Pavonis. Which is a very long way from Earth.

Mama was proud too. She squeezed me so hard before she laid down with Papa and went to sleep. She was crying, but told me it was OK. She wasn't upset. She just doesn't want to miss anything while I am awake—she thinks I will be older by the time she sees me again. I suppose she is right. She made me promise to keep this journal while she is asleep. So that she can go back and hear my voice, and know all about the time in-between.

Audio Journal Transcript: Day 8

Kroger is the other boy, besides me. I never met him before all the families boarded the *Osprey*. I'm not sure I like him much, and it doesn't seem like he likes much either. So the two adults—Kevin and Cassie—have kept Kroger and me apart during the first few days. I help at one end of the ship, he helps at the other. Which is fine. The

Osprey is big! Cassie showed me a computer model of our ship, compared to a skyscraper. If our ship could stand on its end it would be far taller than anything in New York or Hong Kong.

I'm not lonely, though.

Leah and Molly are the two girls. One short and round like me, the other tall and skinny like Kroger. At first the girls didn't seem to want to have much to do with me. But by the third day Leah smiled at me in the lunch room—what Kevin keeps calling the *galley*.

Back on Earth the girls didn't pay any attention to me. But Leah pays attention. I found out she likes kitty cats. I like kitty cats too. I wish they'd let us bring some on the ship.

Molly is more like Kroger. Rude. She told me I was fat, and I told her to shut up because it's mean to call someone that. Molly said the truth hurts, and stuck her tongue out at me. Just like my classmates back home. I got angry, but Cassie told me to not let it bother me. She was going to talk to Molly and would get Molly to be nice.

The teachers on Earth always said the same thing.

It never worked.

Tomorrow Kevin is going to begin showing me how the navigation and nuclear fusion drive computers work. He says the *Osprey* has the best computers money can buy. They run just about everything onboard, including the machines that make the air and keep it clean and full of oxygen. Kevin says he will be teaching me how to program the computers, once I understand how they function. I think that ought to be fun.

Audio Journal Transcript: Day 35

The computers are better than anything I ever had in school. You can talk to them and they actually understand you, and will talk back. They all sound like grown-up women with nice voices. I told Kevin and Cassie that we ought to start naming each of them. Cassie asked me why, when the computers are just machines. Not real people. I told her that if our trip to Delta Pavonis is as long as she keeps saying it is, the computers will learn to be people. They seem smart enough for it.

Leah wants to know why there are only girl computers, and no boy computers. Cassie said it's because girls are smarter than boys, which made Leah and Molly smile big. I think Cassie was just being funny, but Leah and Molly spent all day feeling proud of themselves. I keep telling them that boys are just as smart, otherwise the adults would have kept four girls awake, instead of two, but Leah and Molly aren't listening.

I asked Kevin why we have gravity on the *Osprey* when all the videos I saw in school told me that there was no gravity in space. Kevin says it's because the nuclear motor at the back of the ship is pushing us constantly towards Delta Pavonis, and this makes our bodies press down against the deck. Not as much as on Earth. Yet. But a little more each day. Until we get up to a full *gee*—Kevin's word for it.

I said before that the *Osprey* is taller than a skyscraper. It's like a building on the inside too, with decks instead of floors. The Intra-Ship Transit is like elevators—if you've ever ridden an elevator that goes a mile high, and back. Everything runs on electricity from the nuclear motor, which takes a lot of gas to work. Cassie said most of the ship is actually one giant fuel tank. We're supposed to have enough to take us all the way, with gas to spare.

Audio Journal Transcript: Day 78

I'm sorry I missed a few days. I've not been feeling very well, and Cassie let me stay in bed today, rather than go out and help with chores. Cassie doesn't think there's anything wrong with me, she just says I'm homesick. Maybe she is right? A few days ago I had a really good dream about going to the park and playing with my kite. The sky was bright blue and there were pretty white clouds, and all three of us—Mama, me, and Papa—were running across the green grass and laughing, just like we used to do back home. When I woke up, I wanted so badly to be with Mama and Papa at the park, I cried. And I cried some more. And I kept crying. Enough so that Kevin got worried, but Cassie said it was normal, and would pass.

Meanwhile I have the day to rest.

The Earth is very, very far away now. Kevin can still find it using the computers and the telescopes that are outside on the ship's skin—

what Kevin calls the *hull*. But if the Earth was huge on the first day, now it's a little ball not much bigger than a pea. Kevin has to tell the computers to magnify a bunch of times for us to see home with any detail.

Cassie says she can't wait to see our *new* home. The planet the astronomers found at Delta Pavonis is supposed to have lots of water and lots of plants. Weeds and bushes and trees and forests. Or at least that's what the astronomers think. When I look at the fuzzy pictures Kevin showed me, I wonder if that's how the Earth looked a long time ago? Kevin thinks maybe so, though the new planet doesn't have big continents like Earth does. Just hundreds of smaller green and brown blotches—big islands, covered in forests. All over the world. And clouds. Half the planet is white in any given image. Cassie thinks it must rain a lot.

Though, I sure hope there are a few sunny days too. I've been looking at the pictures again, while I'm in bed, and wondering what it will be like to fly a kite in the new sky.

Audio Journal Transcript: Day 149

Mama and Papa have been asleep for almost half a year. Some days I miss them so much that I want to tell Kevin and Cassie to go down to the medical bay and wake them up. Because I can't stand it anymore. But I don't. I know Kevin and Cassie will just say no.

I think Kevin and Cassie are a good team. I think maybe this is why they got married before we left Earth?

I asked Cassie if she's going to have a baby soon.

Cassie laughed, and said she already has four babies.

Me, Leah, Molly, and Kroger.

I told her that it was my birthday in another month and that 8 years old is way too old to be a baby!

Cassie just laughed some more. But I don't think she was being mean. Cassie has kind eyes and kind hands. She gives me hugs when she can tell I miss Mama and Papa. Cassie is soft and warm and reminds me of Mama, but younger.

Kevin's got all four of us kids going up to the gymnasium now. He says that even though the nuclear motor gives us gravity for awhile, there will come a time in the middle of the journey when we'll have to turn the motor off and coast for a great distance. Otherwise we'll have used too much fuel, and won't have enough left to stop ourselves when we get to Delta Pavonis.

So we have to get used to using the gym, because when there is no gravity the gym will be the only thing that keeps us from getting weak, and unable to do things.

Kroger shows off in the gym. Taller than me, with muscles. He thinks he is so tough. He especially makes fun of me when I use the treadmills, because my stomach jiggles and I get sweaty faster than anyone else. I almost hit him for it, but Mama always said never to hit other boys who hadn't hit me first, so I just told Kroger to shut up and leave me alone.

Molly laughs when Kroger makes fun of me, so I told her to shut up too.

Cassie told us all—over and over again—to be nice and to learn to work together. But it doesn't seem to be doing much good. Wherever Leah is, Molly is not. And Kroger spends more time with Molly these days. Which is okay. I like spending time with Leah. She has trouble on the treadmill too, though not as much as me. I don't think Molly teases Leah the way Kroger teases me, but I don't think Molly and Leah are friends.

Kevin says if Leah and I both work hard on the treadmill, and also on our stretches and our hand-weight exercises, then we'll both get in better shape. Then the gym won't be so hard for us anymore.

Leah and I have made a promise to each other, that we will get so good at the gym that nobody will ever make fun of either one of us again.

Leah is my best friend.

Audio Journal Transcript: Day 288

Kevin had to go outside for our first repair. The *Osprey* has what Cassie calls *articulated* space suits, so that there isn't any time wasted changing the air pressure between the inside of the ship, and when someone has to take a suit outside to work on something that's broken. The suit also has motors in the joints, for strength. Kevin looked like a big insect, with balls at his elbows and shoulders and knees. He smiled at me through the window on his helmet, then went out the airlock using strong magnets on his hands and boots to keep him from falling off the ship.

I asked Cassie what was wrong.

Cassie told me not to worry. It was nothing serious.

But Kevin was out there for a very long time, and Cassie had to keep getting additional instructions from Earth, which she spoke to Kevin over the microphone in the *Osprey's* control room. I kept trying to ask Cassie what was the matter, but she shewed me away and asked me to please not bother her while she was trying to help Kevin with a very important problem.

That hurt my feelings. I am smart. I can help!

Cassie told me I wasn't old enough to help.

I told her that someday I will be the best-trained person on the ship. I know I will. Better than anyone. I will know how to run and repair every single part of the *Osprey*.

And then Kroger will be sorry. He's smart like me, but he's also kind of lazy too. He doesn't like learning to work with the computers the way I do. He has been spending more and more time goofing off on the Intra-Ship Transit, or having tantrums in the gym when he thinks no one is around.

Once, after I snuck up to the gym door, I heard Kroger saying bad words and slamming his foot into one of the big rubber exercise balls over and over and over again. He was saying his papa's name in between the bad words. I am not sure Kroger likes his papa very much? From what I heard, I don't think so.

I can't imagine ever saying those things about my Papa.

I went somewhere else until Kroger was done.

One thing's for sure. Kevin was right. The more I use the gym, the easier it gets. And my stomach isn't jiggling so much anymore. Though Molly still tells me I am fat.

Audio Journal Transcript: Day 440

I'm going to be ten years old soon.

It seems like such a long time since we left home.

This morning I went down to the medical bay and looked at Mama and Papa through the glass of their stasis bed. They don't move, and they don't breathe, though their eyes and mouths are closed like they're sleeping. I wonder very much if they are having dreams? I hope so. I hope they are having the kind of dreams I've been having lately. About Earth. About where we used to live.

There have been messages from Uncle Burt and Aunt Filly, and Gramma too. They say they miss us all very much and are very sad that we were chosen to leave Earth. Because they know this means they'll never see us again. But they are proud of us too, because all our names are going to be in the history books. The first people to live on a world belonging to a star other than the Sun.

Cassie says this audio journal might wind up being more than just a memento for Mama and Papa when they wake up. She thinks that historians will some day listen to it, to learn what it was like growing up on the long flight to Delta Pavonis. That makes me nervous. I don't know what I want to say to the future. Which is why it's been a week since my last entry. I have to make myself only think about my parents, when I talk. I put a picture of them on the wallvid in my cabin and I imagine that they're talking to me over breakfast.

I wish there was a way for them to tell me what's on their minds right now, the way I've been telling my journal what's on mine.

Audio Journal Transcript: Day 576

Something hit the *Osprey* yesterday.

Not a big thing, otherwise Cassie says we'd all be dead. In fact she thinks it was very, very small. But this far from Earth there are a lot of pieces of rock and dust all traveling very fast. There's a giant mushroom-shaped shield at the front of the *Osprey* that's designed to protect us while we're moving towards Delta Pavonis. It absorbs all the small pieces that get in our way. The piece that hit us was coming at an angle, from the side. Dumb luck, Kevin said. But it was serious enough that both Kevin and Cassie had to put suits on and go outside to fix the hole.

I've studied the electronic blueprints of the Osprey. The part of the ship we all move around in, is actually a very narrow column that runs up and down the center. Outside of that is a wide, hollow tube. And that's where all the fuel is kept: in the tube, between us and outer space. Liquid-slush isotope, Kevin calls it. Very cold. But if there's a hole in the hull it means some of the fuel might *sublimate,* which is what Cassie calls it when the liquid-slush turns immediately to gas and goes out the hole.

When Cassie and Kevin came back inside, they were exhausted. All four of us kids helped them get their suits off and made them food and coffee in the galley. Cassie's hands were shaking so badly that she almost dropped her cup. She said the hole had been a lot bigger than they'd expected, and that they'd had to burrow through the fuel to find the thing that hit us, so that it didn't contaminate the isotope. Then they had trouble sealing the hole from the outside. Despite the fact that we have lots of extra hull panels stored on the outside, just in case something like this happened.

Kevin said they finally got it fixed. But he looked scared.

I asked him why.

He said that if the thing that hit us—a rock the size of a softball—had been any bigger, or going any faster, it might have penetrated all the way through to the center. And then we'd have had a *real* problem. Somebody could have even been hurt, or killed.

Leah wanted to know why we don't just turn on the deflectors.

That made Cassie smile. She said deflectors only exist in movies and on shows. Real astronauts can't flip a switch and be safe. Real astronauts have to always be ready for the worst.

Audio Journal Transcript: Day 888

It's triple-eight day.

Kevin and Cassie said that means it's a holiday for us. No work. Just play. Though I am getting kind of tired of video games and puzzle contests with the others. So I decided to build a kite. Even though there are no parks to fly it in. I spent all day on it, using some plastic sheeting and thin, hollow tubes from the ship's stores. It's a big one, with a tail. When we get to where we're going, I think it will fly well. Until then, I am going to just keep it under my bunk in my cabin.

I went down to look at my parents again.

It's as if no time has passed for them at all.

I can definitely tell time's passed for me.

I'm a lot taller than I was when I came onboard, and not nearly so round. I'll be eleven in a few months. Kevin has pulled me aside a couple of times to warn me—man to man—that things are going to start changing soon. I think Cassie gave Leah the same talk. Leah and I rode the Intra-Ship Transit up to the big room just under the bow shield—where we can be alone when we want—and we talked about it. We both agree, it's got something to do with making babies.

The birds and the bees, my Papa would call it.

I didn't believe my Papa when he told me about the birds and the bees the first time. But now that I am a little older, I think I am starting to believe him. Enough so that I wonder if Kevin and Cassie do the birds and the bees when they are in their cabin together. Is it fun? I wonder.

Speaking of birds and bees, Leah is getting very curious about our new planet. Will there be animals? Kevin seems sure that there will be. Cassie disagrees, and thinks that if there are animals, they might only be in the water. Or they might be microscopic, like the cells Cassie has shown me under the medical lab computer scope.

The astronomers think Delta Pavonis is older than the Sun. So old that Delta Pavonis is just starting to move into its red giant phase. I asked Cassie what that means and she said that all stars burn hydrogen, a lot like the motor for the *Osprey,* but when a star is very old, it runs out of hydrogen and starts to change.

Like me and Leah, I guess. We're going to change too.

Audio Journal Transcript: Day 1,000

I can't believe it's been one thousand Earth days since we left home.

And yet we're still so far away from Delta Pavonis that it still looks just like all the other stars in space. No bigger. We know which one it is because it's the star our navigational computer keeps track of every second of every day. We're aimed right at it. Though Cassie said we're not going in a straight line. We're actually following a curved line, because Delta Pavonis and Earth are moving relative to each other.

Where Delta Pavonis was when we left home is not where Delta Pavonis is now. And it won't be where it is now in six months, and not in six years, and not in sixty years. So the computer has to constantly watch, and make small adjustments in our course.

Kevin took me down to the big maintenance bay that has all the space suits and other equipment in it. There are small vehicles and tools and things lined up neatly in racks, or in rows on the walls. He told me he's making it my job to check the maintenance bay every day, and to make sure everything is in its place. So that when I turn 12 he can assign me to the job of Maintenance Bay Chief.

I told Kevin I didn't know we had rank on the *Osprey*.

Kevin said that Maintenance Bay Chief was a very big, very important job, and that I was the right man for it. Which made me feel very proud. So proud that I went down to the medical bay and told Mama and Papa.

I know they can't hear me. They look like they're frozen in time. But I think Papa especially would be glad for me. I am growing up.

Though I wonder if Kroger is growing up?

We've been having fights lately. Not kicking or hitting. But yelling and name-calling. Nasty words. Cassie has sent us to our separate cabins several times. She yelled at us during the last one. Probably the first time I can ever remember Cassie getting that mad. I think she is tired of Kroger and I not getting along. But I don't know what to do? I can't make Kroger like me. And at this point I don't even want to try. It would be too much work. I think Kroger will always hate me. I talk wrong, walk wrong, think wrong, my breath smells wrong, everything about me, Kroger doesn't like. What am I supposed to do about that?

But we're all stuck with each other.

So Kevin tries to keep Kroger and I working on different stuff in different places. Otherwise he's afraid things might get serious. Though what he means by *serious* I am not sure.

Audio Journal Transcript: Day 1,500

Being Maintenance Bay Chief is a lot of work. Not only do I have to inventory everything and check the inventory against lists, I have to pull all the parts out on a schedule and check them to make sure they work. Big parts. Small parts. In-between parts. Anything that might break, has to be inspected. And Kevin's slowly been showing me how to do this, so that I can make sure that all of the space suits and maneuvering units are in order, along with all of the winches and one-man extravehicular sleds. Everything we need any time someone has to go outside, especially to fix something.

It made me nervous, at first.

But Kevin's been very patient about showing me.

He says it's one of the most important jobs.

Right up there with Nuclear Reactor Chief.

Which is Molly's job.

Cassie says that in a couple of years, we will each rotate jobs. And then, in a couple of years after that, we'll rotate again. And so on. Until each of us—all of the kids—have learned how to do essentially everything on the *Osprey* that needs doing. In case the adults get sick or hurt or even killed, and we have to run things. Maybe even all the way to the end of the trip.

Kevin thinks the estimate of 80 Earth years, one-way travel time, is still more or less accurate. I told Kevin that I didn't want to be an old man by the time we got to our new planet. I also told him that I thought it wasn't fair for them to keep four kids awake, just to train them to do all the jobs, so that the adults could sleep peacefully in stasis.

Kevin laughed, and reminded me that just like when we switch jobs, people would be switching in and out of stasis too. Like taking turns. So that if everything went as planned, by the time each of us arrived at the new planet, we'd be roughly the same age, biologically. Which made me think for a minute. Do I want to be the same age as my parents when they wake up? That idea seems very strange to me. Will I still know them like I knew them when we left Earth? Will they know *me?* I couldn't get this question out of my head today, so as always, I went down to the medical bay and I looked at the rows and rows of stasis beds, and I thought about how different everything is becoming as I get older.

Kevin has been right about one thing.

My body is getting ready for the birds and the bees.

And so is Leah's, and Molly's.

They're each getting bumps under their shirts, and their butts are wider. Leah even told me about how Cassie sat Leah and Molly down and had a very serious talk with them about something called *that time of the month*. Leah says she and Molly are going to bleed. Out of the same place where they pee! I said Leah was trying to be funny, but she wasn't smiling. She seemed as unhappy about the idea as I did. And when I cornered Kevin and demanded to know the truth, he said it was fact: once a month, girls bleed from their vaginas.

I think Leah wants very badly not to believe it.

I don't blame her. If I had blood coming out of my penis once a month, I don't know what I'd do.

Audio Journal Transcript: Day 2,500

We all got shots today. All of us teenagers.

Kevin says it's a nodule designed to slowly dissolve in our blood over the course of the year, and that next year, each of us will need to get another one. It doesn't hurt. But Leah and I are pretty sure it's supposed to keep us from getting pregnant.

Not that Leah and I have … done it. You know.

Kroger and Molly? I think they've done it a few times. Cassie and Kevin have told us over and over that it's a mistake to have sex at our age, but those injections today tell me that Cassie and Kevin aren't taking any chances. There's only so many resources to go around. The hydroponics farms and waste recyclers can only handle a certain number of people being awake at any given time. Introducing a baby into the environment at this point would be a very bad idea. Which is why Cassie finally admitted to me that this is why she's never had a child the whole time we'd been underway. Because she doesn't dare risk it.

I asked her if she wants to have a baby when we get to the new planet. She said she hopes she can have many babies. She said that all of the women, including Leah and Molly, are going to need to have as many babies as they can stand. To ensure that there are enough people in the first generation to survive what might come.

I asked Kevin if he thinks something bad might happen when we land. He said that nobody can say for sure because nobody has any idea what the new planet is like. There could be storms or earthquakes or tsunami or even diseases that kill people. Settling on the new planet is going to be hard, often dangerous work.

I've had to do a lot of thinking about that. I'm old enough now that I can handle any tool onboard. But there are no guns. Why don't we have any guns?

Cassie told me that guns were strictly forbidden. There would be absolutely no need for them, and she was glad to have gotten away from guns on Earth, because guns were a big part of what made life on Earth scary for her.

I'm not so sure Cassie's right. I've been looking at the fuzzy images of our new planet and wondering what might live in those endless forests on all those endless islands. I've gone through the computer libraries and seen all the images of all the dinosaurs from Earth's prehistoric past. If anything even remotely like a dinosaur—especially the carnivorous kind—lives on our new world, we're probably going to need all the rifles we can get. Hell, we'll need rocket launchers.

There are machining and milling workstations connected to the maintenance bay. I've looked at some of the cylindrical steel stock we have onboard. Could it be drilled out? And cut with grooves inside? What could we use for propellant? And bullets?

A long-term project, I've decided. But definitely something for me to look into, though it won't make Cassie happy if she finds out. So I'd better keep it quiet.

Audio Journal Transcript: Day 3,650

Ten years, trip time.

I've now spent more of my life on this ship, than I did on Earth.

I'm really hoping I get to fly that kite under my bed some day.

Kevin and Cassie have literally taught us everything we need to know about the *Osprey* and its operations. We know how to use the tools and equipment to do repairs, how to use the spacesuits and the maneuvering units outside. I've even gone out with Kevin to patch holes. One last year, and two more this year. Cassie thinks we must be passing through a debris field. This is the Oort Cloud after all. We're not even an eighth of the way to Delta Pavonis, and nobody knows how thick the Oort Cloud really is. Light-years thick?

There may be more holes to come. I've been out on top of the bow shield. It's riddled with divots from all the dust and larger junk that's been in our way all this time.

Kevin and Cassie will be going to sleep soon, and two of the other adults will be woken up. There will be a year of overlap with the new adults. Just to be sure that stasis has not harmed them physically or mentally, and that both of them are capable of taking on their respective jobs. Then Leah, myself, Molly, and Kroger will go to sleep, and the adults will wake up four new kids, and the process will begin all over again.

Audio Journal Transcript: Day 3,787

Ben and Laura are older than Kevin and Cassie were when the voyage began. Ben was an military man back in his day. He's big, and has a beefy body. First thing he went to look at was the Osprey's gym. I take it he's going to be spending a lot of time in there.

I told him about how I'd been pretty chubby as a little kid, but that using the gym has shaped me up. Ben seemed to like that, and I liked giving him a tour of the ship while Molly gave Laura a tour. Not that these new adults don't know the Osprey from memory. They do. It's just that knowing a thing—static—is different from knowing a thing real-time. The *Osprey* is 99.8% the same ship she was when she left Earth orbit. But there have been little adjustments and modifications along the way. Small and occasionally subtle, but also important, differences in how stuff operates. Such that Ben and Laura are having to go through a bit of a train-up cycle of their own, before us first-run kids get to take our turns in stasis, and the next batch gets woken up for duty.

Which is what I've realized the last ten-plus years have actually been: duty. I didn't sign up for it, and there have been many mornings when I've laid in my bunk and stared at the ceiling and resented the fact that no matter how much I don't *want* this, I'm stuck with it.

I've become especially annoyed with the fact that there are no women. At least not women I could maybe call my *girlfriend*.

I've known Leah and Molly so long, we're sort of sick of each other. And while I do think Molly and Kroger were boinking each other for awhile, I believe that got old pretty quickly, so that they've each gone back to being celibate again.

Leah and me ... well, we never got to be anything other than friends. And I think we've both come to agree that this is for the best. We'll still want to be friends when we get to the new world, and introducing sex or romance into the equation ... that would complicate things more than either of us wants.

Besides, with Leah, there's no mystery. No adventure. No getting to know somebody for the first time. When I decide I want to be with someone, I want it to be fresh. I want her to be brand new. At least to me. And hopefully me to her, too.

Ordinarily I'd have chatted about all of this with Kevin, but now that Kevin is asleep I am realizing I don't know Ben well enough for he and I have to have the kinds of talks Kevin and I used to have. Which makes me very sad. Kevin wasn't quite a dad to me, but he was the only other man onboard with whom I could sit down and have a frank, honest discussion. And now that he's in stasis, I find myself missing him terribly.

And Cassie too, though for different reasons.

I hope they are each having wonderful stasis dreams. Either, of the new life waiting for us when we land, or of the life they left behind. Back on Earth. Which is now so far away from us even the ship's telescopes have to spend several minutes carefully looking, in order to find it.

Audio Journal Transcript: Day 4,000

I'm still awake.

I'm almost 20 years old, and I am still awake.

Laura told me they had to pull me out of the stasis bed because of irregularities in the readings, once I was under. I don't remember anything about that. Going to sleep for stasis felt just like going to sleep in normal life, only I was hooked up to a nest of wires and other medical stuff that constantly fed data to the ever-watchful medical bay computer.

Leah's down. Nice and peaceful. I was staring at her in her stasis bed today, with her own nest of wires, and her body gently immersed in the special stasis jelly that they developed for us back on Earth—to help slow down the human metabolic process to a fraction of its ordinary rate.

Ben calls it being one degree warmer than dead.

I've learned Ben can have an occasionally bleak sense of humor.

Laura blames it on Ben's time in the military.

Ben is an altogether different guy, compared to Kevin. Ben's got a quicker temper, talks in shorter sentences, and often phrases things as commands, rather than requests. But he's really got a talent for working with hardware. He spends almost more time patrolling the internals of the ship, doing manual inspections, than he does in the gym. Laura tells me that Ben used to be a Navy man. Submariner. Worked on the missile boats. The kind of lifestyle and pedigree that had earned him a spot on the trip to Delta Pavonis.

Therefore I did what I could not do when Cassie was awake: I showed Ben my three-dee designs for the guns I was sure we'd need when we got to the new world.

Ben slapped me on the back and was grinning ear to ear. He liked the idea so much. He also said that while Cassie was a fine lady, she had some odd ideas about how the universe ought to work, as opposed to how it *actually* works, and that I was right to be concerned about what awaited us when we landed. Ben and I have thus been refining my designs—with his practical knowledge and input—and we're probably going to actually try to build a prototype before too long. That is, unless Laura can figure out what's causing the problems when I try to go into stasis.

Audio Journal Transcript: Day 4,513

That's it. I'm screwed.

Laura has officially diagnosed me with stasis instability syndrome.

There's no cure for it, and there's no way to screen for it in advance. Back on Earth the statistics are that one in ten thousand have the potential for it. After three tries in the stasis bed, I can't risk a fourth try without putting my life on the line. My body can't handle it, apparently.

What would Kevin have called it? *Dumb luck.*

Ben can barely look me in the eye. Not because of anything he did or I said, but because he knows that I've been handed a death sentence. The average healthy human male on Earth lives to 84. By the time we get to Delta Pavonis I will be pushing 90. And there sure as hell isn't any chance of going back to the solar system.

I've been sitting in my cabin for two days now.

Contemplating suicide.

Seems like the most rational course of action at this particular point in time. So maybe it's a good thing for me that Ben and I haven't actually put together a working gun yet? I'd probably have the barrel in my mouth right about now. The only other option is to go down to the maintenance bay, step into the airlock without a suit, and press the CYCLE button.

If ever there was a time I wish that I had my father—Papa, who slumbers blissfully and without awareness—it's now.

Audio Journal Transcript: Day 4,515

We were supposed to have woken up four more children.

Turns out Laura woke up three kids … and one woman.

Li is one of the rare adults: single.

And she's a solid dozen years older than I am.

Look, I get it. I've been pretty messed up since Laura gave me the news about not being able to use the stasis beds. I think Ben and Laura both were getting desperate. In their position I might have done the same thing. But what the hell is Li supposed to do for me? Sing a song? Do a puppet show? I'm not a child anymore. I'm a man. Who has been told that his entire life is going to be lived out on an interstellar prison, with no possibility for parole.

Laura says Li is a medical doctor with specific training in longevity treatments, geriatric therapy, and knows her way around the stasis bed technology. Li's already hard at work in the medical bay labs trying to come up with a "cure" for my problem. Not that I think there's a hell of a lot one person can do that all of the specialists and doctors and technicians on Earth can't. If Earth hasn't been able to puzzle out the solution, I am thinking Li's just going to frustrate herself.

And I'm having a wickedly difficult time slapping on an optimistic face. There's simply no way to "fix" this. It is what it is. All that's left for me now is to decide: is my life worth living even if it's spent living inside a steel can slowly hopping from one star to the next?

Audio Journal Transcript: Day 4,518

Ben's taken me off all technical and maintenance duty. I am not sure how or why he thought he had the authority, but I'm in no state of mind to argue with the man. Instead he's asked—not ordered, and that spooks me—me to devote my time to the three kids. Since I was in their place over a decade ago, it stands to reason that I'll have a connection to them that the other adults may not. Sounds perfectly reasonable. Presuming I can make myself presentable and decent. I've not been shaving, nor bathing. And I am pretty sure last time Li had me come down for some tests, I peeled the paint off the walls with my demeanor. I am not a good guy to be around when I am still trying to figure out if I should *off* myself.

But I'm going to try my best.

The new kids are named Carlos, Tanika, and Edward.

All between 8 and 10 years old; or roughly the same age I was when I boarded the shuttle to Earth orbit.

I think the original plan is a good plan: get the kids used to their new world—altogether different from what they knew before—and phase them into added areas of responsibility that will not only make them feel like they have a purpose, but will help train them to operate and maintain the *Osprey*, in the event that me and the other adults get taken out of the equation at some point.

I won't know—until I've worked with them a little—how intelligent these kids are. Supposedly the selection process for the trip involved testing the children as well as the adults, so there shouldn't be any dull bulbs in the bunch. But you never know. Kroger was a dick to me for ten years, and there were times I considered doing him harm. Would either of the two new boys wind up being another Kroger? Could I resist the urge to murder if such were the case?

Murder. There I go again. Happy thoughts, happy thoughts.

My God, I need to talk to my parents.

Things are really going to hell in a handbasket.

Audio Journal Transcript: Day 4,525

I have to admit, I am starting to like these three kids.

Unlike Leah, Kroger, and me, these kids apparently know each other from before we left Earth, and while they're not related by blood, they behave more or less like two brothers and a sister. Oh, to be sure, a squabble here and there. But all in all they behave themselves, they help each other out, and miracle of miracles, I have even observed them saying the words *I am sorry* without being prodded to it by an adult.

Laura came to my cabin and visited.

She notes that I am not looking quite so devilish as before.

Yeah, well, don't go thinking it's all better, lady.

The most aggravating thing about my situation is that it's out of my hands to resolve. I can't get out and push the *Osprey* faster. I can't go down and wave a wand over one of Li's test simulators and make it come up with the magical answer to stasis instability syndrome. And now that I am getting to know these kids … well, let's just say I don't have the heart to whack myself while they're aware of what's going on. Lord knows how it would have affected me if Kevin or Cassie had committed suicide while I was younger. And as much as I hate life right now, I can't hate these kids enough to inflict my pain on them out of selfish fear.

So I am just kind of taking it day by day.

Audio Journal Transcript: Day 4,545

Li has asked me on a date.

That sounds quite ridiculous, given the circumstances. And I am pretty sure Laura put Li up to it. But I had an e-mail from Li waiting for me this morning, asking me if I'd like to go spend some time in the third observation bubble—which is one of five scattered across the exterior of the ship. We'll have to take suits outside to get there. No way to use an internal crawl space or corridor. We'll pack a dinner, and a blanket, and have a picnic. Or at least that's what the e-mail says.

Would it be silly of me to admit I am nervous?

I've never been on a date.

I've heard about them. Read about them in books and articles and news from Earth. Seen them in movies. Although Ben informs me that the movies are mostly bullshit about that kind of stuff. He and I were in the gym earlier and I confessed my anxiety. He laughed, but then he got serious and told me he thought it was one of the best pieces of news he'd heard since being woken up—that I'd be a fool to not take Li up on it.

So, I wrote Li back, and now we're committed.

For the entire time she's been awake, Li's been entirely clinical in her appraisal of me. A bona fide date suggests romantic interest. Or at least interest of a kind so personal I am not sure I am prepared to go there with her. Last woman I knew on any sort of level like that was Leah, and we'd known each other so well we'd become like gloves to one another. Or smelly socks, depending on how you look at it. What could I possibly have to talk to Li about? Our lives, our experiences, are so different, it's like we're aliens to each other.

Well, I've got the rest of the week to figure myself out.

The kids? They're all giggling about it.

Teacher has a girlfriend!

Yah. Riiight.

Teacher has a complex, compounded by a morbid problem.

I think I'll skip journal entries until the date's over.

For better, or for worse.

Audio Journal Transcript: Day 4,550

Li is actually pretty cool. With a sense of humor that she keeps wrapped up tightly when she's working. Not a talkative sort.

While we ate—out under the stars of the observation bubble—she came out of her shell. Showed me a side of herself I'd not seen before. And honestly, as hard as I tried to stay grumpy, she had me smiling by the time we were suiting back up and leaving for our return across the hull to the maintenance bay airlock.

So if Ben and Laura's ultimate plan was to get me to take the proverbial razor blade off my wrist—and return to the land of the truly living—it might actually be working.

The kids have been a lot of fun so far, and Li …

Well, we've arranged to do a second, similar date—and one each week thereafter, for however long we feel like it.

Goodness, does that mean we'll be going *steady?*

I'm actually recording this with my portable digital recorder; while down in the medical bay. Li's gone to sleep for the night, after this last session of labs on one of my blood samples. And I'm just staring into the stasis beds my parents have occupied for the last twelve and a half years.

When I put my hand on the glass, right about where my father's hand is, I realize that I am his size now. With the same thick fingers. How old was he when we left? Maybe 36? Maybe? I honestly can't remember Papa's age. When I look in the mirror, I see Papa's face, but younger. Like in the old photos from the family digital album that began when Papa and Mama first got married.

Which is, perhaps, another reason I can't put myself into an airlock without a suit.

Neither of my parents would ever forgive me.

Worse yet, they wouldn't forgive themselves.

I suspect the key to pulling people back from the abyss is to remind them that however hopeless they may be, or however hurting, their permanent absence will hurt the lives of many. And that there are other things to live for, besides purely selfish motives.

Okay, enough with the self-psych speculations.

I am sleepy, and it's time to get some rest. Tomorrow's a big day with the kids. And Ben's challenged me to a double workout in the gym.

Audio Journal Transcript: Day 5,000

Li is almost ready to throw in the towel.

It's been over a year, and she's still no closer to solving my problem than when she woke up. She tries to put on a brave face, but … well, there's nothing she can tell me at this point that's a surprise. I've had plenty of time to adjust to the fact that the *Osprey* is likely to be the only home I'll ever know. If that idea used to terrify me, now it just sort of … is. Like getting a brain cancer pronouncement, but the cancer's not spreading and it can't be operated on. Maybe one day the tumor will kill me, but for the moment I'm perfectly healthy. So I'm stuck trying to find usefulness and meaning onboard this great big vessel—which has also suddenly become very, very small.

Ben and Laura don't talk about it.

I don't talk about it to them.

The kids? They talk about it when they think I can't hear them. They feel sorry for me because they know if I live to see our new planet, I'll be too old to enjoy colonizing a virgin world.

Speaking of virginity, something else I don't talk about is how Li and I have been … ummm, you know, *doing it.*

Mama and Papa would have preferred that I be married first, but then if things had worked out the way they preferred I'd be in stasis right next to them. Nobody planned for me to be stuck in limbo like this. And while I suspect Li is partially doing it out of sympathy, I think she enjoys it too. It helps cure the loneliness. For a little while. When all the rest of the ship is asleep and the computers have taken over and the only sound you can hear are your lover's hot gasps of appreciation in your ear as you work up a naked sweat with her in your bunk.

So at least I can say that my life on this tub isn't celibate.

Sorry, Mama. Sorry, Papa.

I hope you can forgive me.

Audio Journal Transcript: Day 7,500

It'll be time to wake up the next batch soon.

Like me, Kroger, Molly, and Leah before them, the new kids aren't exactly kids anymore. They've worked hard, and paid their dues. Just like Ben and Laura. All of them are anxious to go back to sleep. Let someone else take the reins for awhile.

Li says she's going to stay awake with me.

I've told her many times that I can't allow it. She's a medical doctor, and where we're going all medical doctors will be worth their weight in platinum-coated diamonds. For the colony to succeed, Li must sleep. Whether either one of us likes it, or not.

She tells me I can't stop her.

I tell her that she'll be dead long before I am, assuming she can stay sane for the entire trip. Something I am not even sure about myself, much less someone else.

She's already got lines on her face. And I've seen the little silver strands in her black hair—when we're curled up together and she's fast asleep. Leaving me wide awake and wondering how it's going to be for me when I take the only woman I've ever held in my arms and loved, and put her back into stasis for the remainder of the voyage.

Ben and Laura have agreed to help me.

It won't be difficult.

One of these nights after Li and I have made love, I'll slip some sleeping agent into her electrolyte drink. Then when I'm certain she's out for keeps, I'll call Ben and Laura on the comm, we'll all carry Li down to the medical bay, and I'll resign myself to watching her through the lid of a living coffin—for the rest of my days.

Audio Journal Transcript: Day 8,500

With Ben, Laura, Li, and the kids all safely put away—down in the medical bay—Chris and Janicka came next.

Dealing with them is different than dealing with Ben, Laura, or any of the other adults to date. *Because I've become an adult too.* Just a few years younger than Chris and Janicka, biologically speaking. Though I'm feeling far older—and less charitable—than when Ben and Laura took charge.

Now *I'm* the point man. The one with the experience. So that I feel like I'm devoting my time to managing 6 children, instead of 4.

Which is not to say the arrangement remains precisely unchanged from the way it was before. I told them all that while I was perfectly happy to help show everyone the ropes—and do a little baby-sitting now and again—since I'm the odd man out for this particular phase of the voyage, I play by my own rules, and would remove myself from the pell-mell of the daily chore list whenever I pleased.

This does not exactly cheer Chris or Janicka, but then I didn't ask for their permission either. After all, they are going to go back to sleep eventually. I'm not. Therefore they *owe* me. Just as everyone else onboard owes me. Even my parents.

Unlike Ben and Laura, Chris and Janicka weren't husband and wife when they boarded the *Osprey*.

In fact, they don't get along that well.

Though Janicka surprised me in one specific way.

She likes to work out with me in the gym the same way Ben and I liked to work out in the gym, whereas Chris is a bit on the pudgy side and loathes anything that makes him break a sweat. So while Janicka and I don't have much else in common, over a few weeks we've gotten to understand each other the way gym rats everywhere understand each other.

Audio Journal Transcript: Day 8,525

Spending time with Janicka in the gym, I've learned that she prizes physical fitness. And admires people who can stick to a regimen. Something I've been doing for years. She wouldn't believe me when I told her I was soft as a kid. Even made me show her pictures as proof.

When I got done giving her a brief tour of my flabby childhood, there was a little mischievous twinkle in her eyes.

Thus Janicka's sneak visit to my after-workout shower was not precisely unanticipated. One moment I was all by myself—the curtain zipped up and hot water pounding across my tired muscles. The next moment I heard the curtain unzip. With soap in my hair I didn't dare open my eyes. I felt strong female hands on my shoulders, arms, chest, biceps, and … other places.

All the rest was automatic.

Now, I won't lie. Having to put Li into stasis still hurts too much. This thing with Janicka … we're not a couple. Not really. Janicka is a different kind of woman altogether. Not nearly as sensitive nor hidden as Li is. Janicka knows what she wants, and isn't afraid to say it. Or take it.

Janicka is also on the kinky side—nobody ever told me the birds and the bees could be as interesting as it's been since Janicka and I hooked up. I don't love her. And she doesn't love me. That much we've made clear. But the sex is its own kind of bond, helping each of us to escape from different problems. We are, for each other, the most wonderful kind of distraction.

I think the technical term I once saw used in an old movie is *fuck buddy*.

Of course, sometimes I think having a fuck buddy is sowing some unfortunate seeds with Chris. Especially when it's obvious that Chris is feeling sorry for himself: left out of the mix, the poor bastard.

So what? It's not my fault he's a fatass.

Janicka likes buff.

And buff is the one thing I've got in ample supply.

I guess Chris will just have to get over it?

Audio Journal Transcript: Day 8,613

I hurt a man today. Badly.

I suppose I should have seen it coming.

Janicka and I had been getting gradually more adventurous and flagrant with our behavior. In different parts of the ship. In places where someone might walk in and catch us. It was fun. It was exciting. The more risks we took, the greater the heightened emotional and physical pleasure.

What was it Mama always said? It's all fun and games ... until someone gets hurt.

Chris came into the galley late one night—to find Janicka and I going at it rather frenetically and noisily on one of the tables.

He started screaming at us. And called her a whore.

So I clocked him.

One shot, to the face. I didn't even think twice about it.

Broke his nose, his cheek, and put him into a coma ...

Now I'm sitting at his side in the medical bay every day while Janicka scours the medical computer trying to find out what to do about his condition. We don't dare put him back in stasis like this, but we're not exactly sure that letting him float along at the edge of death is a good idea either. Neither of us has the kind of medical training that someone like Li has. I've even considered waking Li long enough to ask for her help. I resist the idea only because I can't face admitting to her that I've done what I've done—to Chris in rage, or with Janicka in lust.

Mama and Papa are still trapped in virtual amber, like always.

As if their son hasn't become an altogether different person than he started out being as a boy, long ago.

All I feel now ... is empty.

Audio Journal Transcript: Day 8,648

Chris came out of it today. Much to my relief.

He was still banged up pretty bad, but he was conscious. And didn't remember a thing about my having put his lights out for him.

Janicka and I haven't yet had the heart to spill the beans.

But I think Chris is smart enough to have figured it out.

All three of us adults are just sort of trying to keep things puttied together, because the kids have been acting out something fierce—since Chris has been down.

If Janicka and I had been overly concerning ourselves with our libidos, Chris had been pouring all of his time into keeping the kids squared away. And in a rather thankless fashion to boot. No wonder he screamed at us. Like a housewife who's logged too many sleepless hours, only to find her husband off drinking and pinching bottoms at a gentleman's club.

I've profusely apologized to Chris, for shirking. I've put myself to work on the daily chores list like never before. Both to keep myself occupied—so that thinking about what's happened doesn't hurt as much—and to make it up to the man however I can.

Janicka?

Janicka ... has withdrawn.

Audio Journal Transcript: Day 8,679

You know what?

The mission planners for this trip totally screwed up.

And do you want to know why?

There's nothing in the *Osprey's* extensive and voluminous operations library that discusses the fixing of *broken people.*

Regardless of whether or not Chris has forgiven me, there's still the question of justice. You can't just hit a man like that, and get away with it.

One of the kids suggested we have a trial. Like on Earth.

I told them it was an excellent idea.

With Chris recused, Janicka reluctantly called the tribunal to order, and the kids all heard my confession, with the medical records as evidence. When it came time for sentencing, Janicka was stumped. But the kids were quick on the uptake. *Put him in time out!*

I'll be departing for one of the observation bubbles soon. For six months solitary confinement. No entertainment, other than one hour of music per day. I'll take a week's worth of rations with me, and someone will come every week thereafter to retrieve trash, give me new food and water, and make sure I haven't done anything unfortunate to myself.

A small part of me dreads the sentence.

But then again, I feel like it's a great object lesson for the kids. When we left Earth behind, we also technically left civilization. But civilization is also something you carry with you in your heart. Your soul. I am afraid I've gradually turned barbarian since I got the news that I can't go to sleep like all the rest. It's time for me to re-learn my manners. So that the kids will know that regardless of where we are in space, the rules are still the rules. And when you break the rules, there are consequences.

Audio Journal Transcript: Day 8,700

It's been hard, being stuck out under the stars all day every day. Nothing to do. Not even the gym. No chance of escape—they didn't let me keep a suit, not even in case I might need it. I don't even have any reading material, because they wouldn't give me a pad or a computer terminal.

But once a day, I do get my music.

Selected at random from the massive MP3 archive that the *Osprey* brought with it from Earth. Millions of recordings. Decades worth of listening. And for one hour each day I'm able to partake.

Sometimes it's classical, like Mozart.

Sometimes it's jazz.

Other times it's the latest—at the moment of our launch—pop stuff from any dozen Earth cultures: Japanese, Chinese, Korean, North American, French, et cetera.

And still other times it's spoken word.

I think I like that best of all.

Not exactly audio books. But poetry and short stories.

There was an old actor named Geoffrey Lewis who told wonderful tales set to music. I recognize his distinctive voice from some of the old movies I've seen over my long years of being permanently awake on the ship. *Celestial Navigations,* they're called. Haunting pieces, in that I sometimes hear myself in them: the eternal wandering man, in search of himself, or his idea of the perfect woman.

Speaking of which, it's been difficult not having access to Janicka.

Chris is the only one who comes to see me every week, bringing fresh food and hauling out my waste in sacks which I've filled and tied off: sorted by color, for recycling.

He doesn't say much, and neither do I.

But I dream about Janicka.

And, sometimes, I dream about Li too.

The stars are crystal clear all day and all night.

When I get to go back inside, with the others, I want things to be different.

Audio Journal Transcript: Day 8,860

I'm a free man again.

Whatever hard feelings there might have been, between Chris and I, they seem to be settled. He's healthy, and appears no worse for wear. And none of us can say that I wasn't given ample time to consider my sin, and reform. Which I was determined to prove was the case.

And Janicka is still distant.

Which is, I suppose, to be expected.

I think both of us were more than a little ashamed of ourselves, for what happened, and why. There haven't been any sexual encounters since I came back inside. Nor have I desired any, really. Janicka and Li are like night and day: the one soft and gentle and earnest, the other muscular and forceful and daring. I can't say I regret having been physical with either one of them. But I think Janicka and I both believe that it's for the best that we don't try to pick up again right where we left off.

Our fuck buddy days are over.

So I've gone back to work, and the kids are working with me, and while I still have a blank, terrified spot in my heart over the fact that I am essentially trapped on the *Osprey*, a man without a world, it's easier to ignore that spot when I am busy.

Audio Journal Transcript: Day 9,082

Janicka is dead.

Stupid accident. None of us could have predicted it. Janicka went outside for routine maintenance on one of the external radiation sensors when a piece of dark interstellar debris clipped her helmet. Just, *slice*, one second Janicka was alive and working, the next ... half her head was gone and she was dangling backwards along the hull by her safety tether.

I demanded to be the one to go out and get her.

I got her all the way back to the maintenance bay, her corpse limp, before it hit me.

Our first bona fide casualty.

Nobody had been naïve, about the risks. When we left Earth. All of the adults had been volunteers, and while those of us who'd been kids hadn't necessarily understood the danger, coming of age on the *Osprey* meant becoming intimately familiar with that danger. We were totally dependent on the ship, and on each other, to keep us alive. Not a lot of margin for error. And while an interplanetary voyage of a few weeks was now as safe and routine as intercontinental airline travel had become in my great-great-grandfather's time, traveling from star to star is brand new. Never been done. Totally without precedent.

We got Janicka's body into a man-sized sack, sealed it up, then Chris and I both suited up and took her back outside. To the very rear of the ship, where the glow of the fusion drive lit the edges of the radiation shield and push-plate that formed an inverted twin to the mushroom-shaped bow shield at the front of the ship.

We debated who should cast Janicka into the void.

As the only person aboard who'd been intimate with her, I mumbled a few words on her behalf. Then cursed myself for not having anything more eloquent to say. Just as nobody in the planning stages had thought to consider what might happen if the people went haywire, there was nothing in the training nor the library for dealing with death.

Janicka was too stark a reminder to me that it would probably be me in that sack some day: a relic of the trip, soon to be disposed of.

Which made up my mind for me.

I told Chris we aren't doing any space burials.

Janicka is going to stay in cold storage on the outside of the ship until we reach our new home, and then she's going to be goddamned buried in the goddamned soil like the pioneer woman that she is.

Chris nodded his head through the clear face plate of his helmet.

He likes the idea too.

And so it is.

There's a "graveyard" on the *Osprey* now. A graveyard for one, right down at the base of the pusher-plate where we seldom ever have to go. Janicka will be tethered there, frozen by the blackness of space, until we get to Delta Pavonis—and she can be given proper honors under a new sun.

Audio Journal Transcript: Day 10,000

Ten-kay Day.

Just like any other day.

After Janicka's death, Chris and I decided not to wake up any other adults. Not before it was his turn to go back to sleep, and the cycle would begin all over again.

Lately the kids have been pestering me about Earth.

For them, it's been just four years.

For me ... ?

I'm probably older than my parents now. Biologically, as well as emotionally.

Each year that passes, my memories of Earth become more like hardcopy photos: still possessing the same colors and shapes that they always have, but flat. Yes, flat. And so very, very far away.

I've started running a contest with the kids to see who can draw, each week, the most imaginative example of a possible animal we might meet when we land on our new world at Delta Pavonis. The kids have really taken the idea and run with it, too. Now all the screen savers all over the control room and, indeed, all over the ship, are filled with drawings of rampaging two-headed tyrannosaurs, unicorn snakes with rainbow wings, gargantuan proto-whales with eight flukes, and still other creatures too imaginative or even disturbing to adequately describe.

I've archived all of the drawings with my journal, so that anyone listening in the future can take a look. I like what the kids have done. I hope our new planet doesn't let them down.

I think I am going to miss these kids when they go back to sleep.

Audio Journal Transcript: Day 12,150

It's time. Not only for Chris and the boys and girls—young men and women, really—to re-enter their long, quiet night of stasis, but also to turn the engine off.

We're going to spend the next twenty years coasting. Having burned the fusion reactor for the last three decades, we've got three-fifths of our original fuel load left. And the math is holding steady: with two decades of free flight, we can turn the drive back on for braking, dropping gradually back down the relative velocity curve to something approaching normal interplanetary speed.

We haven't gone that slow in many a year.

Yet, we've only ever reached a fraction of the ultimate velocity: the speed of light.

I've been thinking that if they're going to build more ships like the *Osprey*, it's going to be like building time capsules in each instance. Oh, we get radio messages from Earth and are more or less up to date on what's going on, but the further we've traveled the more detached from home we've become.

Or, I should say, the more detached *I* have become.

Chris still suffers from a shade of homesickness.

I think he truly regrets coming on the trip; some days.

Which I thoroughly and completely understand.

But at this point there is only one way to go, with only one way to get there, and all anybody who is awake can do is muddle through his or her assigned tasks, make sure the broken stuff gets fixed, and hope that when we finally do touch soil again, it's as promising and marvelous a landscape as I think all of us have unconsciously come to hope it will be.

Audio Journal Transcript: Day 15,000

I don't check in with my journal much these days.

Turning 50 means not having to say you're sorry.

I'm the grandpa on the boat now. Or maybe an eccentric uncle?

The rotation schedule got fouled up when we had three more deaths. Extra people had to be woken up early. Now there are four bodies in the graveyard, including a child's. Which made me quite sad. The little ones deserve to see their new home even more than the adults who started out on the trip fully-grown.

Watching a child die was about as hard as seeing Janicka die, or putting Li to sleep knowing that when she woke up again, it would probably be me who'd have passed on.

But I eat right and I use the gym and I do what I can to make sure the grim reaper stays far away. One thing about a trip like this: it's a test case in seeing how much interstellar radiation a body can absorb before the cancers explode and take over. Even with shielding, I figure I've absorbed far more gamma rays than is reasonably healthy. And while the stasis beds could keep a tumor from sprouting full-bloom, my metabolism is alive and well and churning at 100%. If a metastasis chooses to present itself, I am not sure there's a hell of a lot I can do to slow it down.

No worries.

In the past I've had to get dental work done. If I need to have a tumor mass of any sort removed … there are people that can be woken up for that.

What matters most right now is that we're over halfway to Delta Pavonis. Not that you'd notice it from looking outside. Delta Pavonis is still just a star in space, like the Sun. We're out of the Oort Cloud by a good ways, and things in interstellar space are just a whole lot of black nothing. But knowing that there's now less time in front of us than behind us is somehow … invigorating. I don't know. I think it's a little like taking a long family car trip: *are we there yet? No, not yet, but soon.*

Hah. Soon. Indeed.

How warped my sense of time has become, as I've gotten older.

The days pass much more quickly than I remember them passing when I was 25, or 15 for that matter.

I am friendly with the new crew, but not intimate.

Certainly not to the degree I've been with past crews.

It's hard to relate to the kids—regardless of whether they woke up as children, or woke up as adults.

Lately I spend most of my time just wandering the ship. Passing through all the corridors and passageways, riding the IST up and down, up and down. Visiting all the familiar spaces and trying desperately to recapture that feeling I had when I was 8 years old, and everything was exciting and new.

Audio Journal Transcript: Day 17,500

I've been accused of playing favorites.

I can live with that accusation.

So what if I rigged the wake-up schedule to my liking?

There are some people who were never going to spend any significant time awake anyway.

To prove my point I showed the plaintiff a roster of all names currently in stasis: 48 men, 49 women, 112 girls, and 83 boys. All of the adults drew lots when they volunteered to come on the trip, and all of them swore to uphold their part of the bargain, if they happened to be one of the ones assigned to an "awake" shift in support of the *Osprey*. Did it really matter if I scrubbed my parents from the next stint? Or Li, who was actually supposed to be awake *now*—for the first time, not the second.

I once read that a military general on Earth said: *no battle plan survives contact with the enemy.* The trip to Delta Pavonis is a war of attrition. Fuel dwindles, supplies get used up, reserves are recycled, re-used, recycled, and re-re-used, to the point that waste must inevitably be jettisoned. Frankly I am amazed we haven't had worse problems than we've already experienced.

And if a couple of untimely deaths gave me an excuse to swap a few names around on the list, who are the newbies to argue with *me* about it?

I'm old enough to be their father for Christ's sake.

Of course, my list of names did not include the 10,000 embryos also being carried in stasis: an entire, healthy human gene pool, with plenty of room to spare.

Not that all 10,000 are expected to be implanted in wombs the instant we arrive. If the medical science is right, those embryos will be good for at least a hundred years or more, on top of the total trip time. So that as new generations of Delta Pavonians—my Lord, that is clumsy, we simply must come up with a better word for ourselves— come of age, the women can have some original offspring, and at least one or two "stasis babies" originally carried from Earth.

Inside of two centuries, if everything progresses according to the plan, there'll be no fear of inbreeding. For anyone. And there will be so many people living on the new world that even a significantly major disaster won't be able to wipe us all out.

Much depends on those first 25 years. When we'll be digging in. Putting down roots. Staking our claim.

To that end I've been slowly and methodically constructing my arsenal of weaponry. Using the rifle designs Ben and I first finalized way back when I was in my 20s. I've taken them outside and test-fired the lot of them, and am satisfied that they will suffice. Unless the new planet is literally infested with bloodthirsty monsters bigger than the biggest elephant, we ought to be able to fend off whatever nasties may be lurking in those jungles and forests.

Which we still can't see—as anything more than a green blur.

It takes hours for the telescopes to find the planet circling Delta Pavonis, and then it's impossible to get a clear shot because of relative drift. Even when we're getting closer and closer all the time.

Audio Journal Transcript: Day 20,000

Twenty-kay day.

I'll turn 63 soon.

In a few more years we will begin our downthrust into the gravity well of Delta Pavonis.

I'm not paying much attention to the names of the people to be woken up next. They are babies, basically, and I've gotten tired of changing diapers. Metaphorically-speaking.

I now spend as much time away from the youngsters as I can.

My jobs on the maintenance schedule are forgotten.

There are younger people to do all of it now. Quicker, smarter, stronger. I try to keep up with them in the gym, but it's tough. I'm not the man I used to be. If only I could talk to my grandfather now, I know he'd understand. But he's been dead for a long time. In fact, most of the people I knew on Earth when I was a boy, are gone. Memories only. Washed away by time and distance.

Once in awhile I still go to the medical bay and talk to Li, or my parents. Sometimes I even talk to Leah, who still looks like a young teenager. Or is it that I've gotten so old, everyone around me seems impossibly youthful? I can't really say for sure. All I know is that I seem to have an easier time talking to the near-dead, than I do to the alive.

The kids think I am the strangest sort of creature: odd, annoying, occasionally funny, but also occasionally scary. One of the older crew yelled at me one day when he caught me chasing a crop of little ones down the corridor, roaring like a beast and wagging my arms and legs about: my tongue flapping, and my eyes huge.

Apparently I'd caused one of the little ones to cry!

A menace, I was.

Fuck 'em. It's not my fault if they don't have a sense of humor.

Audio Journal Transcript: Day 25,000

I'm old.

Old, and tired.

And they turned the goddamned gravity back on.

Not that you can "turn on" gravity. It's just that the *Osprey* has done an about face, and we've been burning the engine again. Bleeding off relative velocity as we close on Delta Pavonis. It's been a long time in coming. But I am resenting having the full weight of my body—not to mention my years—pressing down on me a little bit more each passing day.

If the math holds we should reach our target in about a dozen years.

Enough time for one more awake shift.

Joy. Another patch of snot-noses to wrangle with. This last group almost did me in. Thought they knew everything. Even the tots. It was enough to drive a man crazy.

I'll be glad when everyone finally gets off this stinking ship.

Audio Journal Transcript: Day 28,900

One of the little ones came jumping up to me today and exclaimed, "We can see home!"

Ordinarily I'd have ignored such ruckus, but I decided to humor the child and allowed myself to be lead away to the control room where the telescopes were capturing high-quality, high-resolution images of the Earth-type world which has been drawing us onward like a bulb draws moths in the summer evening.

Even with the better part of a year still in front of us, I have to admit, the view is fairly spectacular.

The planet is a ball of mostly-blue from pole to pole, with fantastic archipelagos and island chains wrapping and re-wrapping the planet from east to west, and back again. As if all the world has become Indonesia. But unspoiled. Pure. Each small land mass covered in lush, green vegetation. Mountains and valleys, rivers and river deltas, masses of white clouds and broiling storms and, yes, there in the southern hemisphere, the tell-tale whorl of a typhoon.

Room enough for ten thousand nations, I thought.

Give people enough time …

But will we get it right? I mean, any more right than we got it the *first* time, back home on Earth?

Wait, this *is* home now. Or rather, it will be.

I must admit to being surprised I made it this far.

My health is fragile and my bones are thin and my hands and face are covered with spots. There's no hair on my head, and I've got to use a cane I built from a piece of mill stock in the maintenance bay.

Whole generations of crew have passed through the bowels of the *Osprey,* one after the next, and I'm the only one to have seen and experienced them all. I am like the biblical Methuselah: the living hourglass by which the entire mission has been measured. Can I hold out for just one more year? What will it be like to actually stretch my toes out into the sand on those new beaches? Of which there will doubtless be an endless variety.

Audio Journal Transcript: Day 29,199

We're in orbit, by God.

500 miles up, and doing fine. Not a single fleck of space debris—nor any artificial satellites. A clean slate in space, as well as on the ground. The new planet has a moon about the size of Callisto. Much bigger than Earth's moon. But roughly about as dense. We're seeing evidence of active volcanism on that moon, as well as on the planet below. Which doesn't necessarily mesh with our expectations, given the estimated age of the Delta Pavonis system. But then, that's part of the fun, right? To come all this way and have assumptions overturned?

Magical.

With everyone being woken up and the aerospace shuttles officially unpacked from their bulbous conformal cocoons amidships, the *Osprey* is suddenly alive with chattering and laughter and arguments—both civil and not-so-civil.

I have retreated to the room just underneath the bow shield.

Where Leah and I used to come.

I haven't had the heart to find or talk to her yet. I've mostly kept out of the way and let the kids do all of the work. This is their party, not mine.

Li found me sulking.

If she was mad at me for putting her back into stasis against her wishes, she didn't show it. She simply ran a finger along my chin and over my jaw, then leaned in and gave me a very gentle kiss on the lips. Before tears pooled at the corners of her eyes and she floated away from me, back towards the IST that would take her down to where the action was.

It wasn't the kind of steamy kiss I'd last gotten from her, but it was sufficient to get my blood moving. I sat there for a long time, remembering how things had been when she'd still held out hope that my stasis instability syndrome could be cured. She'd wanted so many things for us then. Things we'd now never get to have, despite having made it to the new star.

My mother and father found me next.

It was like seeing ghosts.

Their smiles faltered when they saw how decrepit I'd become.

"What have we done to you?" Mama said, tears fluttering from her eyes.

"It wasn't your fault," I told her. "Neither of you had any idea this would happen to me. Come now, there's work to be done. A new life to be lived. You and Papa are still young. You have plenty of time for a new son. Go. Down to the new planet. Be happy."

Papa braced my shoulders with his manly, strong hands, and squeezed tightly.

He understood.

He was crying too, but he understand.

I hugged him close to me, then hugged my mother.

I didn't watch them go as they left me to my silence.

Audio Journal Transcript: Day 29,235

They've started a fresh calendar down on the new world. The days are much longer: by about six Earth hours. Perhaps a blessing, or perhaps a curse? I'm pretty sure the tradition of *siesta* will be alive and well on this, the official second home of humanity in the galaxy.

When all but a few of the landing craft departed the ship, and there was barely anyone left onboard the *Osprey*, Leah came and asked me to come down.

Molly, and Kroger too.

And Ben and Laura. And Chris. And Kevin and Cassie.

I'm older now than all of them.

We packed up all of my belongings, to include an ancient kite which had been under my bunk for almost eight decades. The plastic had become brittle. I wasn't sure it would fly. But I figured I would give it a shot.

Everyone ushered me to the precipice—the docking tunnel that would take me over to the aerospace shuttle, which sat fully-fueled and ready to streak down towards the planet's surface.

I stopped there, considering.

It would be hard, the new world. So much work to do. If I'd hated the gee exerted on the ship during downthrusting, I'd hate the real gravity twice as much. My old body might last a week or two in such an environment, but probably no more than that. I'd have a stroke, or my heart would give out, or I'd fall and bust a hip. That was no way to go. Not when they still needed the *Osprey* to remain functional in orbit. As a satellite relay, both for on-world communication and for pitching messages back towards Sol System—our far away brothers and sisters on the old world.

"No," I finally said to my friends. "I can't go down. But you can do one thing for me. Take Janicka's body and bury it in a sunny place, with the others who died. Where the trees grow tall and the noise of the ocean is in the wind."

I gave them my kite.

"Make sure one of the children gets to fly this too."

There was, of course, much protest.

But I waived them off.

"Are you going to argue with your senior?" I said, half-joking. "I will stay here. It'll be just the *Osprey* and me. Together. She's my woman now. We are the only ones old enough to understand each other."

Their faces showed concern and sorrow, but they ultimately left me in peace.

Audio Journal Transcript: Final Entry

And here onboard the *Osprey* I remain.

The ship is all but empty. Nobody comes up anymore, though occasionally I do send something down when they need it—in one of the numerous emergency re-entry pods. Eventually I'll run out of those, but not before the ship has been stripped of virtually every usable piece of technology that can be put to work below. There's only enough left onboard these days to keep the power, the air, and the hydroponics farm running.

My lovely farm.

Where I grow just enough for me to eat, which isn't much.

And where I suppose someday I'll lay down and let the universe take me.

To be totally honest, it's not been a bad life. I've had responsibilities and I've taken lovers and I've made amends for my wrongs. I've also helped bring a miracle to fruition. There's a new civilization going on down there, on that new world. I think they named it something lofty-sounding, but I can't remember what. A pretty name. Doesn't really matter. They're doing what needs to be done. And I am fully confident that a thousand years from now, this place will be vibrant and alive with people. Maybe launching their own ships towards still more distant stars? Maybe cracking the light-speed barrier altogether, and turning voyages like mine into a question of months, weeks, or even days.

Who knows?

I've got the *Osprey's* long-range radio dishes fine-tuned for communication traffic with Earth. Broadcasts back to Sol System take a long time. I let them know that the *Osprey* has arrived, and that her mission is officially accomplished to satisfaction.

I don't expect anything in return. I won't be alive to listen to their reply.

One thing, though.

Today Leah sent me a high-resolution image of Janicka's grave, where the four bodies of our fallen starfarers now rest.

It's a monument, actually. A huge stone obelisk twenty meters high watches over a gorgeous bluff that looks out across an amazing, endless, wave-tumbled sea.

The plants look a bit strange. Not like Earth plants.

But green is still green.

And the clouds are bright white.

And the sky is true blue.

NOTE: to date, no Analog story has gotten me as much kind mail as "Life Flight" has gotten me. By a country mile. All of it overwhelmingly complimentary. Well, save for one letter. What follows is my magazine-printed response, to an astute reader comment received by the Brass Tacks column, which has run in the back of Analog magazine since long before I was born. Trevor Quachri was nice

enough to give me space for a pleasant rejoinder. In short? Oops. Even us "Hard SF" guys don't always get it right.

January 2014

Steve Gray is correct to complain that my math in "Life Flight" was not precise. As a devotee (and collaborator) of Larry Niven, I take my "hard" science fiction very seriously. Still, even Larry himself was not perfect. There's a filk song about Larry's most famous example: *oh, the Ringworld is unstable, the Ringworld is unstable, did the best that he was able, and that's good enough for me!*

For my short works, I usually don't invest the kind of calculating time one might log on a full novel. And if ever I do novelize "Life Flight" I will absolutely be taking Steve's notes and using them to refine the specifics of the *Osprey's* journey. Just as Larry used criticism of the first *Ringworld* novel to greatly inform the descriptions and events of the second. To that franchise's credit.

Suffice to say that for "Life Flight" the novelette, I was satisfied with what I call back-of-the-creative-envelope educated guesses. Which are reasonably informed by the realities of the physics in question, without dwelling so much on the physics that the human aspect of the story gets swamped by the equations.

I imagined the *Osprey* as a thick, super-skyscraper-sized fuel tank filled with slush hydrogen isotope. The crew module is a very long, insulated, relatively thin cylinder running centerline through the slush. At one end of the *Osprey* is the bow shield, to protect against induced cosmic rays and other interstellar debris. At the other end is a pusher/shield plate punctured by the exhaust nozzle of a supremely efficient, yet necessarily very-low-thrust fusion drive. A drive that consumes reaction mass and reactor fuel at an amazingly miserly rate. So, it takes a *long* time for such a drive to push the *Osprey* up the relative acceleration curve, and then brake accordingly on the other end of the journey. How long—precisely?—was something I didn't feel the story needed to worry about. Nor did I factor in total time spent at one gee, in a per-second-per-second cumulative sense. Just that the ship would never, ever come close to reaching truly relativistic speeds.

Again, all back-of-the-creative-envelope guesswork. Sorry if the way I described the action rang too many physics alarm bells, for those with better arithmetic skills than myself. Hopefully Steve (and anyone else who noticed my imprecision) will forgive me.

Steve, for what it's worth, if the novelization does reach fruition, you can expect a nice credit for having done my homework for me. Where the *Osprey's* journey is concerned. Thank you, sir.

Now, to the instability syndrome that keeps our hero from being able to sleep out the trip to his new world. For this plot point, I made a single, key assumption: even well-funded, highly engineered operations sometimes can't plan for all possible contingencies.

In the body of the story I dropped the hint that the syndrome is fantastically rare and cannot reasonably be tested for. Why not? Well, maybe it takes different lengths of time for the problem to manifest in different people? Time the pre-mission planners didn't have? Or maybe the testing is prohibitively expensive? So much so that it wasn't in the mission budget? Or maybe medical science assumes that if the parents don't have it, their kids won't either? But the science got it wrong in our hero's case? Or maybe our hero just didn't have the problem when he boarded, but later grew into the problem post-puberty? I left it as a mental puzzle for readers to invent (using their own imaginations) why this problem would have gone unchecked before the *Osprey's* launch.

As with the math surrounding the *Osprey's* journey, I didn't dwell so much on the technical details of the instability syndrome so much as I dwelt on its human impact: the way such a discovery would virtually destroy a young man, and condemn him to a life not of his own choosing. How would any of us, faced with such a thing, react? What might our choices entail? How would we derive meaning from living out our days on a ship in a proverbial bottle? I found these questions much more engaging than the actual question of why the syndrome went undetected. And again, I hope Steve (and anyone else who wrinkled his or her brow at the issue) will forgive me.

Cheers, Analog! I look forward to seeing you all next time. And thank you for being the sharpest SF readers in the literary quadrant!

Afterword

As of the writing of these words, it's been approximately one year since I released my very first short fiction collection, *Lights in the Deep,* through WordFire Press. The tremendously positive audience reaction to that book, and its subsequent financial success, are precisely responsible for this new volume coming into being. As with *Lights,* I hope that you've enjoyed *Racers of the Night.* This collection represents the best of my most recent short science fiction, and continues my personal tradition of telling tales which are (I hope) robustly optimistic about the human future, despite potentially disastrous or dire circumstances.

Again, as with *Lights,* I have to offer my most profound thanks to Kevin J. Anderson, Rebecca Moesta, and the whole crew at WordFire Press, for their kindness, diligence, and patience. It's not been an easy year for me, trying to juggle a writing career, a part-time military career, and an increasingly challenging civilian career. *Racers of the Night* should have been done months before it actually got done. Thus I put an added burden on WordFire's crew.

Ladies and gentlemen of WordFire Press, my hat is off to you all. It's been a tremendous treat doing business with you, and I look forward to working with you all on additional short fiction volumes in the future.

And to the readers, eager to see more from me, do please check out my novel *The Chaplain's War,* from Baen Books! Also, take a look at my collaboration with Larry Niven, called *Red Tide,* from Arc Manor!

Additional Copyright Information

Other Books by Brad R. Torgersen

Lights in the Deep
The Chaplain's War

Other WordFire Press Titles

Our list of other WordFire Press authors and titles is always growing. To find out more and to see our selection of titles, visit us at:

wordfirepress.com

www.ingramcontent.com/pod-product-compliance
Lightning Source LLC
Chambersburg PA
CBHW020255120726
47904CB00001B/207